Meems&Feets

Ferrets from Planet Ferretonia!

OCT - - 2023

brjc

Andrews McMeel Publishing
a division of Andrews McMeel Universal
1130 Walnut Street, Kansas City, Missouri 64106

www.andrewsmcmeel.com

23 24 25 26 27 SDB 10 9 8 7 6 5 4 3 2 1

Paperback ISBN: 978-1-5248-7670-8
Hardcover ISBN: 978-1-5248-8451-2

Library of Congress Control Number: 2022947524

Editor: Erinn Pascal
Art Designer: Brittany Lee
Production Editor: Julie Railsback
Production Manager: Chuck Harper
Flat Colors: Aleksey Anisimov

Made by:
RR Donnelley (Guangdong) Printing Solutions Company Ltd
Address and location of manufacturer:
No. 2, Minzhu Road, Daning, Humen Town,
Dongguan City, Guangdong Province, China 523930
1st Printing – 5/1/23

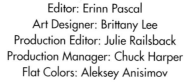

ATTENTION: SCHOOLS AND BUSINESSES

Andrews McMeel books are available at quantity discounts with
bulk purchase for educational, business, or sales promotional use.
For information, please e-mail the Andrews McMeel Publishing
Special Sales Department:sales@amuniversal.com.

Meems & Feefs
Ferrets from Planet Ferretonia!

Liza N. Cooper

Andrews McMeel
PUBLISHING®

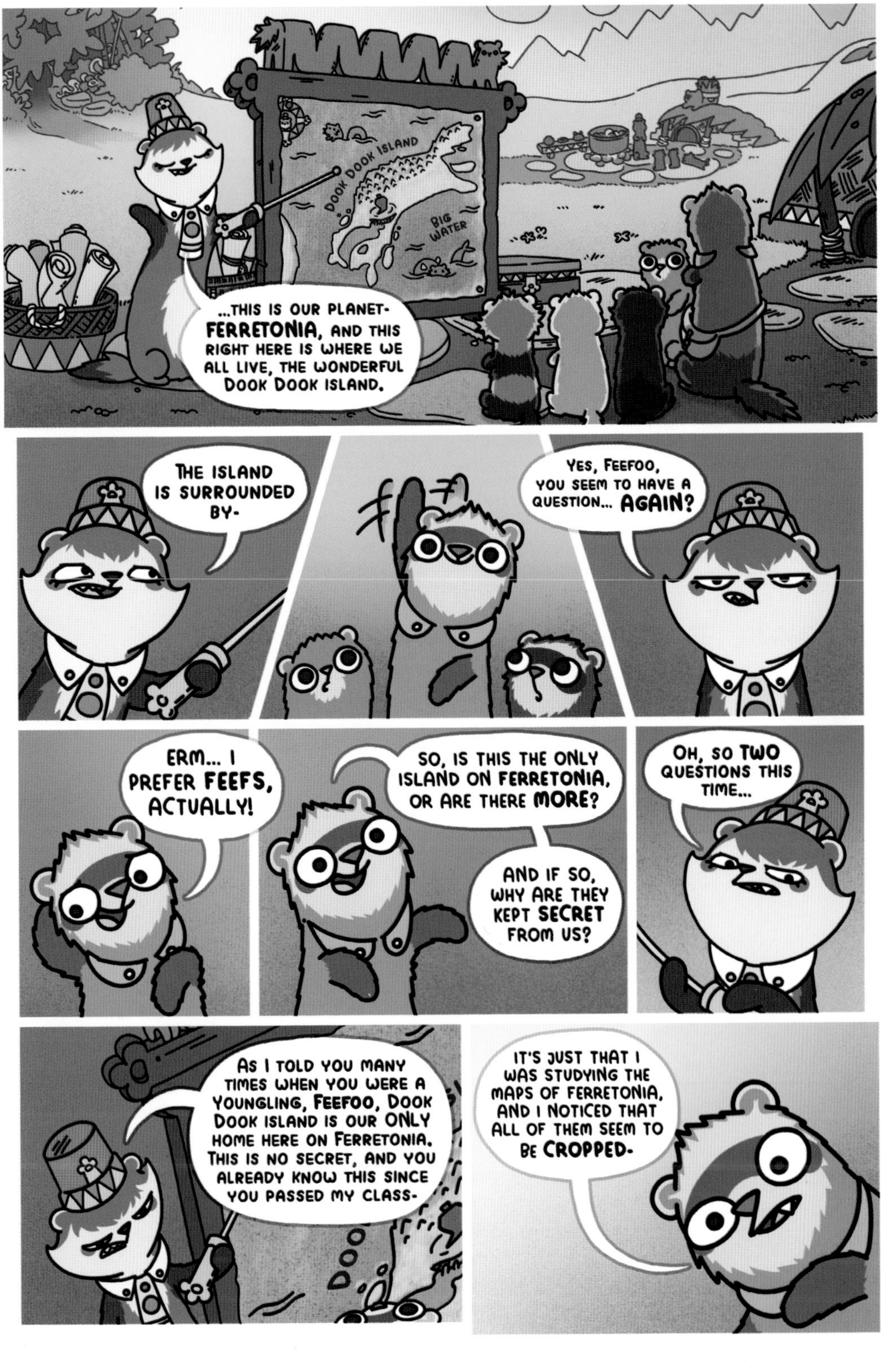

DOOK DOOK ISLAND
BIG WATER
...THIS IS OUR PLANET- FERRETONIA, AND THIS RIGHT HERE IS WHERE WE ALL LIVE, THE WONDERFUL DOOK DOOK ISLAND.
THE ISLAND IS SURROUNDED BY-
YES, FEEFOO, YOU SEEM TO HAVE A QUESTION... AGAIN?
ERM... I PREFER FEEFS, ACTUALLY!
SO, IS THIS THE ONLY ISLAND ON FERRETONIA, OR ARE THERE MORE?
AND IF SO, WHY ARE THEY KEPT SECRET FROM US?
OH, SO TWO QUESTIONS THIS TIME...
AS I TOLD YOU MANY TIMES WHEN YOU WERE A YOUNGLING, FEEFOO, DOOK DOOK ISLAND IS OUR ONLY HOME HERE ON FERRETONIA. THIS IS NO SECRET, AND YOU ALREADY KNOW THIS SINCE YOU PASSED MY CLASS-
IT'S JUST THAT I WAS STUDYING THE MAPS OF FERRETONIA, AND I NOTICED THAT ALL OF THEM SEEM TO BE CROPPED-

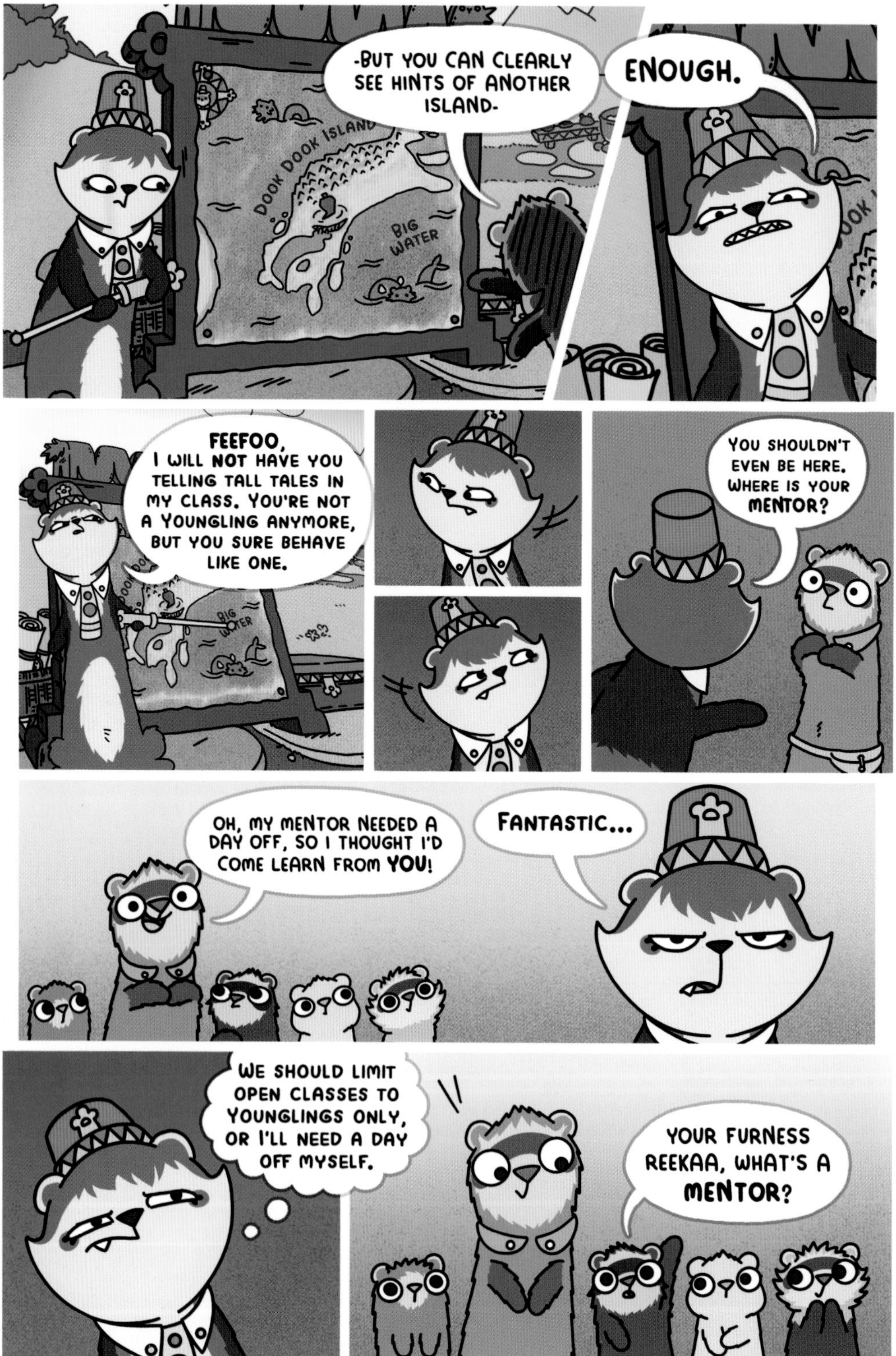
-BUT YOU CAN CLEARLY SEE HINTS OF ANOTHER ISLAND-
DOOK DOOK ISLAND
BIG WATER
ENOUGH.
FEEFOO, I WILL NOT HAVE YOU TELLING TALL TALES IN MY CLASS. YOU'RE NOT A YOUNGLING ANYMORE, BUT YOU SURE BEHAVE LIKE ONE.
BIG WATER
YOU SHOULDN'T EVEN BE HERE. WHERE IS YOUR MENTOR?
OH, MY MENTOR NEEDED A DAY OFF, SO I THOUGHT I'D COME LEARN FROM YOU!
FANTASTIC...
WE SHOULD LIMIT OPEN CLASSES TO YOUNGLINGS ONLY, OR I'LL NEED A DAY OFF MYSELF.
YOUR FURNESS REEKAA, WHAT'S A MENTOR?

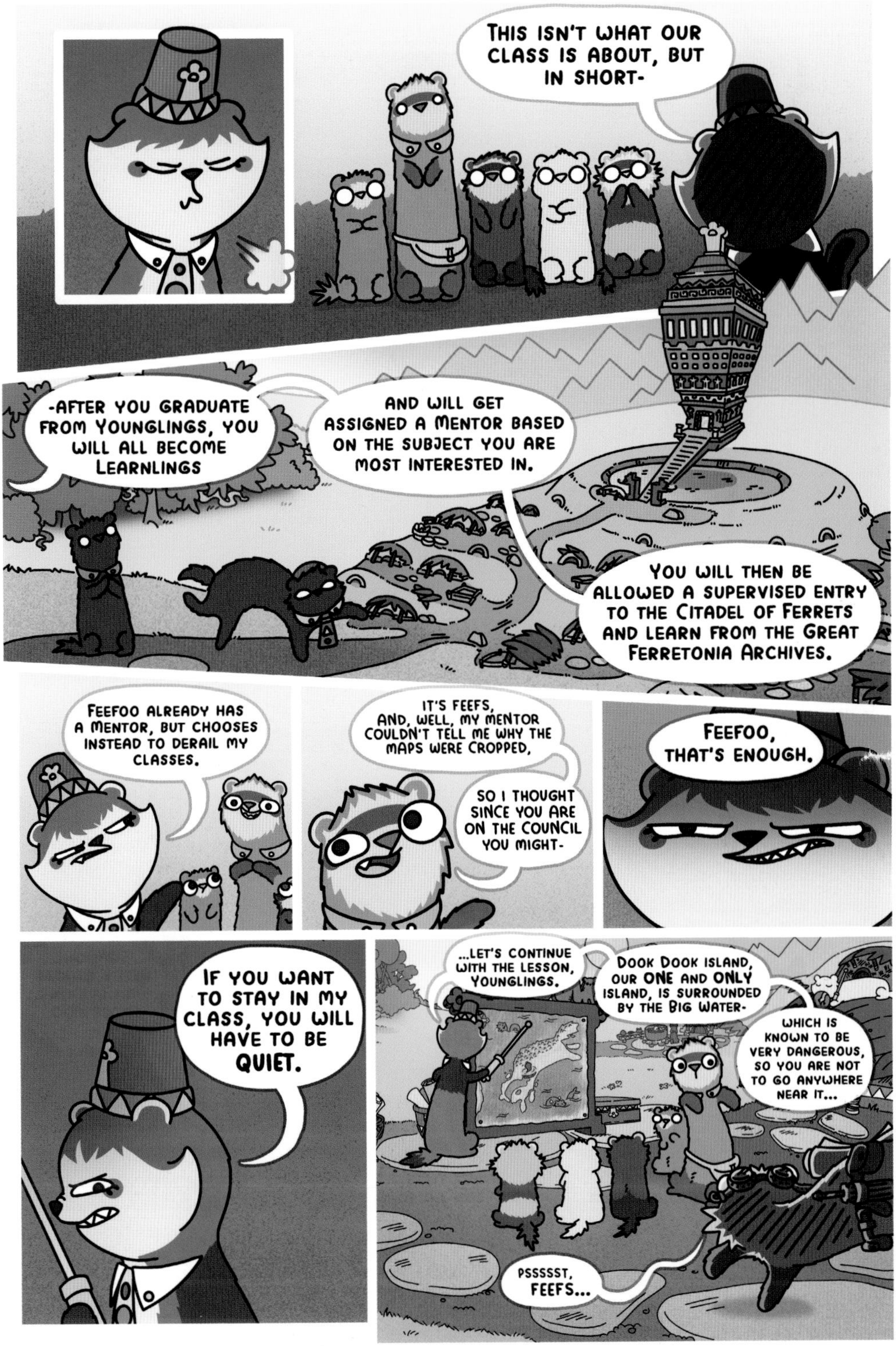
THIS ISN'T WHAT OUR CLASS IS ABOUT, BUT IN SHORT-
-AFTER YOU GRADUATE FROM YOUNGLINGS, YOU WILL ALL BECOME LEARNLINGS
AND WILL GET ASSIGNED A MENTOR BASED ON THE SUBJECT YOU ARE MOST INTERESTED IN.
YOU WILL THEN BE ALLOWED A SUPERVISED ENTRY TO THE CITADEL OF FERRETS AND LEARN FROM THE GREAT FERRETONIA ARCHIVES.
FEEFOO ALREADY HAS A MENTOR, BUT CHOOSES INSTEAD TO DERAIL MY CLASSES.
IT'S FEEFS, AND, WELL, MY MENTOR COULDN'T TELL ME WHY THE MAPS WERE CROPPED,
SO I THOUGHT SINCE YOU ARE ON THE COUNCIL YOU MIGHT-
FEEFOO, THAT'S ENOUGH.
IF YOU WANT TO STAY IN MY CLASS, YOU WILL HAVE TO BE QUIET.
...LET'S CONTINUE WITH THE LESSON, YOUNGLINGS.
DOOK DOOK ISLAND, OUR ONE AND ONLY ISLAND, IS SURROUNDED BY THE BIG WATER-
WHICH IS KNOWN TO BE VERY DANGEROUS, SO YOU ARE NOT TO GO ANYWHERE NEAR IT...
PSSSSST, FEEFS...

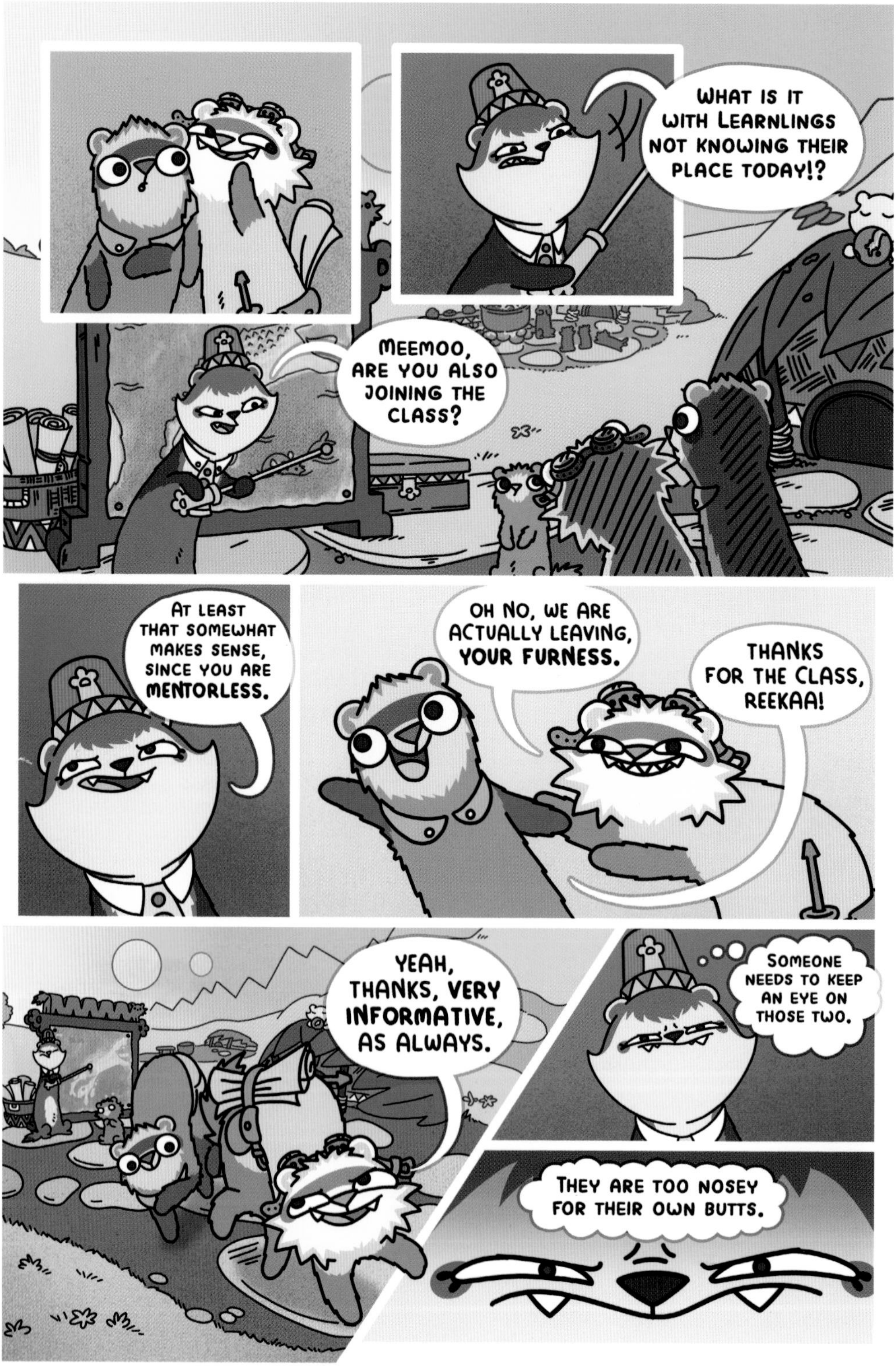
WHAT IS IT WITH LEARNLINGS NOT KNOWING THEIR PLACE TODAY!?
MEEMOO, ARE YOU ALSO JOINING THE CLASS?
AT LEAST THAT SOMEWHAT MAKES SENSE, SINCE YOU ARE MENTORLESS.
OH NO, WE ARE ACTUALLY LEAVING, YOUR FURNESS.
THANKS FOR THE CLASS, REEKAA!
YEAH, THANKS, VERY INFORMATIVE, AS ALWAYS.
SOMEONE NEEDS TO KEEP AN EYE ON THOSE TWO.
THEY ARE TOO NOSEY FOR THEIR OWN BUTTS.

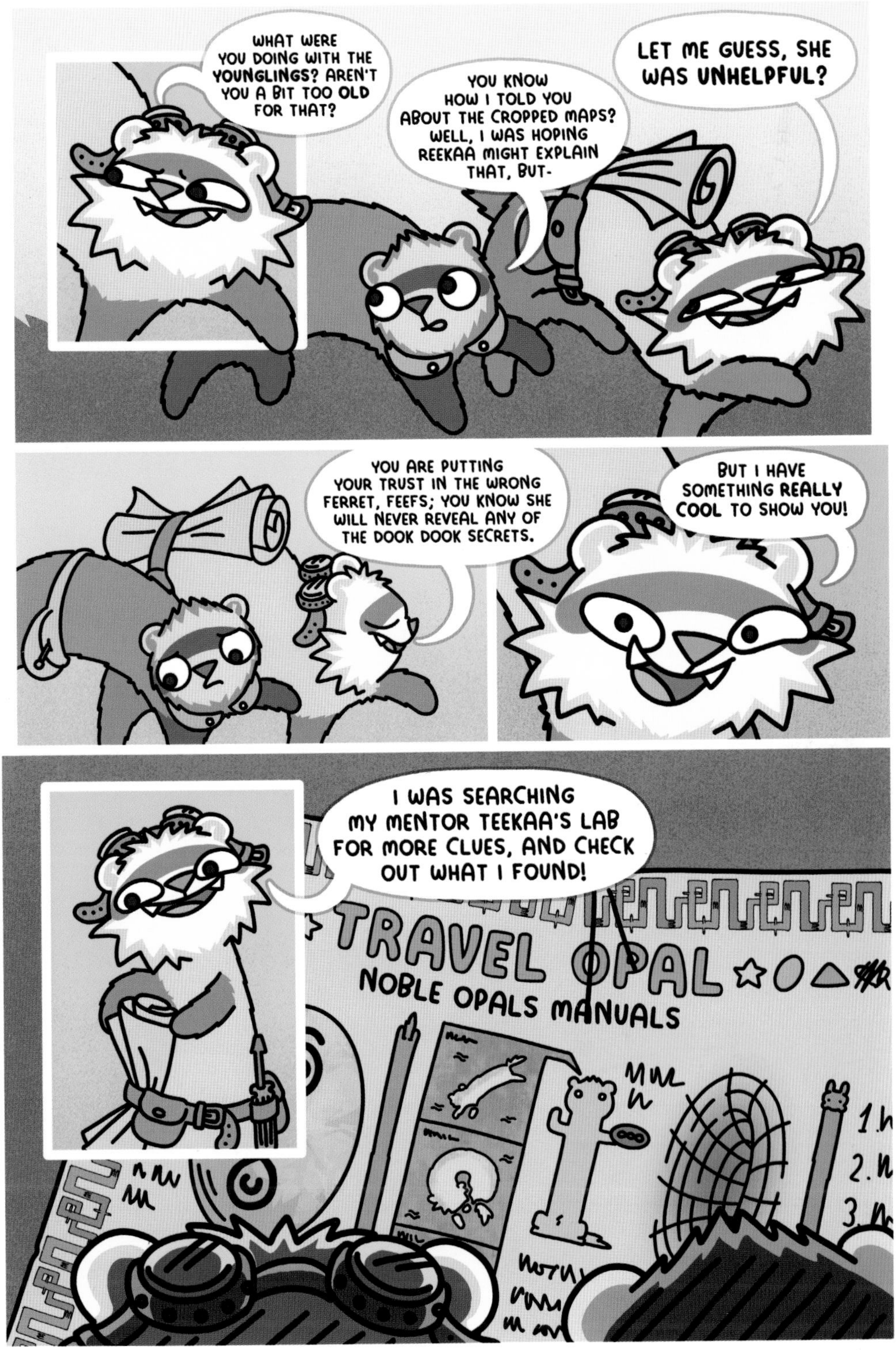
WHAT WERE YOU DOING WITH THE YOUNGLINGS? AREN'T YOU A BIT TOO OLD FOR THAT?
YOU KNOW HOW I TOLD YOU ABOUT THE CROPPED MAPS? WELL, I WAS HOPING REEKAA MIGHT EXPLAIN THAT, BUT-
LET ME GUESS, SHE WAS UNHELPFUL?
YOU ARE PUTTING YOUR TRUST IN THE WRONG FERRET, FEEFS; YOU KNOW SHE WILL NEVER REVEAL ANY OF THE DOOK DOOK SECRETS.
BUT I HAVE SOMETHING REALLY COOL TO SHOW YOU!
I WAS SEARCHING MY MENTOR TEEKAA'S LAB FOR MORE CLUES, AND CHECK OUT WHAT I FOUND!
TRAVEL OPAL
NOBLE OPALS MANUALS

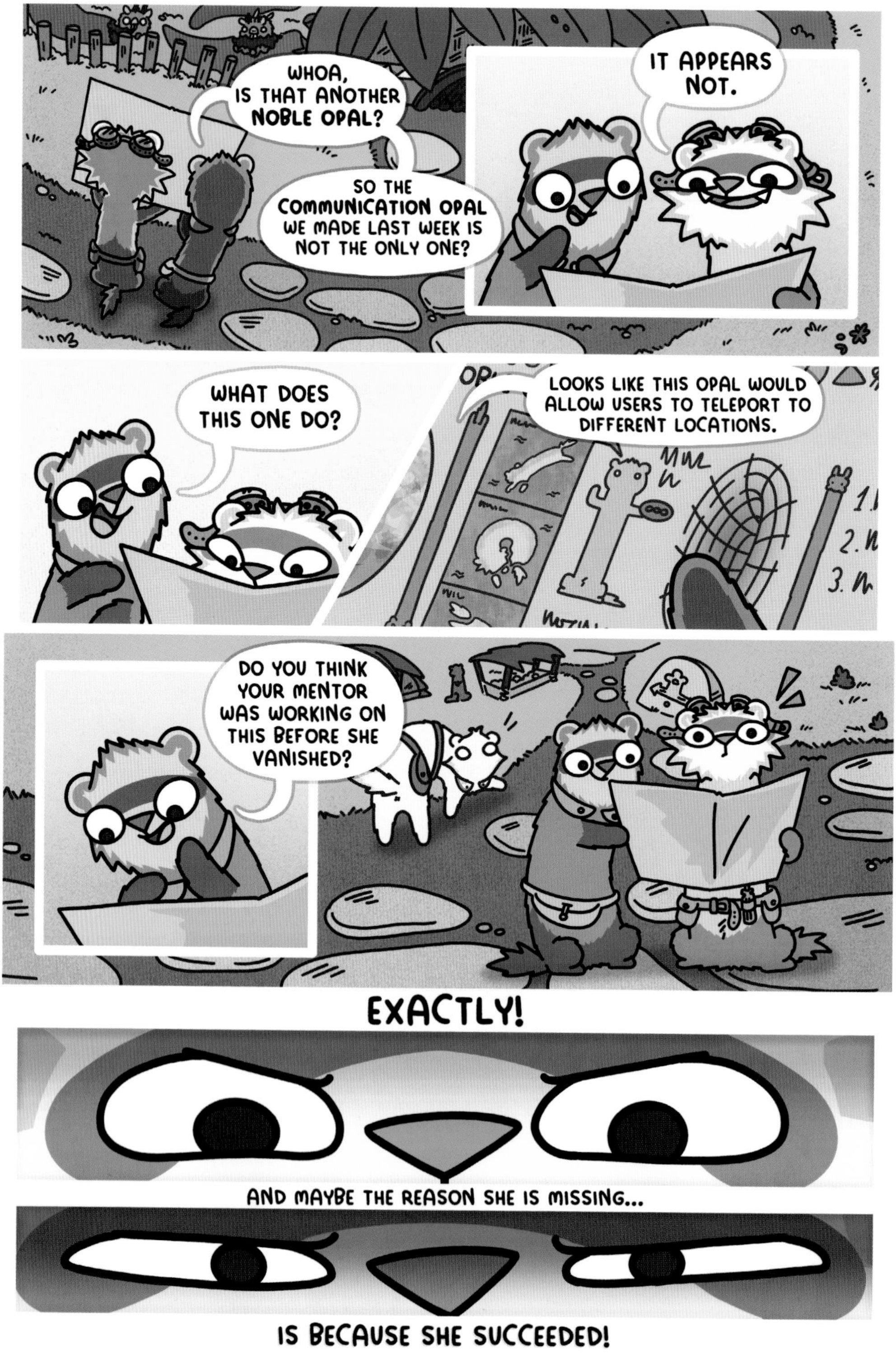
WHOA, IS THAT ANOTHER NOBLE OPAL?
SO THE COMMUNICATION OPAL WE MADE LAST WEEK IS NOT THE ONLY ONE?
IT APPEARS NOT.
WHAT DOES THIS ONE DO?
LOOKS LIKE THIS OPAL WOULD ALLOW USERS TO TELEPORT TO DIFFERENT LOCATIONS.
DO YOU THINK YOUR MENTOR WAS WORKING ON THIS BEFORE SHE VANISHED?
EXACTLY!
AND MAYBE THE REASON SHE IS MISSING...
IS BECAUSE SHE SUCCEEDED!

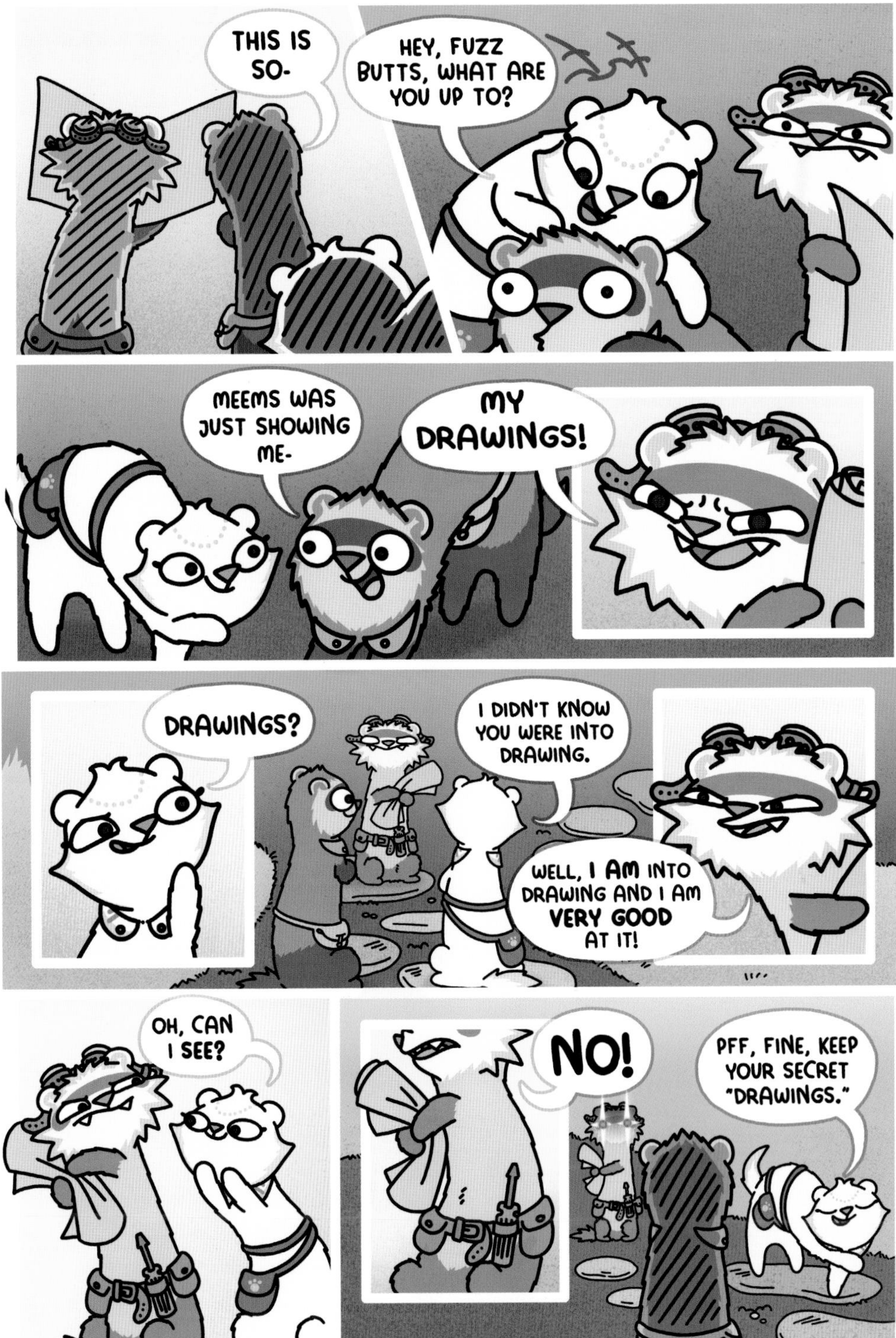
THIS IS SO-
HEY, FUZZ BUTTS, WHAT ARE YOU UP TO?
MEEMS WAS JUST SHOWING ME-
MY DRAWINGS!
DRAWINGS?
I DIDN'T KNOW YOU WERE INTO DRAWING.
WELL, I AM INTO DRAWING AND I AM VERY GOOD AT IT!
OH, CAN I SEE?
NO!
PFF, FINE, KEEP YOUR SECRET "DRAWINGS."

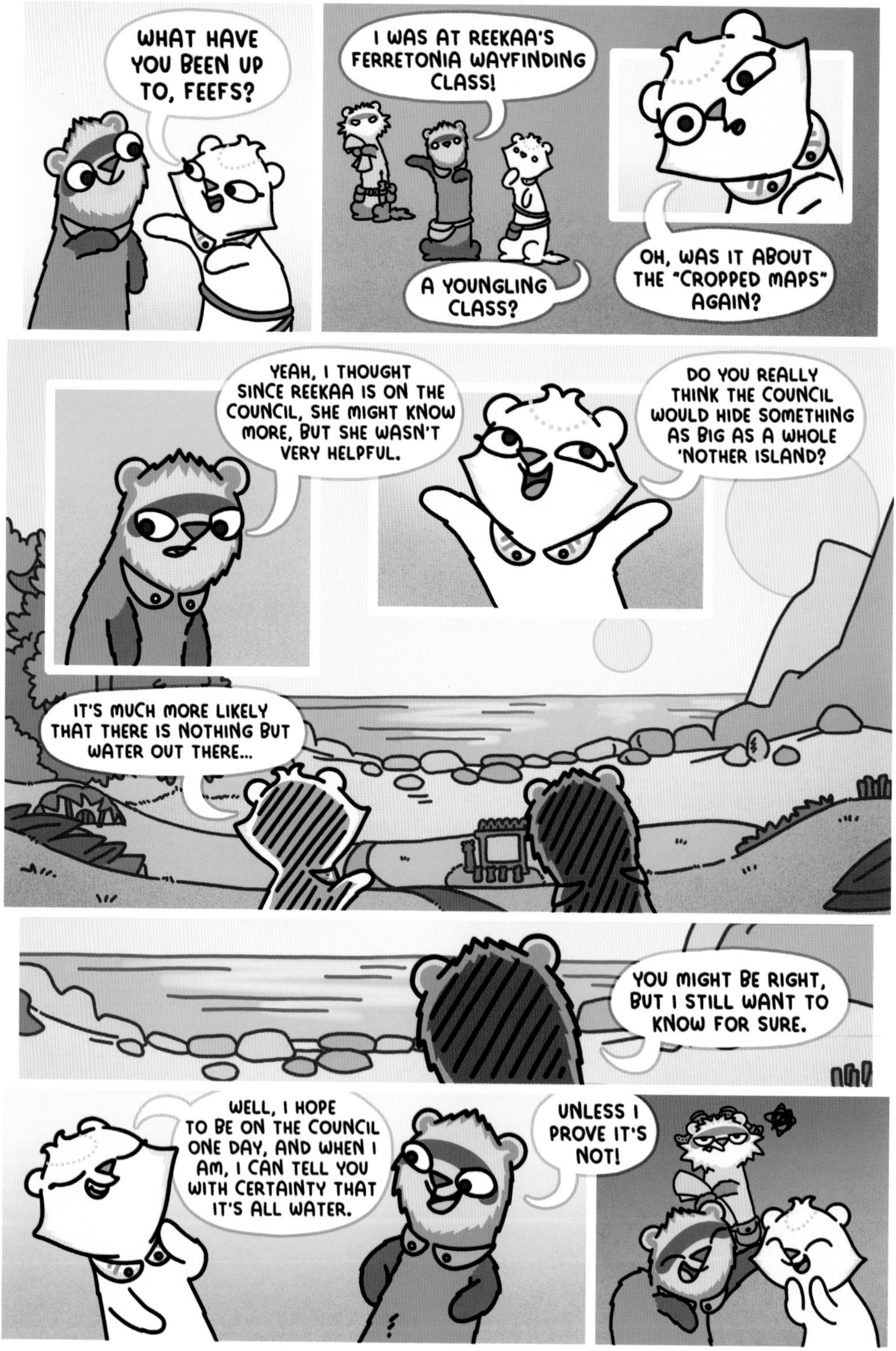
WHAT HAVE YOU BEEN UP TO, FEEFS?
I WAS AT REEKAA'S FERRETONIA WAYFINDING CLASS!
A YOUNGLING CLASS?
OH, WAS IT ABOUT THE "CROPPED MAPS" AGAIN?
YEAH, I THOUGHT SINCE REEKAA IS ON THE COUNCIL, SHE MIGHT KNOW MORE, BUT SHE WASN'T VERY HELPFUL.
DO YOU REALLY THINK THE COUNCIL WOULD HIDE SOMETHING AS BIG AS A WHOLE 'NOTHER ISLAND?
IT'S MUCH MORE LIKELY THAT THERE IS NOTHING BUT WATER OUT THERE...
YOU MIGHT BE RIGHT, BUT I STILL WANT TO KNOW FOR SURE.
WELL, I HOPE TO BE ON THE COUNCIL ONE DAY, AND WHEN I AM, I CAN TELL YOU WITH CERTAINTY THAT IT'S ALL WATER.
UNLESS I PROVE IT'S NOT!

OH, BY THE WAY, A BUNCH OF LEARNLINGS ARE HEADING TO THE BURROWS TO PLAY TUNNEL TAG LATER, DO YOU TWO WANNA JOIN?

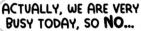

ACTUALLY, WE ARE VERY BUSY TODAY, SO **NO**...

IS THAT SO? WHAT ARE YOU UP TO?

PFF, YOU DON'T HAVE TO BE SO CRYPTIC, I ALREADY KNOW ABOUT THE **COMMUNICATION** OPAL YOU TWO MADE!

NONE OF YOUR BUSINESS, BUT IT'S WAY COOLER THAN TUNNEL TAG!

YOU **TOLD** HER!

ERM- YE-YES, WAS I NOT MEANT TO?

NO!

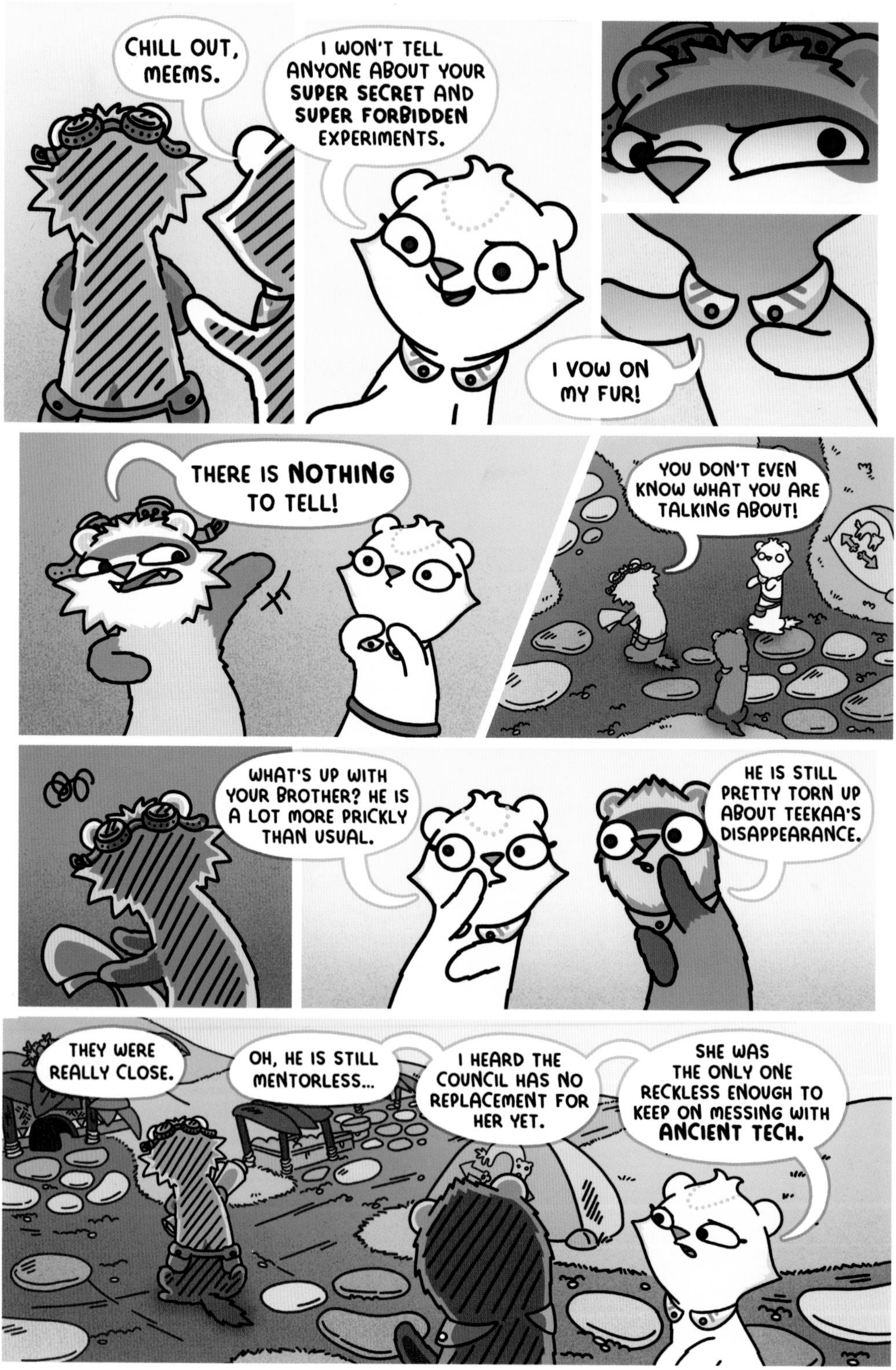
CHILL OUT, MEEMS.
I WON'T TELL ANYONE ABOUT YOUR SUPER SECRET AND SUPER FORBIDDEN EXPERIMENTS.
I VOW ON MY FUR!
THERE IS NOTHING TO TELL!
YOU DON'T EVEN KNOW WHAT YOU ARE TALKING ABOUT!
WHAT'S UP WITH YOUR BROTHER? HE IS A LOT MORE PRICKLY THAN USUAL.
HE IS STILL PRETTY TORN UP ABOUT TEEKAA'S DISAPPEARANCE.
THEY WERE REALLY CLOSE.
OH, HE IS STILL MENTORLESS...
I HEARD THE COUNCIL HAS NO REPLACEMENT FOR HER YET.
SHE WAS THE ONLY ONE RECKLESS ENOUGH TO KEEP ON MESSING WITH ANCIENT TECH.

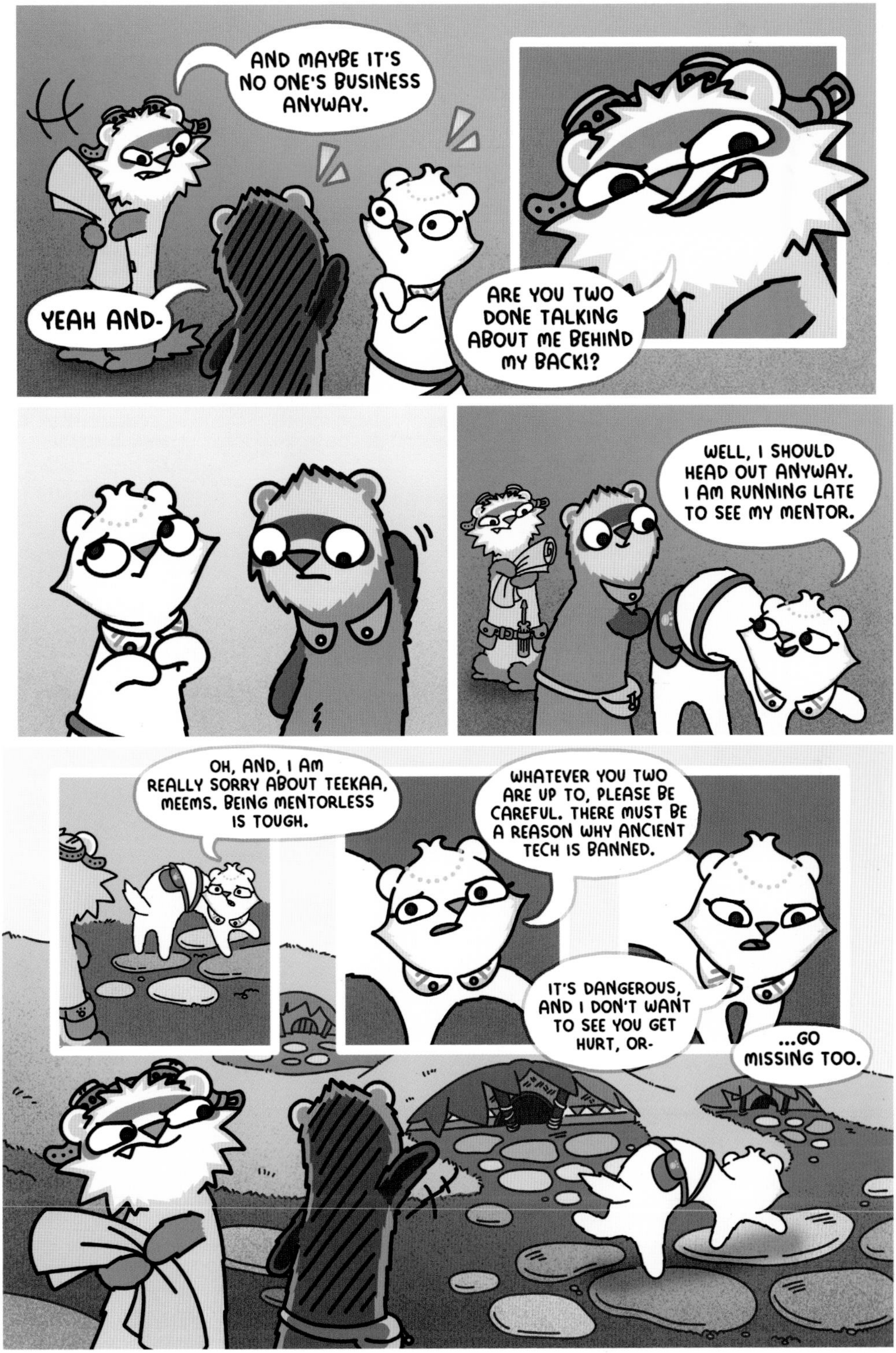
AND MAYBE IT'S NO ONE'S BUSINESS ANYWAY.
YEAH AND-
ARE YOU TWO DONE TALKING ABOUT ME BEHIND MY BACK!?
WELL, I SHOULD HEAD OUT ANYWAY. I AM RUNNING LATE TO SEE MY MENTOR.
OH, AND, I AM REALLY SORRY ABOUT TEEKAA, MEEMS. BEING MENTORLESS IS TOUGH.
WHATEVER YOU TWO ARE UP TO, PLEASE BE CAREFUL. THERE MUST BE A REASON WHY ANCIENT TECH IS BANNED.
IT'S DANGEROUS, AND I DON'T WANT TO SEE YOU GET HURT, OR-
...GO MISSING TOO.

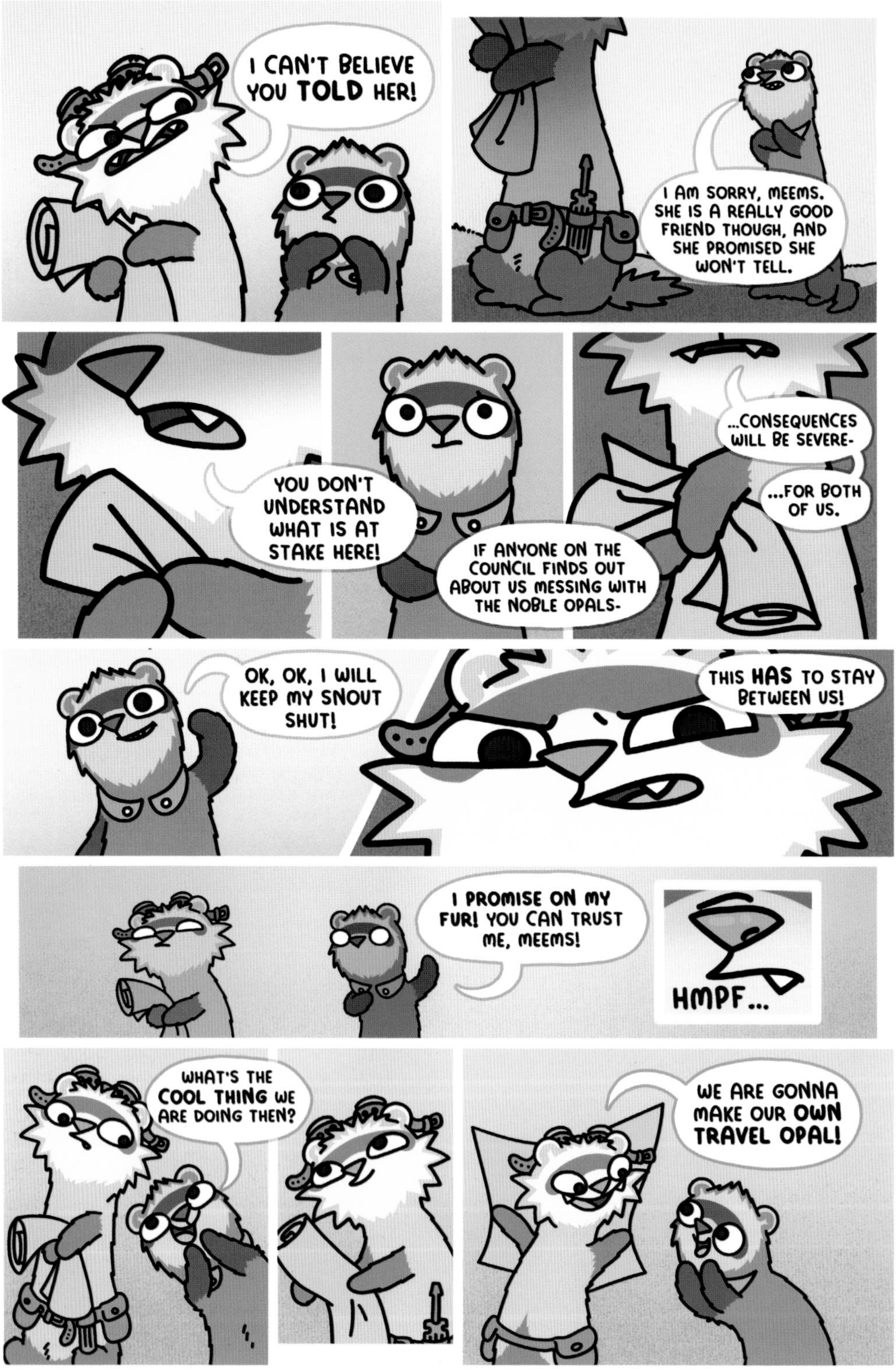
I CAN'T BELIEVE YOU TOLD HER!
I AM SORRY, MEEMS. SHE IS A REALLY GOOD FRIEND THOUGH, AND SHE PROMISED SHE WON'T TELL.
YOU DON'T UNDERSTAND WHAT IS AT STAKE HERE!
IF ANYONE ON THE COUNCIL FINDS OUT ABOUT US MESSING WITH THE NOBLE OPALS-
...CONSEQUENCES WILL BE SEVERE-
...FOR BOTH OF US.
OK, OK, I WILL KEEP MY SNOUT SHUT!
THIS HAS TO STAY BETWEEN US!
I PROMISE ON MY FUR! YOU CAN TRUST ME, MEEMS!
HMPF...
WHAT'S THE COOL THING WE ARE DOING THEN?
WE ARE GONNA MAKE OUR OWN TRAVEL OPAL!

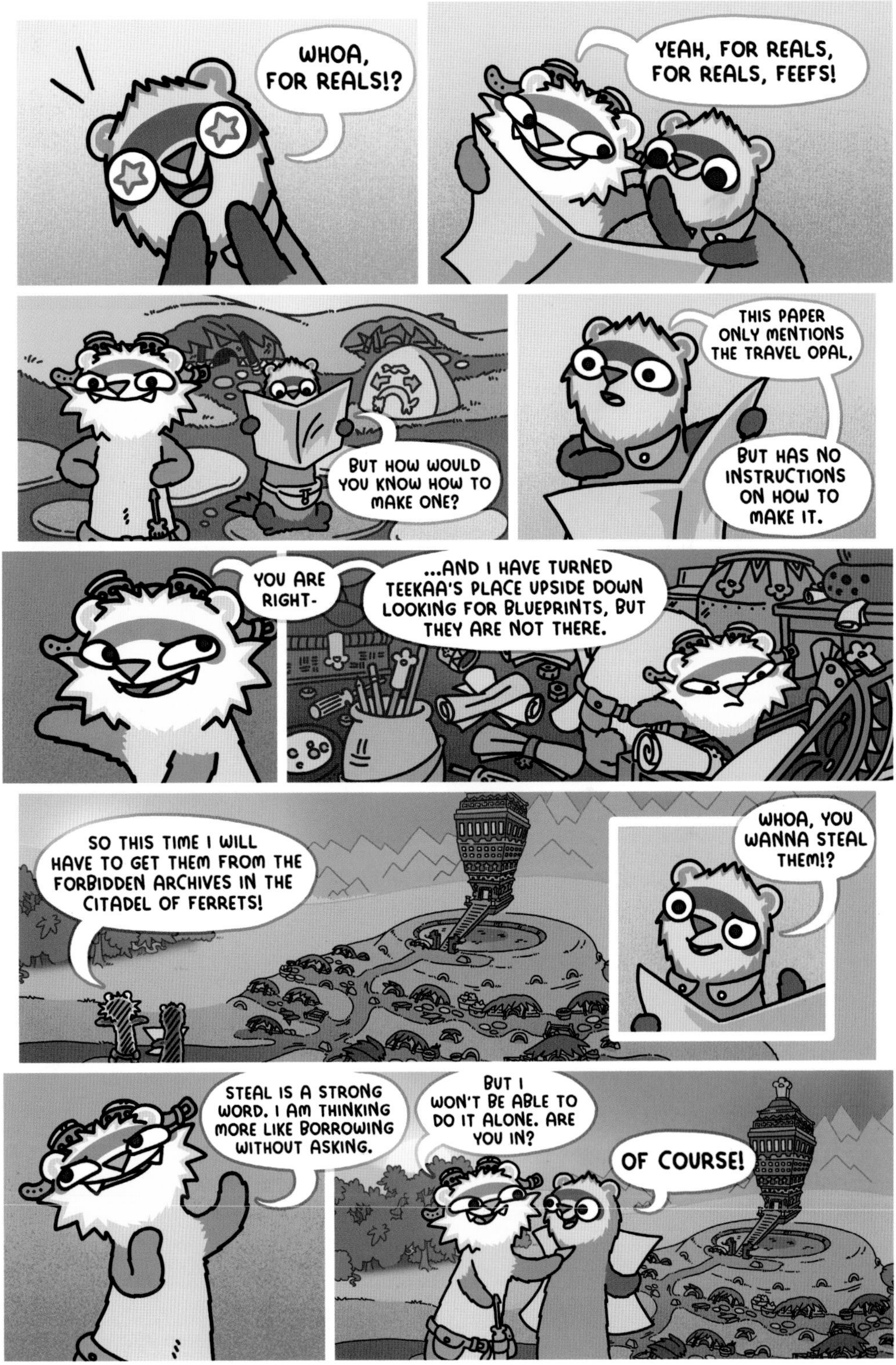
WHOA, FOR REALS!?
YEAH, FOR REALS, FOR REALS, FEEFS!
BUT HOW WOULD YOU KNOW HOW TO MAKE ONE?
THIS PAPER ONLY MENTIONS THE TRAVEL OPAL,
BUT HAS NO INSTRUCTIONS ON HOW TO MAKE IT.
YOU ARE RIGHT-
...AND I HAVE TURNED TEEKAA'S PLACE UPSIDE DOWN LOOKING FOR BLUEPRINTS, BUT THEY ARE NOT THERE.
SO THIS TIME I WILL HAVE TO GET THEM FROM THE FORBIDDEN ARCHIVES IN THE CITADEL OF FERRETS!
WHOA, YOU WANNA STEAL THEM!?
STEAL IS A STRONG WORD. I AM THINKING MORE LIKE BORROWING WITHOUT ASKING.
BUT I WON'T BE ABLE TO DO IT ALONE. ARE YOU IN?
OF COURSE!

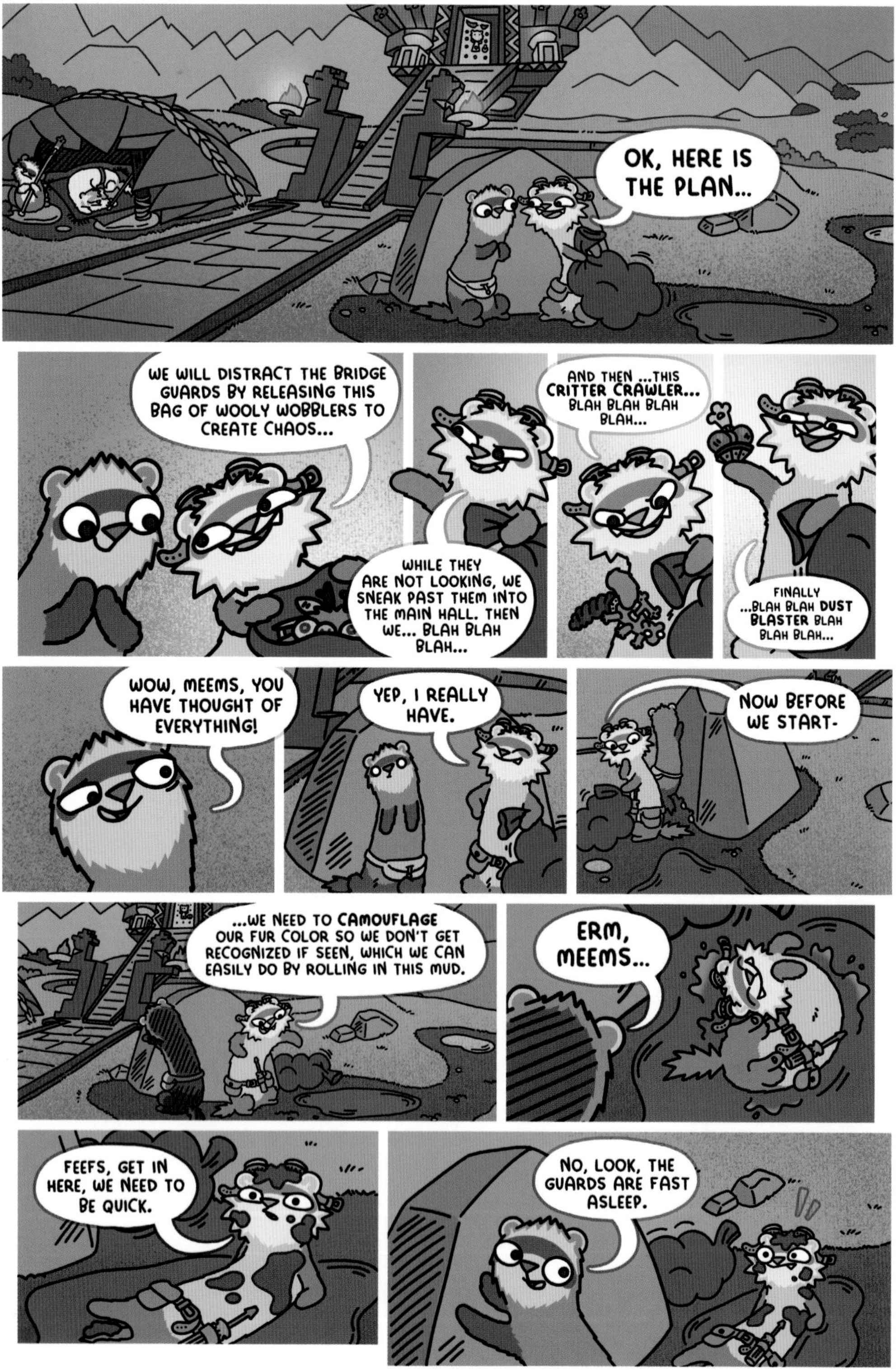
OK, HERE IS THE PLAN...
WE WILL DISTRACT THE BRIDGE GUARDS BY RELEASING THIS BAG OF WOOLY WOBBLERS TO CREATE CHAOS...
WHILE THEY ARE NOT LOOKING, WE SNEAK PAST THEM INTO THE MAIN HALL. THEN WE... BLAH BLAH BLAH...
AND THEN ...THIS CRITTER CRAWLER... BLAH BLAH BLAH BLAH...
FINALLY ...BLAH BLAH DUST BLASTER BLAH BLAH BLAH...
WOW, MEEMS, YOU HAVE THOUGHT OF EVERYTHING!
YEP, I REALLY HAVE.
NOW BEFORE WE START-
...WE NEED TO CAMOUFLAGE OUR FUR COLOR SO WE DON'T GET RECOGNIZED IF SEEN, WHICH WE CAN EASILY DO BY ROLLING IN THIS MUD.
ERM, MEEMS...
FEEFS, GET IN HERE, WE NEED TO BE QUICK.
NO, LOOK, THE GUARDS ARE FAST ASLEEP.

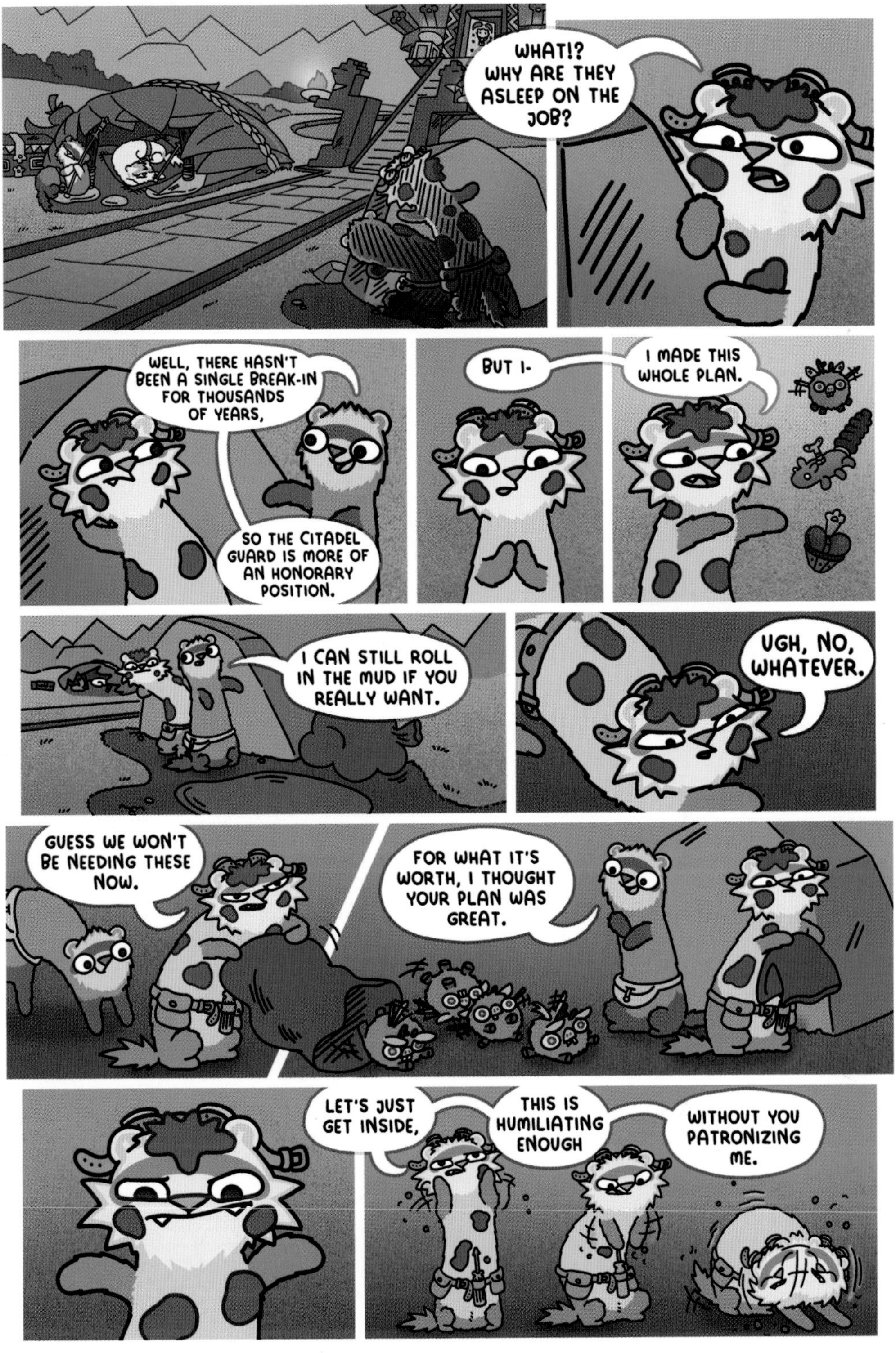
WHAT!? WHY ARE THEY ASLEEP ON THE JOB?
WELL, THERE HASN'T BEEN A SINGLE BREAK-IN FOR THOUSANDS OF YEARS,
SO THE CITADEL GUARD IS MORE OF AN HONORARY POSITION.
BUT I-
I MADE THIS WHOLE PLAN.
I CAN STILL ROLL IN THE MUD IF YOU REALLY WANT.
UGH, NO, WHATEVER.
GUESS WE WON'T BE NEEDING THESE NOW.
FOR WHAT IT'S WORTH, I THOUGHT YOUR PLAN WAS GREAT.
LET'S JUST GET INSIDE,
THIS IS HUMILIATING ENOUGH
WITHOUT YOU PATRONIZING ME.

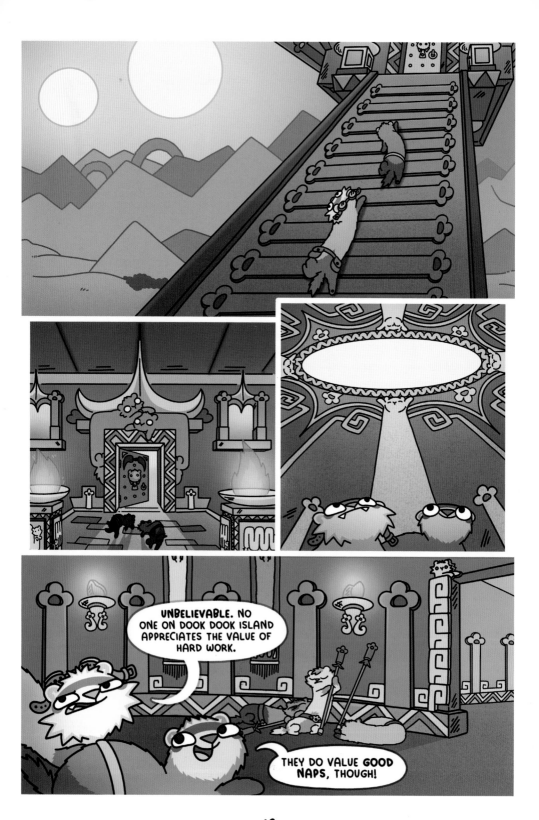

UNBELIEVABLE. NO ONE ON DOOK DOOK ISLAND APPRECIATES THE VALUE OF HARD WORK.

THEY DO VALUE **GOOD NAPS**, THOUGH!

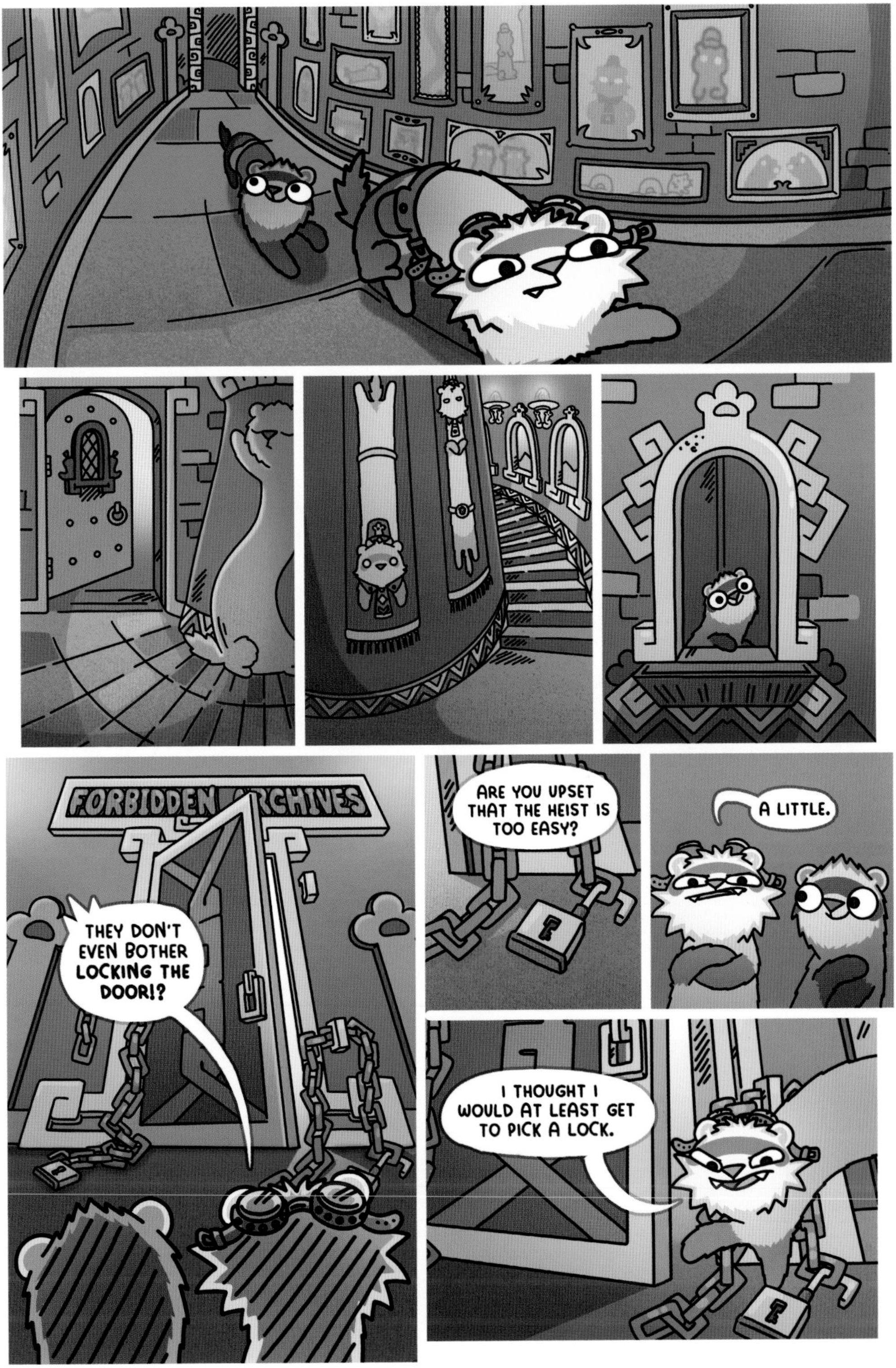
FORBIDDEN ARCHIVES
THEY DON'T EVEN BOTHER LOCKING THE DOOR!?
ARE YOU UPSET THAT THE HEIST IS TOO EASY?
A LITTLE.
I THOUGHT I WOULD AT LEAST GET TO PICK A LOCK.

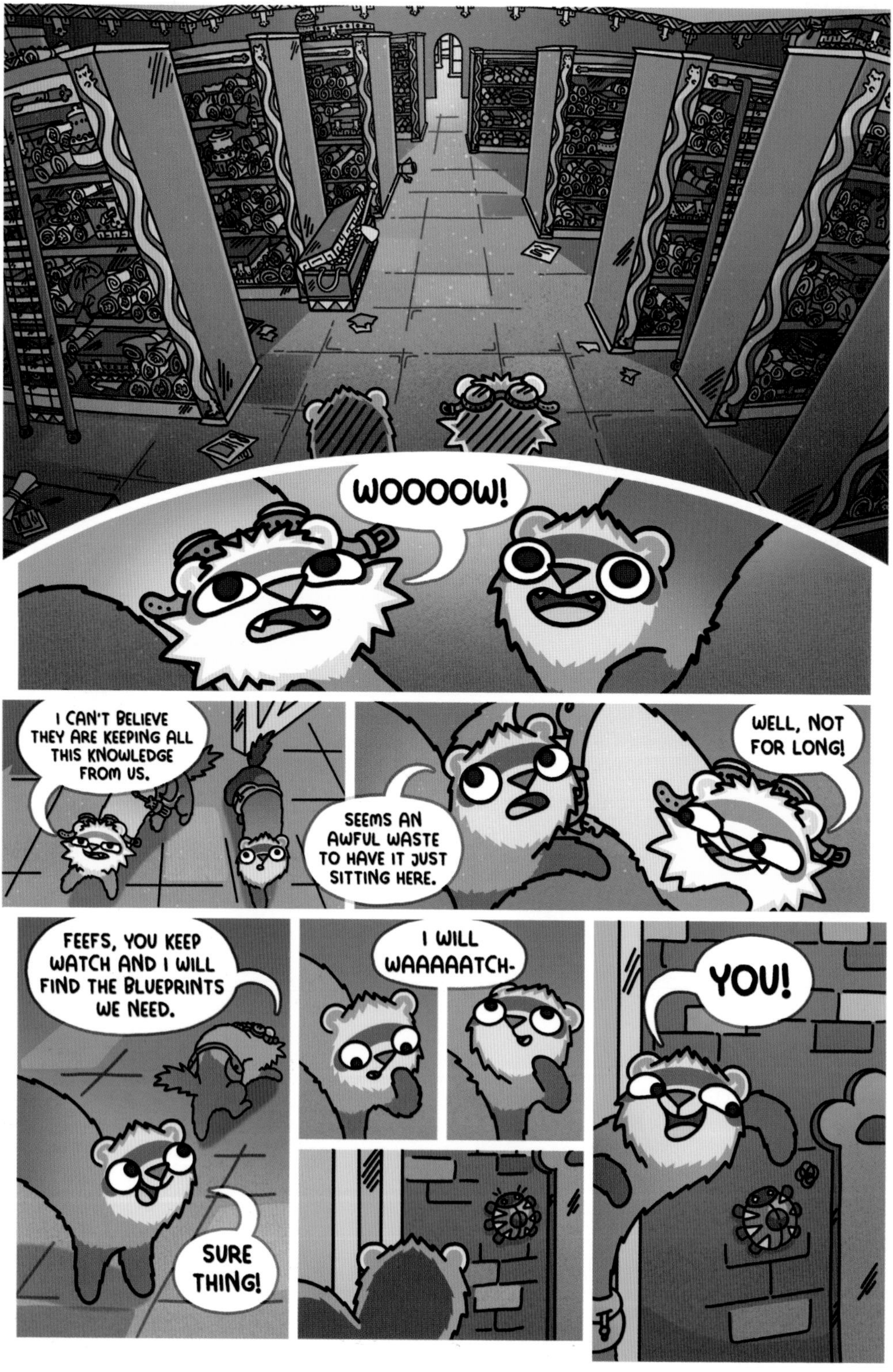
WOOOOW!
I CAN'T BELIEVE THEY ARE KEEPING ALL THIS KNOWLEDGE FROM US.
SEEMS AN AWFUL WASTE TO HAVE IT JUST SITTING HERE.
WELL, NOT FOR LONG!
FEEFS, YOU KEEP WATCH AND I WILL FIND THE BLUEPRINTS WE NEED.
SURE THING!
I WILL WAAAAATCH-
YOU!

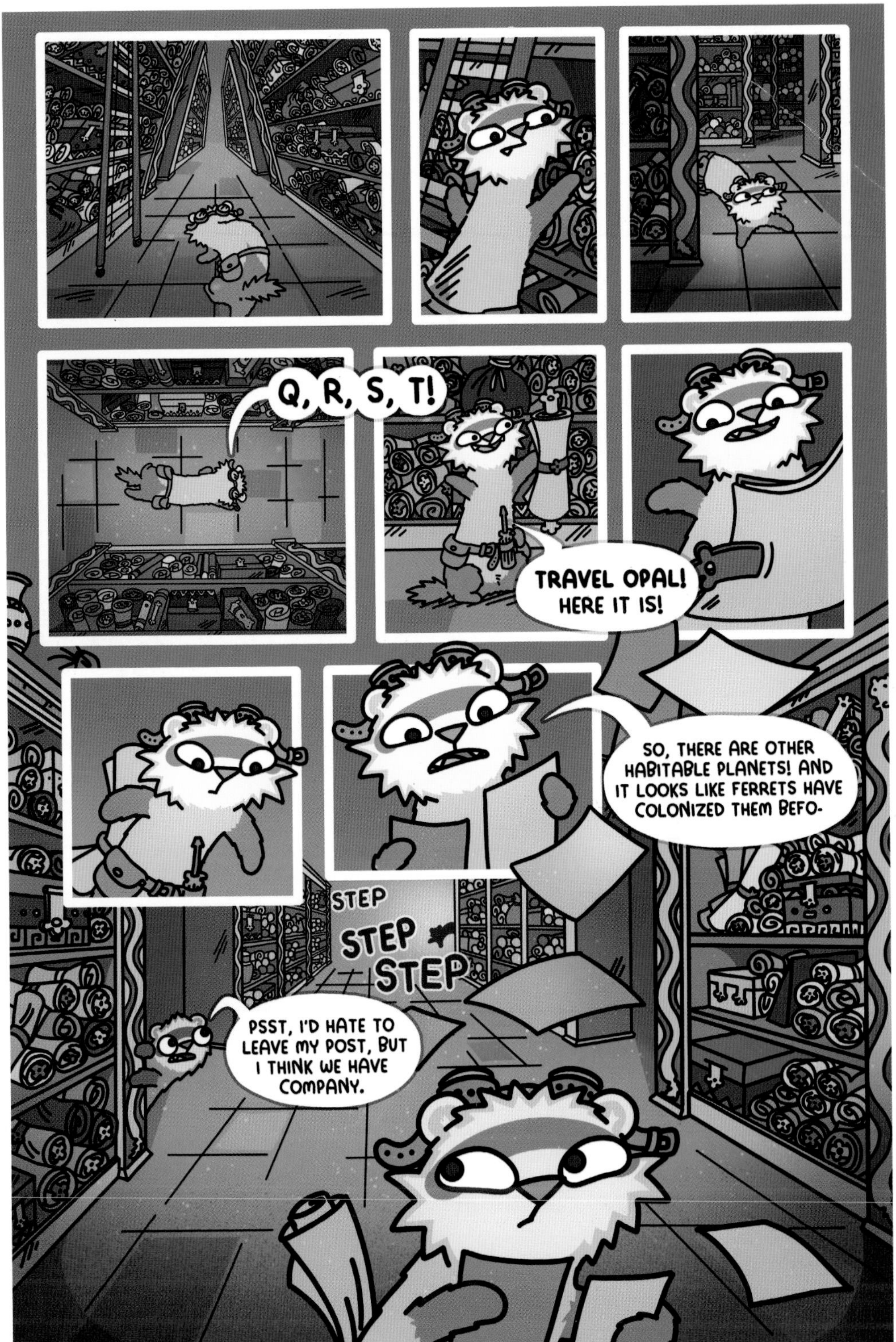
Q, R, S, T!
TRAVEL OPAL! HERE IT IS!
SO, THERE ARE OTHER HABITABLE PLANETS! AND IT LOOKS LIKE FERRETS HAVE COLONIZED THEM BEFO-
STEP
STEP
STEP
PSST, I'D HATE TO LEAVE MY POST, BUT I THINK WE HAVE COMPANY.

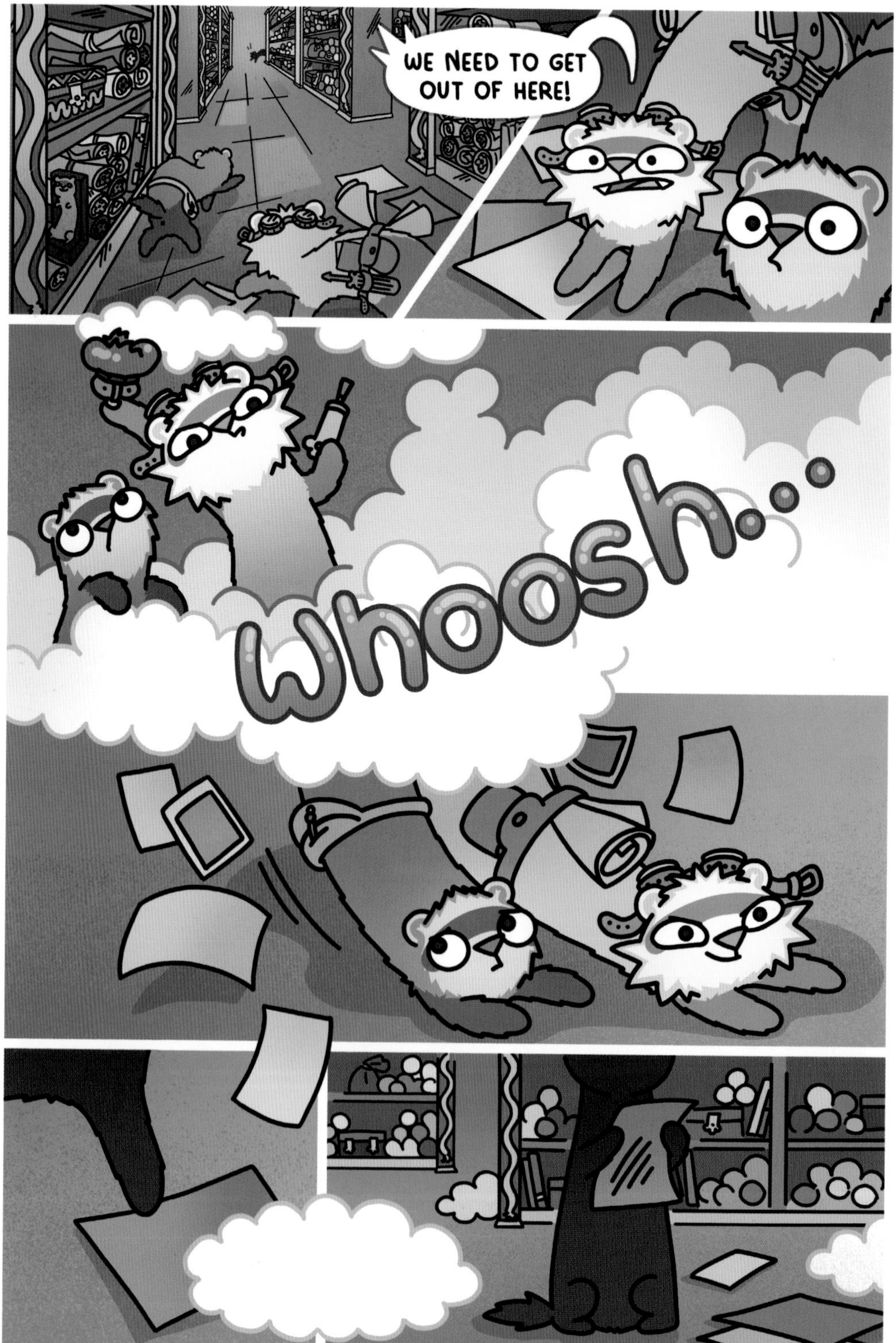
WE NEED TO GET OUT OF HERE!
Whoosh...

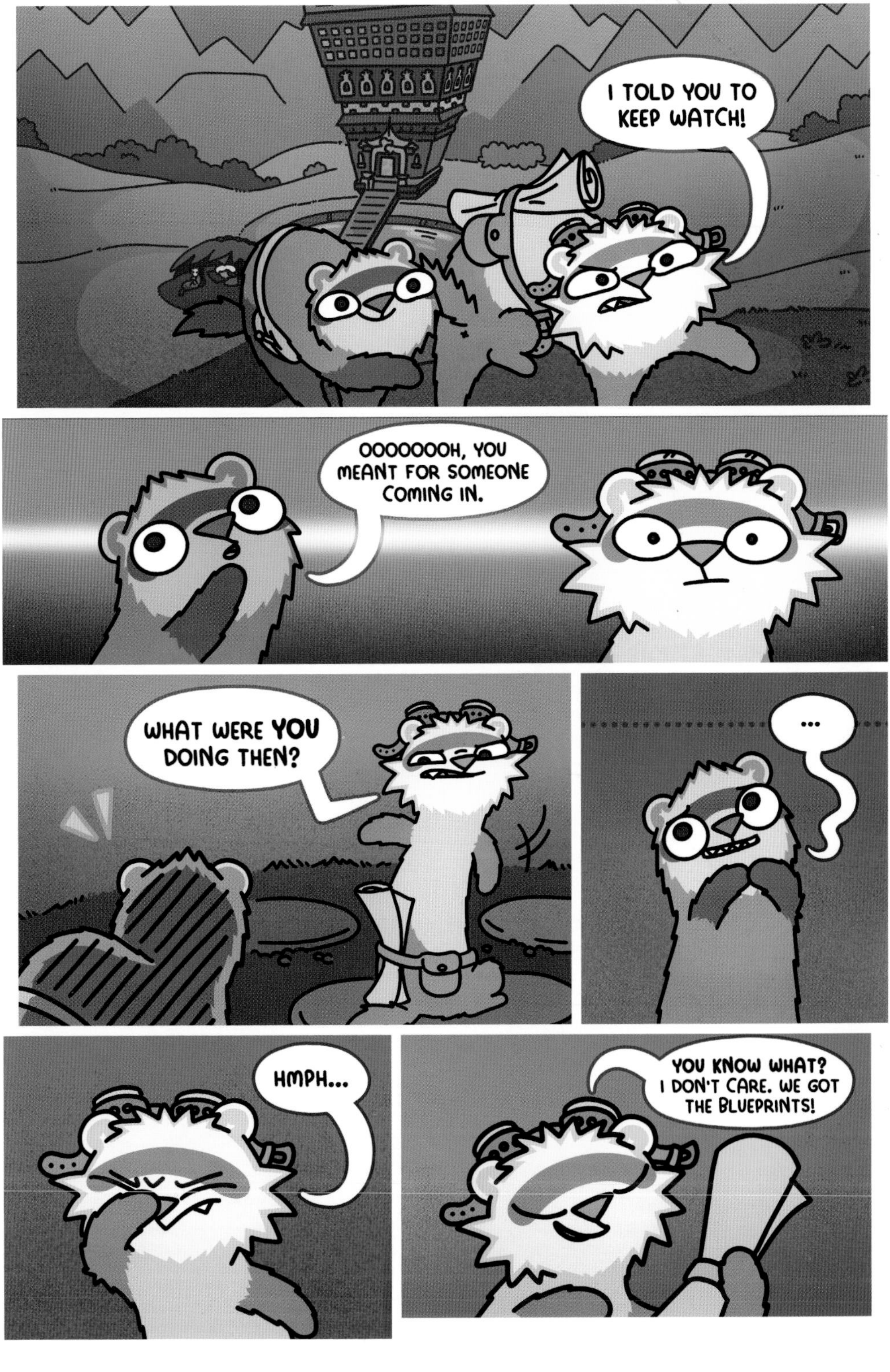
I TOLD YOU TO KEEP WATCH!
OOOOOOOH, YOU MEANT FOR SOMEONE COMING IN.
WHAT WERE YOU DOING THEN?
...
HMPH...
YOU KNOW WHAT? I DON'T CARE. WE GOT THE BLUEPRINTS!

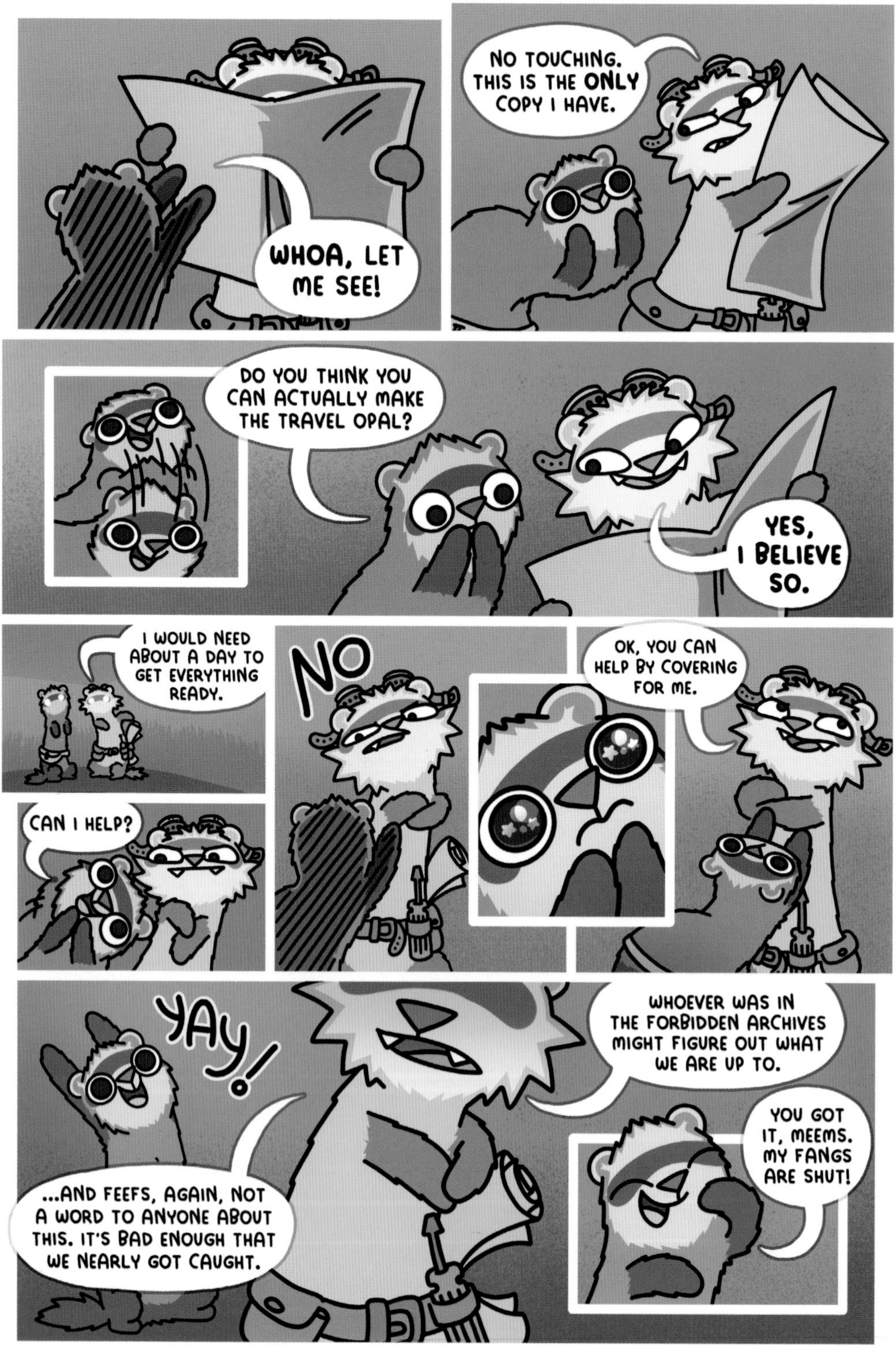
WHOA, LET ME SEE!
NO TOUCHING. THIS IS THE ONLY COPY I HAVE.
DO YOU THINK YOU CAN ACTUALLY MAKE THE TRAVEL OPAL?
YES, I BELIEVE SO.
I WOULD NEED ABOUT A DAY TO GET EVERYTHING READY.
CAN I HELP?
NO
OK, YOU CAN HELP BY COVERING FOR ME.
YAY!
WHOEVER WAS IN THE FORBIDDEN ARCHIVES MIGHT FIGURE OUT WHAT WE ARE UP TO.
...AND FEEFS, AGAIN, NOT A WORD TO ANYONE ABOUT THIS. IT'S BAD ENOUGH THAT WE NEARLY GOT CAUGHT.
YOU GOT IT, MEEMS. MY FANGS ARE SHUT!

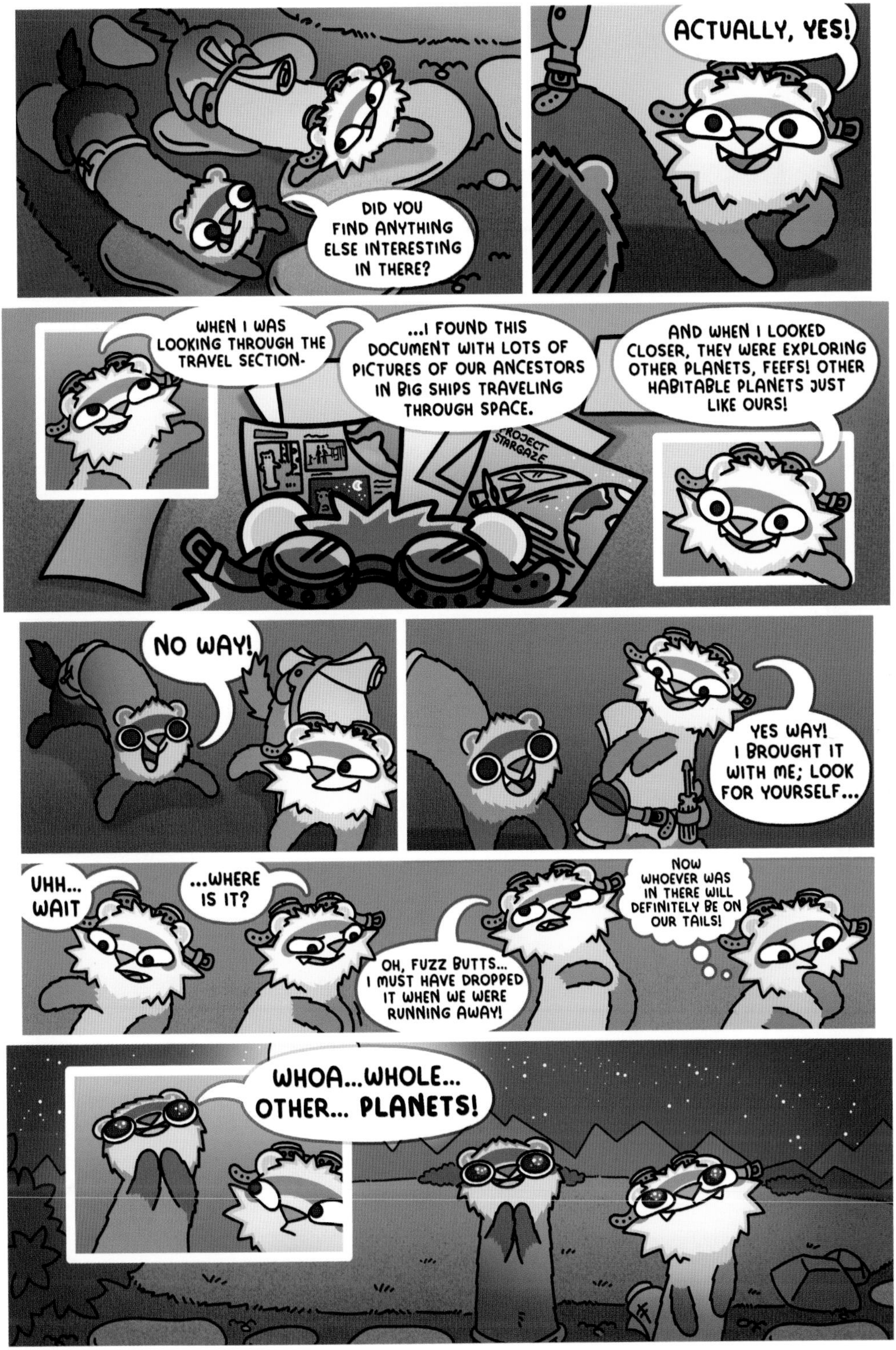
DID YOU FIND ANYTHING ELSE INTERESTING IN THERE?
ACTUALLY, YES!
WHEN I WAS LOOKING THROUGH THE TRAVEL SECTION-
...I FOUND THIS DOCUMENT WITH LOTS OF PICTURES OF OUR ANCESTORS IN BIG SHIPS TRAVELING THROUGH SPACE.
AND WHEN I LOOKED CLOSER, THEY WERE EXPLORING OTHER PLANETS, FEEFS! OTHER HABITABLE PLANETS JUST LIKE OURS!
NO WAY!
YES WAY! I BROUGHT IT WITH ME; LOOK FOR YOURSELF...
UHH... WAIT
...WHERE IS IT?
OH, FUZZ BUTTS... I MUST HAVE DROPPED IT WHEN WE WERE RUNNING AWAY!
NOW WHOEVER WAS IN THERE WILL DEFINITELY BE ON OUR TAILS!
WHOA...WHOLE... OTHER... PLANETS!

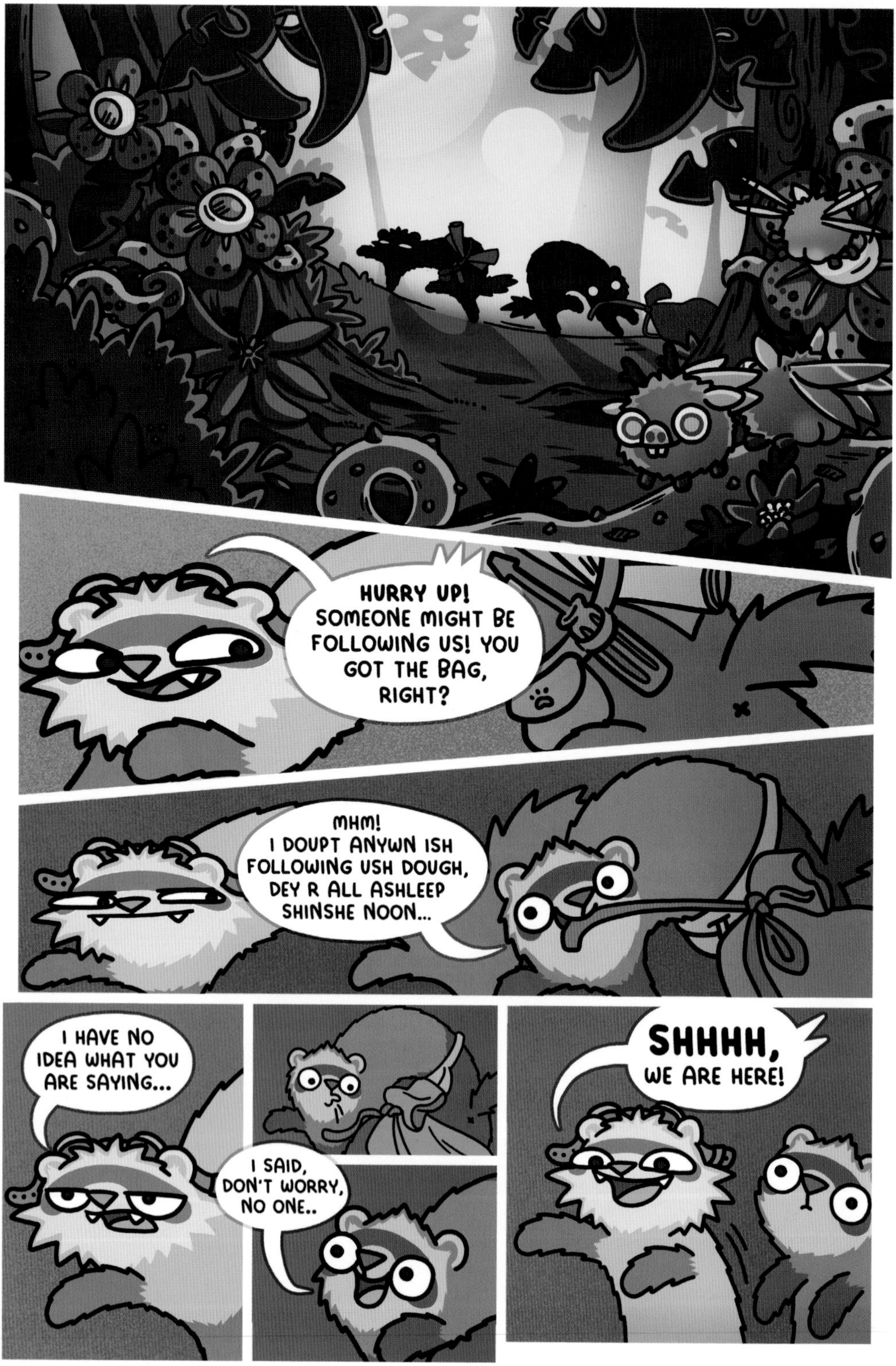
HURRY UP! SOMEONE MIGHT BE FOLLOWING US! YOU GOT THE BAG, RIGHT?
MHM! I DOUPT ANYWN ISH FOLLOWING USH DOUGH, DEY R ALL ASHLEEP SHINSHE NOON...
I HAVE NO IDEA WHAT YOU ARE SAYING...
I SAID, DON'T WORRY, NO ONE..
SHHHH, WE ARE HERE!

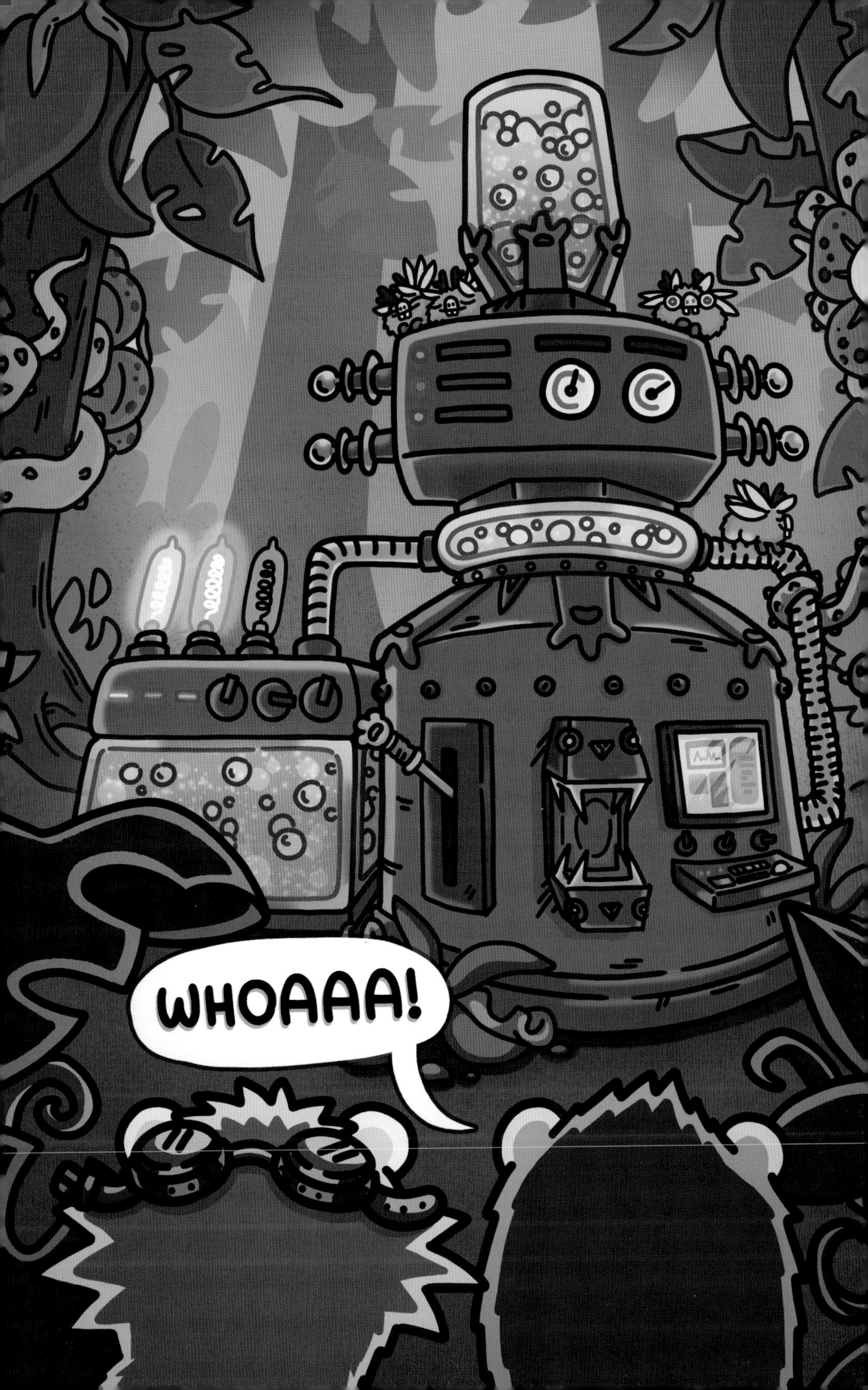
WHOAAA!

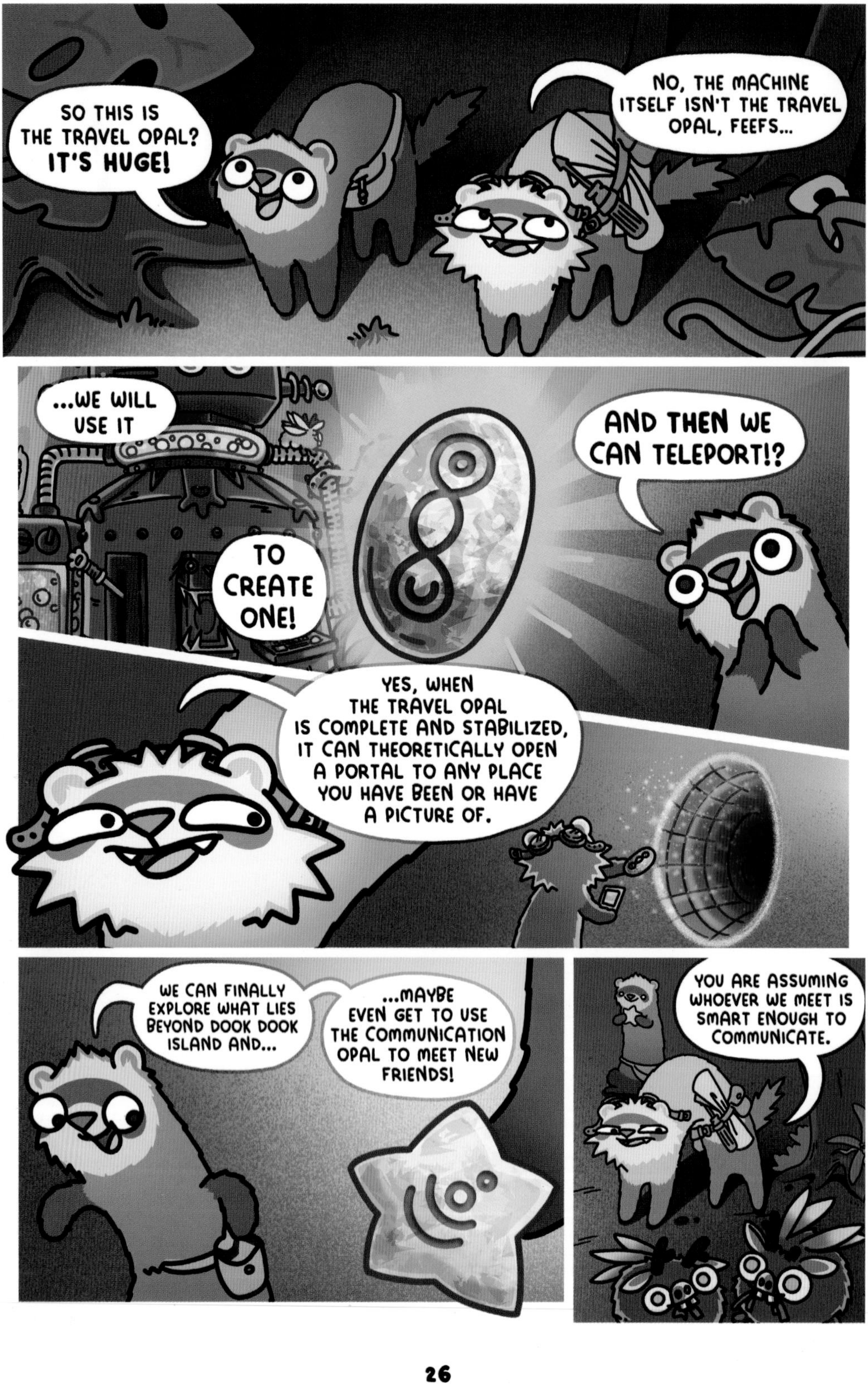
SO THIS IS THE TRAVEL OPAL? IT'S HUGE!
NO, THE MACHINE ITSELF ISN'T THE TRAVEL OPAL, FEEFS...
...WE WILL USE IT
TO CREATE ONE!
AND THEN WE CAN TELEPORT!?
YES, WHEN THE TRAVEL OPAL IS COMPLETE AND STABILIZED, IT CAN THEORETICALLY OPEN A PORTAL TO ANY PLACE YOU HAVE BEEN OR HAVE A PICTURE OF.
WE CAN FINALLY EXPLORE WHAT LIES BEYOND DOOK DOOK ISLAND AND...
...MAYBE EVEN GET TO USE THE COMMUNICATION OPAL TO MEET NEW FRIENDS!
YOU ARE ASSUMING WHOEVER WE MEET IS SMART ENOUGH TO COMMUNICATE.

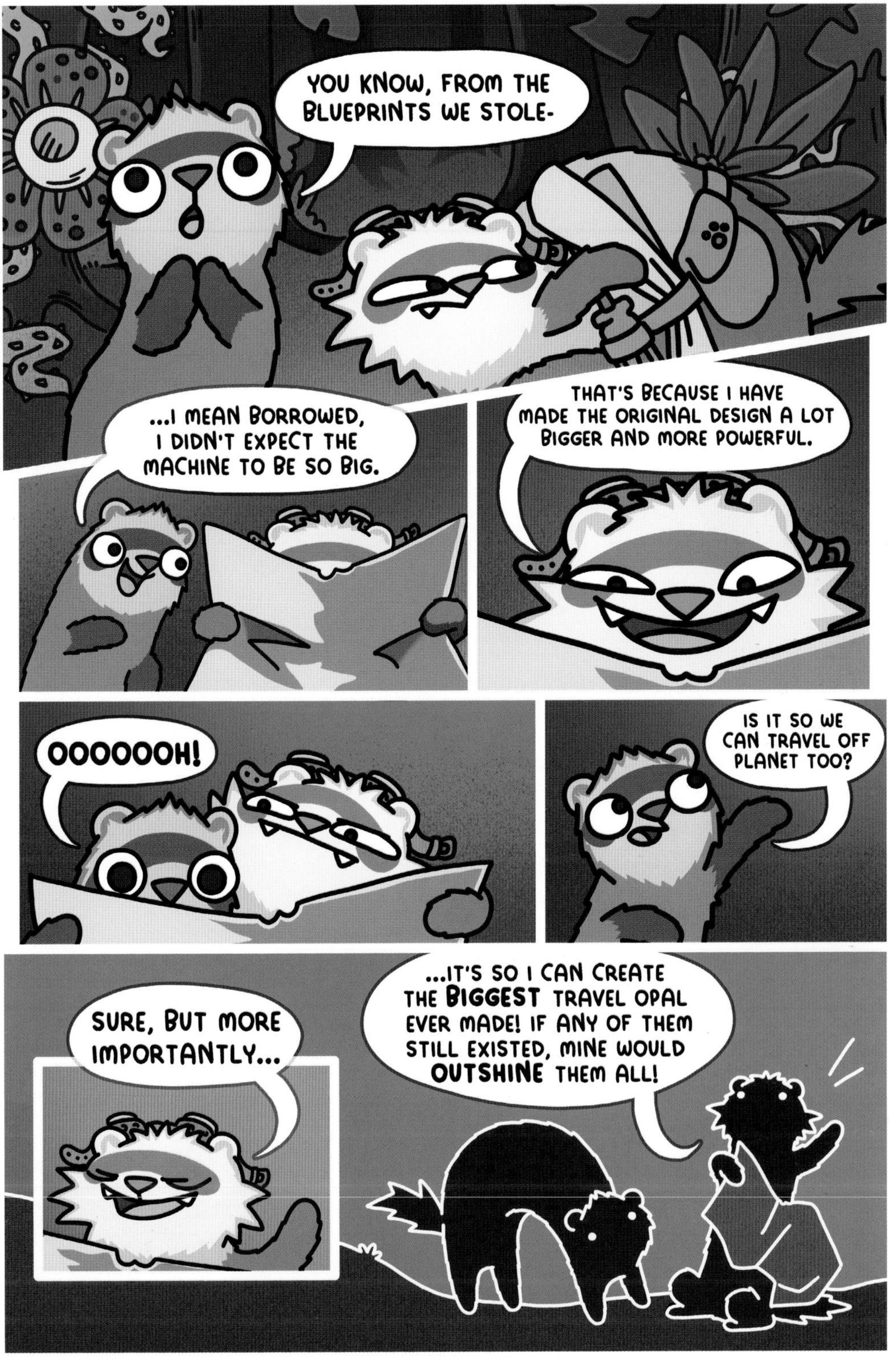
YOU KNOW, FROM THE BLUEPRINTS WE STOLE-
...I MEAN BORROWED, I DIDN'T EXPECT THE MACHINE TO BE SO BIG.
THAT'S BECAUSE I HAVE MADE THE ORIGINAL DESIGN A LOT BIGGER AND MORE POWERFUL.
OOOOOOH!
IS IT SO WE CAN TRAVEL OFF PLANET TOO?
SURE, BUT MORE IMPORTANTLY...
...IT'S SO I CAN CREATE THE **BIGGEST** TRAVEL OPAL EVER MADE! IF ANY OF THEM STILL EXISTED, MINE WOULD **OUTSHINE** THEM ALL!

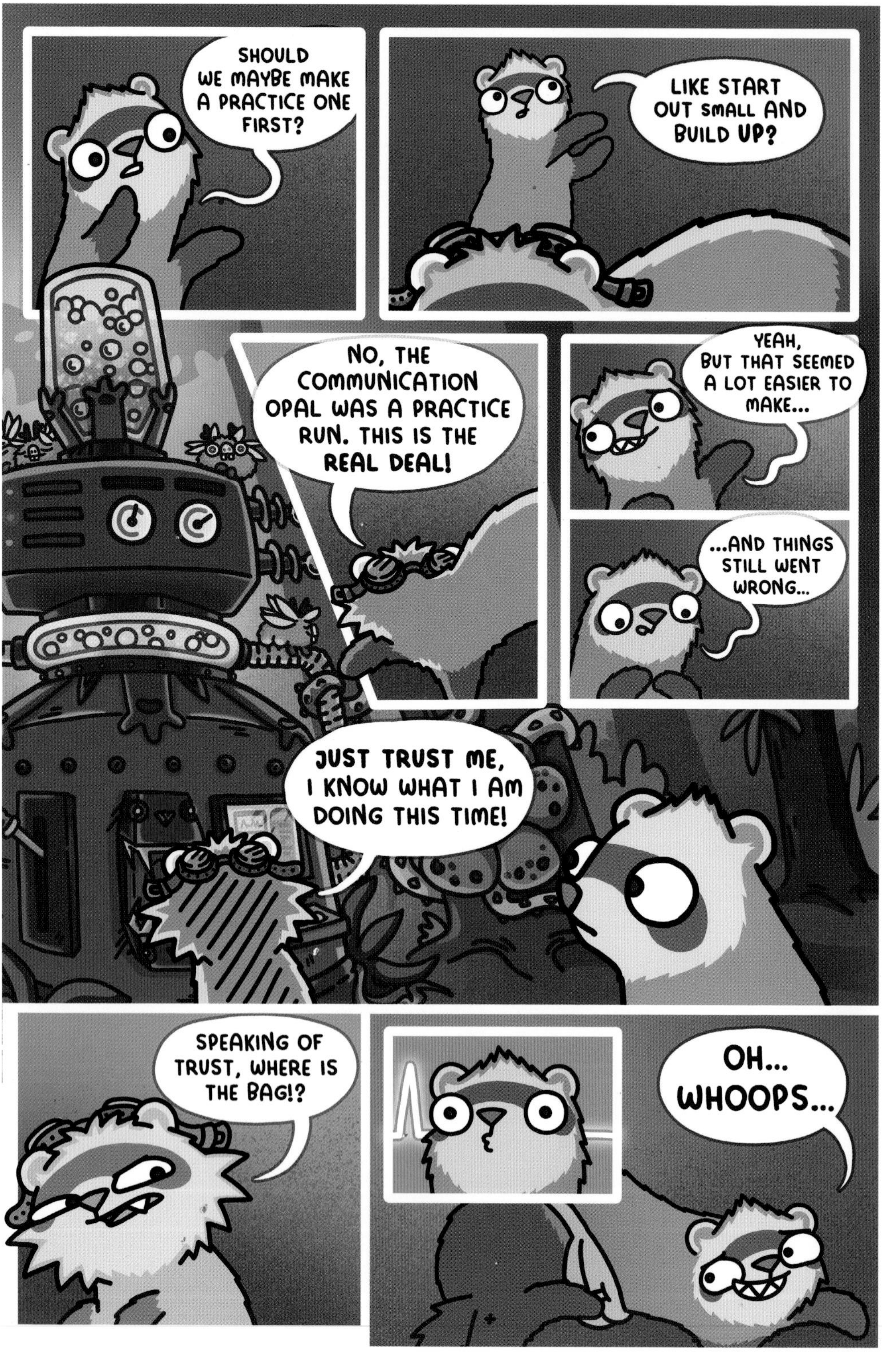
SHOULD WE MAYBE MAKE A PRACTICE ONE FIRST?
LIKE START OUT SMALL AND BUILD UP?
NO, THE COMMUNICATION OPAL WAS A PRACTICE RUN. THIS IS THE REAL DEAL!
YEAH, BUT THAT SEEMED A LOT EASIER TO MAKE...
...AND THINGS STILL WENT WRONG...
JUST TRUST ME, I KNOW WHAT I AM DOING THIS TIME!
SPEAKING OF TRUST, WHERE IS THE BAG!?
OH... WHOOPS...

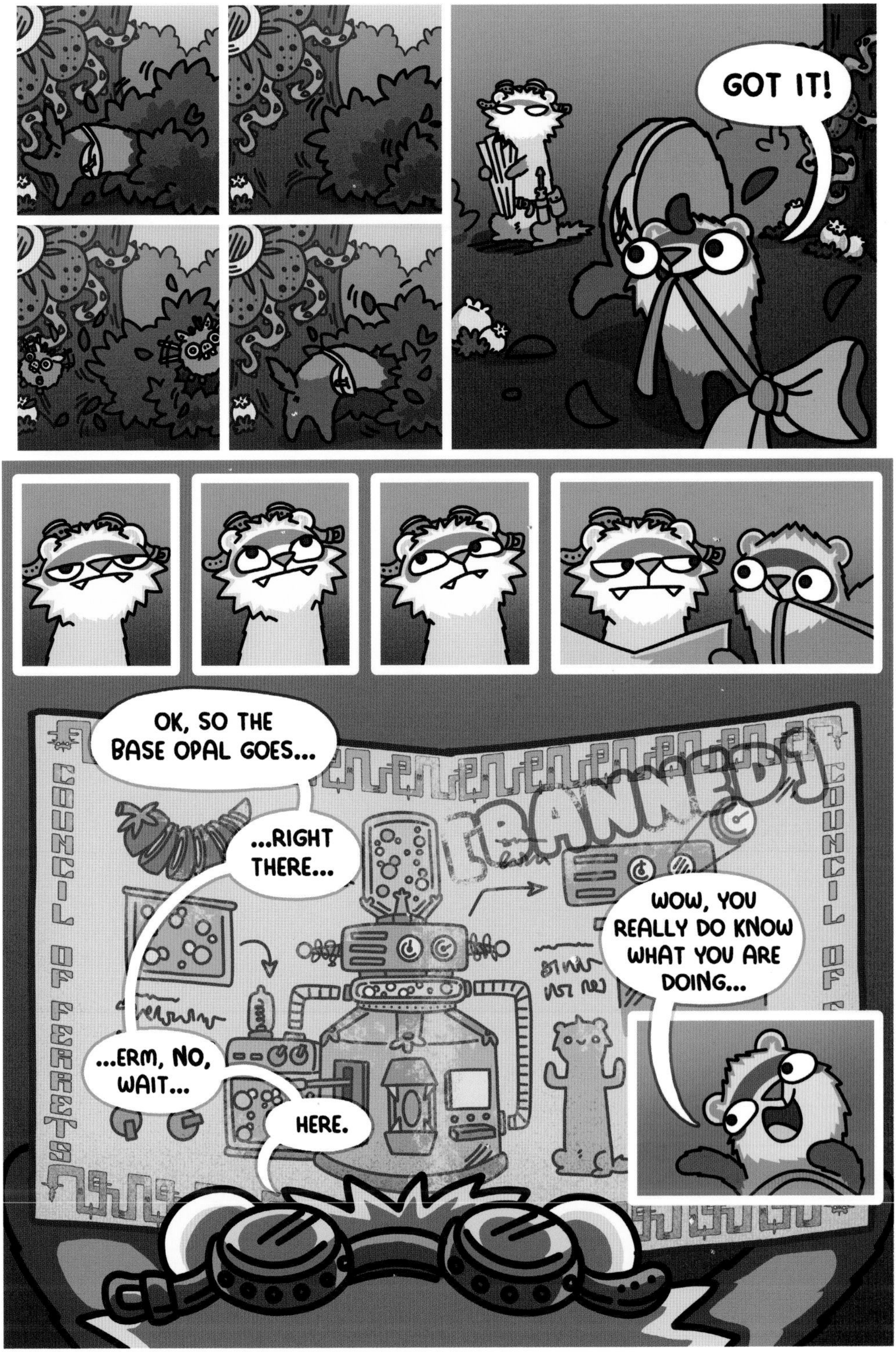
GOT IT!
OK, SO THE BASE OPAL GOES...
...RIGHT THERE...
...ERM, NO, WAIT...
HERE.
WOW, YOU REALLY DO KNOW WHAT YOU ARE DOING...
BANNED
COUNCIL OF FERRETS

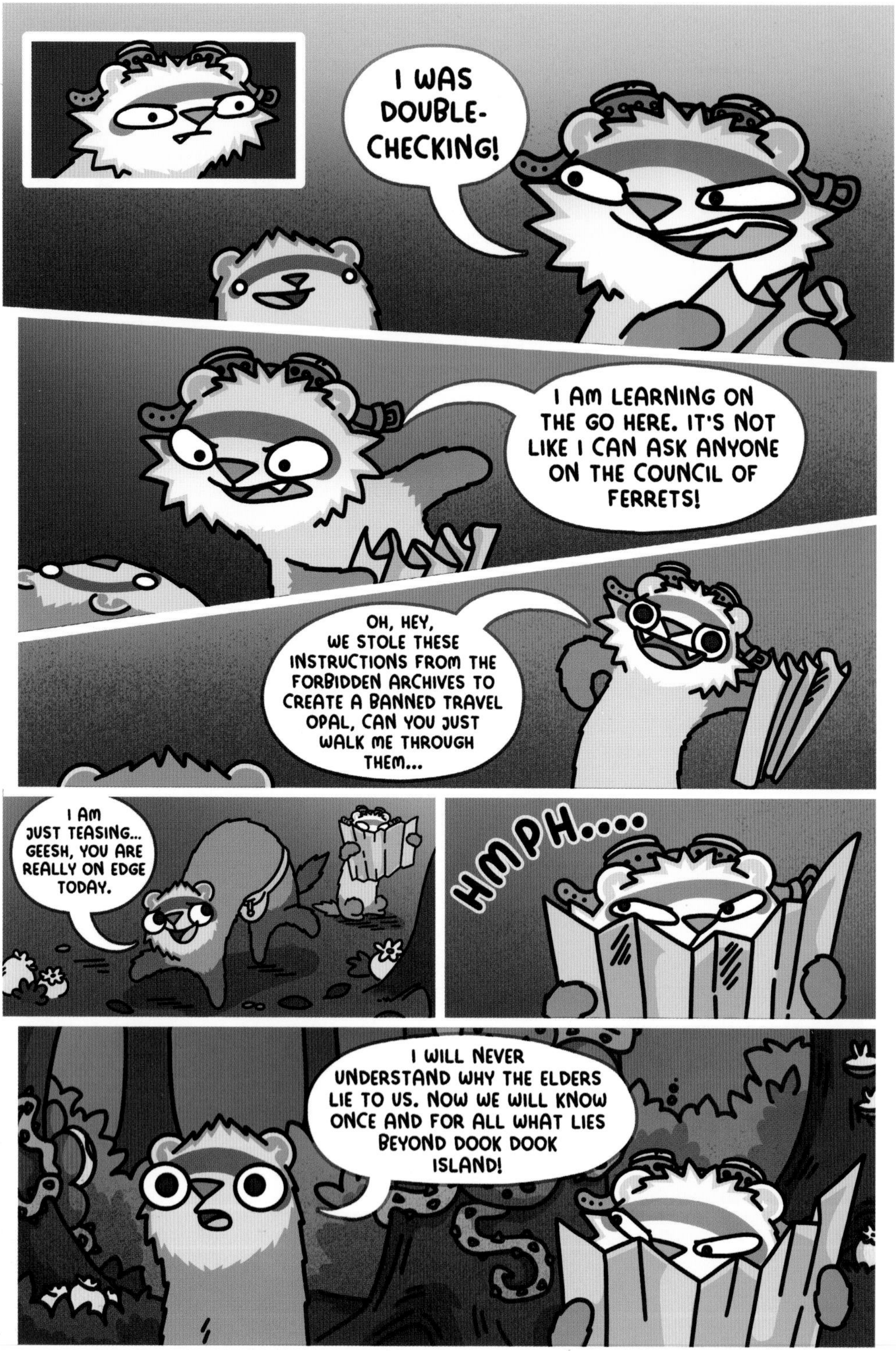
I WAS DOUBLE-CHECKING!
I AM LEARNING ON THE GO HERE. IT'S NOT LIKE I CAN ASK ANYONE ON THE COUNCIL OF FERRETS!
OH, HEY, WE STOLE THESE INSTRUCTIONS FROM THE FORBIDDEN ARCHIVES TO CREATE A BANNED TRAVEL OPAL, CAN YOU JUST WALK ME THROUGH THEM...
I AM JUST TEASING... GEESH, YOU ARE REALLY ON EDGE TODAY.
HMPH....
I WILL NEVER UNDERSTAND WHY THE ELDERS LIE TO US. NOW WE WILL KNOW ONCE AND FOR ALL WHAT LIES BEYOND DOOK DOOK ISLAND!

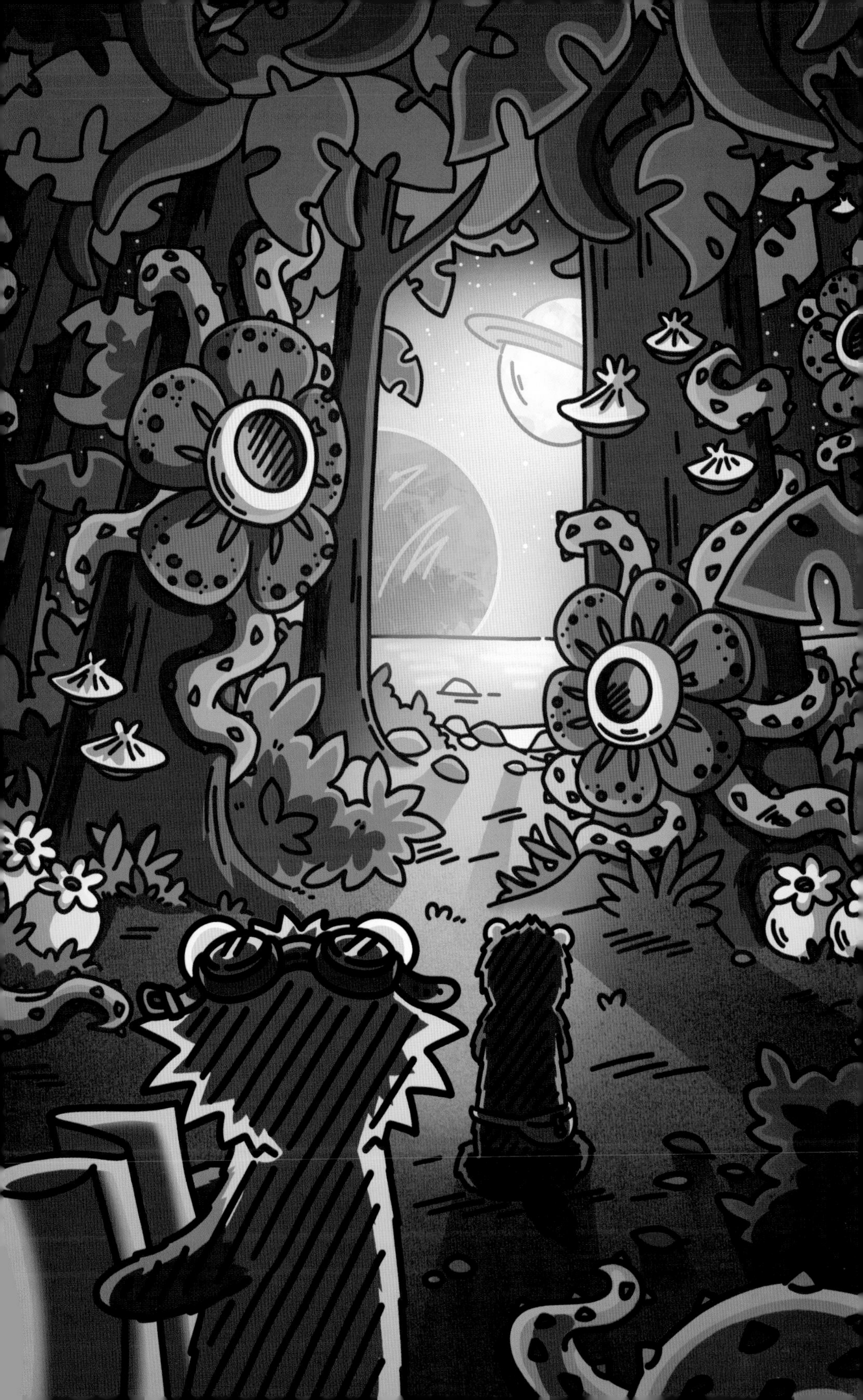

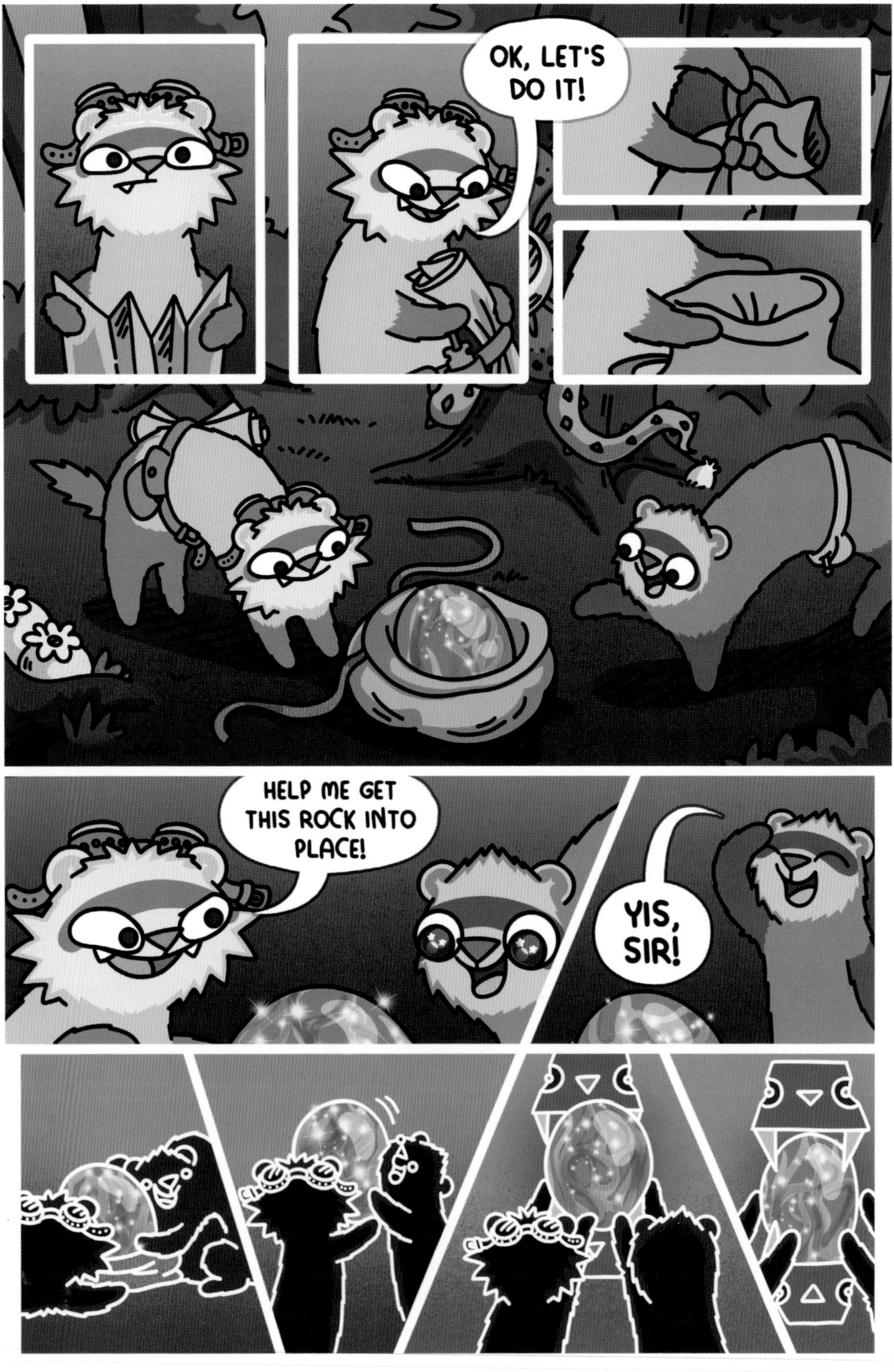
OK, LET'S DO IT!
HELP ME GET THIS ROCK INTO PLACE!
YIS, SIR!

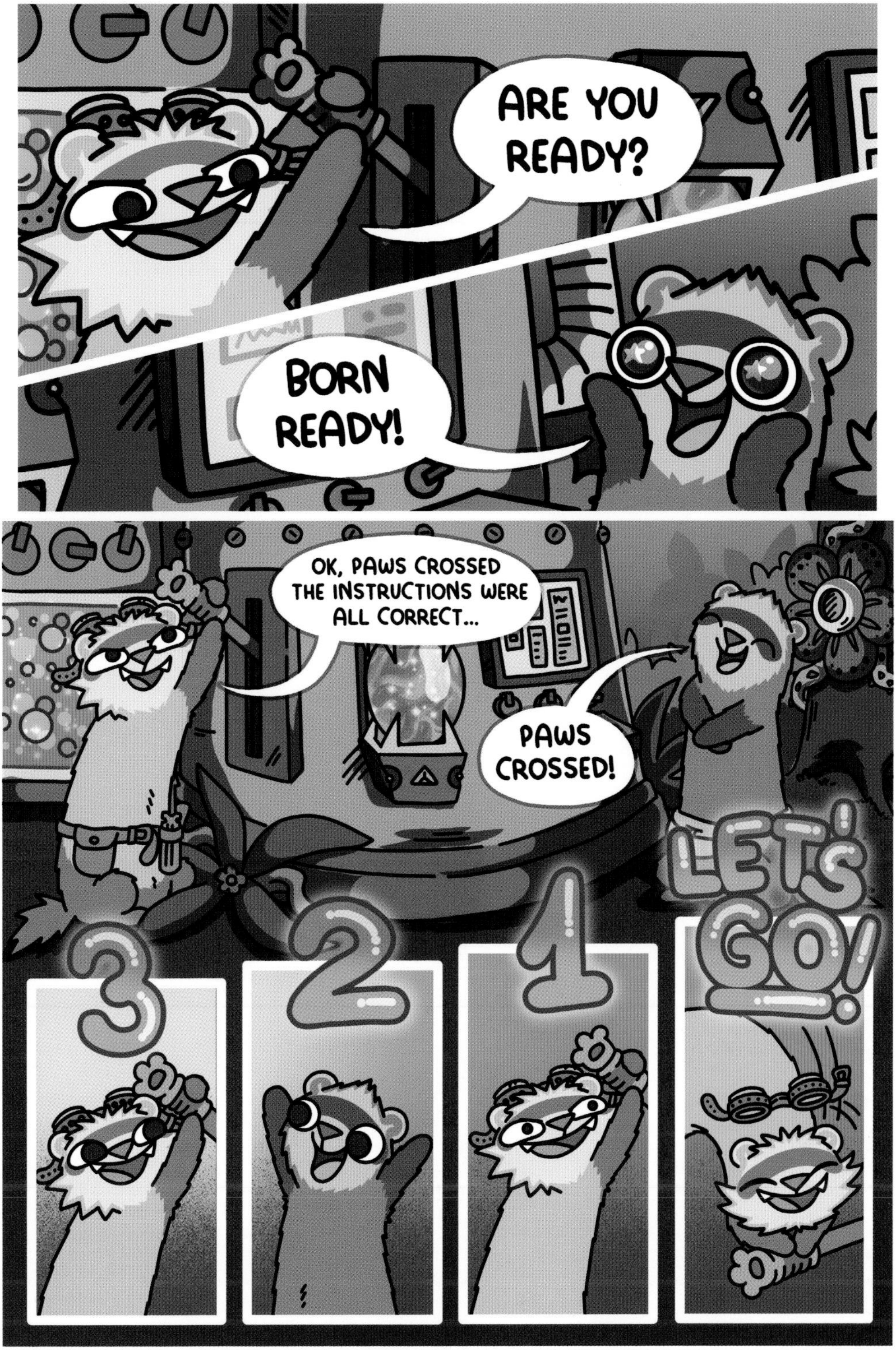
ARE YOU READY?
BORN READY!
OK, PAWS CROSSED THE INSTRUCTIONS WERE ALL CORRECT...
PAWS CROSSED!
3
2
1
LET'S GO!

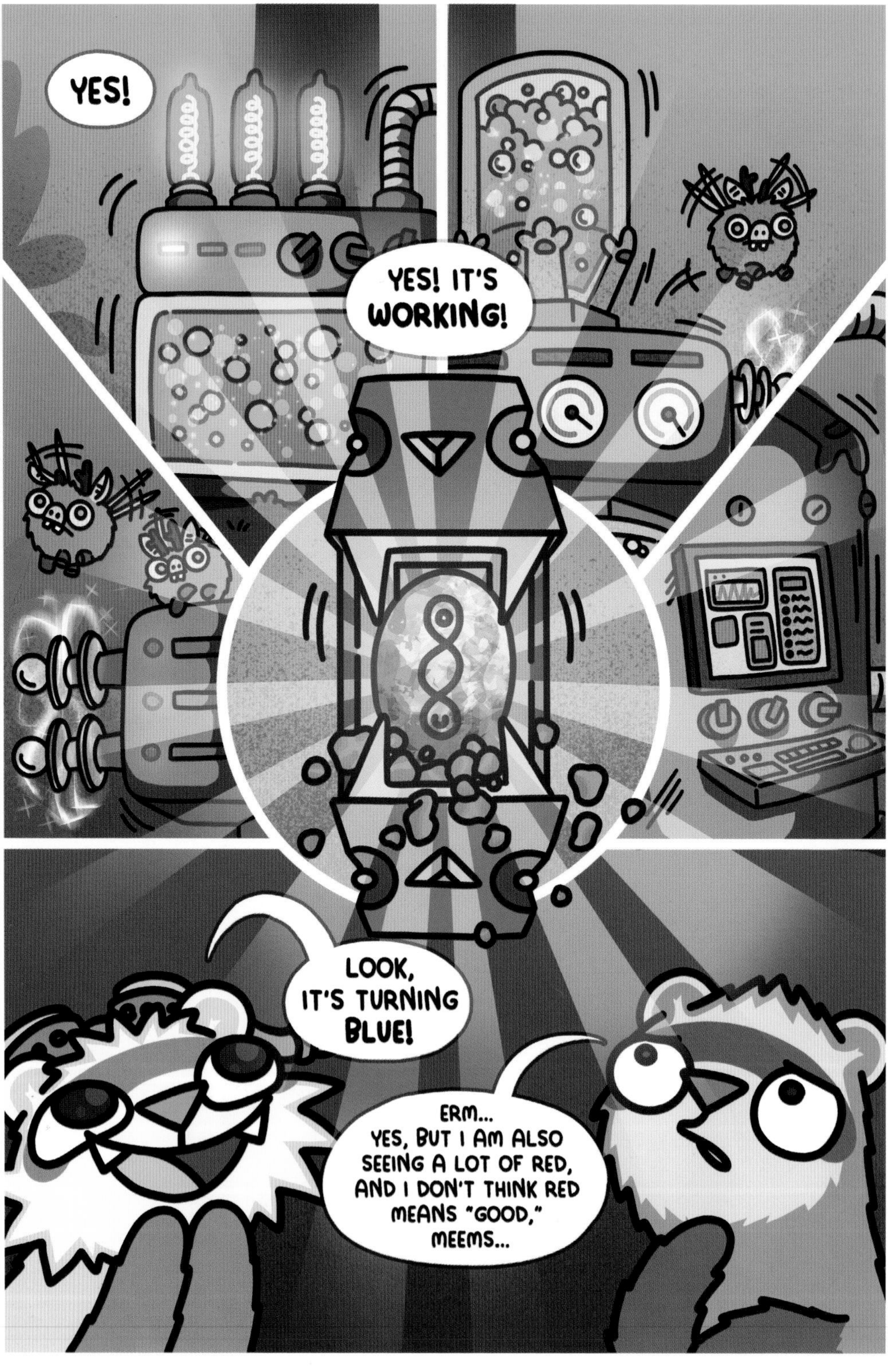
YES!
YES! IT'S WORKING!
LOOK, IT'S TURNING BLUE!
ERM... YES, BUT I AM ALSO SEEING A LOT OF RED, AND I DON'T THINK RED MEANS "GOOD," MEEMS...

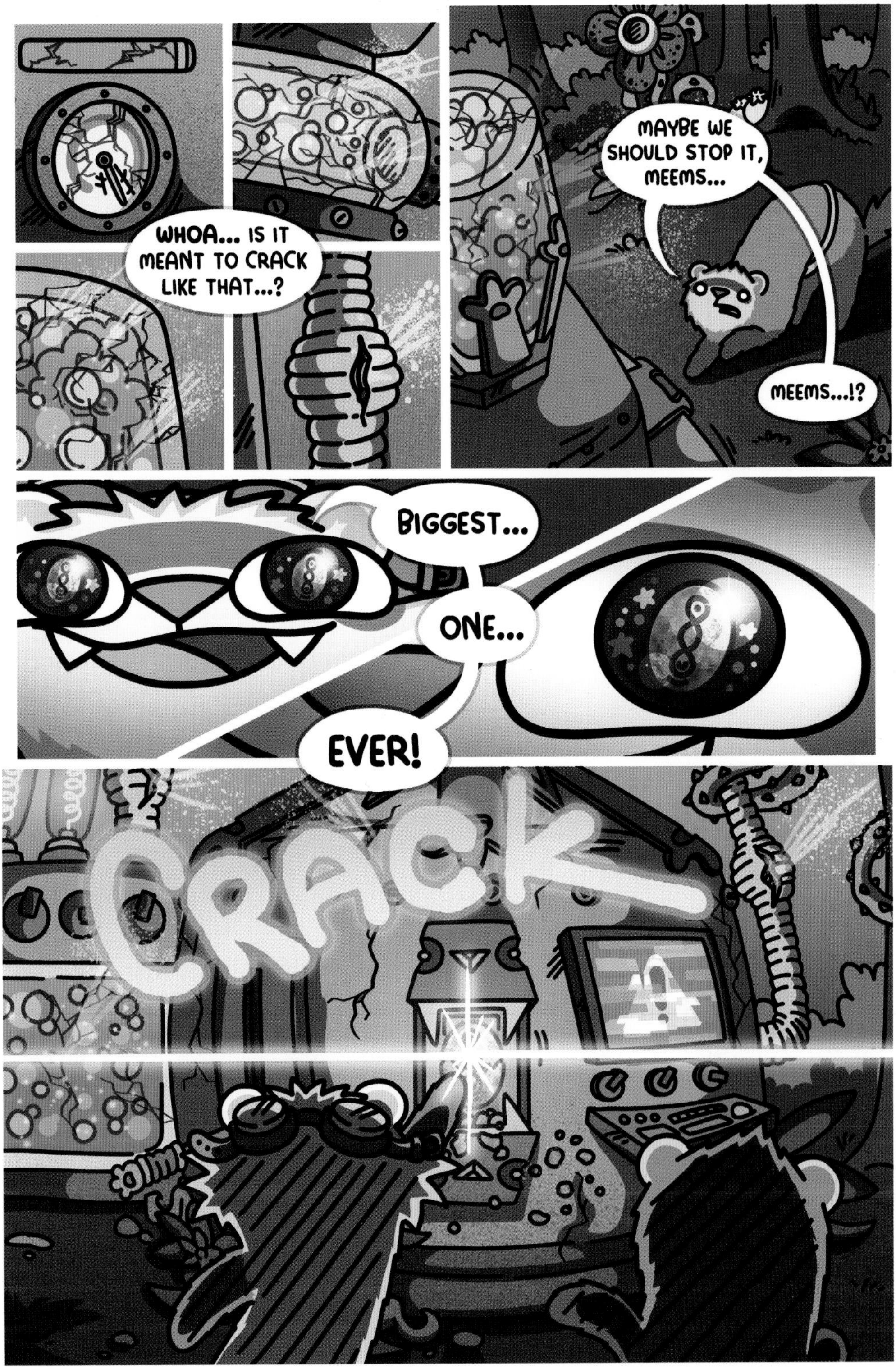
WHOA... IS IT MEANT TO CRACK LIKE THAT...?
MAYBE WE SHOULD STOP IT, MEEMS...
MEEMS...!?
BIGGEST...
ONE...
EVER!
CRACK

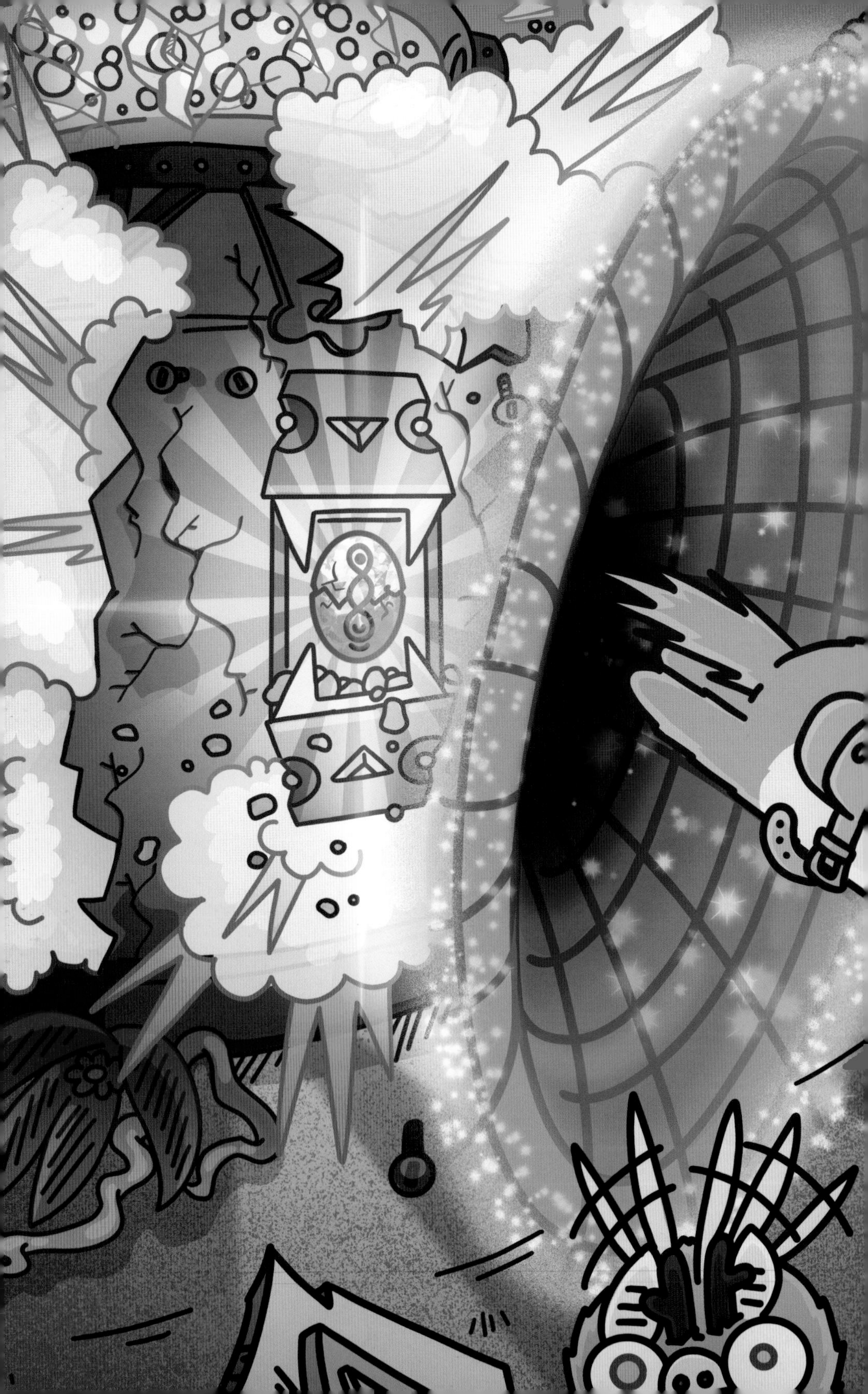

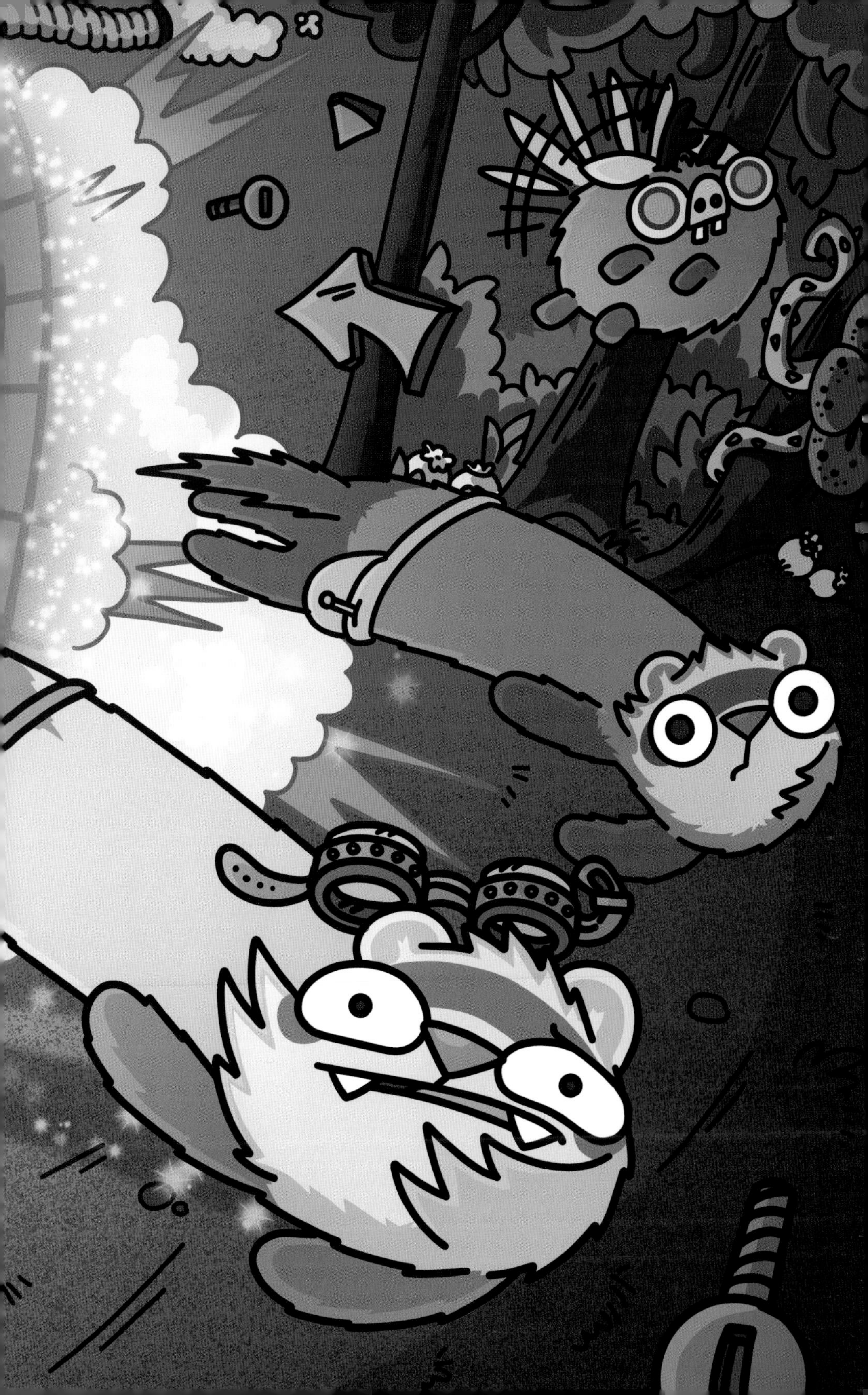

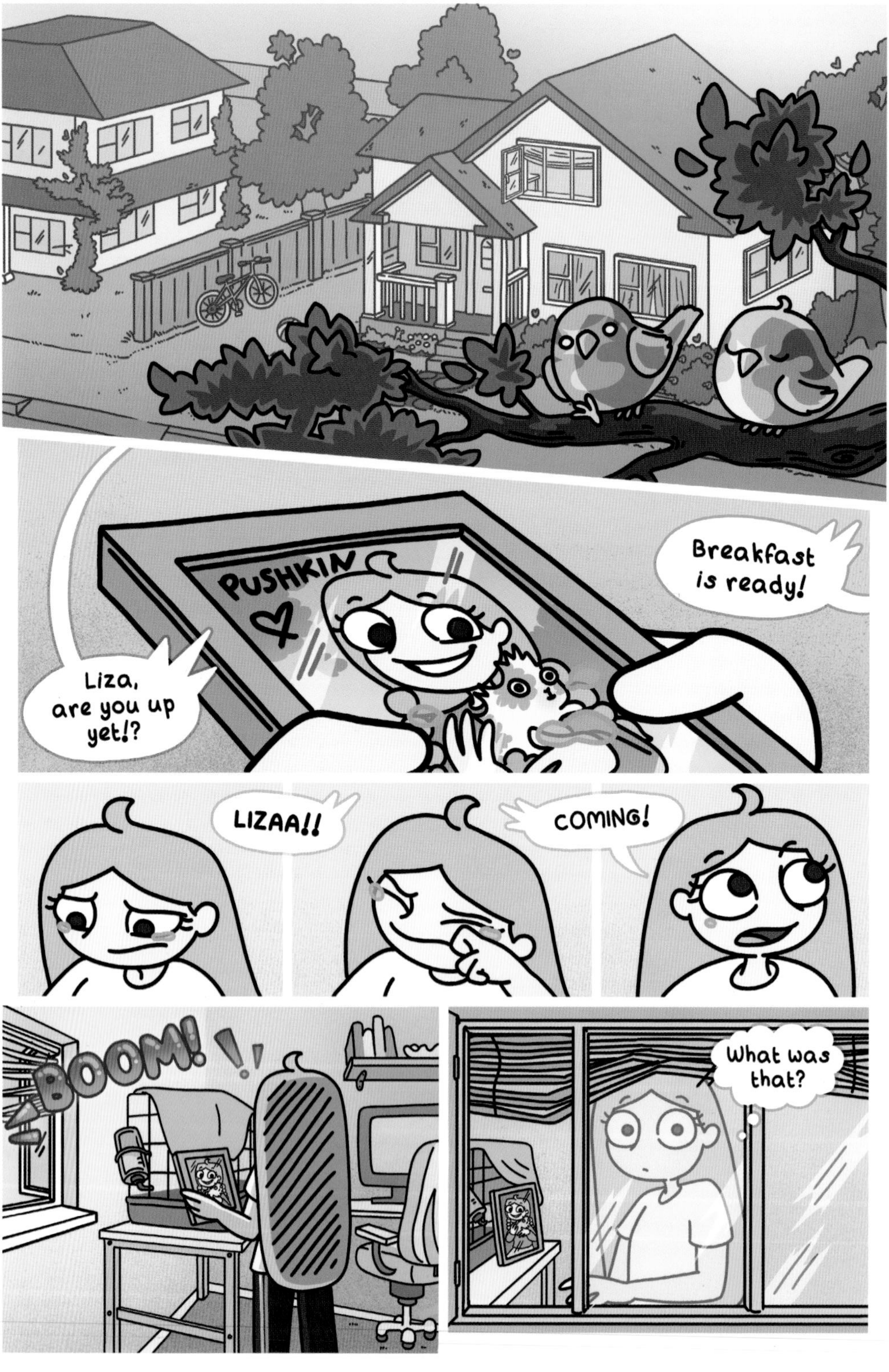
PUSHKIN
Breakfast is ready!
Liza, are you up yet!?
LIZAA!!
COMING!
BOOM!
What was that?

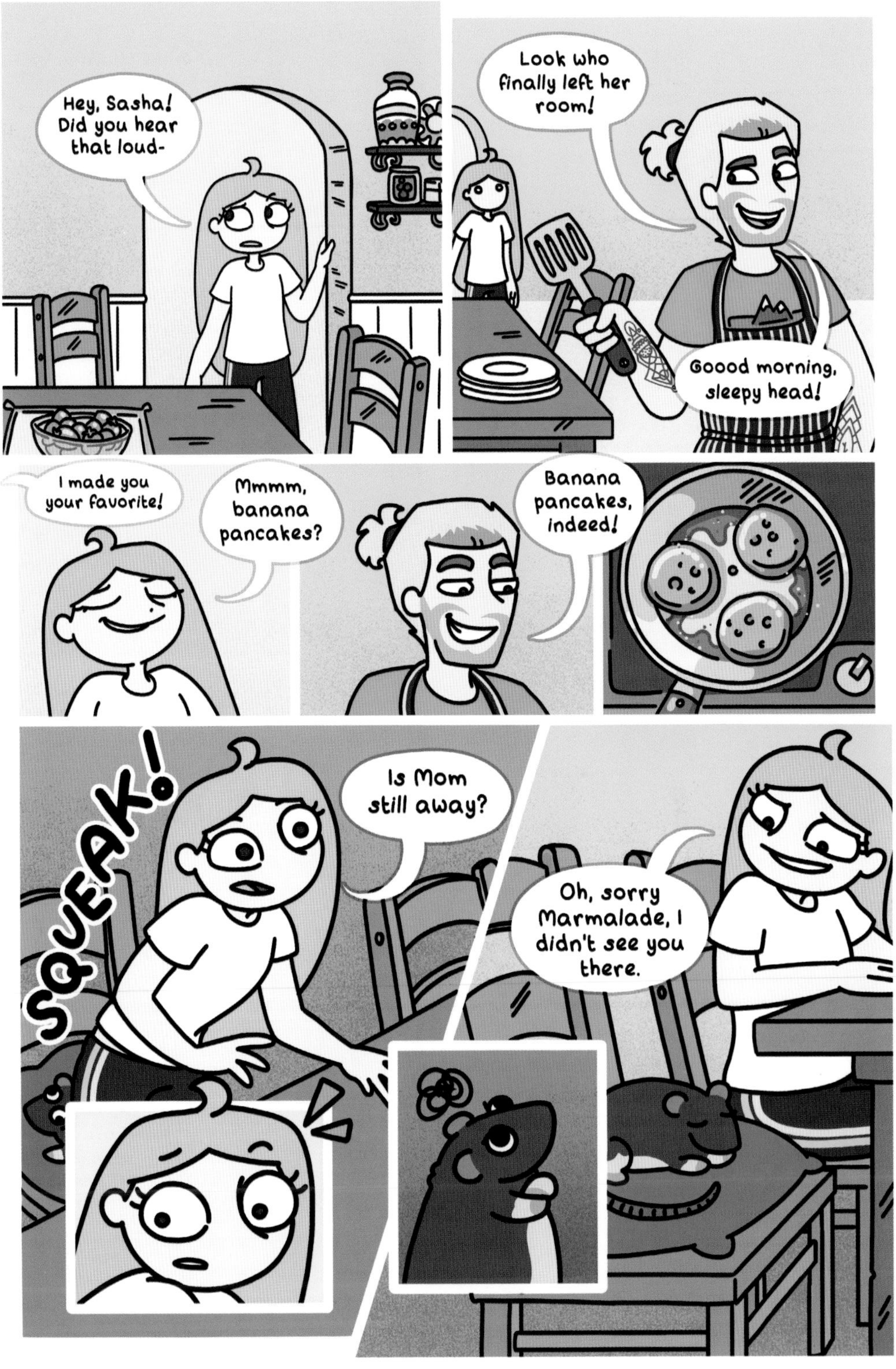
Hey, Sasha! Did you hear that loud-
Look who finally left her room!
Goood morning, sleepy head!
I made you your favorite!
Mmmm, banana pancakes?
Banana pancakes, indeed!
SQUEAK!
Is Mom still away?
Oh, sorry Marmalade, I didn't see you there.

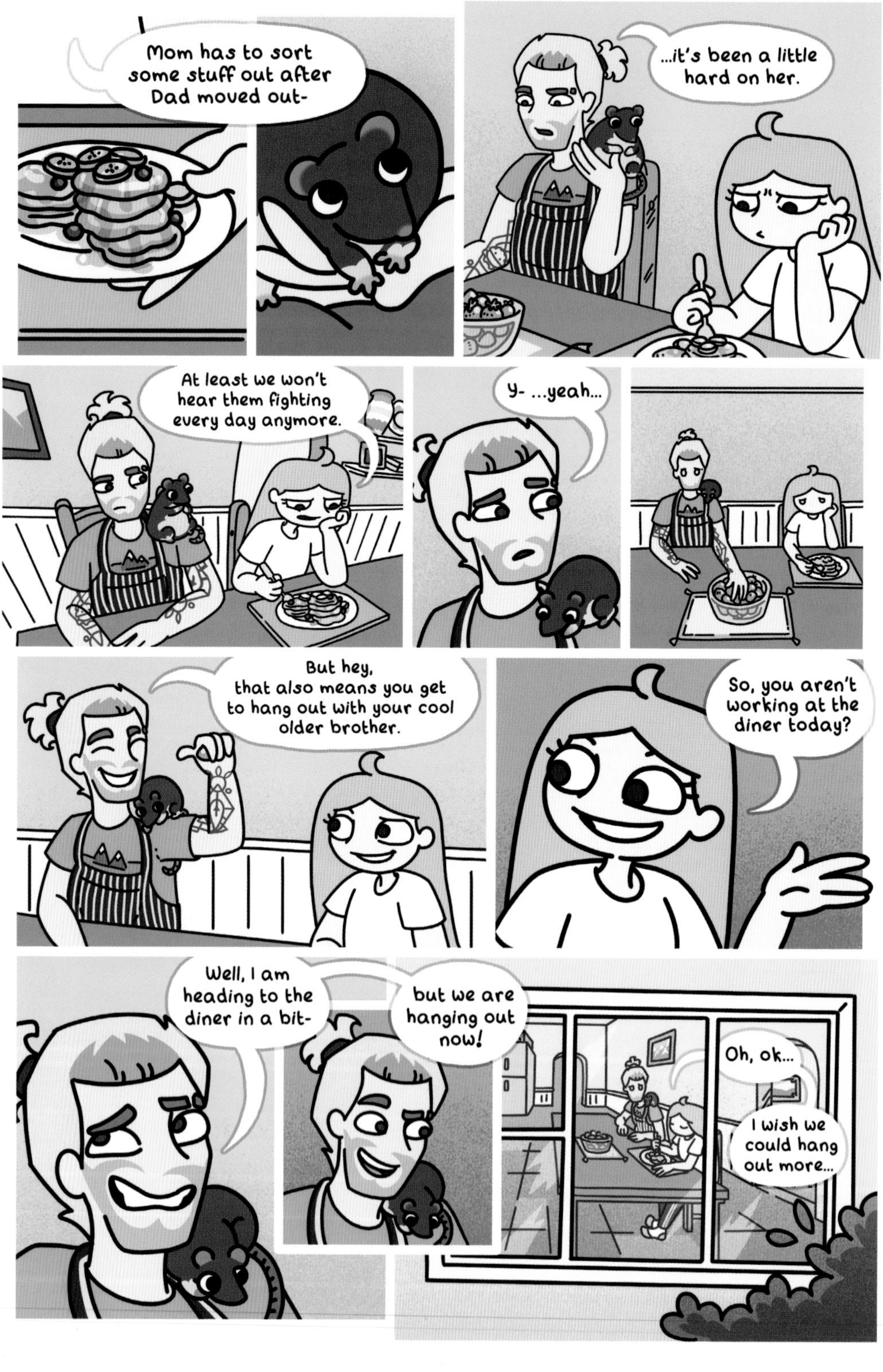
Mom has to sort some stuff out after Dad moved out-
...it's been a little hard on her.
At least we won't hear them fighting every day anymore.
Y- ...yeah...
But hey, that also means you get to hang out with your cool older brother.
So, you aren't working at the diner today?
Well, I am heading to the diner in a bit-
but we are hanging out now!
Oh, ok...
I wish we could hang out more...

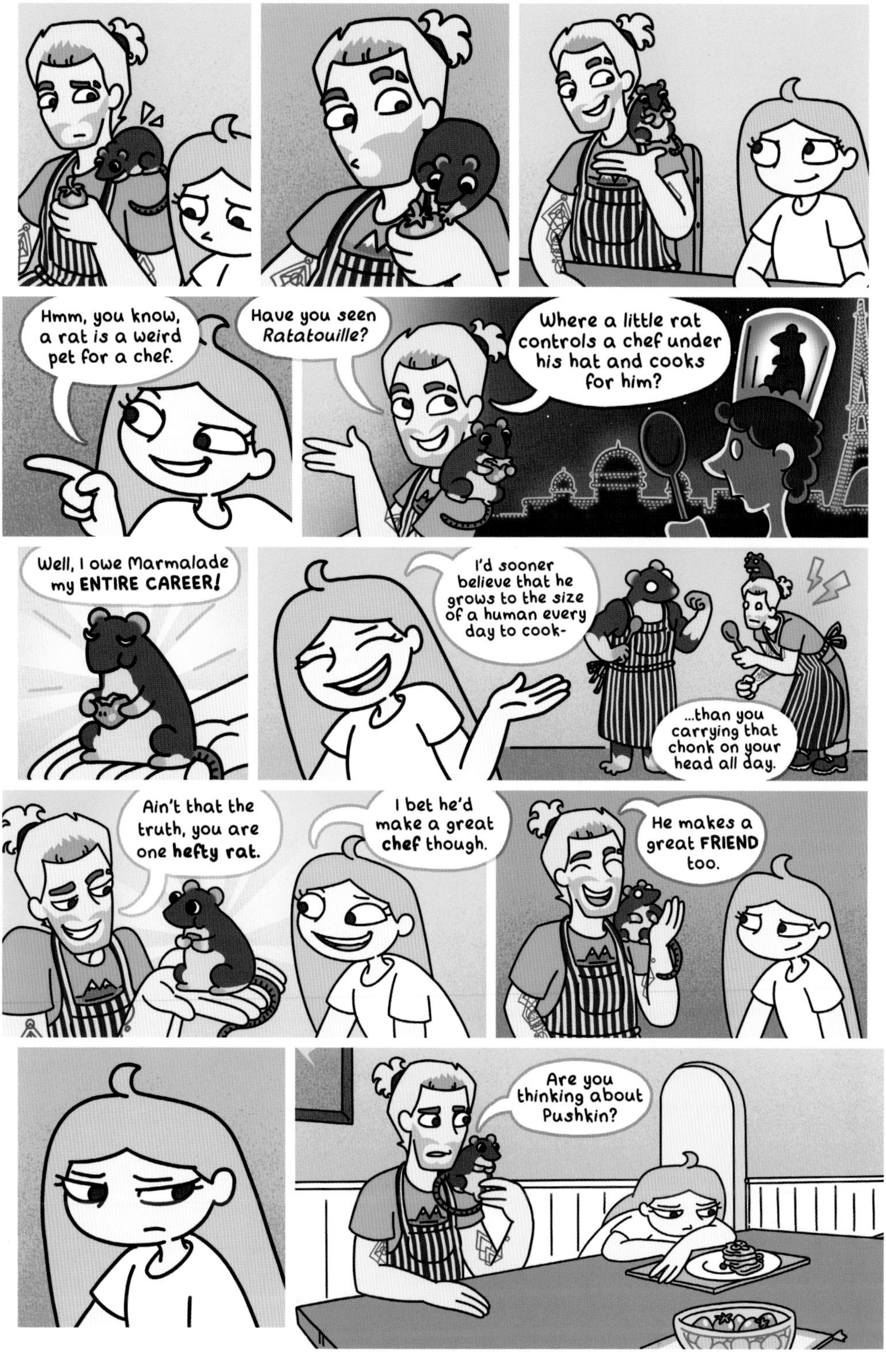
Hmm, you know, a rat is a weird pet for a chef.
Have you seen Ratatouille?
Where a little rat controls a chef under his hat and cooks for him?
Well, I owe Marmalade my ENTIRE CAREER!
I'd sooner believe that he grows to the size of a human every day to cook-
...than you carrying that chonk on your head all day.
Ain't that the truth, you are one hefty rat.
I bet he'd make a great chef though.
He makes a great FRIEND too.
Are you thinking about Pushkin?

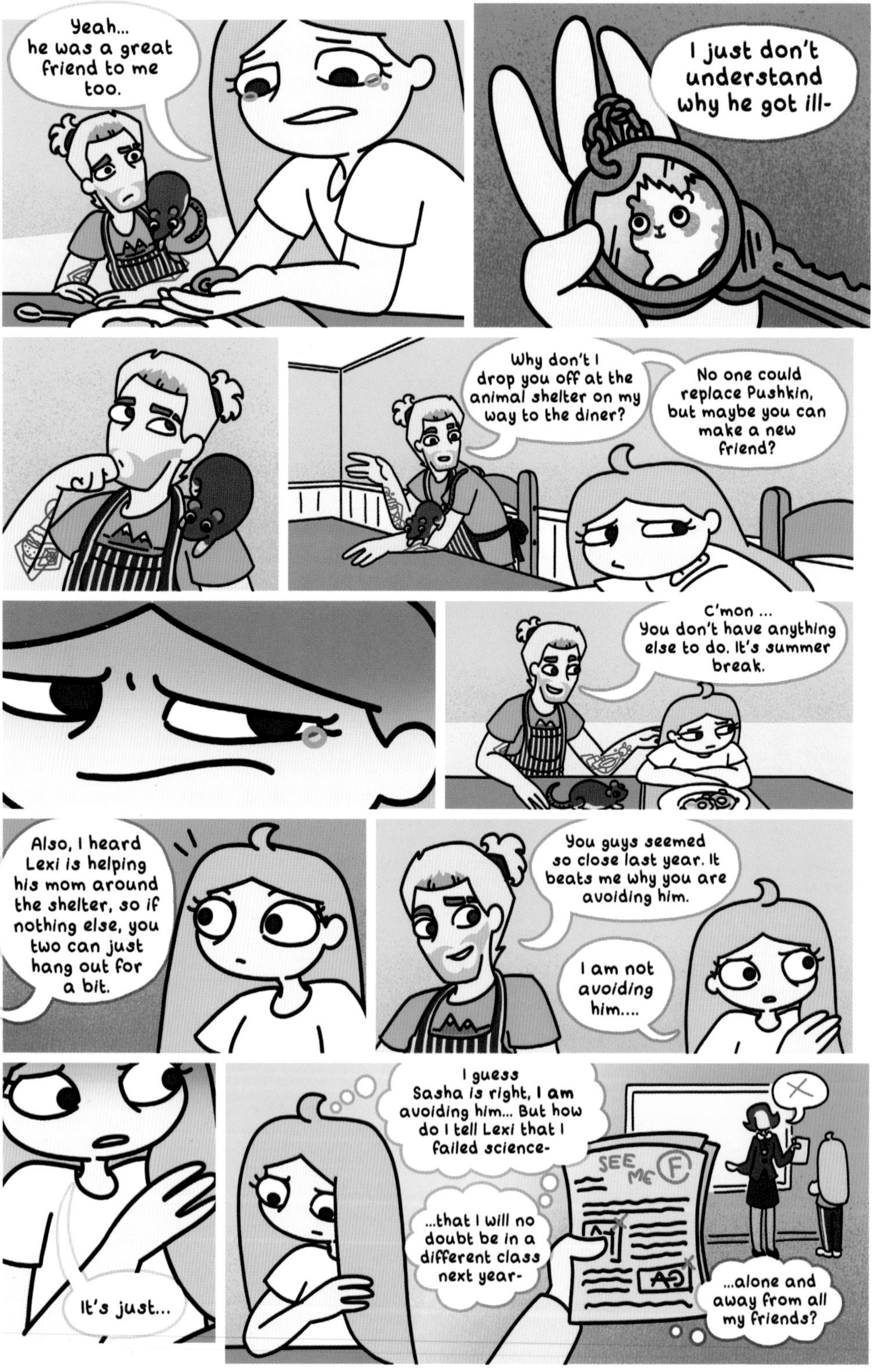
Yeah...
he was a great friend to me too.
I just don't understand why he got ill-
Why don't I drop you off at the animal shelter on my way to the diner?
No one could replace Pushkin, but maybe you can make a new friend?
C'mon ...
You don't have anything else to do. It's summer break.
Also, I heard Lexi is helping his mom around the shelter, so if nothing else, you two can just hang out for a bit.
You guys seemed so close last year. It beats me why you are avoiding him.
I am not avoiding him....
It's just...
I guess Sasha is right, I am avoiding him... But how do I tell Lexi that I failed science-
SEE ME
F
...that I will no doubt be in a different class next year-
...alone and away from all my friends?

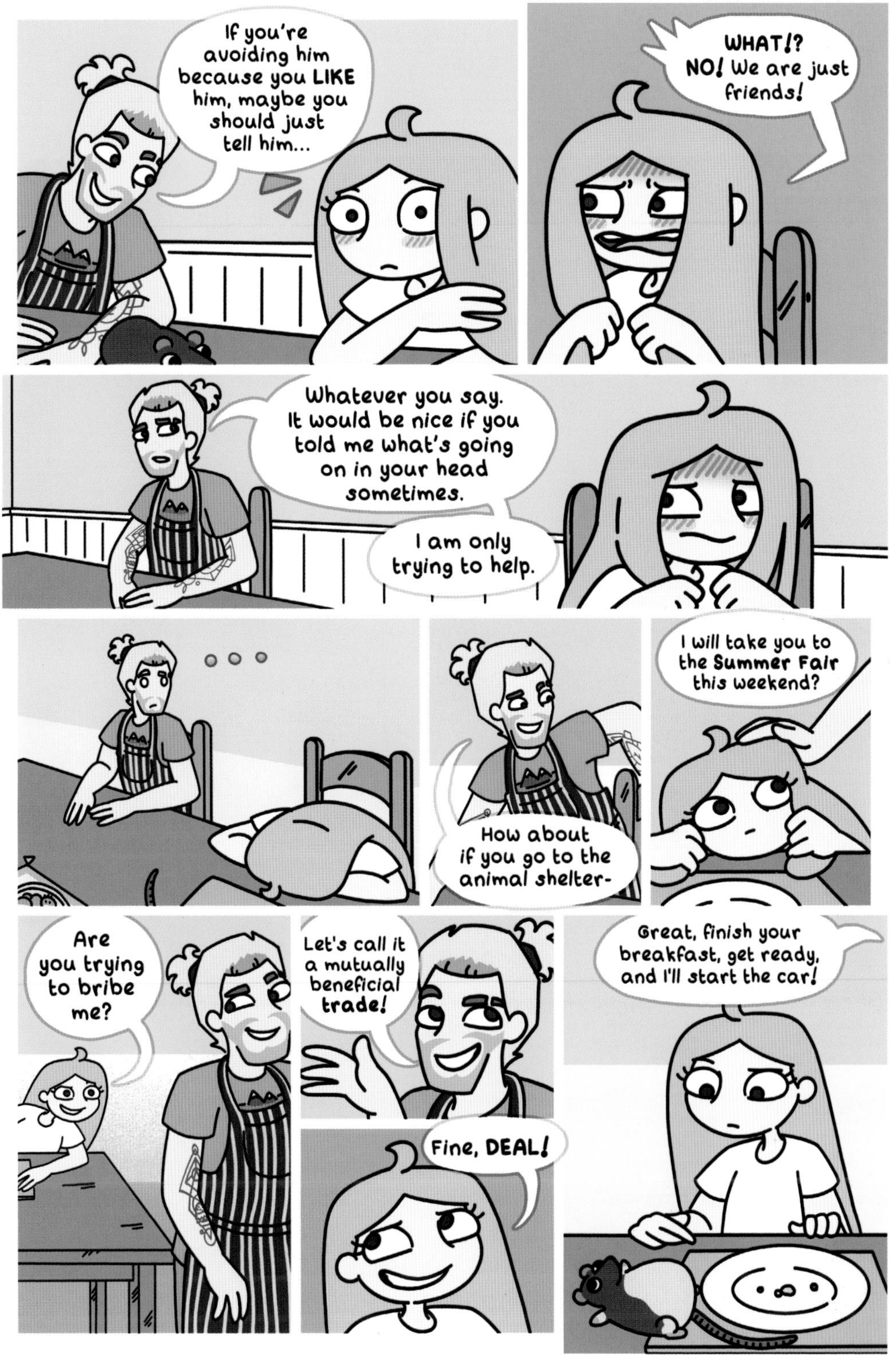
If you're avoiding him because you LIKE him, maybe you should just tell him...
WHAT!? NO! We are just friends!
Whatever you say. It would be nice if you told me what's going on in your head sometimes.
I am only trying to help.
How about if you go to the animal shelter-
I will take you to the Summer Fair this weekend?
Are you trying to bribe me?
Let's call it a mutually beneficial trade!
Fine, DEAL!
Great, finish your breakfast, get ready, and I'll start the car!

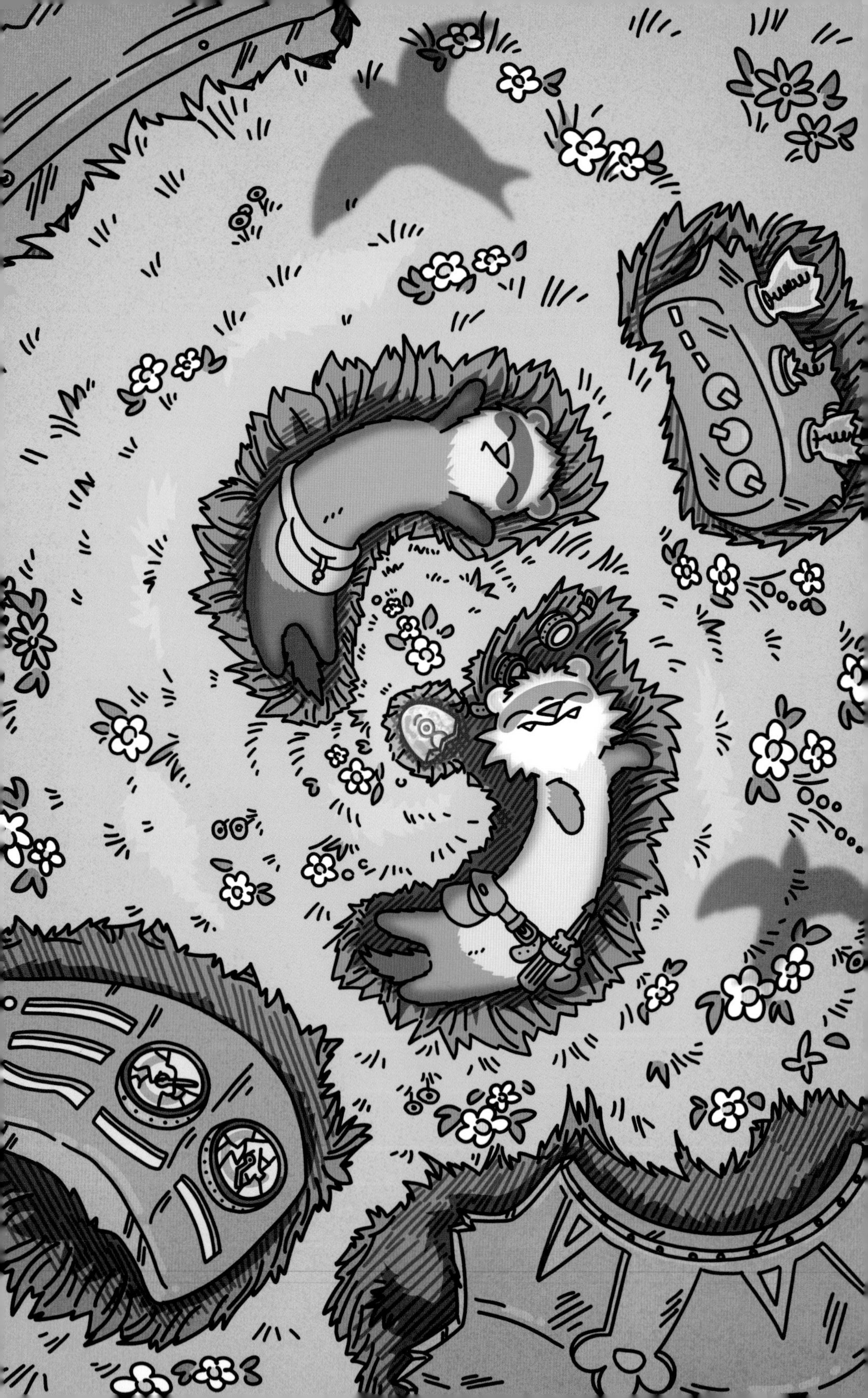

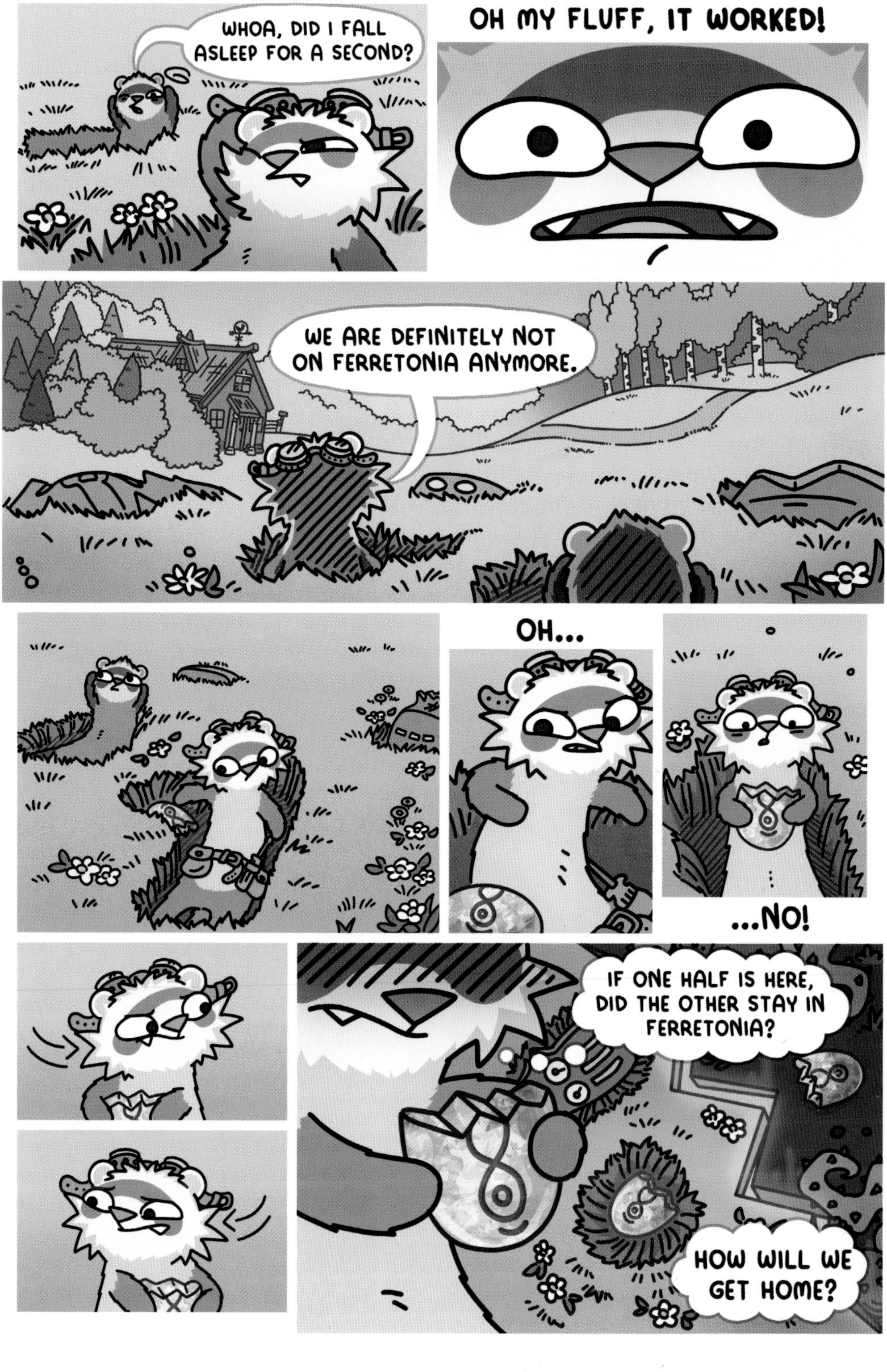
WHOA, DID I FALL ASLEEP FOR A SECOND?
OH MY FLUFF, IT WORKED!
WE ARE DEFINITELY NOT ON FERRETONIA ANYMORE.
OH...
...NO!
IF ONE HALF IS HERE, DID THE OTHER STAY IN FERRETONIA?
HOW WILL WE GET HOME?

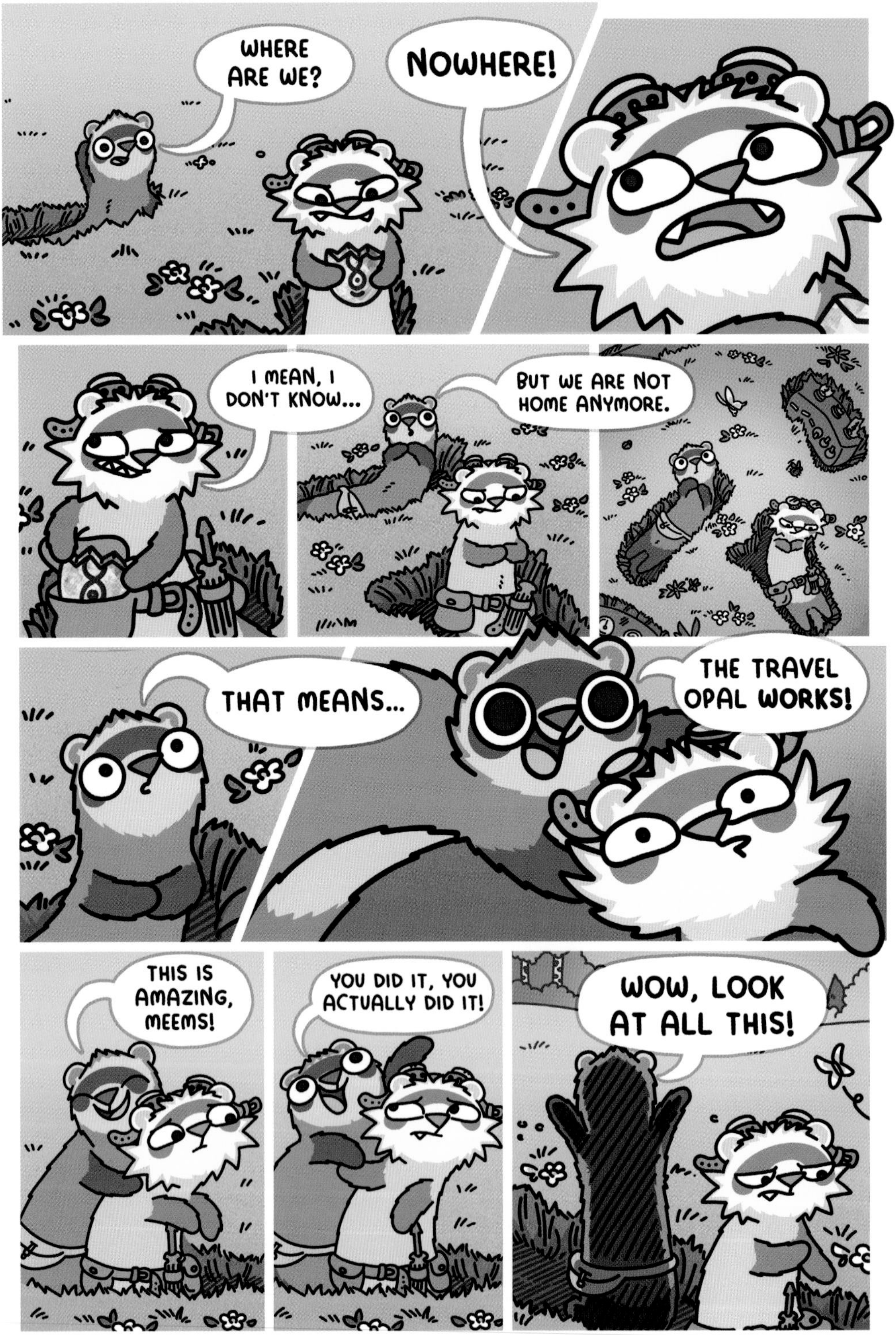
WHERE ARE WE?
NOWHERE!
I MEAN, I DON'T KNOW...
BUT WE ARE NOT HOME ANYMORE.
THAT MEANS...
THE TRAVEL OPAL WORKS!
THIS IS AMAZING, MEEMS!
YOU DID IT, YOU ACTUALLY DID IT!
WOW, LOOK AT ALL THIS!

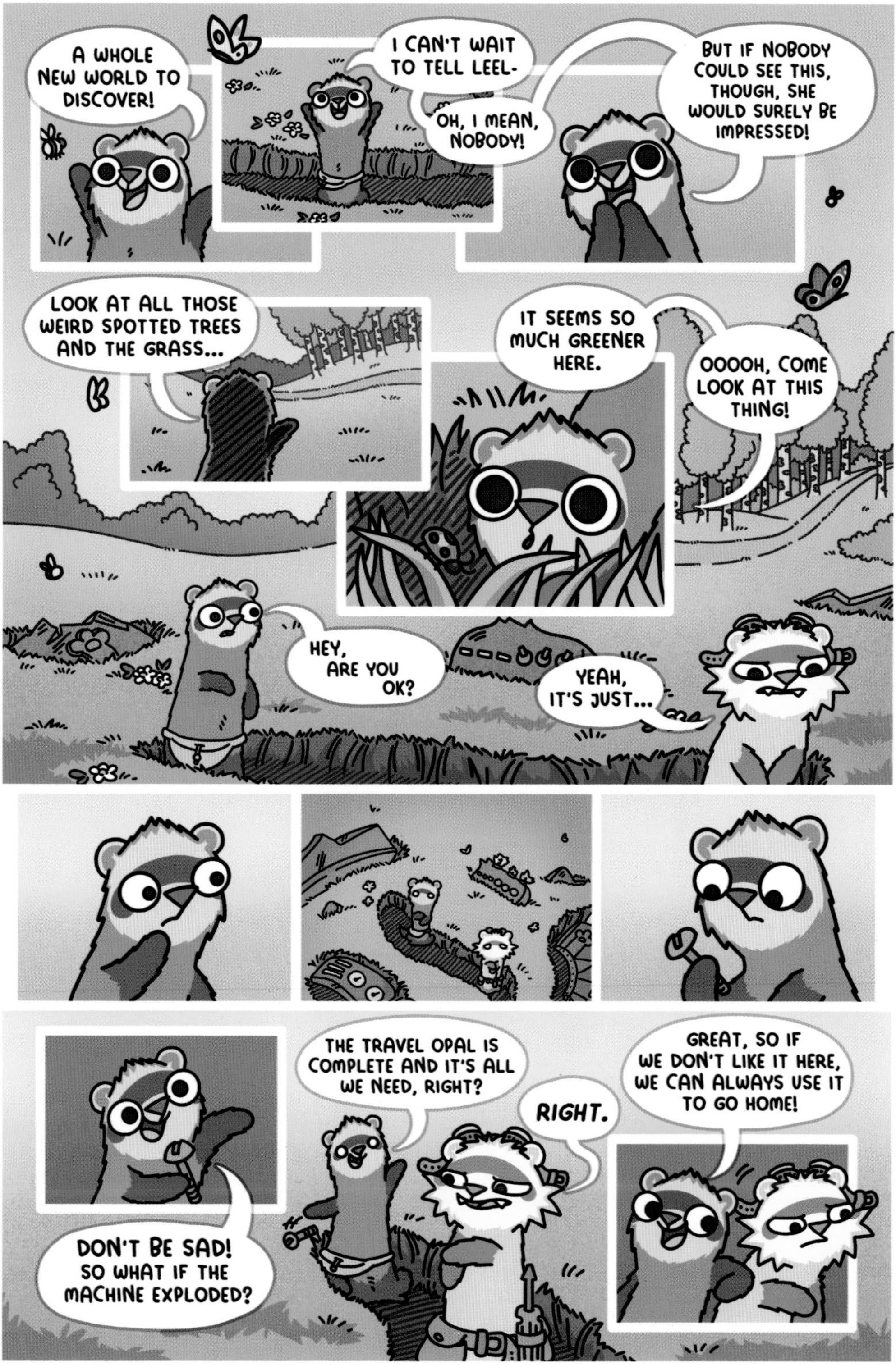
A WHOLE NEW WORLD TO DISCOVER!
I CAN'T WAIT TO TELL LEEL-
OH, I MEAN, NOBODY!
BUT IF NOBODY COULD SEE THIS, THOUGH, SHE WOULD SURELY BE IMPRESSED!
LOOK AT ALL THOSE WEIRD SPOTTED TREES AND THE GRASS...
IT SEEMS SO MUCH GREENER HERE.
OOOOH, COME LOOK AT THIS THING!
HEY, ARE YOU OK?
YEAH, IT'S JUST...
DON'T BE SAD! SO WHAT IF THE MACHINE EXPLODED?
THE TRAVEL OPAL IS COMPLETE AND IT'S ALL WE NEED, RIGHT?
RIGHT.
GREAT, SO IF WE DON'T LIKE IT HERE, WE CAN ALWAYS USE IT TO GO HOME!

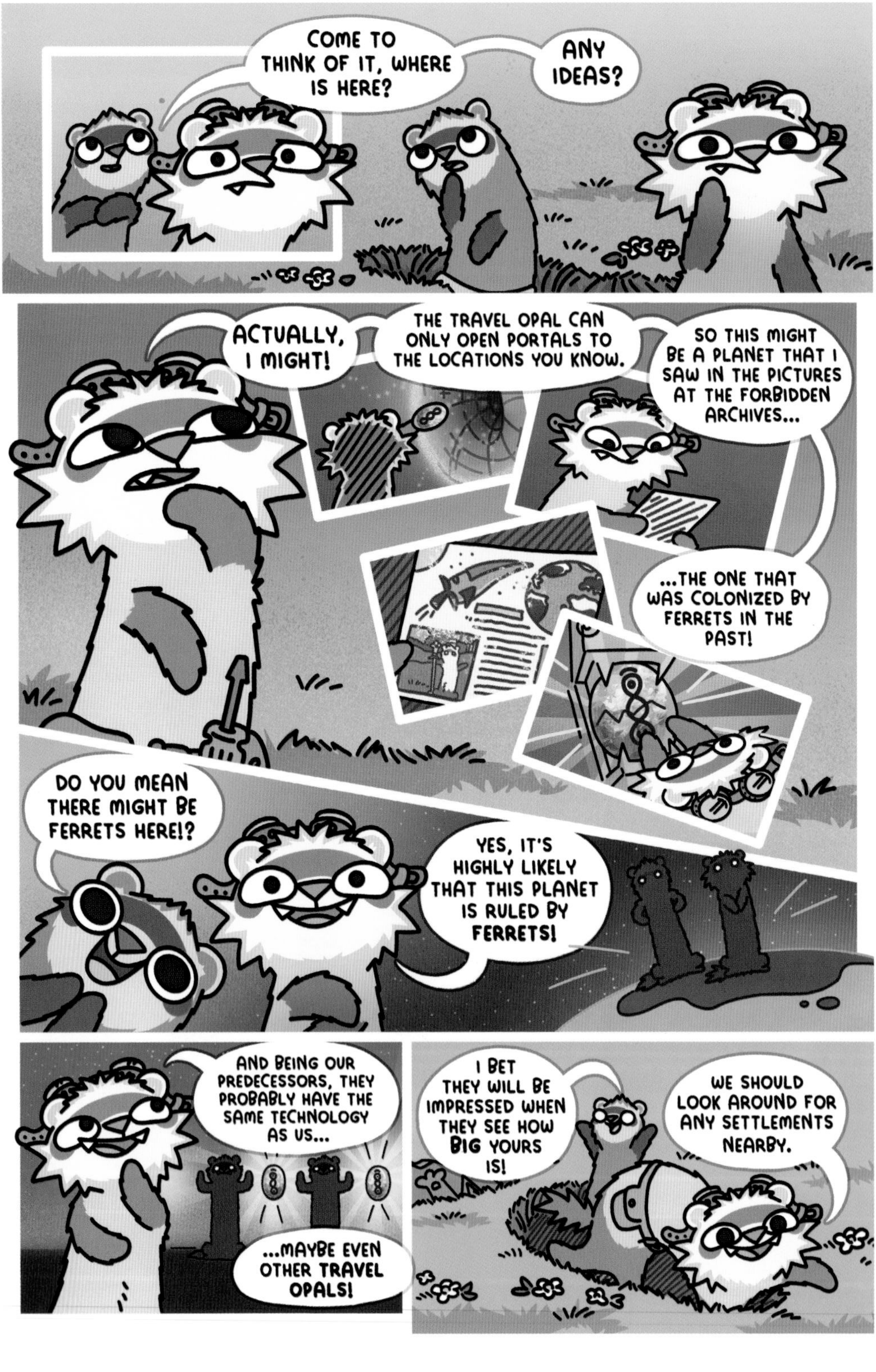
COME TO THINK OF IT, WHERE IS HERE?
ANY IDEAS?
ACTUALLY, I MIGHT!
THE TRAVEL OPAL CAN ONLY OPEN PORTALS TO THE LOCATIONS YOU KNOW.
SO THIS MIGHT BE A PLANET THAT I SAW IN THE PICTURES AT THE FORBIDDEN ARCHIVES...
...THE ONE THAT WAS COLONIZED BY FERRETS IN THE PAST!
DO YOU MEAN THERE MIGHT BE FERRETS HERE!?
YES, IT'S HIGHLY LIKELY THAT THIS PLANET IS RULED BY FERRETS!
AND BEING OUR PREDECESSORS, THEY PROBABLY HAVE THE SAME TECHNOLOGY AS US...
...MAYBE EVEN OTHER TRAVEL OPALS!
I BET THEY WILL BE IMPRESSED WHEN THEY SEE HOW BIG YOURS IS!
WE SHOULD LOOK AROUND FOR ANY SETTLEMENTS NEARBY.

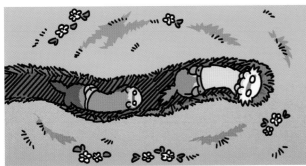

HOW ARE WE GOING TO FIND A SETTLEMENT?

WELL, IF THE FERRETS HERE COME FROM THE PAST, THEY PROBABLY DON'T HAVE THE STUPID ANCIENT TECH BAN THAT WE HAVE ON OUR PLANET NOW.

WHICH MEANS THEY ARE HIGHLY DEVELOPED. I HAVE NO DOUBT WE WILL SEE SOMETHING FERRET-MADE SOON THAT WILL GIVE US A CLUE!

THEIR SETTLEMENT MUST BE AWESOME! THEY WILL PROBABLY HAVE, LIKE, TWO CITADELS AT LEAST.

TRY THOUSANDS!

IF THEY HAVE HAD THIS WHOLE PLANET TO DEVELOP, THEY PROBABLY HAVE **NUMEROUS** SETTLEMENTS ALL OVER! MAYBE AN ENTIRE FERRET EMPIRE!

WHOAA! THIS SOUNDS AMAZING!

49

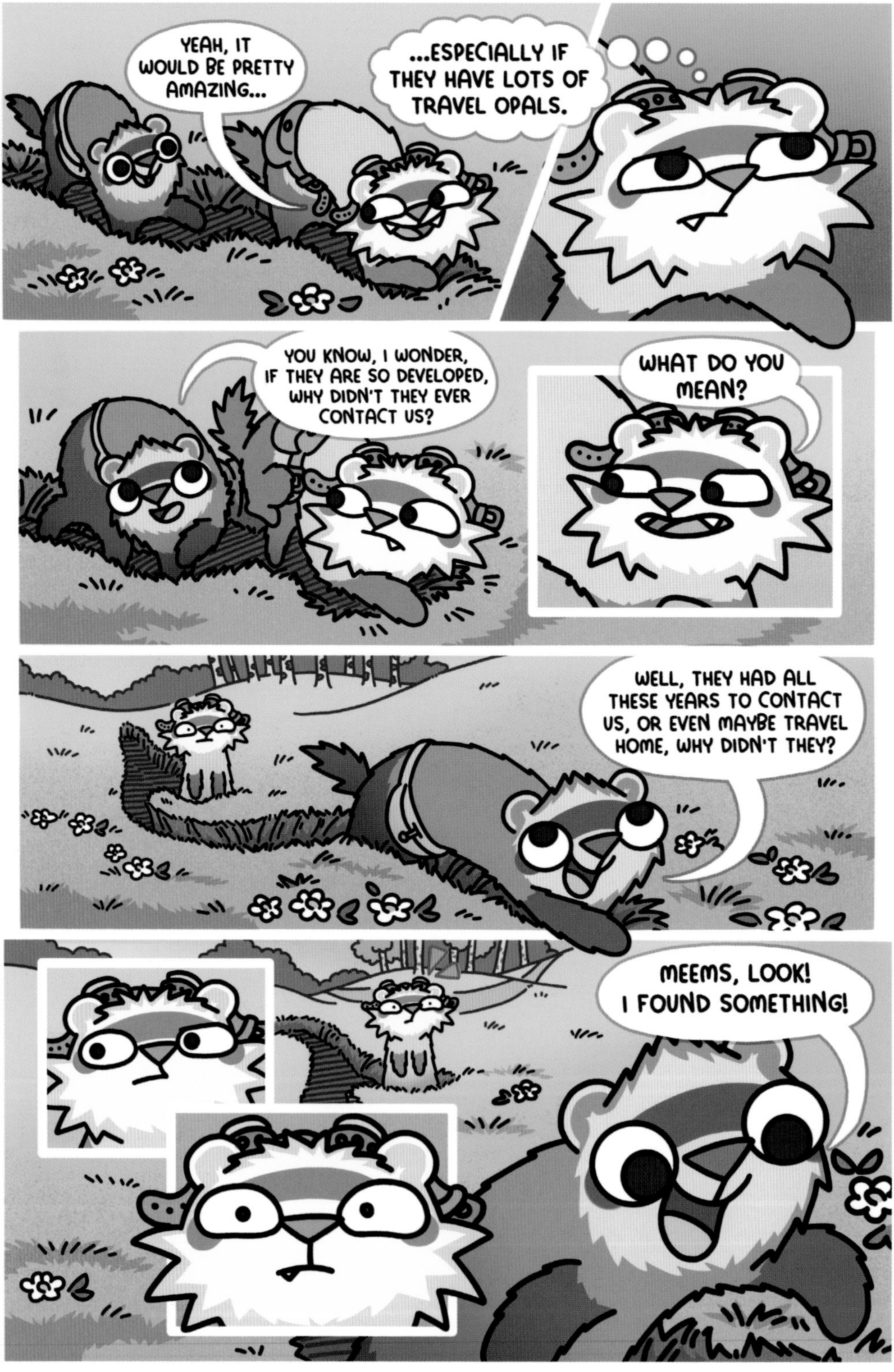
YEAH, IT WOULD BE PRETTY AMAZING...
...ESPECIALLY IF THEY HAVE LOTS OF TRAVEL OPALS.
YOU KNOW, I WONDER, IF THEY ARE SO DEVELOPED, WHY DIDN'T THEY EVER CONTACT US?
WHAT DO YOU MEAN?
WELL, THEY HAD ALL THESE YEARS TO CONTACT US, OR EVEN MAYBE TRAVEL HOME, WHY DIDN'T THEY?
MEEMS, LOOK! I FOUND SOMETHING!

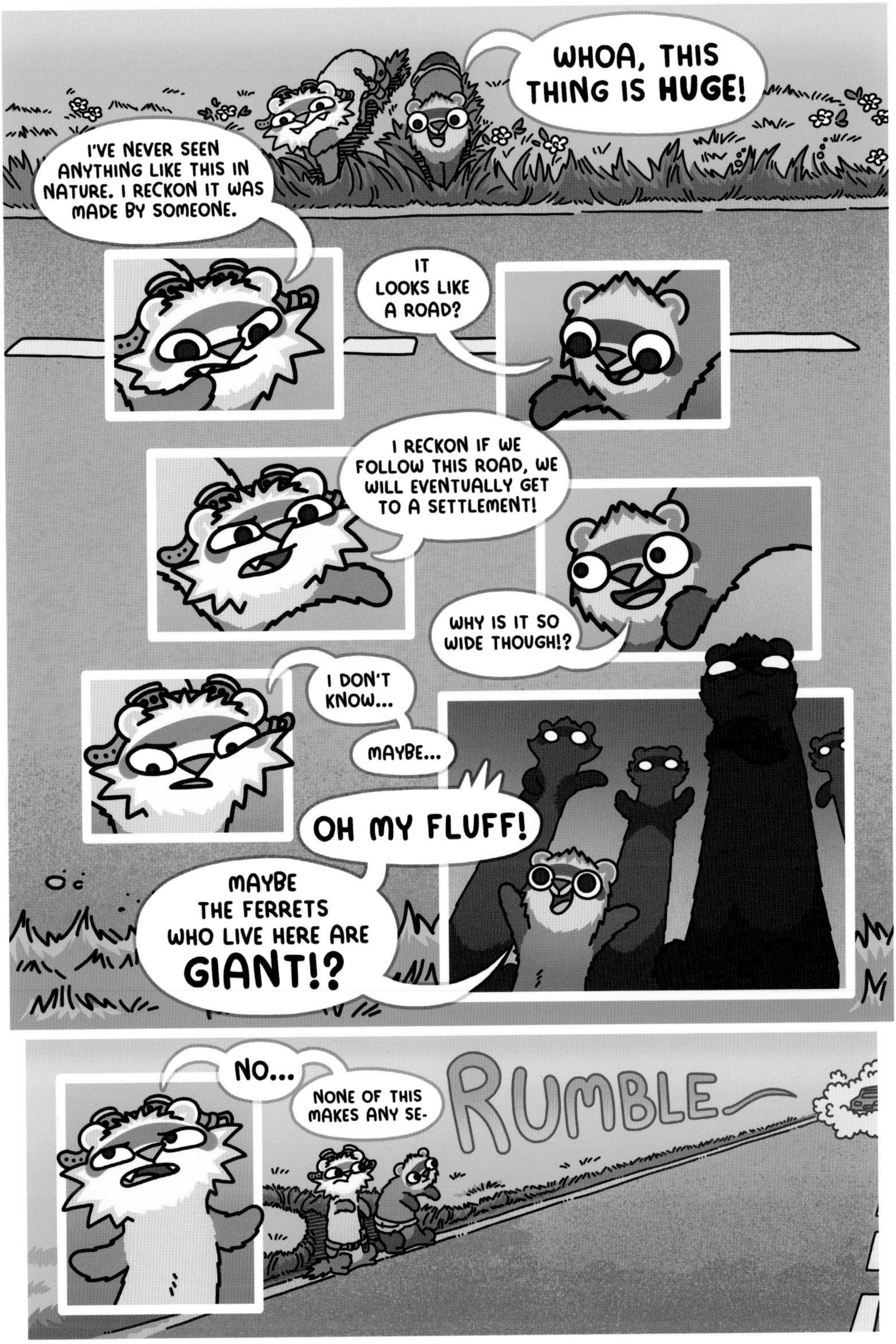
WHOA, THIS THING IS HUGE!
I'VE NEVER SEEN ANYTHING LIKE THIS IN NATURE. I RECKON IT WAS MADE BY SOMEONE.
IT LOOKS LIKE A ROAD?
I RECKON IF WE FOLLOW THIS ROAD, WE WILL EVENTUALLY GET TO A SETTLEMENT!
WHY IS IT SO WIDE THOUGH!?
I DON'T KNOW...
MAYBE...
OH MY FLUFF!
MAYBE THE FERRETS WHO LIVE HERE ARE GIANT!?
NO...
NONE OF THIS MAKES ANY SE-
RUMBLE

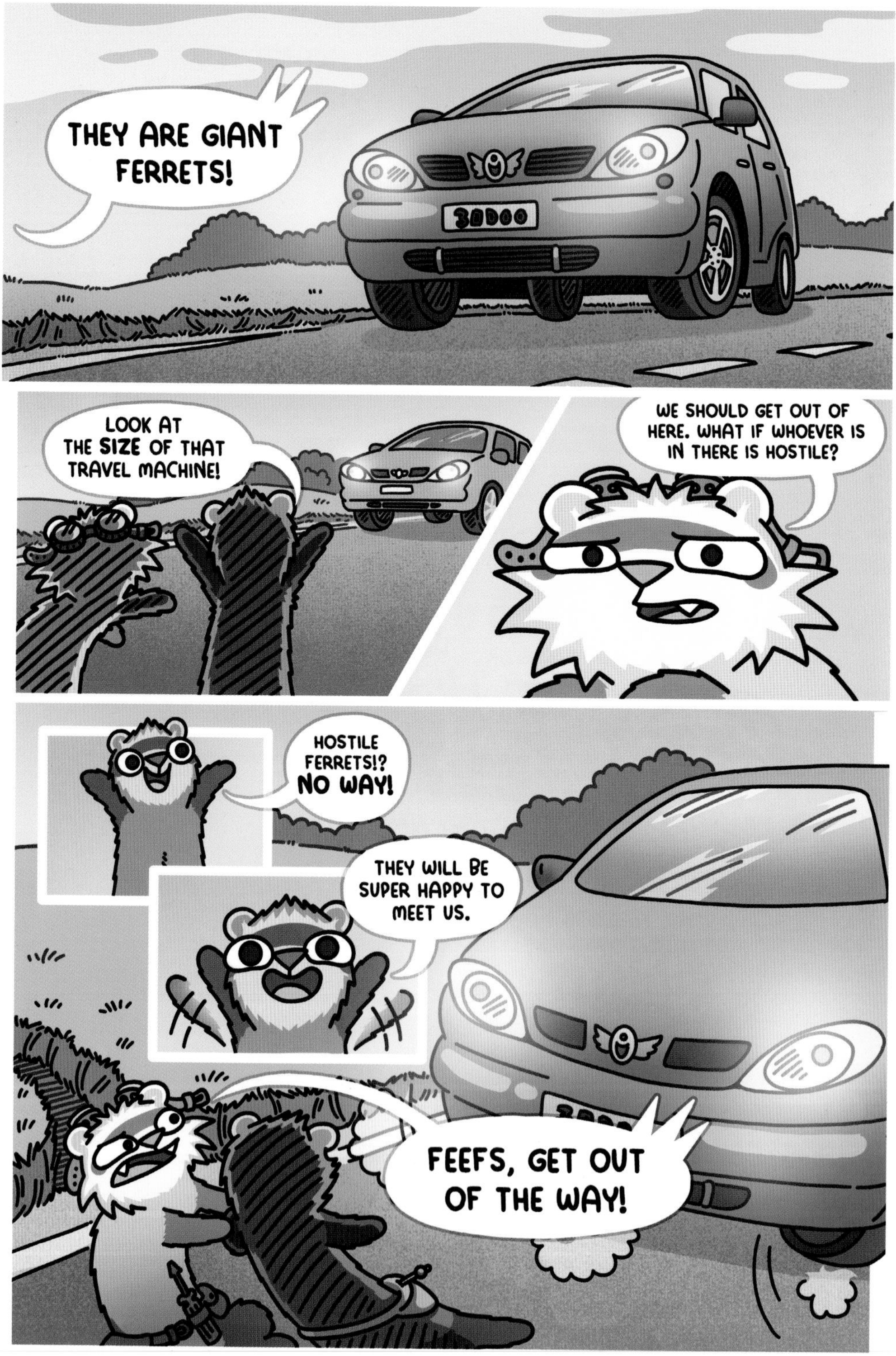
THEY ARE GIANT FERRETS!
3ADOO
LOOK AT THE SIZE OF THAT TRAVEL MACHINE!
WE SHOULD GET OUT OF HERE. WHAT IF WHOEVER IS IN THERE IS HOSTILE?
HOSTILE FERRETS!? NO WAY!
THEY WILL BE SUPER HAPPY TO MEET US.
FEEFS, GET OUT OF THE WAY!

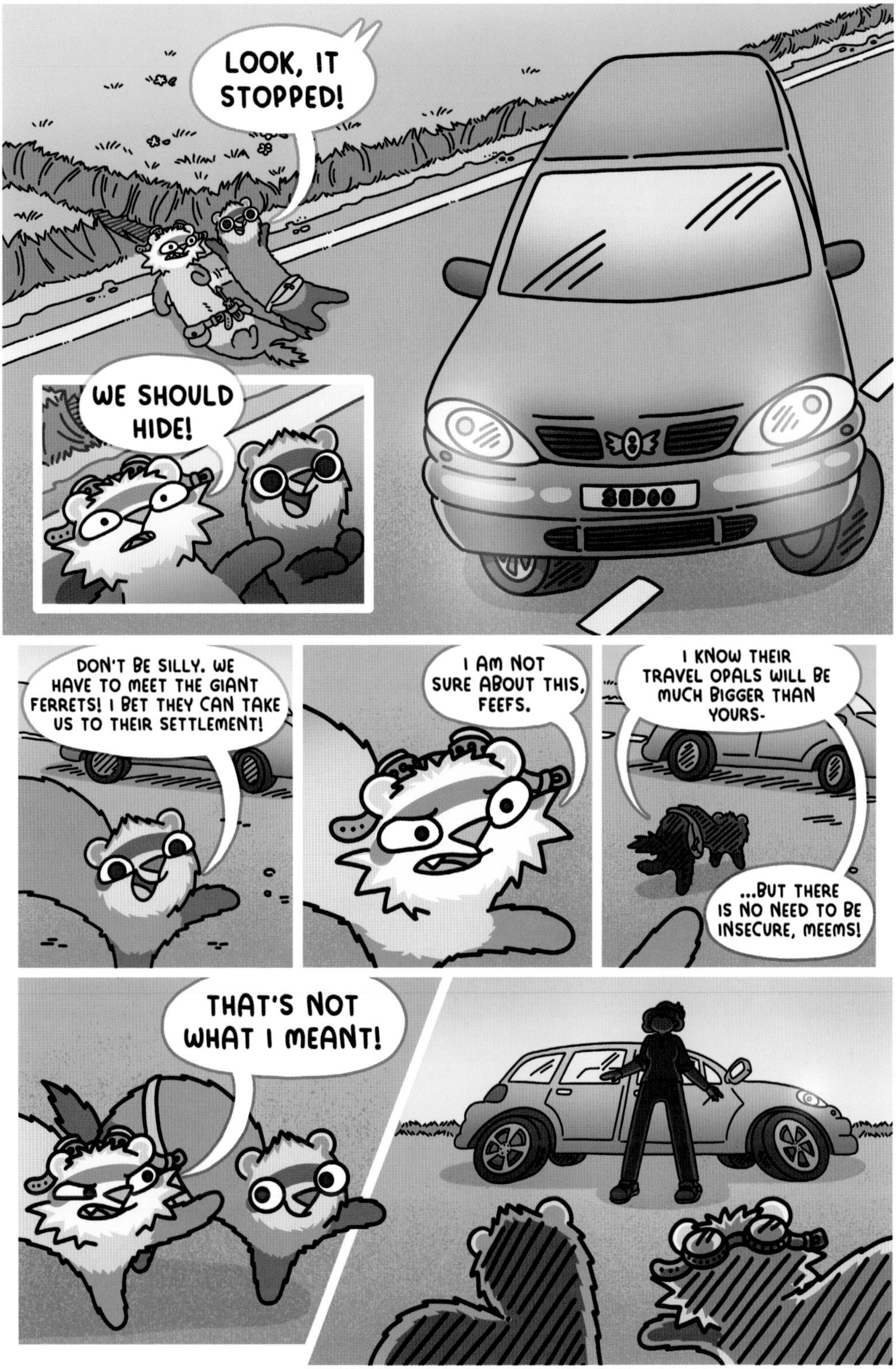
LOOK, IT STOPPED!
WE SHOULD HIDE!
DON'T BE SILLY. WE HAVE TO MEET THE GIANT FERRETS! I BET THEY CAN TAKE US TO THEIR SETTLEMENT!
I AM NOT SURE ABOUT THIS, FEEFS.
I KNOW THEIR TRAVEL OPALS WILL BE MUCH BIGGER THAN YOURS-
...BUT THERE IS NO NEED TO BE INSECURE, MEEMS!
THAT'S NOT WHAT I MEANT!

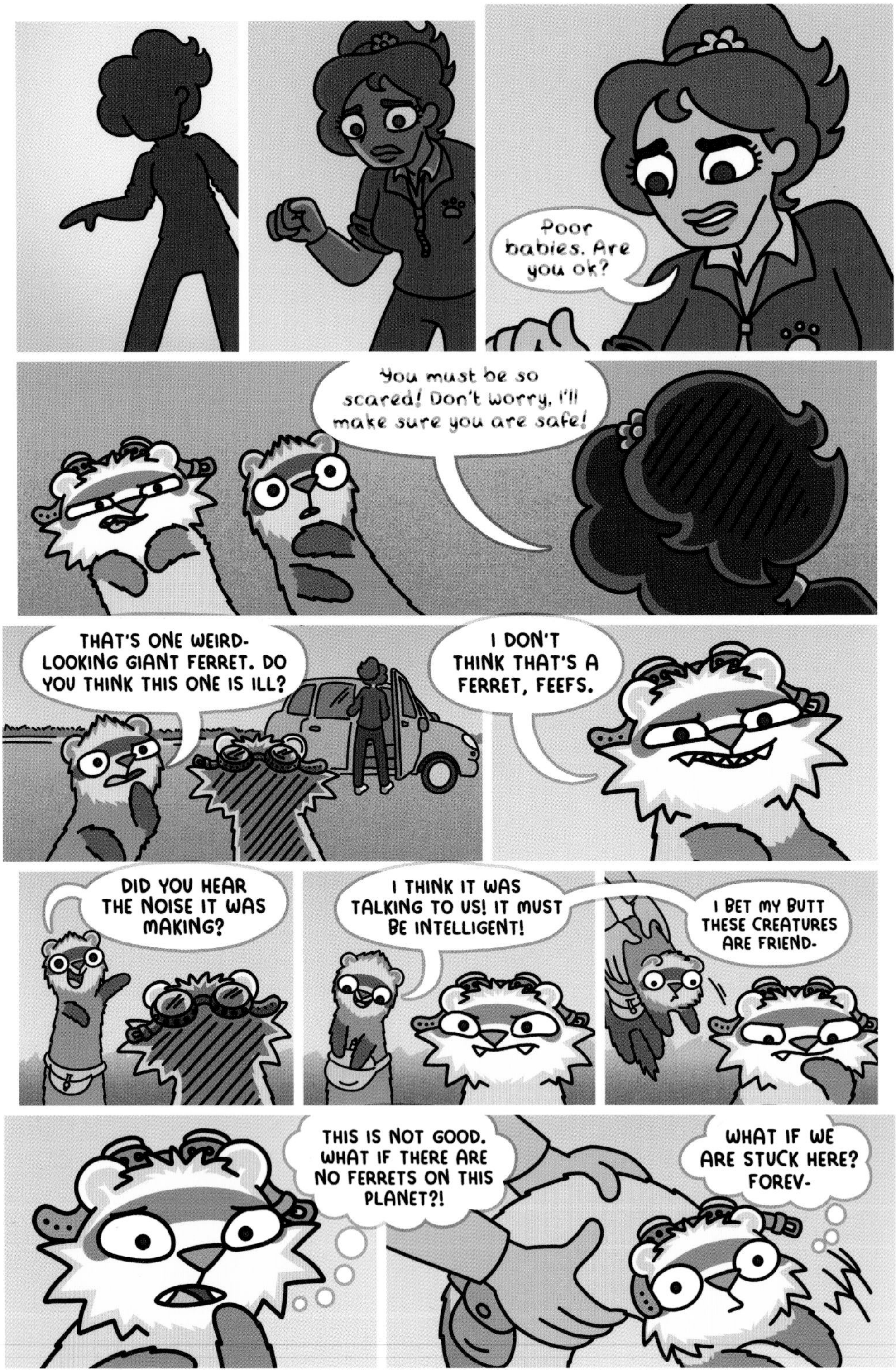
Poor babies. Are you ok?
You must be so scared! Don't worry, I'll make sure you are safe!
THAT'S ONE WEIRD-LOOKING GIANT FERRET. DO YOU THINK THIS ONE IS ILL?
I DON'T THINK THAT'S A FERRET, FEEFS.
DID YOU HEAR THE NOISE IT WAS MAKING?
I THINK IT WAS TALKING TO US! IT MUST BE INTELLIGENT!
I BET MY BUTT THESE CREATURES ARE FRIEND-
THIS IS NOT GOOD. WHAT IF THERE ARE NO FERRETS ON THIS PLANET?!
WHAT IF WE ARE STUCK HERE? FOREV-

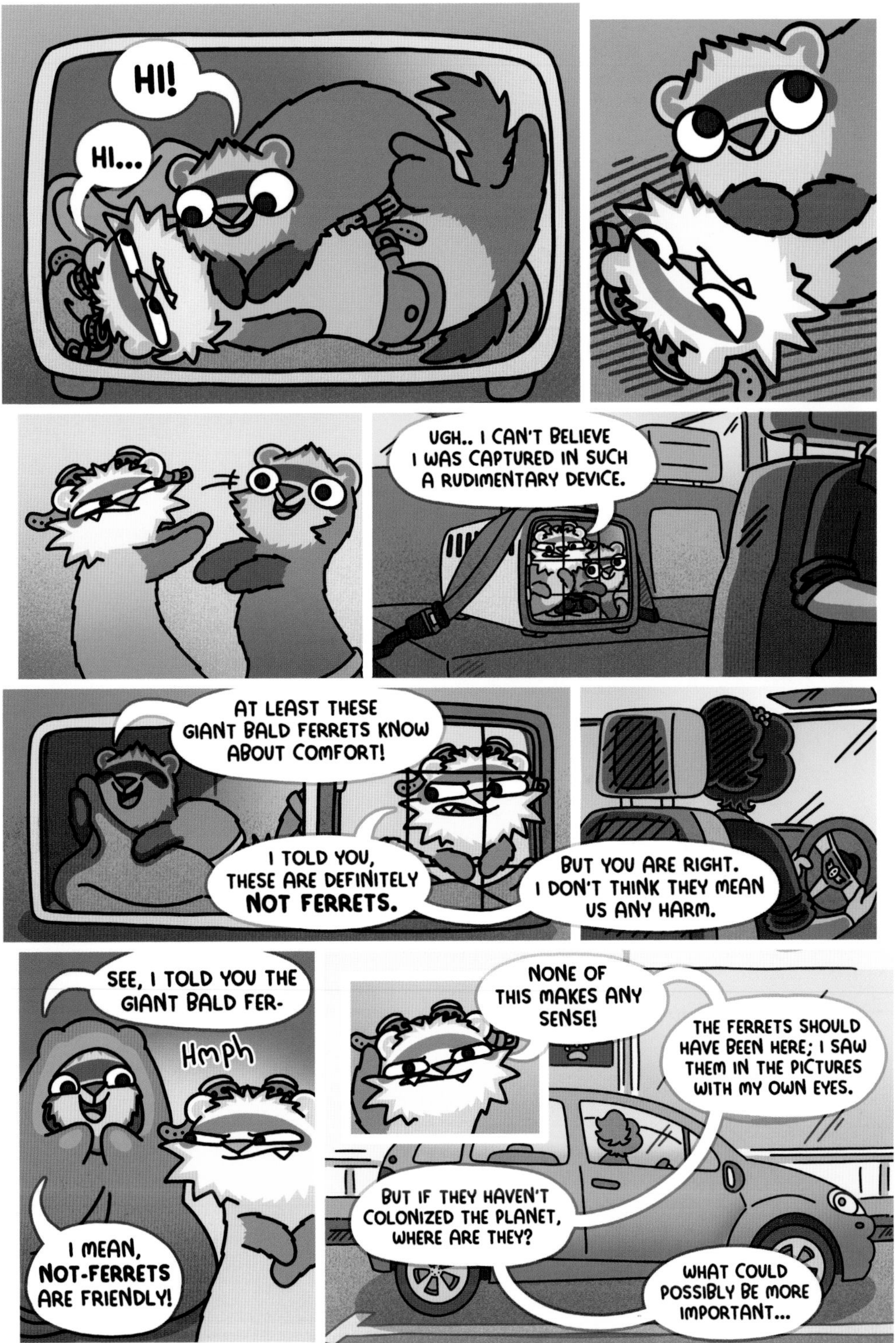
HI!
HI...
UGH.. I CAN'T BELIEVE I WAS CAPTURED IN SUCH A RUDIMENTARY DEVICE.
AT LEAST THESE GIANT BALD FERRETS KNOW ABOUT COMFORT!
I TOLD YOU, THESE ARE DEFINITELY NOT FERRETS.
BUT YOU ARE RIGHT. I DON'T THINK THEY MEAN US ANY HARM.
SEE, I TOLD YOU THE GIANT BALD FER-
Hmph
I MEAN, NOT-FERRETS ARE FRIENDLY!
NONE OF THIS MAKES ANY SENSE!
THE FERRETS SHOULD HAVE BEEN HERE; I SAW THEM IN THE PICTURES WITH MY OWN EYES.
BUT IF THEY HAVEN'T COLONIZED THE PLANET, WHERE ARE THEY?
WHAT COULD POSSIBLY BE MORE IMPORTANT...

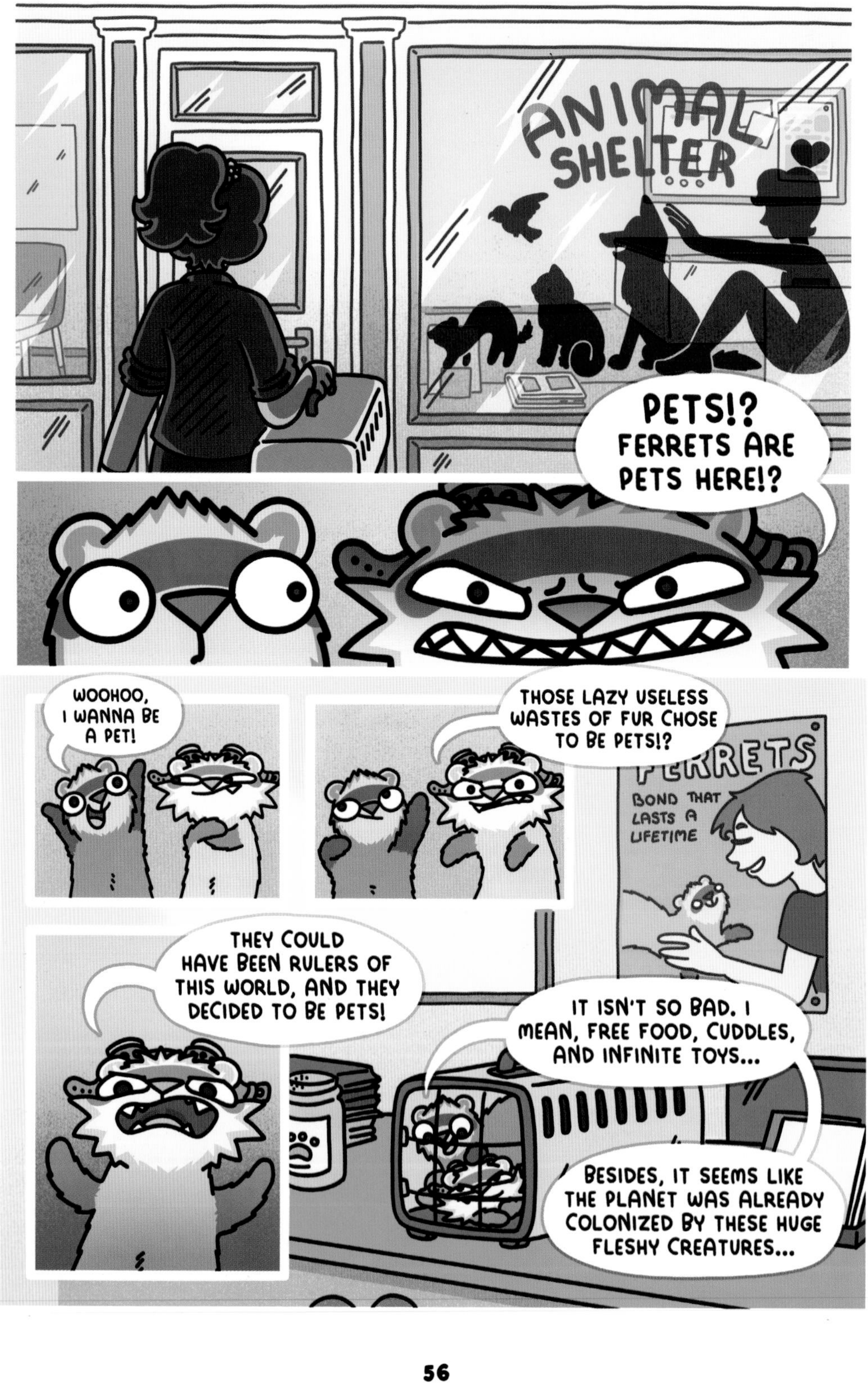
ANIMAL SHELTER
PETS!? FERRETS ARE PETS HERE!?
WOOHOO, I WANNA BE A PET!
THOSE LAZY USELESS WASTES OF FUR CHOSE TO BE PETS!?
FERRETS
BOND THAT LASTS A LIFETIME
THEY COULD HAVE BEEN RULERS OF THIS WORLD, AND THEY DECIDED TO BE PETS!
IT ISN'T SO BAD. I MEAN, FREE FOOD, CUDDLES, AND INFINITE TOYS...
BESIDES, IT SEEMS LIKE THE PLANET WAS ALREADY COLONIZED BY THESE HUGE FLESHY CREATURES...

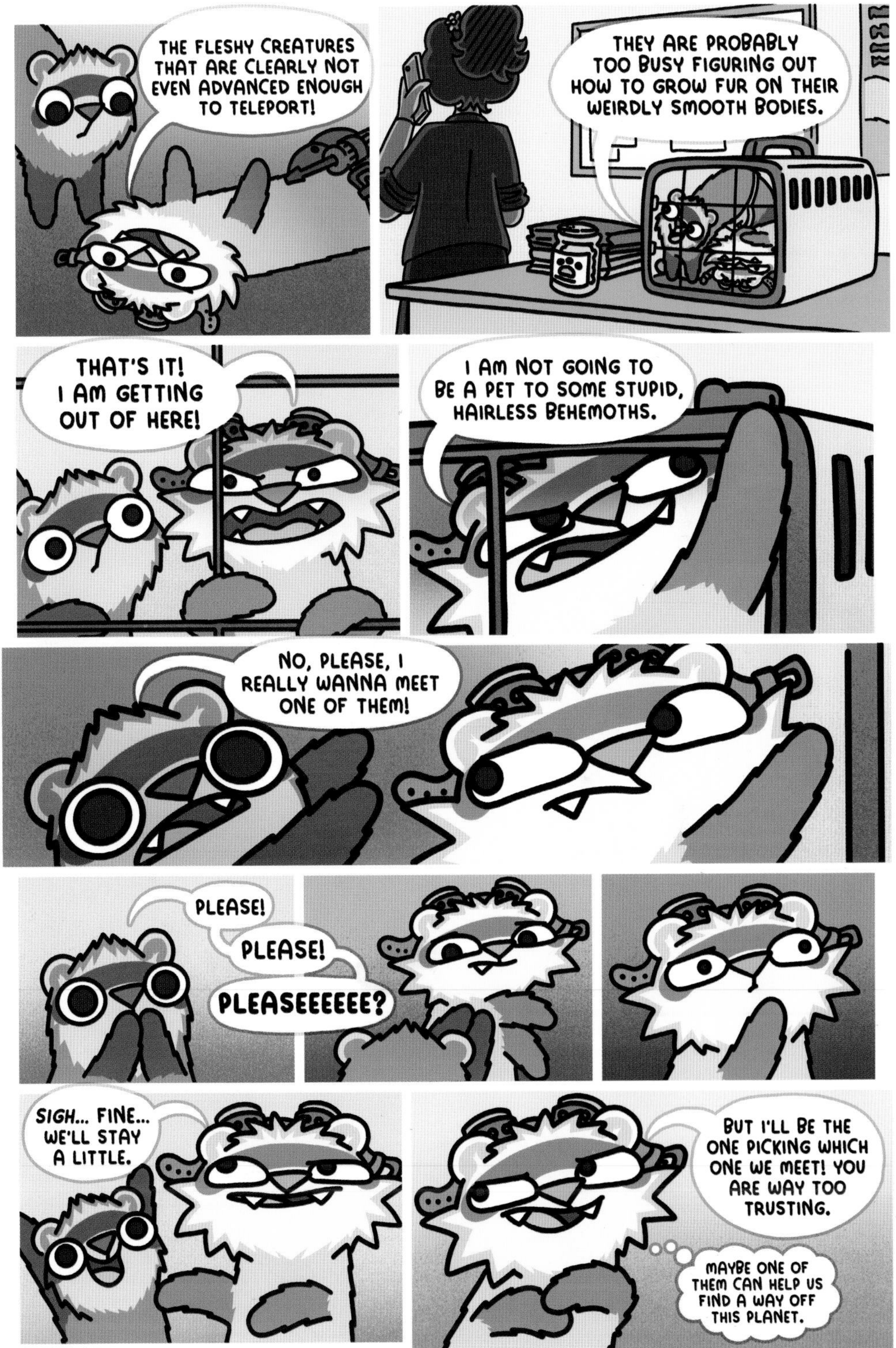
THE FLESHY CREATURES THAT ARE CLEARLY NOT EVEN ADVANCED ENOUGH TO TELEPORT!
THEY ARE PROBABLY TOO BUSY FIGURING OUT HOW TO GROW FUR ON THEIR WEIRDLY SMOOTH BODIES.
THAT'S IT! I AM GETTING OUT OF HERE!
I AM NOT GOING TO BE A PET TO SOME STUPID, HAIRLESS BEHEMOTHS.
NO, PLEASE, I REALLY WANNA MEET ONE OF THEM!
PLEASE!
PLEASE!
PLEASEEEEEEE?
SIGH... FINE... WE'LL STAY A LITTLE.
BUT I'LL BE THE ONE PICKING WHICH ONE WE MEET! YOU ARE WAY TOO TRUSTING.
MAYBE ONE OF THEM CAN HELP US FIND A WAY OFF THIS PLANET.

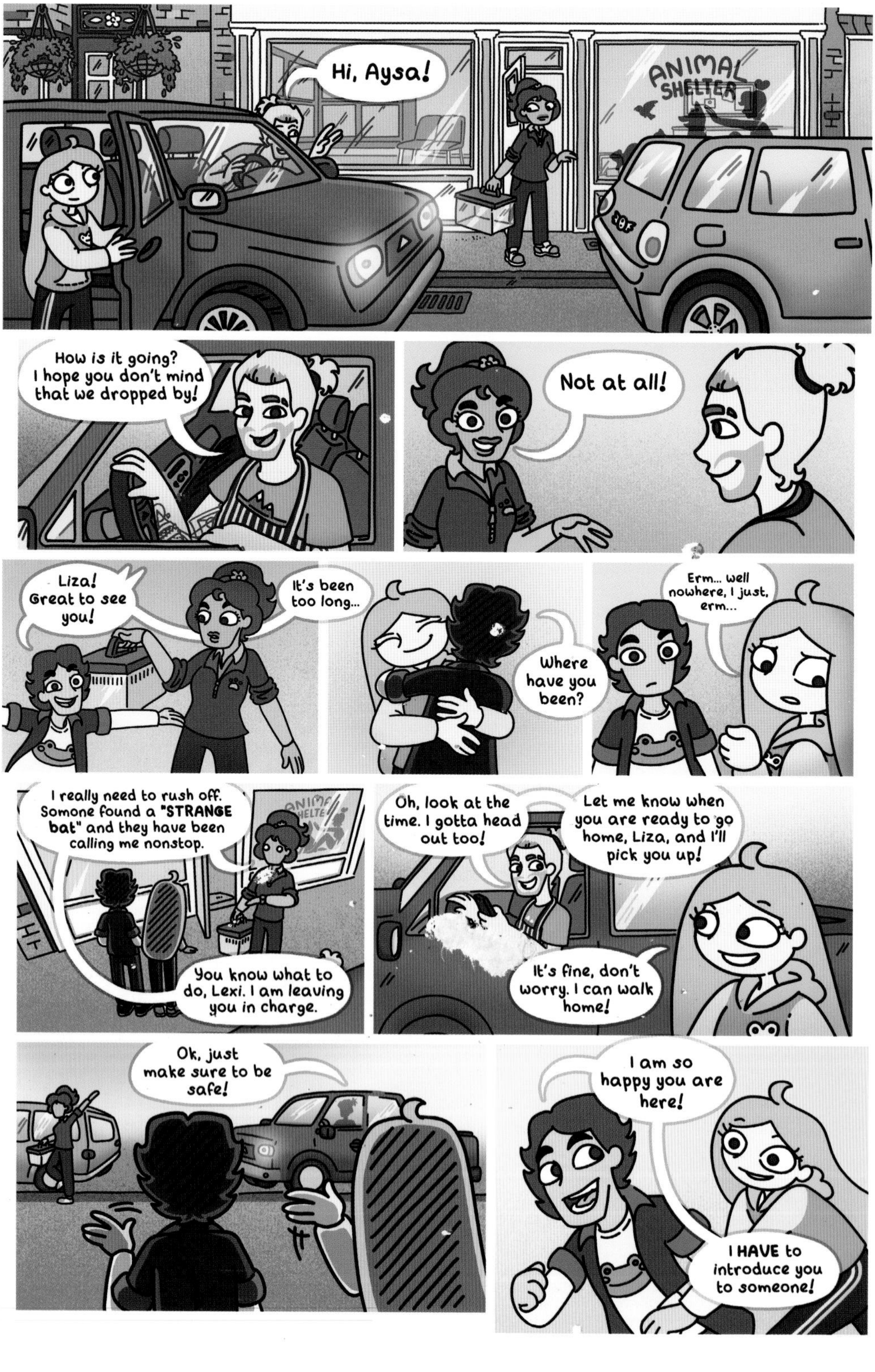

Hi, Aysa!
ANIMAL SHELTER
How is it going? I hope you don't mind that we dropped by!
Not at all!
Liza! Great to see you!
It's been too long...
Where have you been?
Erm... well nowhere, I just, erm...
I really need to rush off. Somone found a "STRANGE bat" and they have been calling me nonstop.
You know what to do, Lexi. I am leaving you in charge.
Oh, look at the time. I gotta head out too!
Let me know when you are ready to go home, Liza, and I'll pick you up!
It's fine, don't worry. I can walk home!
Ok, just make sure to be safe!
I am so happy you are here!
I HAVE to introduce you to someone!

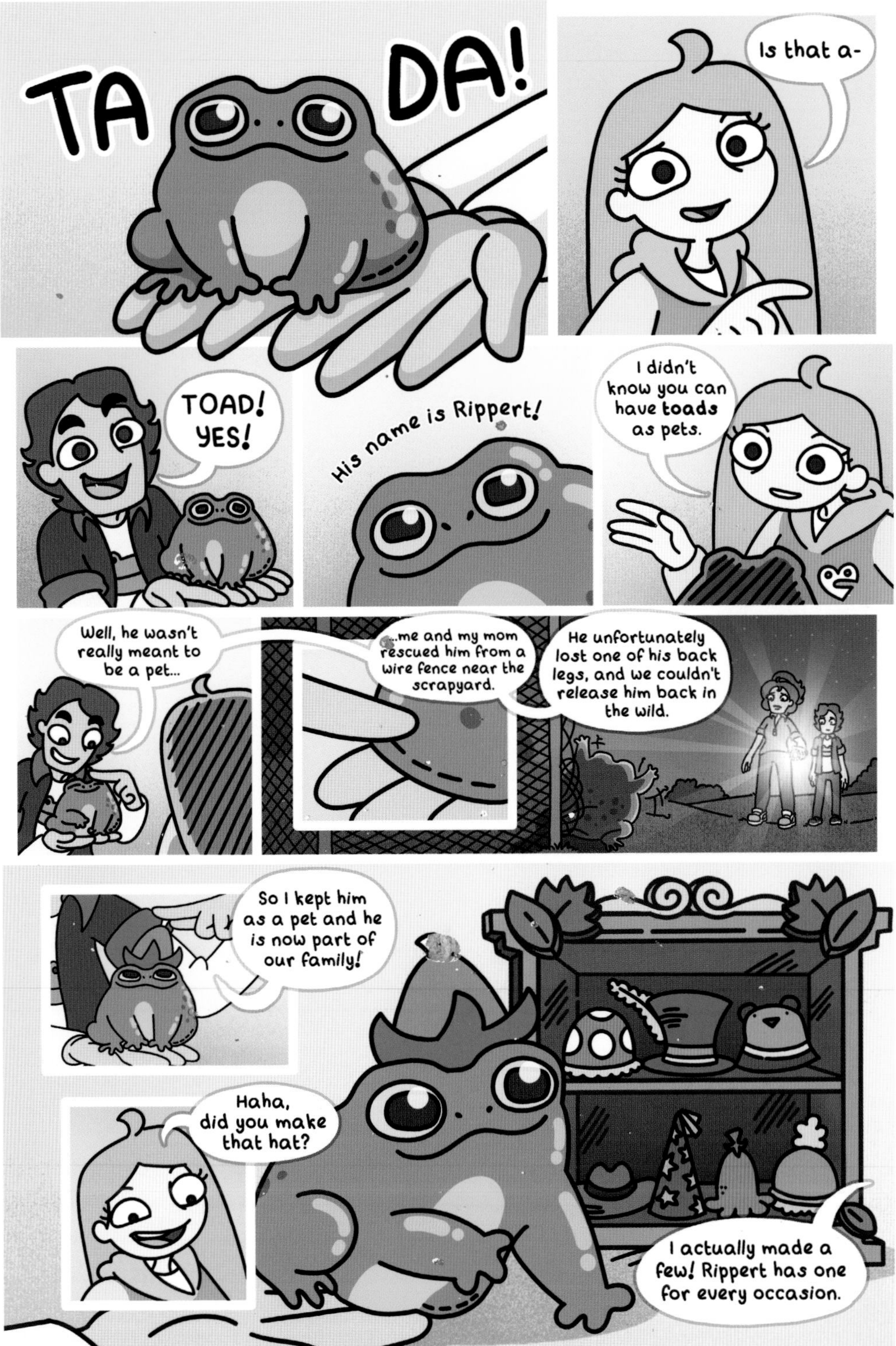
TA DA!
Is that a-
TOAD! YES!
His name is Rippert!
I didn't know you can have toads as pets.
Well, he wasn't really meant to be a pet...
...me and my mom rescued him from a wire fence near the scrapyard.
He unfortunately lost one of his back legs, and we couldn't release him back in the wild.
So I kept him as a pet and he is now part of our family!
Haha, did you make that hat?
I actually made a few! Rippert has one for every occasion.

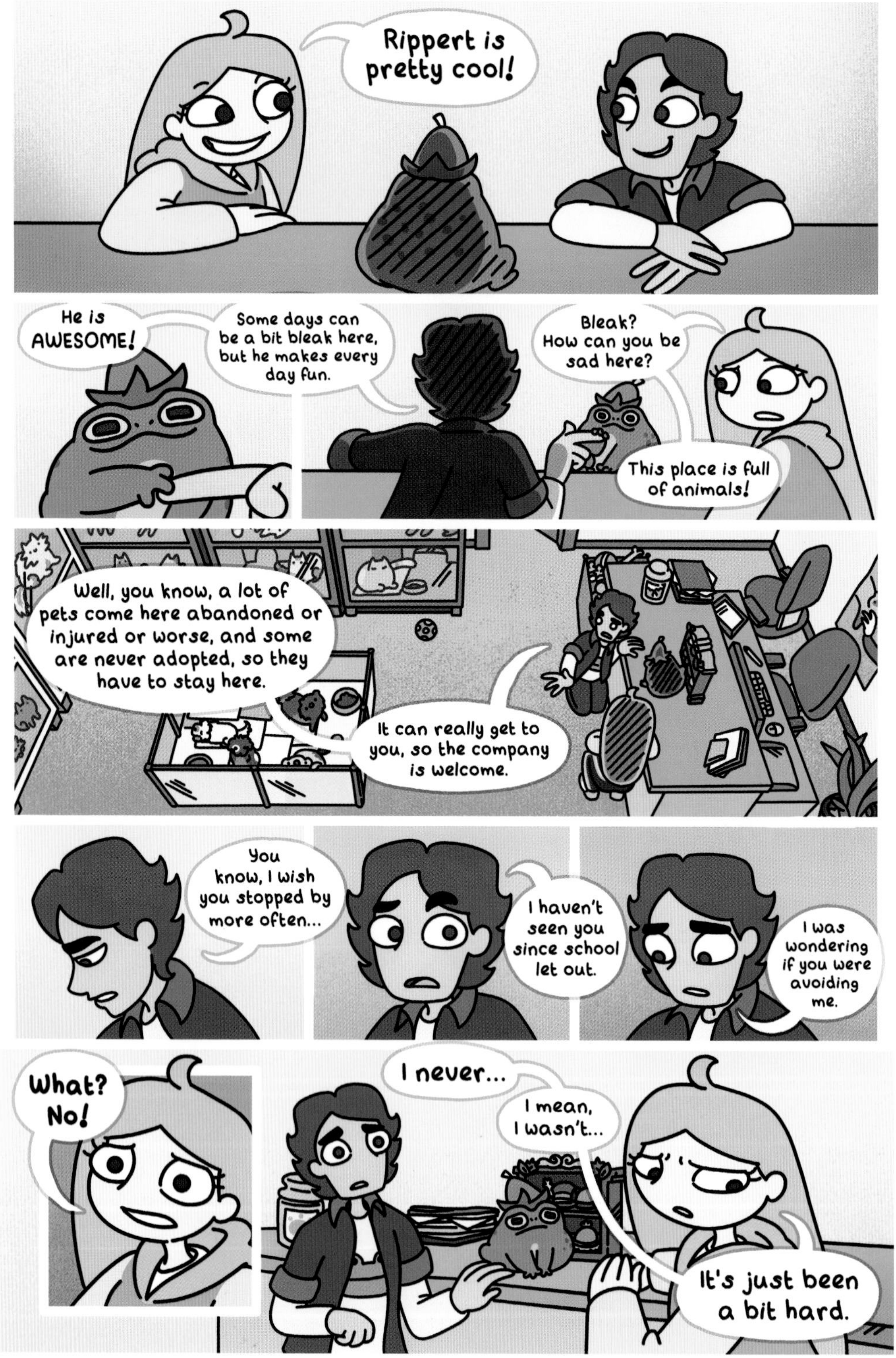

Rippert is pretty cool!
He is AWESOME!
Some days can be a bit bleak here, but he makes every day fun.
Bleak? How can you be sad here?
This place is full of animals!
Well, you know, a lot of pets come here abandoned or injured or worse, and some are never adopted, so they have to stay here.
It can really get to you, so the company is welcome.
You know, I wish you stopped by more often...
I haven't seen you since school let out.
I was wondering if you were avoiding me.
What? No!
I never...
I mean, I wasn't...
It's just been a bit hard.

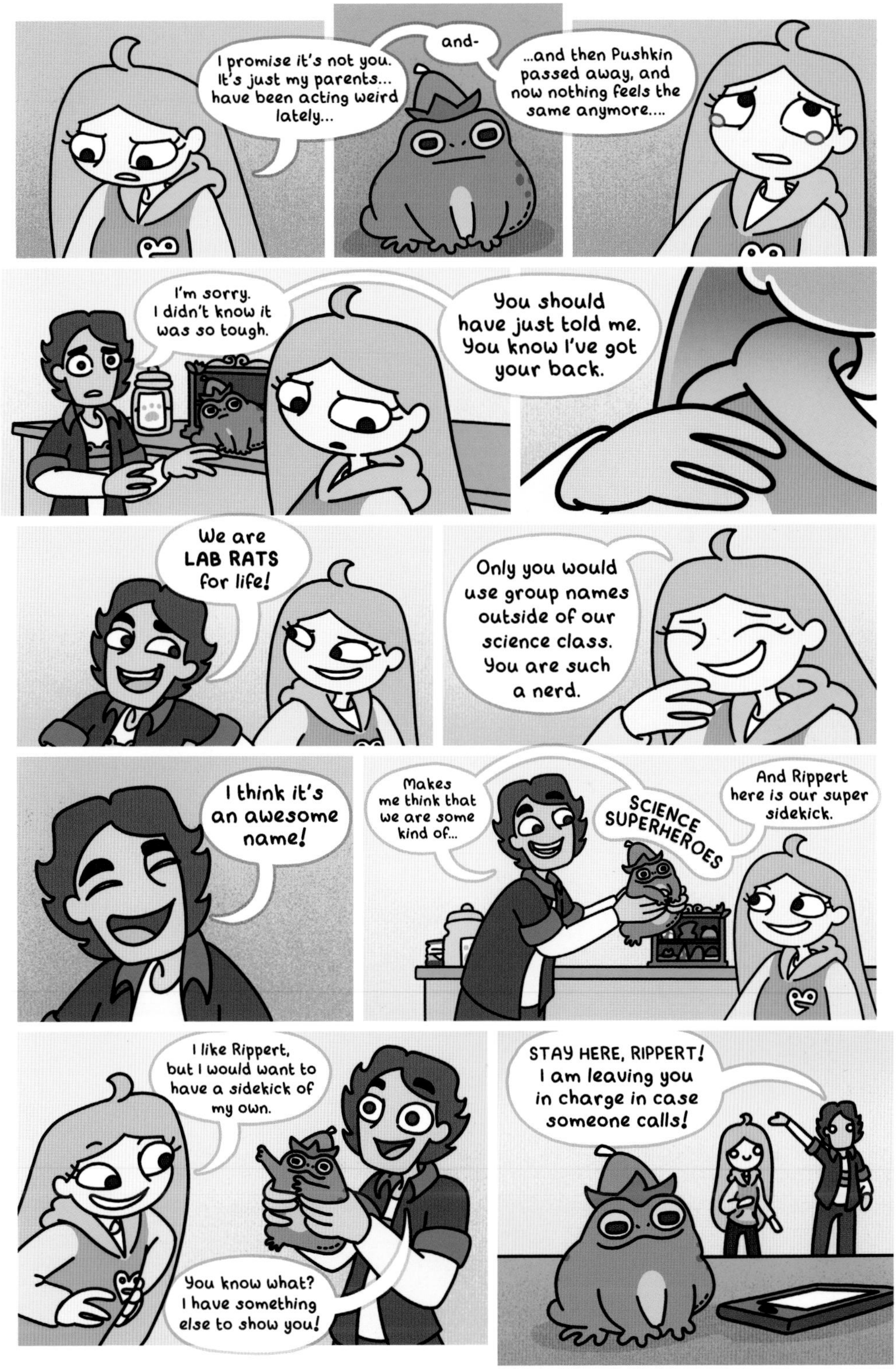

I promise it's not you. It's just my parents... have been acting weird lately...
and-
...and then Pushkin passed away, and now nothing feels the same anymore....
I'm sorry. I didn't know it was so tough.
You should have just told me. You know I've got your back.
We are LAB RATS for life!
Only you would use group names outside of our science class. You are such a nerd.
I think it's an awesome name!
Makes me think that we are some kind of...
SCIENCE SUPERHEROES
And Rippert here is our super sidekick.
I like Rippert, but I would want to have a sidekick of my own.
You know what? I have something else to show you!
STAY HERE, RIPPERT! I am leaving you in charge in case someone calls!

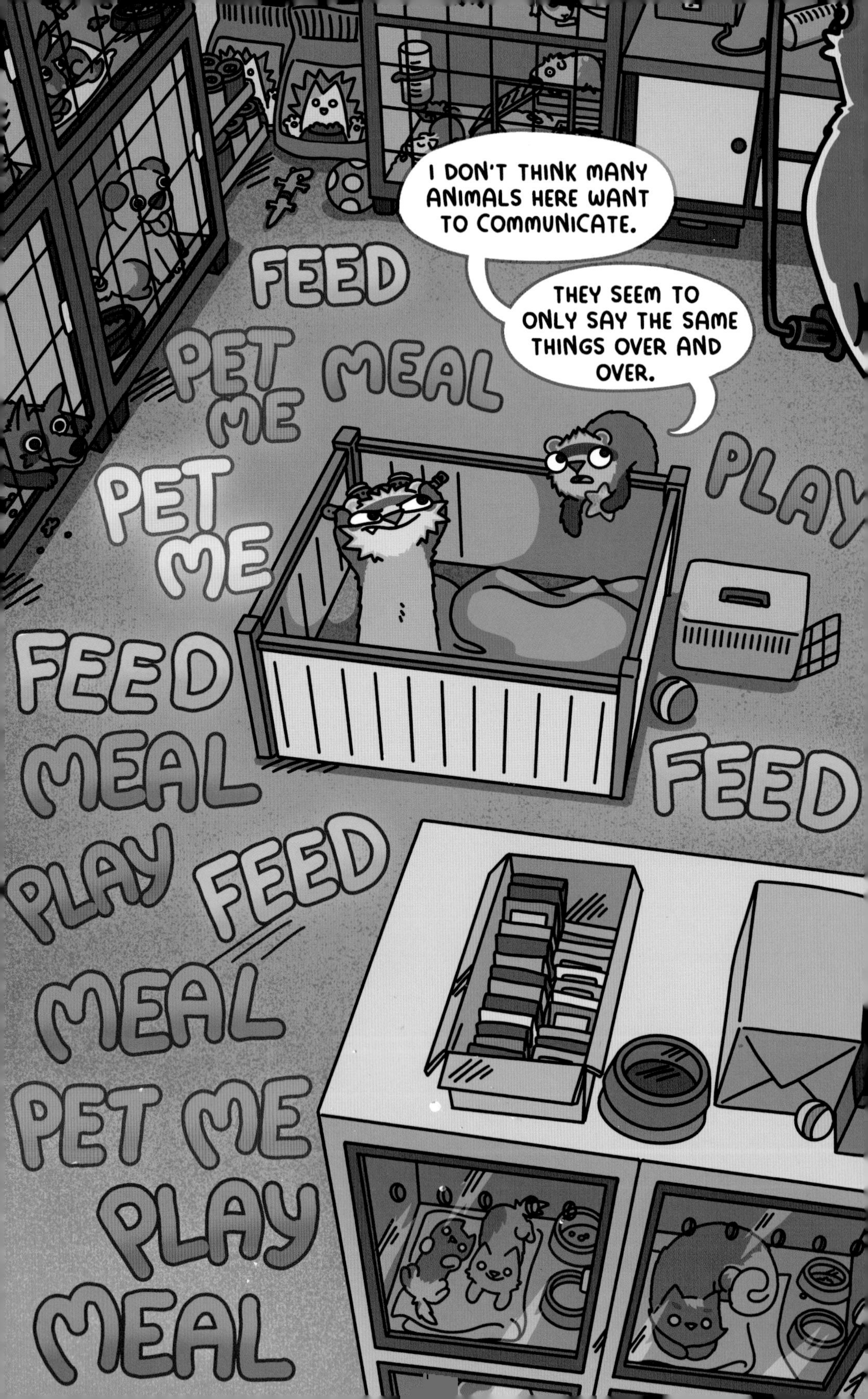
I DON'T THINK MANY ANIMALS HERE WANT TO COMMUNICATE.
THEY SEEM TO ONLY SAY THE SAME THINGS OVER AND OVER.
FEED
PET ME
MEAL
PLAY
PET ME
FEED
MEAL
FEED
PLAY
FEED
MEAL
PET ME
PLAY
MEAL

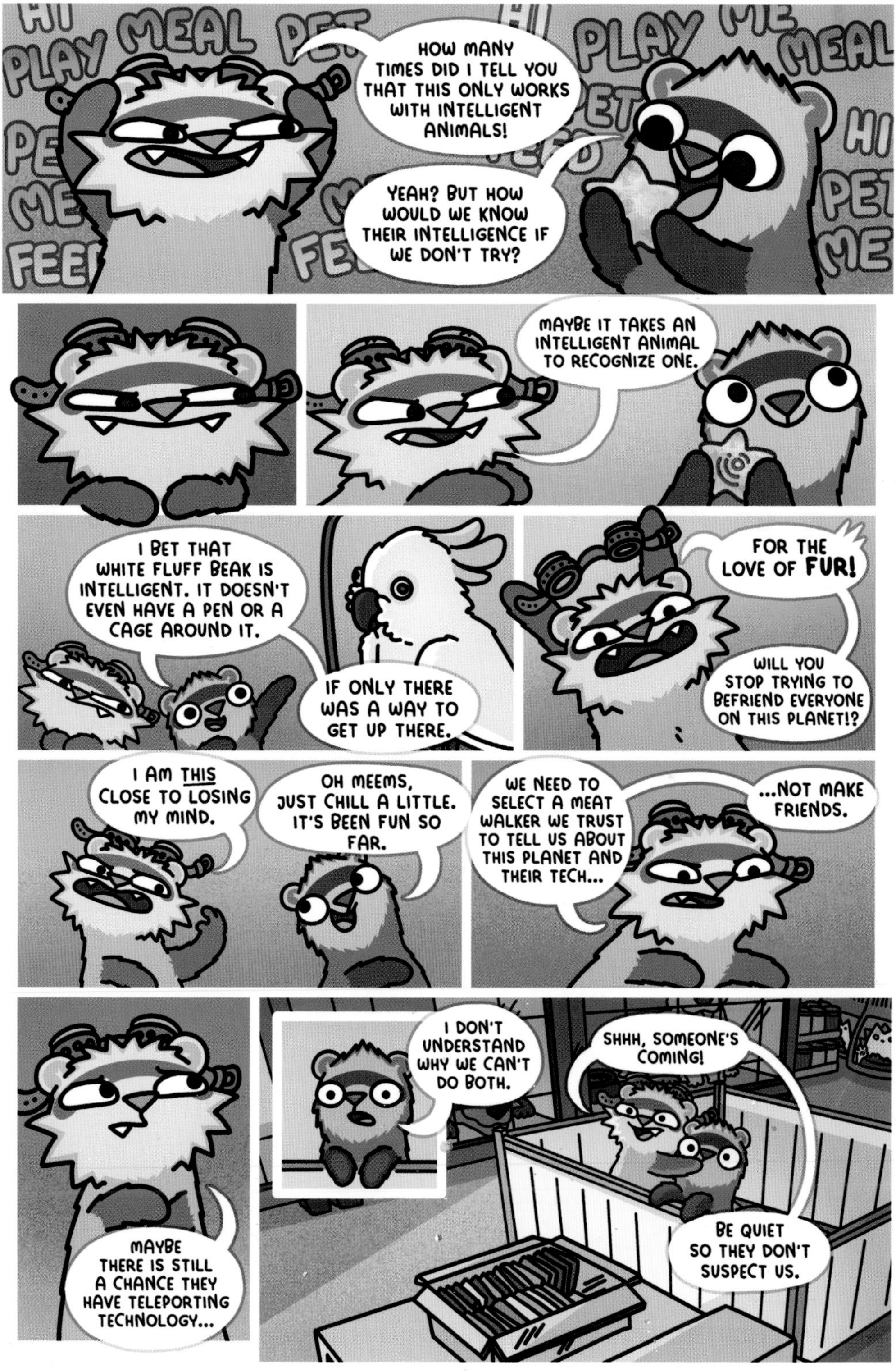
HI
PLAY
MEAL
PET
ME
FEED
HOW MANY TIMES DID I TELL YOU THAT THIS ONLY WORKS WITH INTELLIGENT ANIMALS!
YEAH? BUT HOW WOULD WE KNOW THEIR INTELLIGENCE IF WE DON'T TRY?
MAYBE IT TAKES AN INTELLIGENT ANIMAL TO RECOGNIZE ONE.
I BET THAT WHITE FLUFF BEAK IS INTELLIGENT. IT DOESN'T EVEN HAVE A PEN OR A CAGE AROUND IT.
IF ONLY THERE WAS A WAY TO GET UP THERE.
FOR THE LOVE OF FUR!
WILL YOU STOP TRYING TO BEFRIEND EVERYONE ON THIS PLANET!?
I AM THIS CLOSE TO LOSING MY MIND.
OH MEEMS, JUST CHILL A LITTLE. IT'S BEEN FUN SO FAR.
WE NEED TO SELECT A MEAT WALKER WE TRUST TO TELL US ABOUT THIS PLANET AND THEIR TECH...
...NOT MAKE FRIENDS.
MAYBE THERE IS STILL A CHANCE THEY HAVE TELEPORTING TECHNOLOGY...
I DON'T UNDERSTAND WHY WE CAN'T DO BOTH.
SHHH, SOMEONE'S COMING!
BE QUIET SO THEY DON'T SUSPECT US.

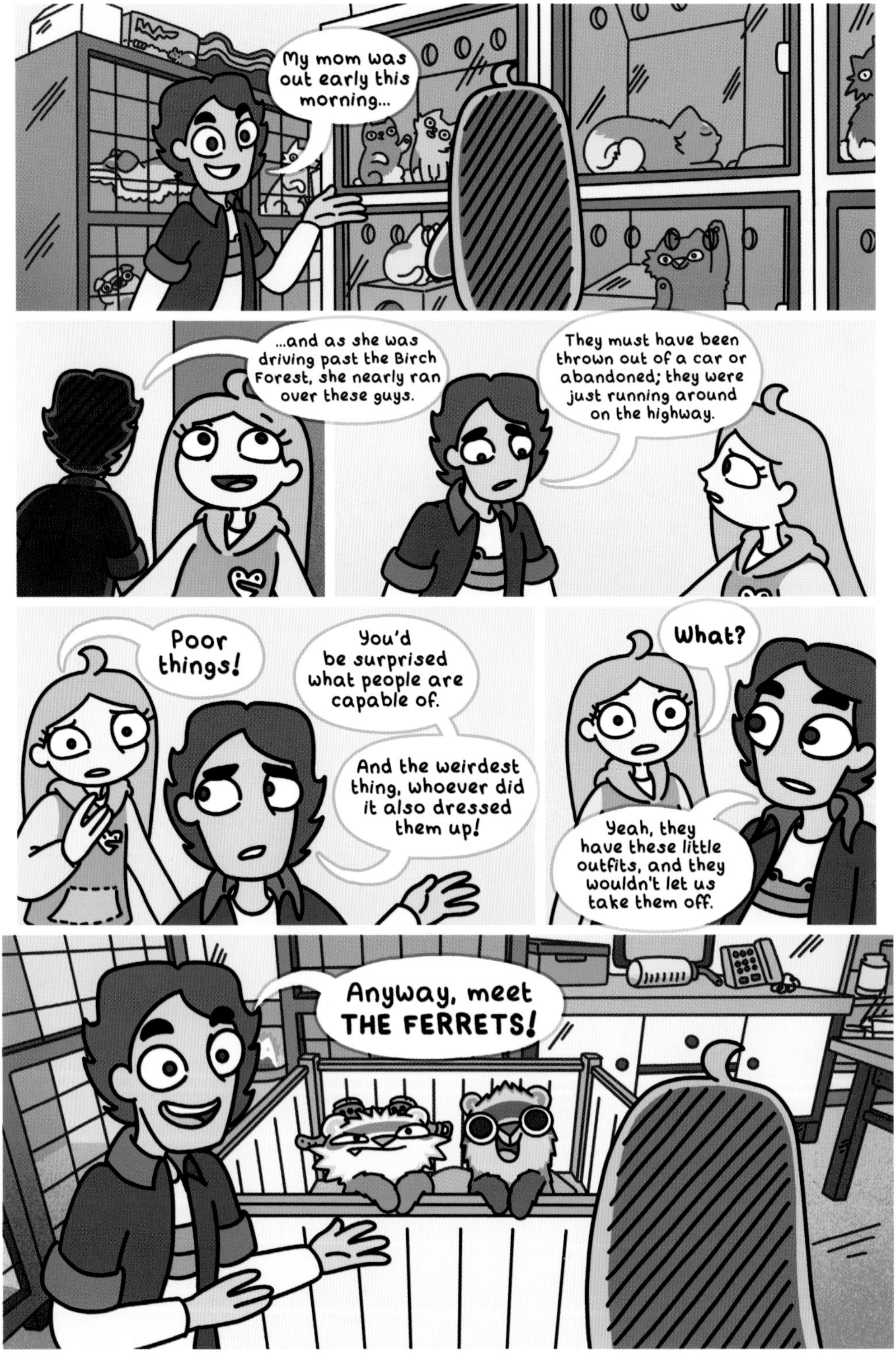
My mom was out early this morning...
...and as she was driving past the Birch Forest, she nearly ran over these guys.
They must have been thrown out of a car or abandoned; they were just running around on the highway.
Poor things!
You'd be surprised what people are capable of.
And the weirdest thing, whoever did it also dressed them up!
What?
Yeah, they have these little outfits, and they wouldn't let us take them off.
Anyway, meet THE FERRETS!

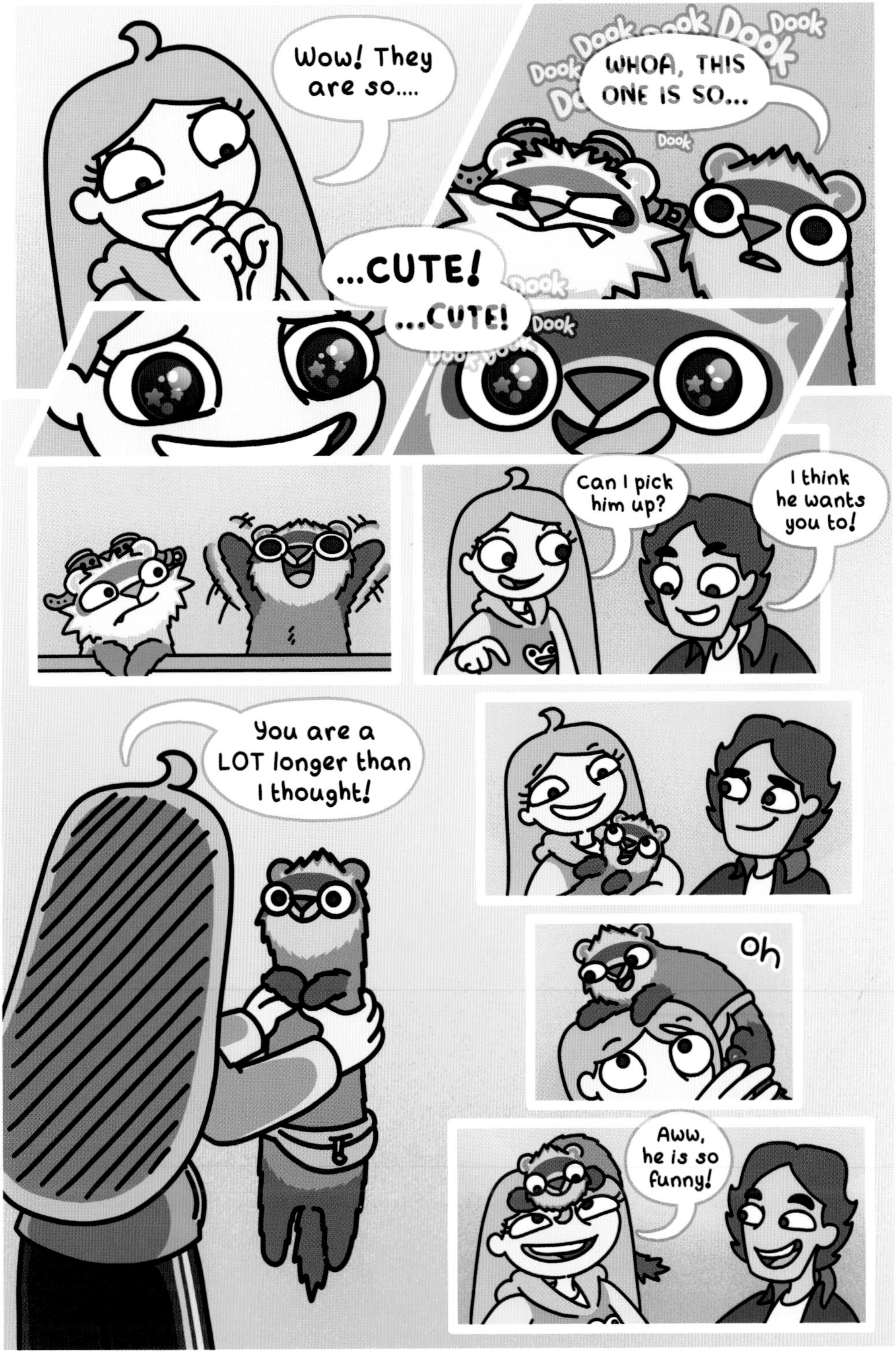
Wow! They are so....
Dook Dook Dook Dook Dook
WHOA, THIS ONE IS SO...
Dook
...CUTE!
...CUTE!
Dook
Can I pick him up?
I think he wants you to!
You are a LOT longer than I thought!
oh
AWW, he is so funny!

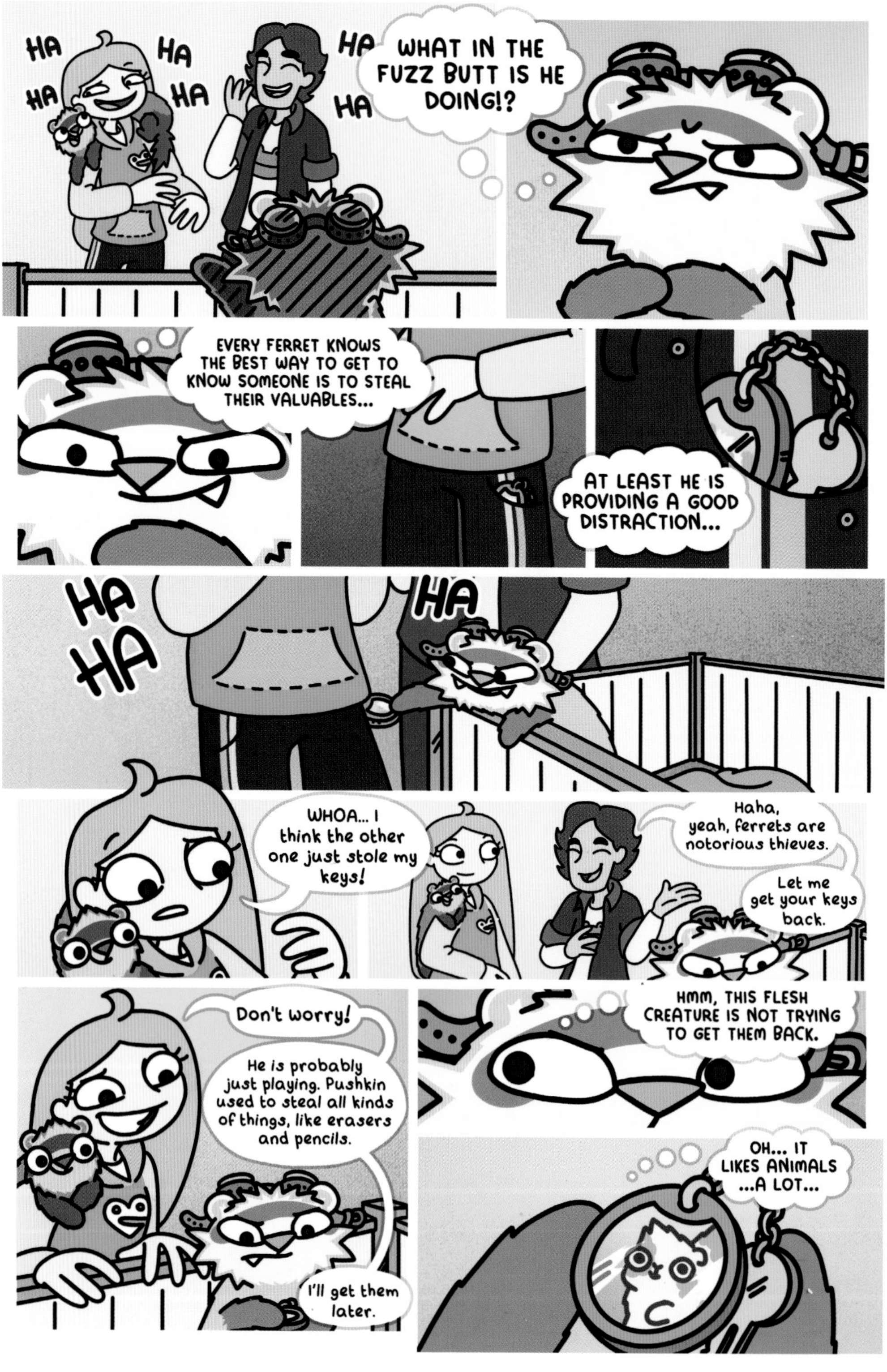
HA HA HA HA
HA HA
WHAT IN THE FUZZ BUTT IS HE DOING!?
EVERY FERRET KNOWS THE BEST WAY TO GET TO KNOW SOMEONE IS TO STEAL THEIR VALUABLES...
AT LEAST HE IS PROVIDING A GOOD DISTRACTION...
HA HA
HA
WHOA... I think the other one just stole my keys!
Haha, yeah, ferrets are notorious thieves.
Let me get your keys back.
Don't worry!
He is probably just playing. Pushkin used to steal all kinds of things, like erasers and pencils.
I'll get them later.
HMM, THIS FLESH CREATURE IS NOT TRYING TO GET THEM BACK.
OH... IT LIKES ANIMALS ...A LOT...

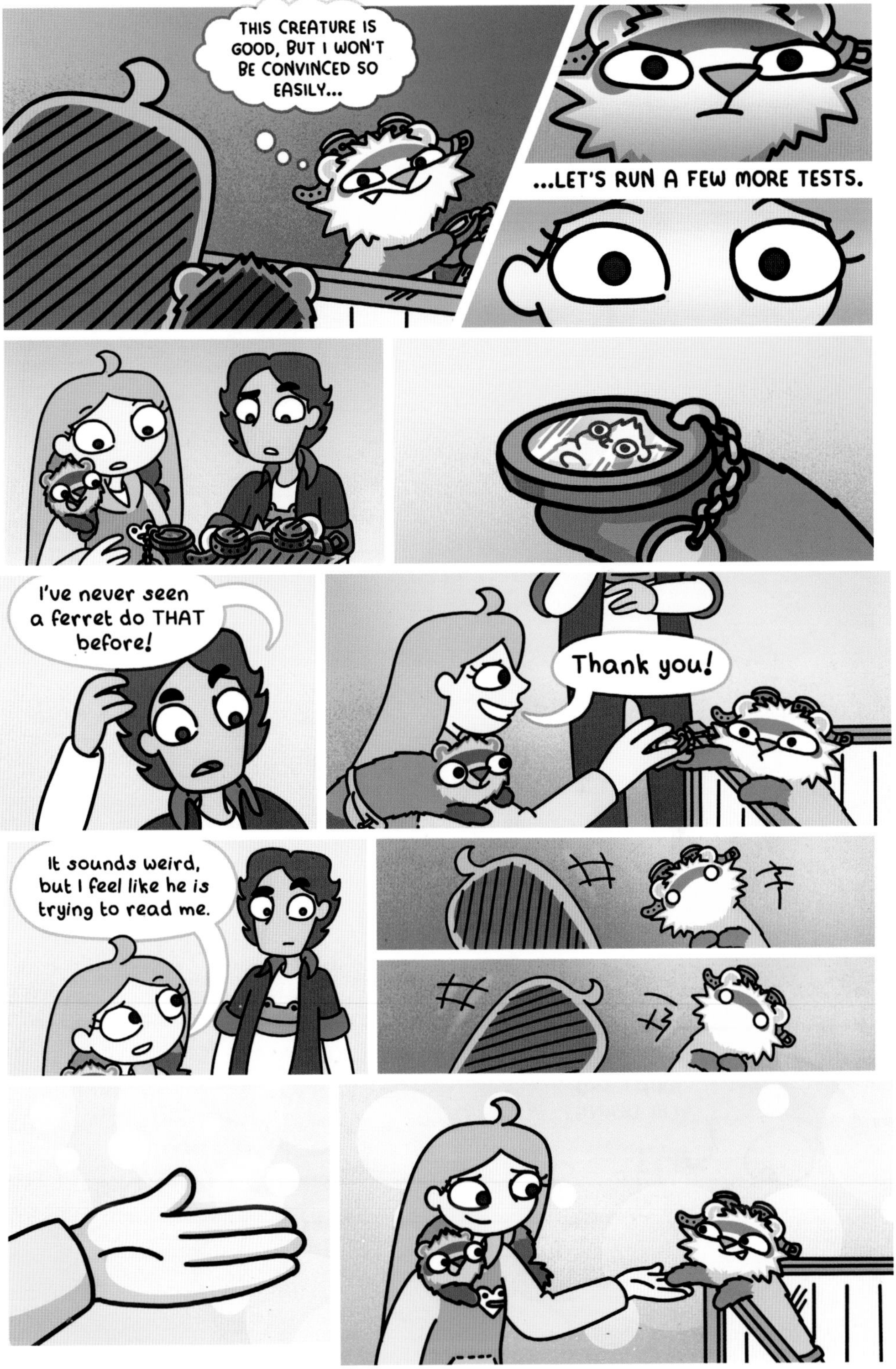
THIS CREATURE IS GOOD, BUT I WON'T BE CONVINCED SO EASILY...
...LET'S RUN A FEW MORE TESTS.
I've never seen a ferret do THAT before!
Thank you!
It sounds weird, but I feel like he is trying to read me.

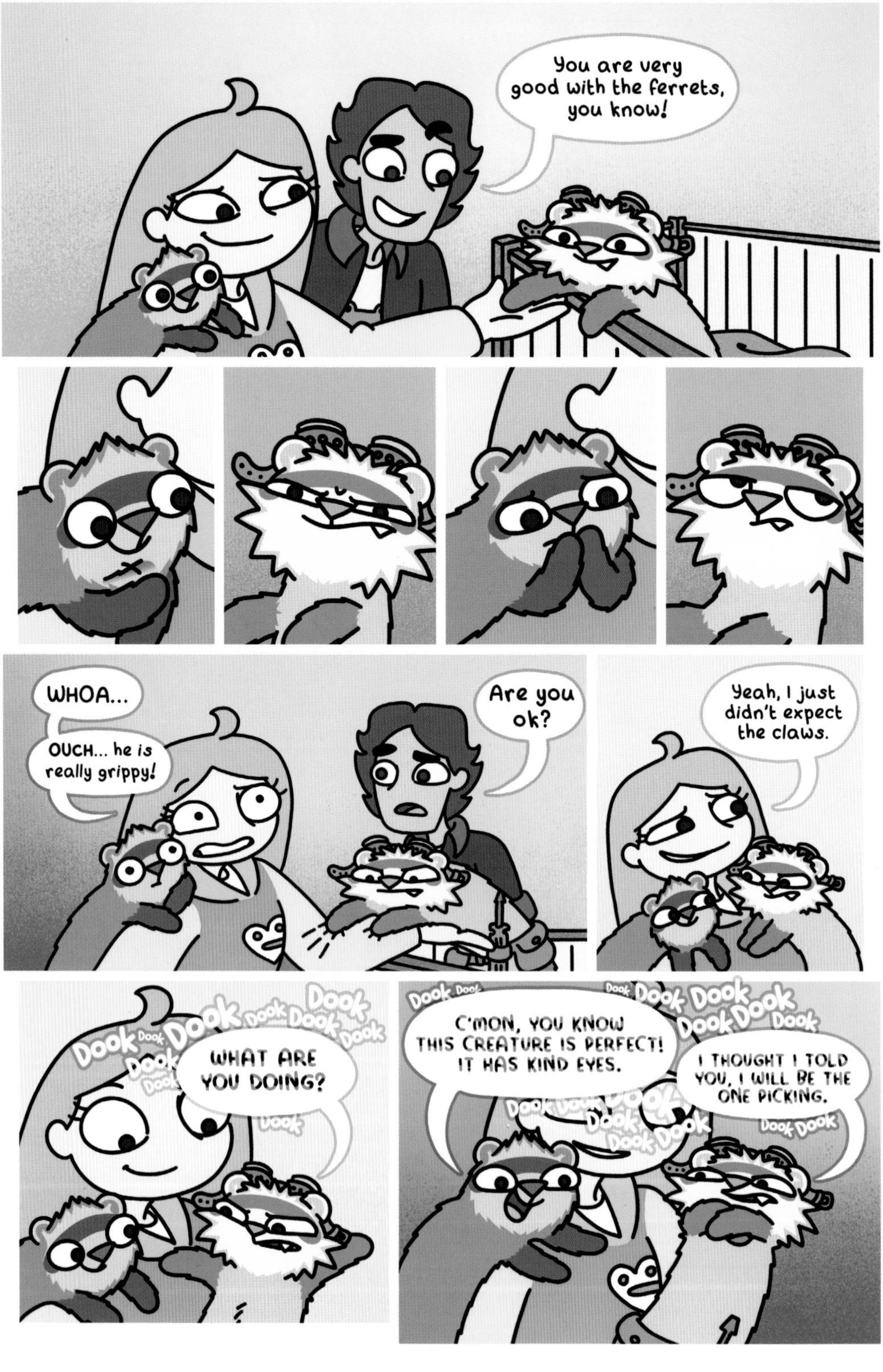
You are very good with the ferrets, you know!
WHOA...
OUCH... he is really grippy!
Are you ok?
Yeah, I just didn't expect the claws.
Dook Dook Dook Dook Dook Dook Dook Dook Dook
WHAT ARE YOU DOING?
Dook Dook Dook Dook Dook Dook
C'MON, YOU KNOW THIS CREATURE IS PERFECT! IT HAS KIND EYES.
I THOUGHT I TOLD YOU, I WILL BE THE ONE PICKING.
Dook Dook Dook Dook Dook Dook Dook

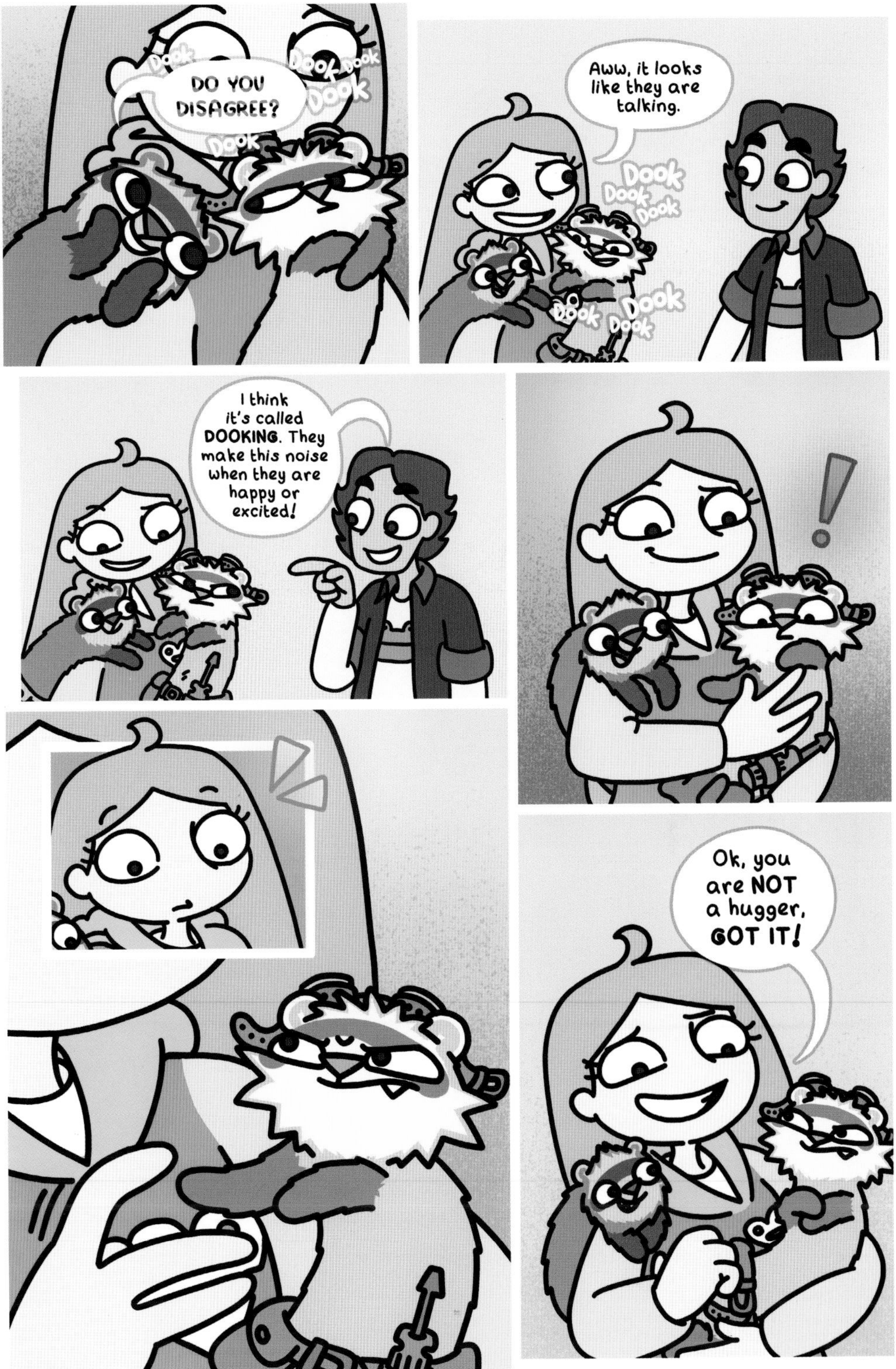
Dook
DO YOU DISAGREE?
Dook Dook Dook
Dook
Aww, it looks like they are talking.
Dook Dook Dook
Dook Dook Dook
I think it's called DOOKING. They make this noise when they are happy or excited!
!
Ok, you are NOT a hugger, GOT IT!

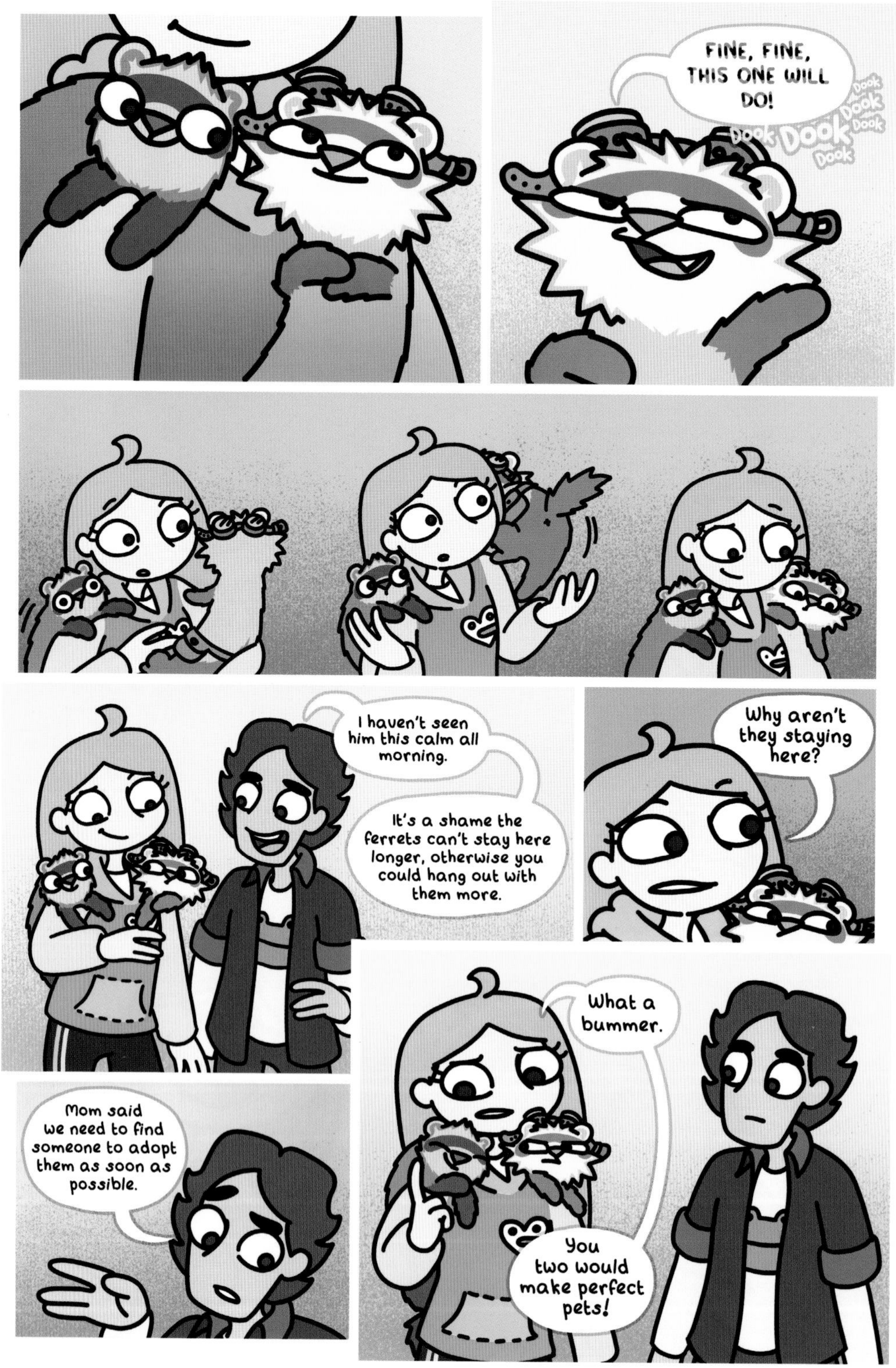
FINE, FINE, THIS ONE WILL DO!
Dook Dook Dook Dook Dook Dook
I haven't seen him this calm all morning.
It's a shame the ferrets can't stay here longer, otherwise you could hang out with them more.
Why aren't they staying here?
Mom said we need to find someone to adopt them as soon as possible.
What a bummer.
You two would make perfect pets!

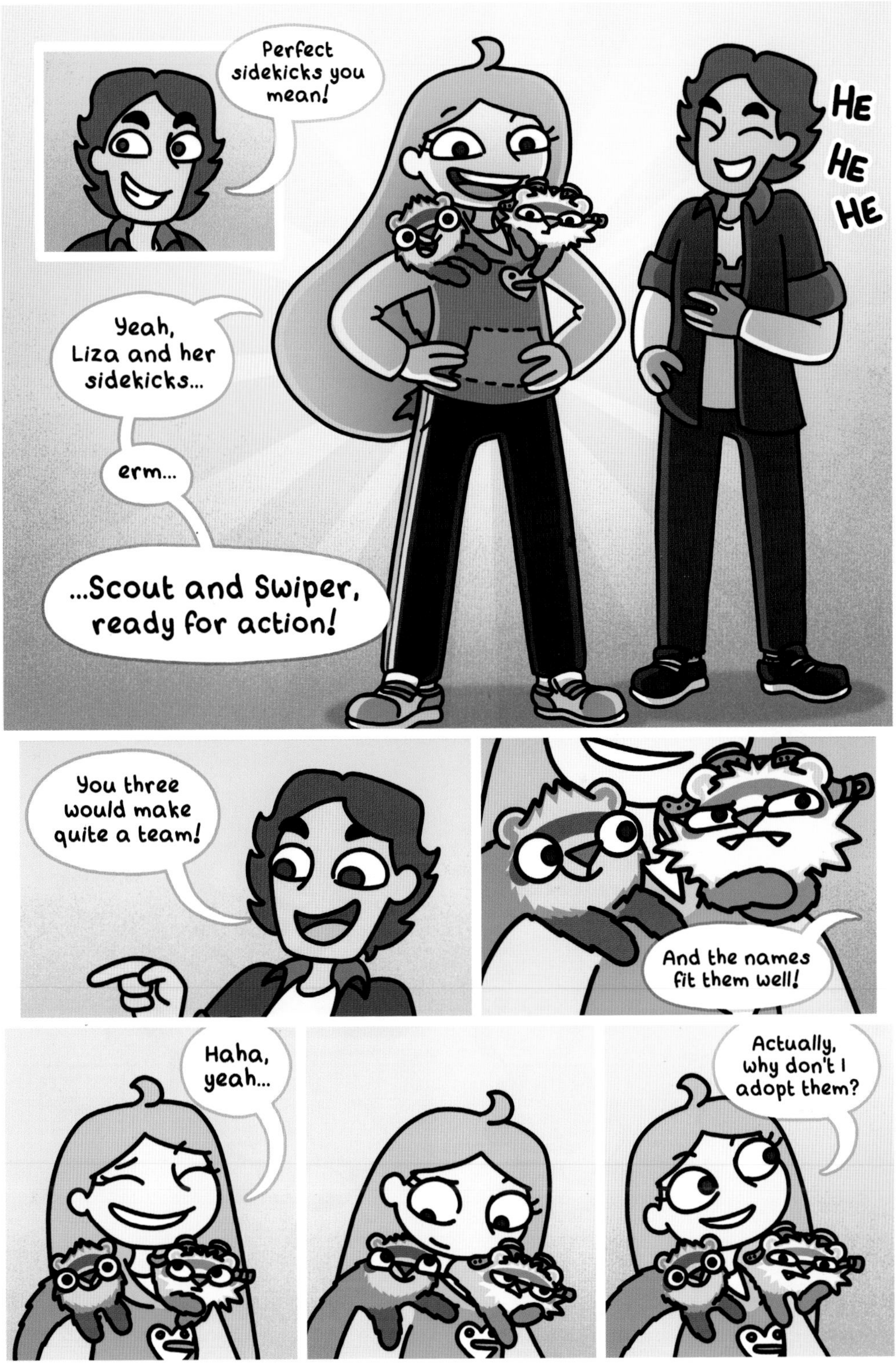
Perfect sidekicks you mean!
HE HE HE
Yeah, Liza and her sidekicks...
erm...
...Scout and Swiper, ready for action!
You three would make quite a team!
And the names fit them well!
Haha, yeah...
Actually, why don't I adopt them?

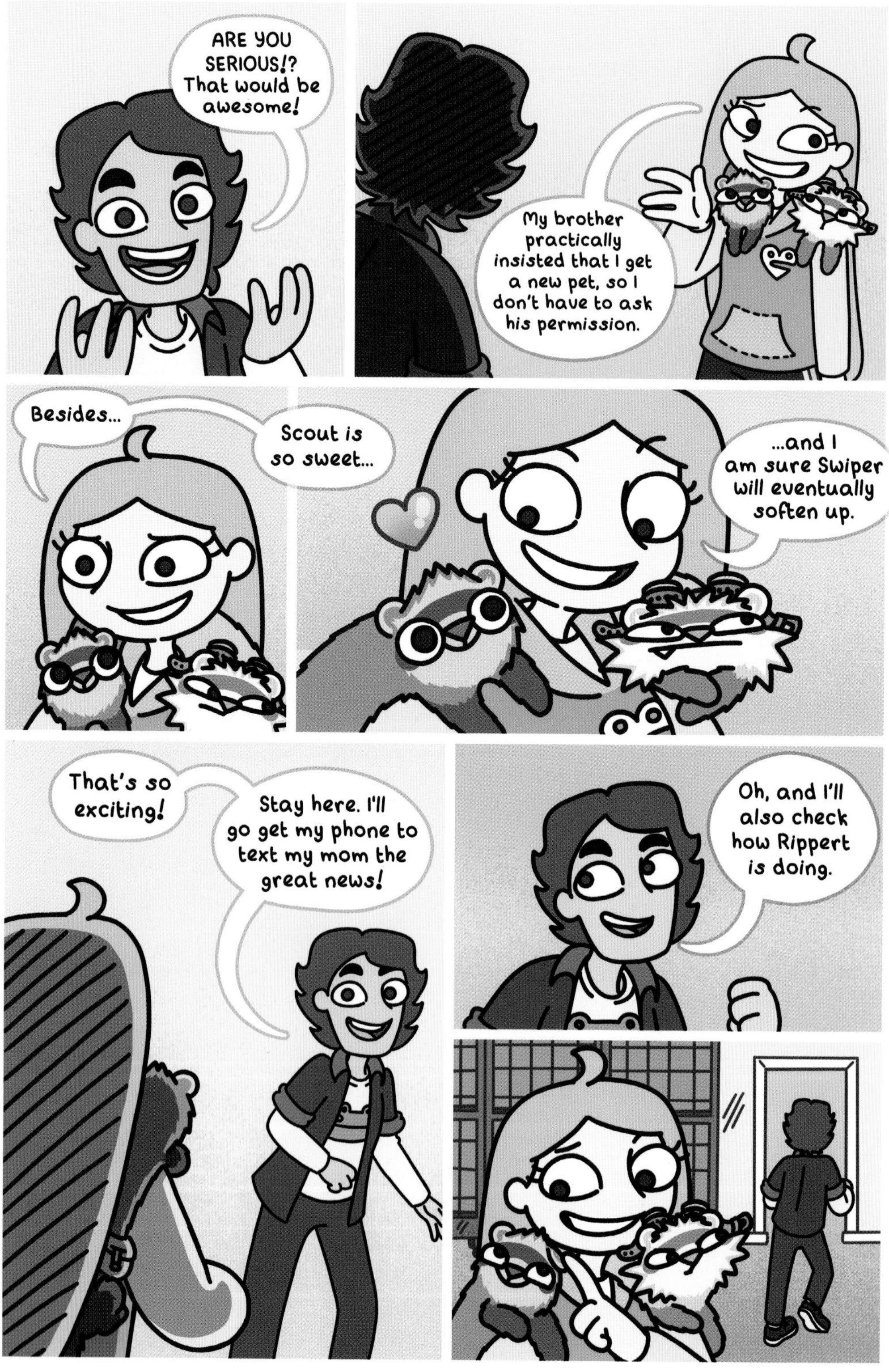
ARE YOU SERIOUS!? That would be awesome!
My brother practically insisted that I get a new pet, so I don't have to ask his permission.
Besides...
Scout is so sweet...
...and I am sure Swiper will eventually soften up.
That's so exciting!
Stay here. I'll go get my phone to text my mom the great news!
Oh, and I'll also check how Rippert is doing.

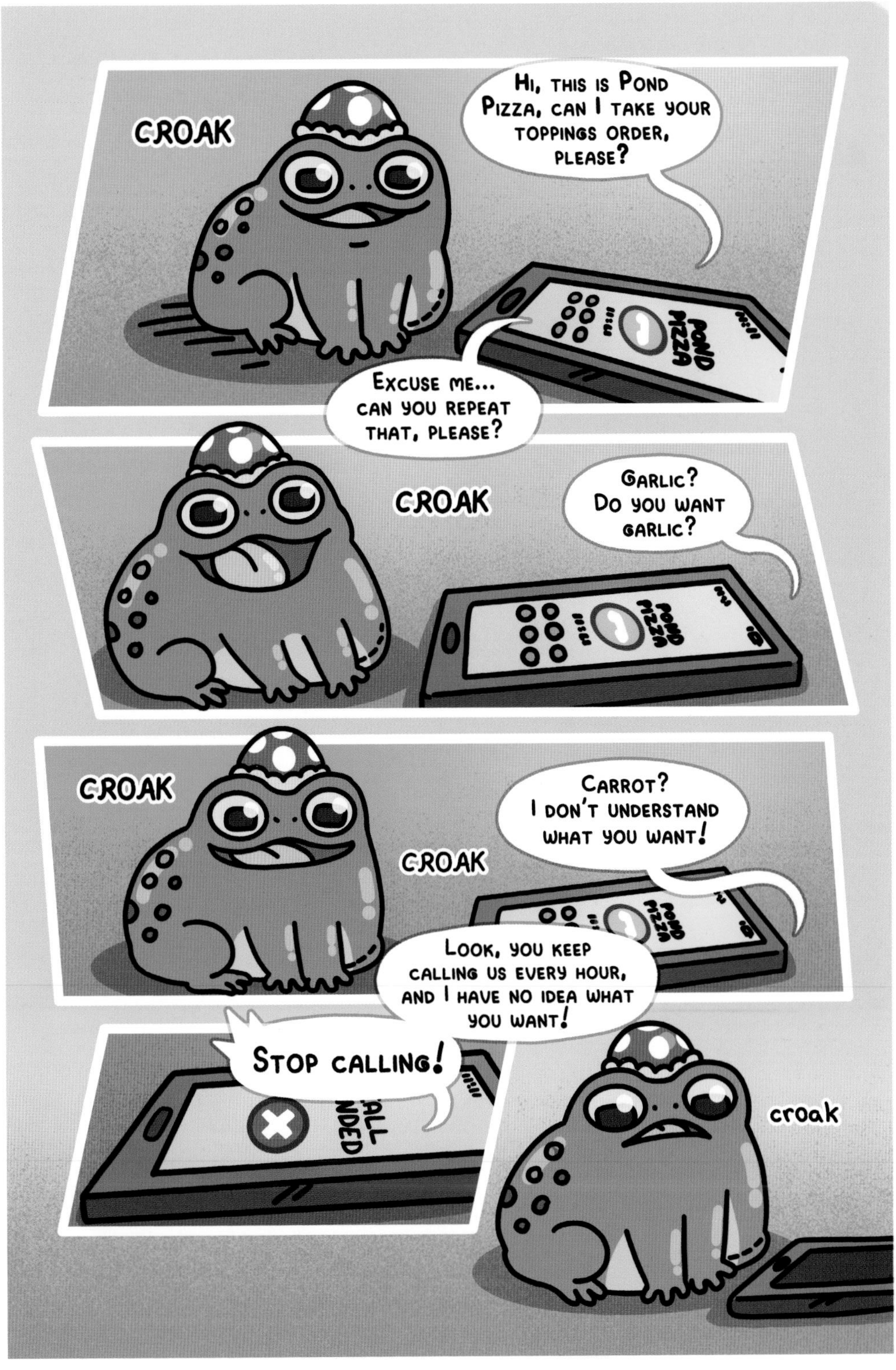
CROAK
Hi, this is Pond Pizza, can I take your toppings order, please?
POND PIZZA
Excuse me... can you repeat that, please?
CROAK
Garlic? Do you want garlic?
POND PIZZA
CROAK
CROAK
Carrot? I don't understand what you want!
POND PIZZA
Look, you keep calling us every hour, and I have no idea what you want!
Stop calling!
croak

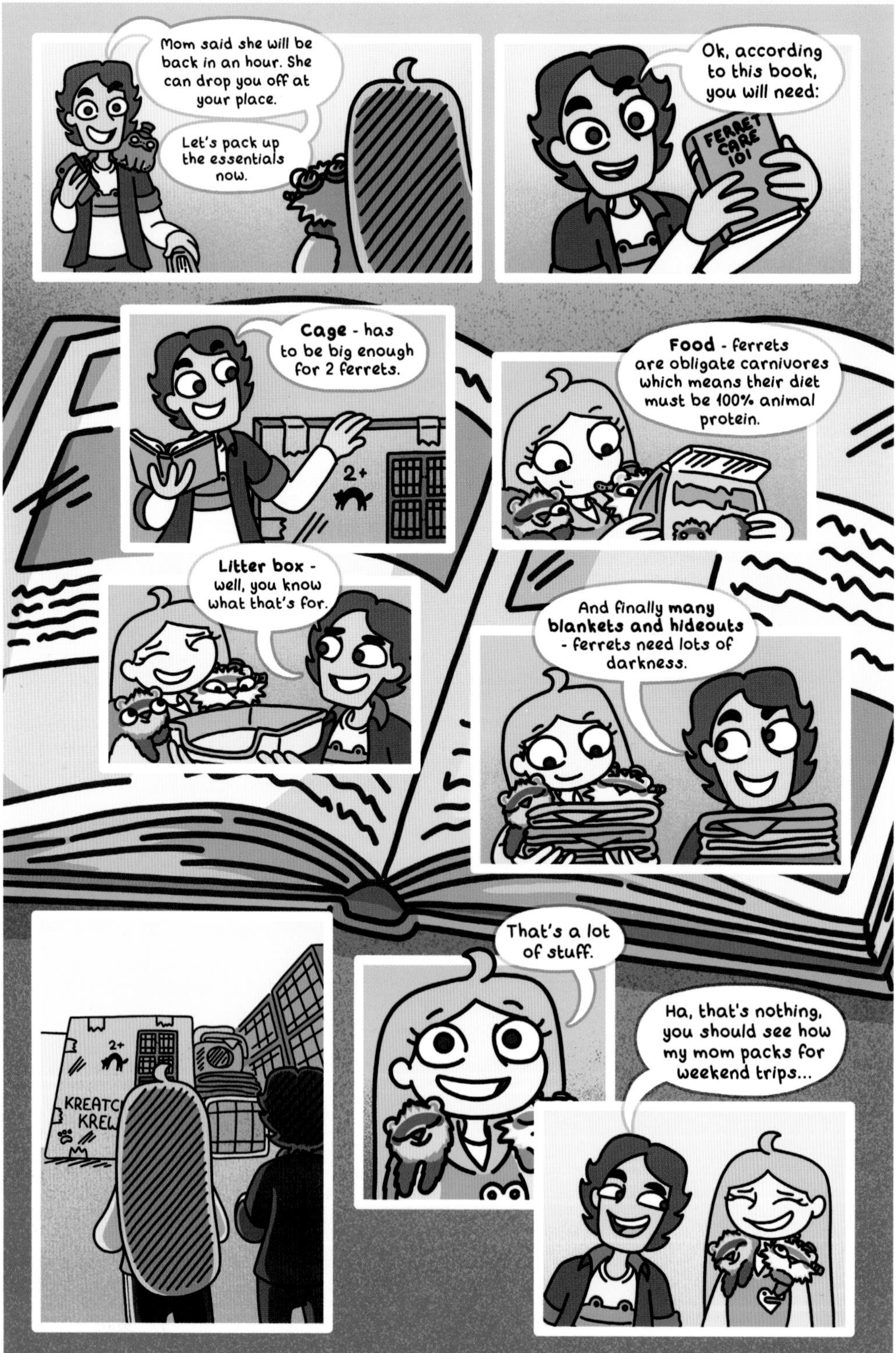
Mom said she will be back in an hour. She can drop you off at your place.
Let's pack up the essentials now.
Ok, according to this book, you will need:
FERRET CARE 101
Cage - has to be big enough for 2 ferrets.
2+
Food - ferrets are obligate carnivores which means their diet must be 100% animal protein.
Litter box - well, you know what that's for.
And finally many blankets and hideouts - ferrets need lots of darkness.
2+
KREATC
KREW
That's a lot of stuff.
Ha, that's nothing, you should see how my mom packs for weekend trips...

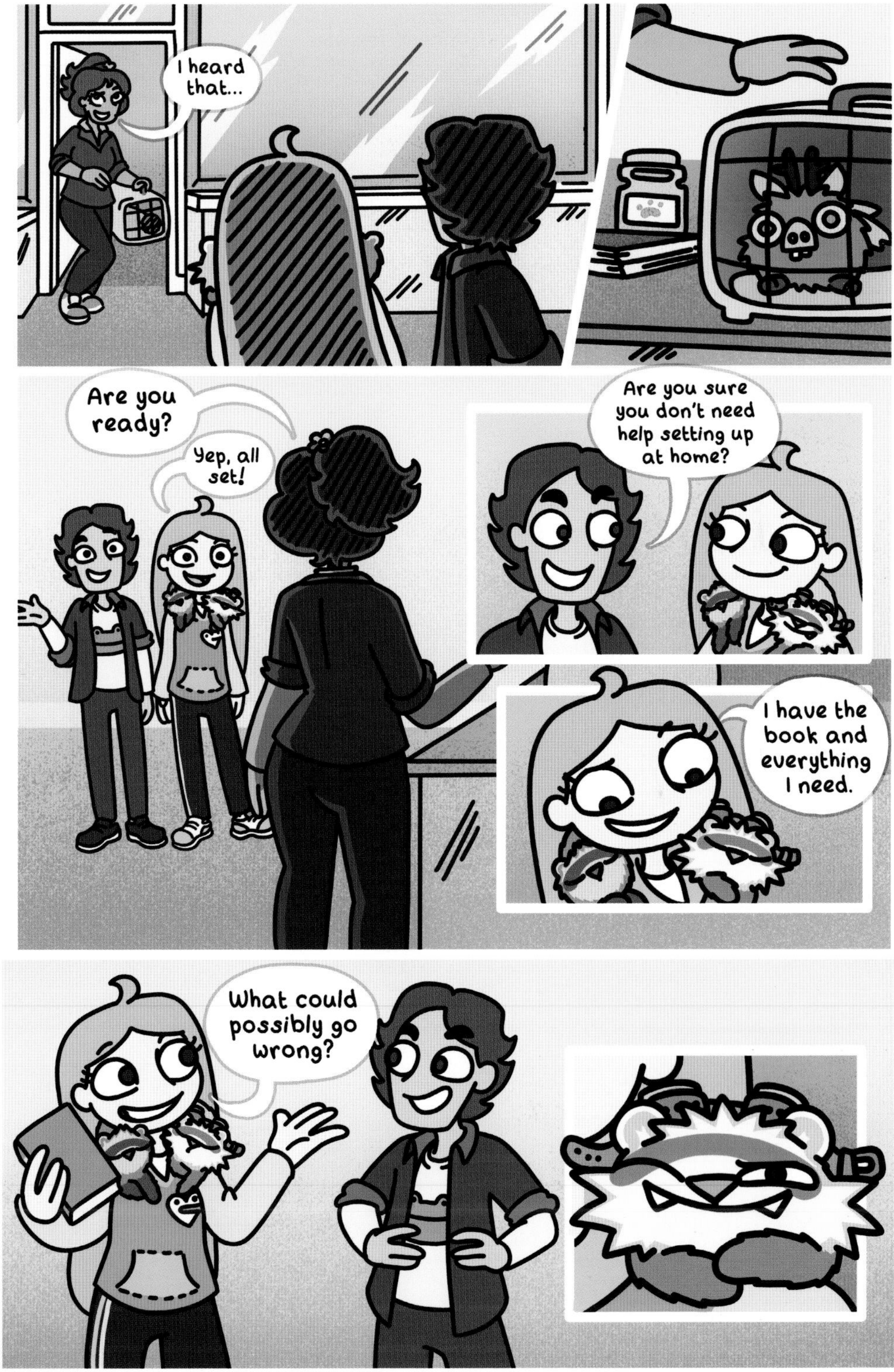
I heard that...
Are you ready?
Yep, all set!
Are you sure you don't need help setting up at home?
I have the book and everything I need.
What could possibly go wrong?

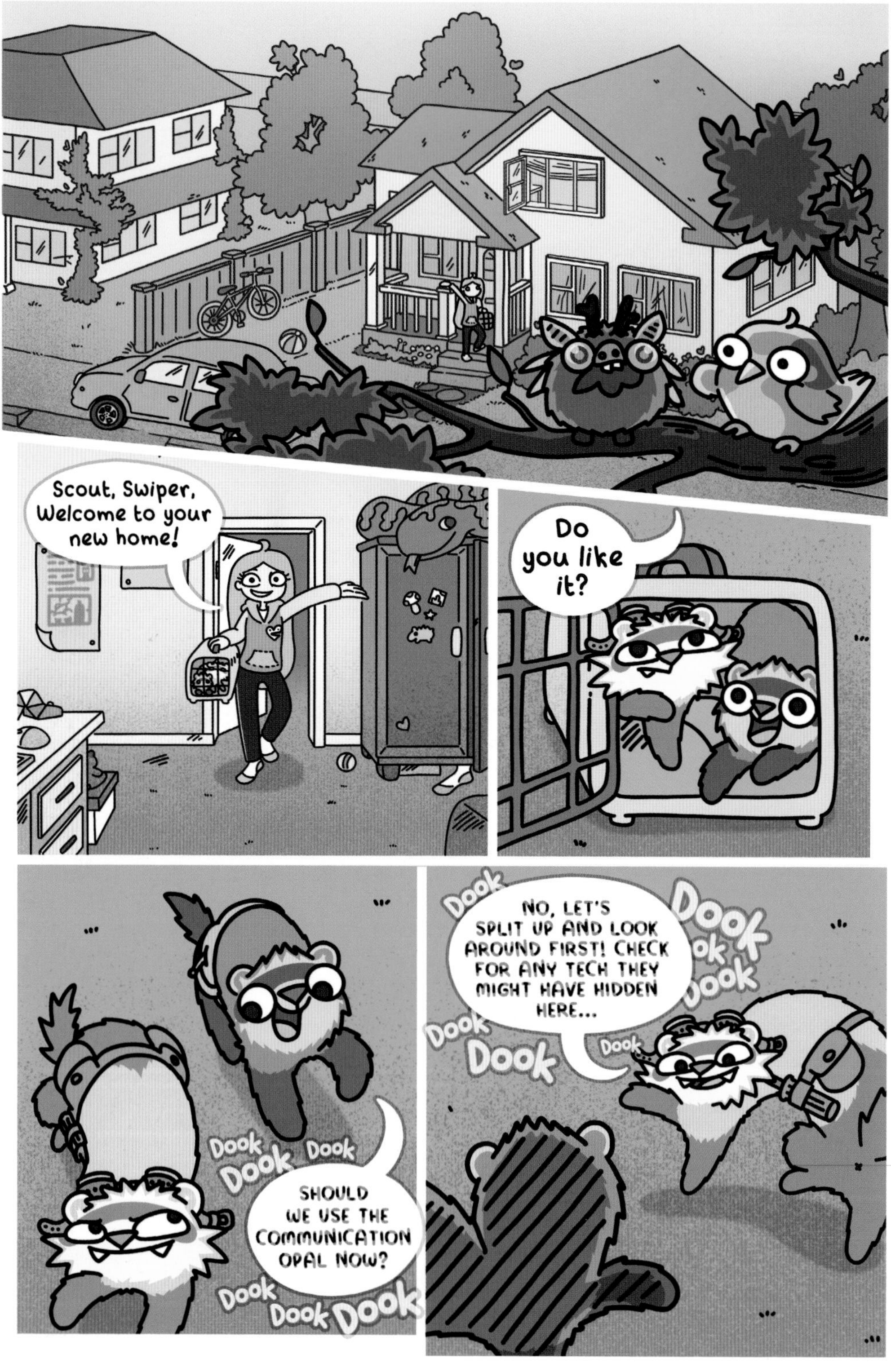

Scout, Swiper, Welcome to your new home!
Do you like it?
Dook Dook Dook
SHOULD WE USE THE COMMUNICATION OPAL NOW?
Dook Dook Dook
Dook
NO, LET'S SPLIT UP AND LOOK AROUND FIRST! CHECK FOR ANY TECH THEY MIGHT HAVE HIDDEN HERE...
Dook ok Dook
Dook Dook
Dook

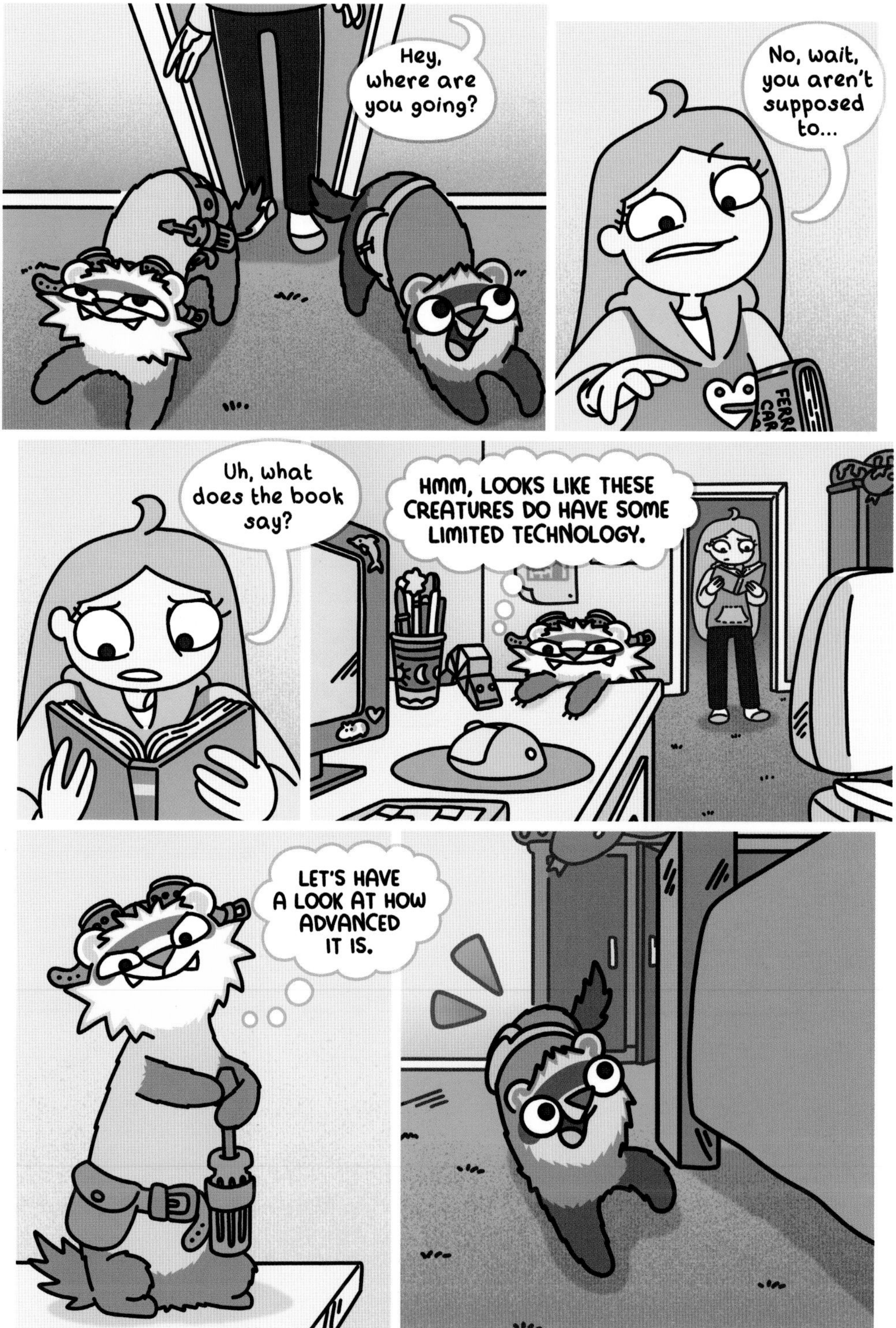
Hey, where are you going?
No, wait, you aren't supposed to...
FERR CAR
Uh, what does the book say?
HMM, LOOKS LIKE THESE CREATURES DO HAVE SOME LIMITED TECHNOLOGY.
LET'S HAVE A LOOK AT HOW ADVANCED IT IS.

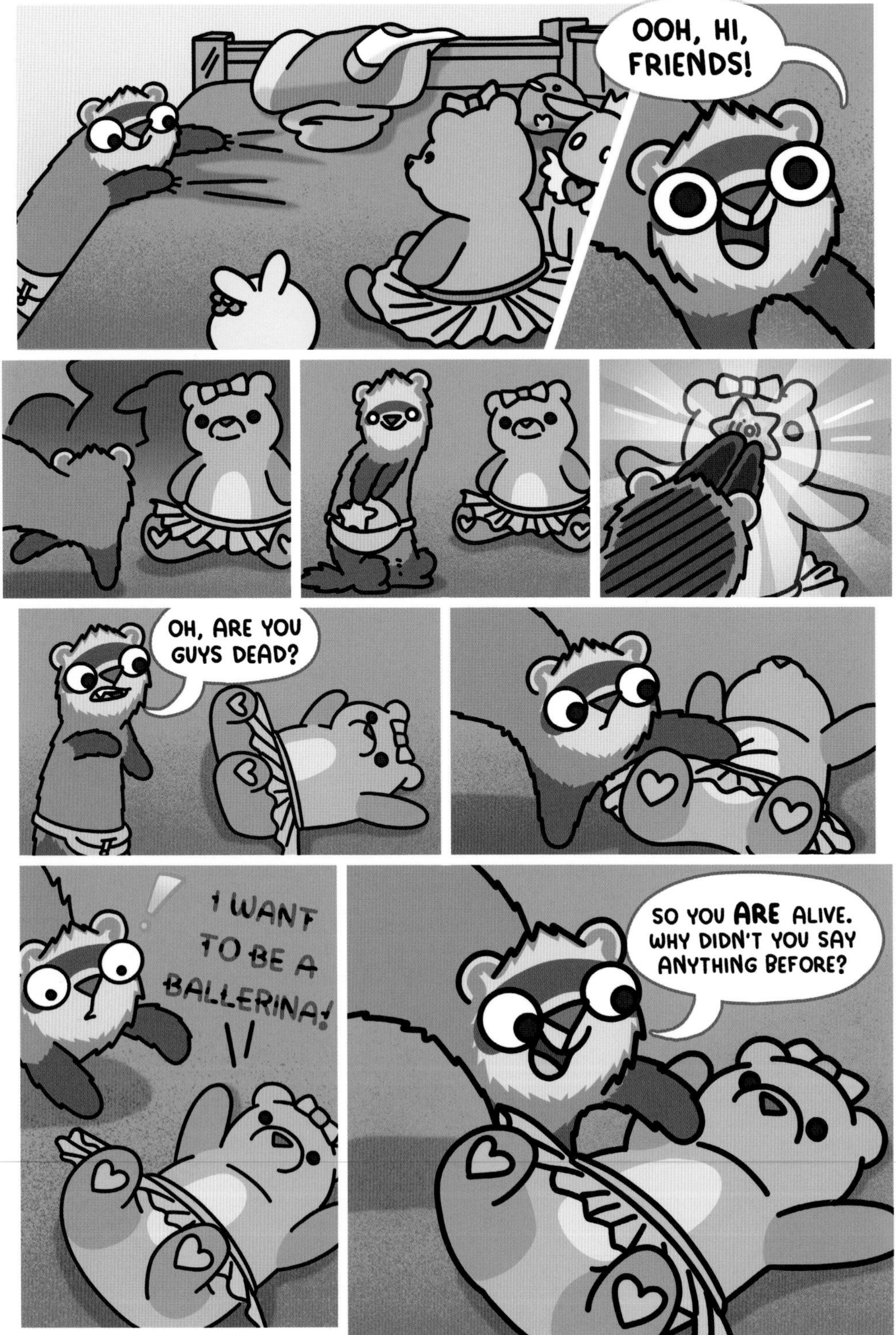
OOH, HI, FRIENDS!
OH, ARE YOU GUYS DEAD?
I WANT TO BE A BALLERINA!
SO YOU ARE ALIVE. WHY DIDN'T YOU SAY ANYTHING BEFORE?

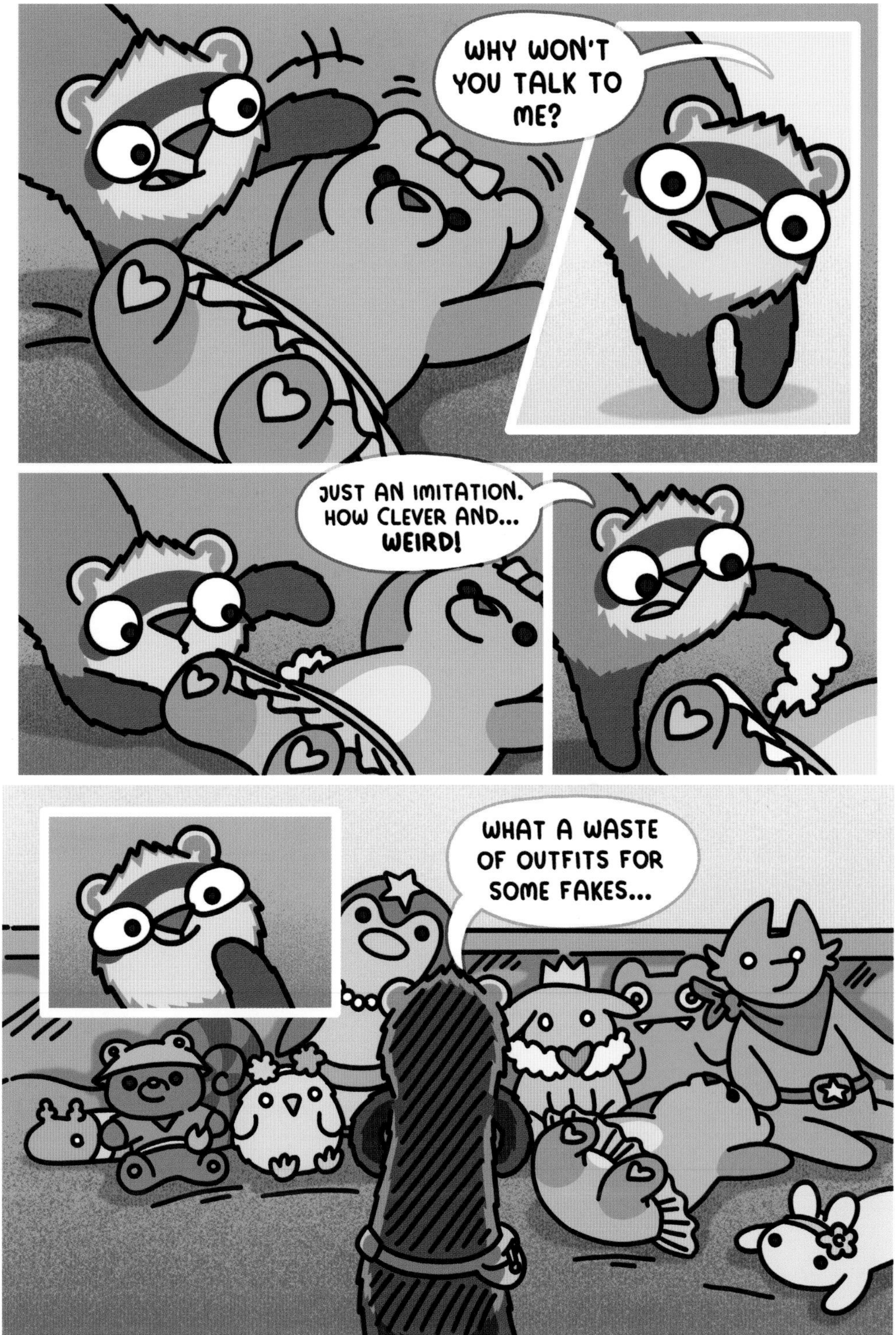
WHY WON'T YOU TALK TO ME?
JUST AN IMITATION. HOW CLEVER AND... WEIRD!
WHAT A WASTE OF OUTFITS FOR SOME FAKES...

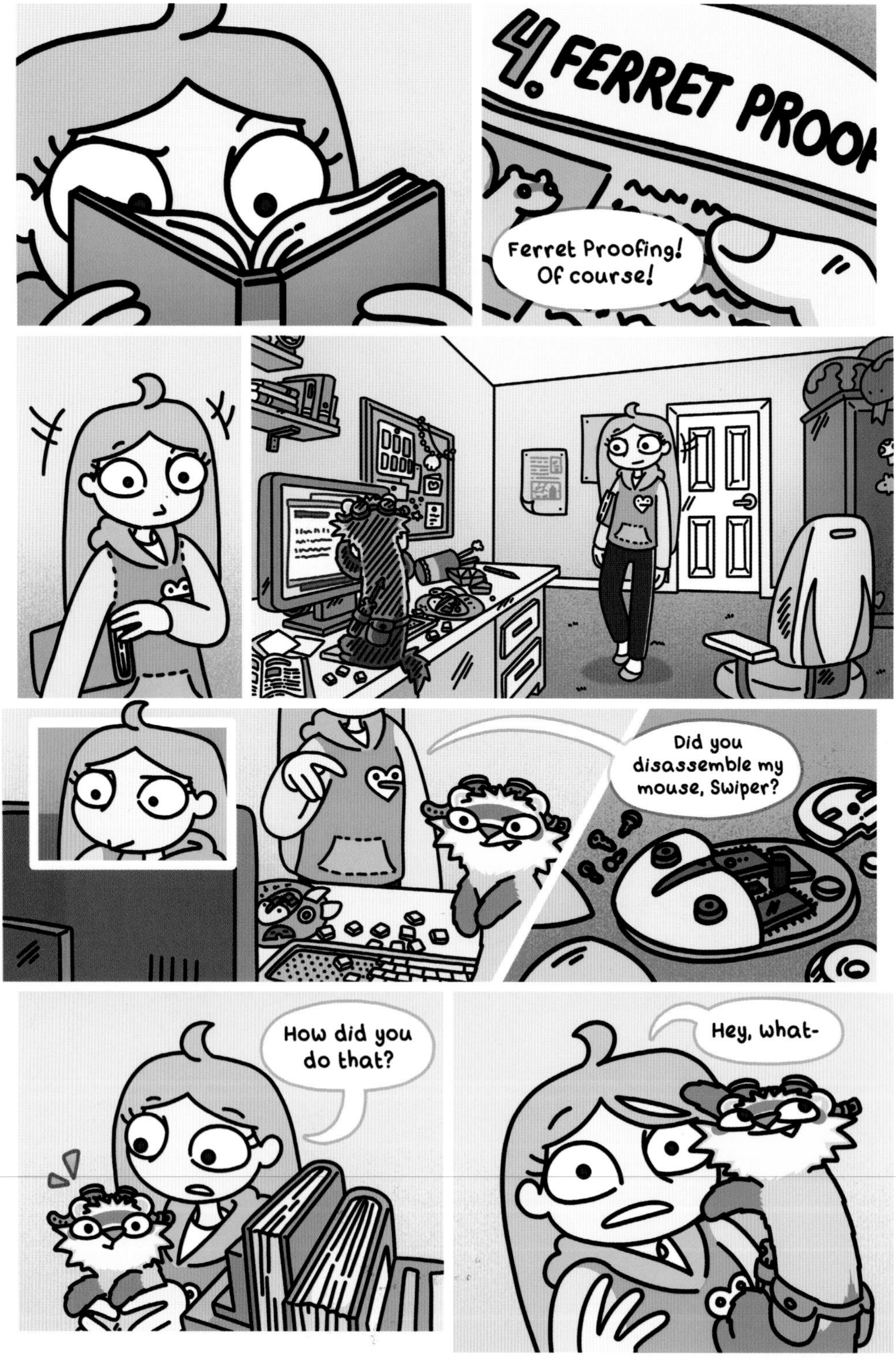
4. FERRET PROOF
Ferret Proofing! Of course!
Did you disassemble my mouse, Swiper?
How did you do that?
Hey, what-

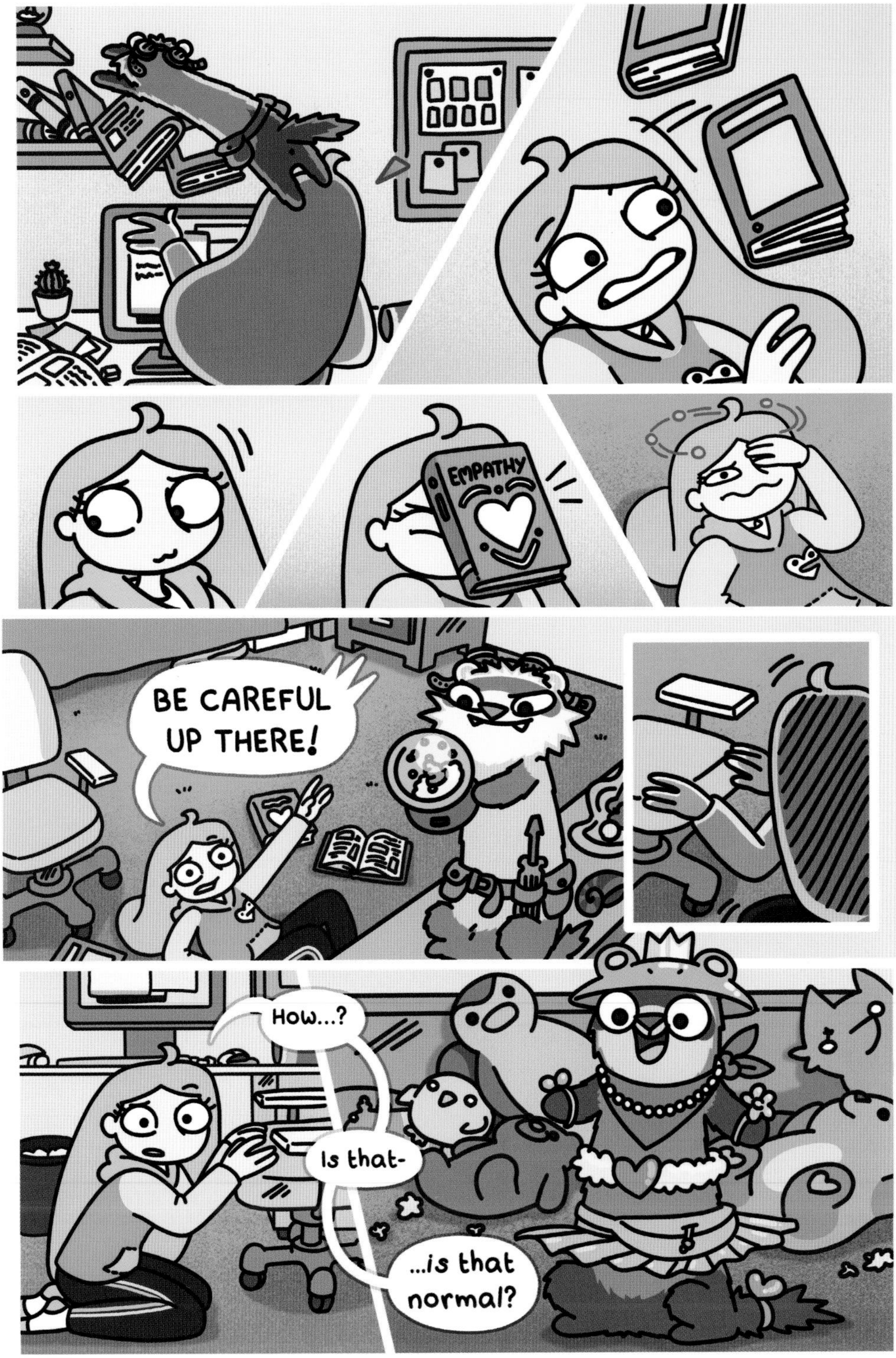
EMPATHY
BE CAREFUL UP THERE!
How...?
Is that-
...is that normal?

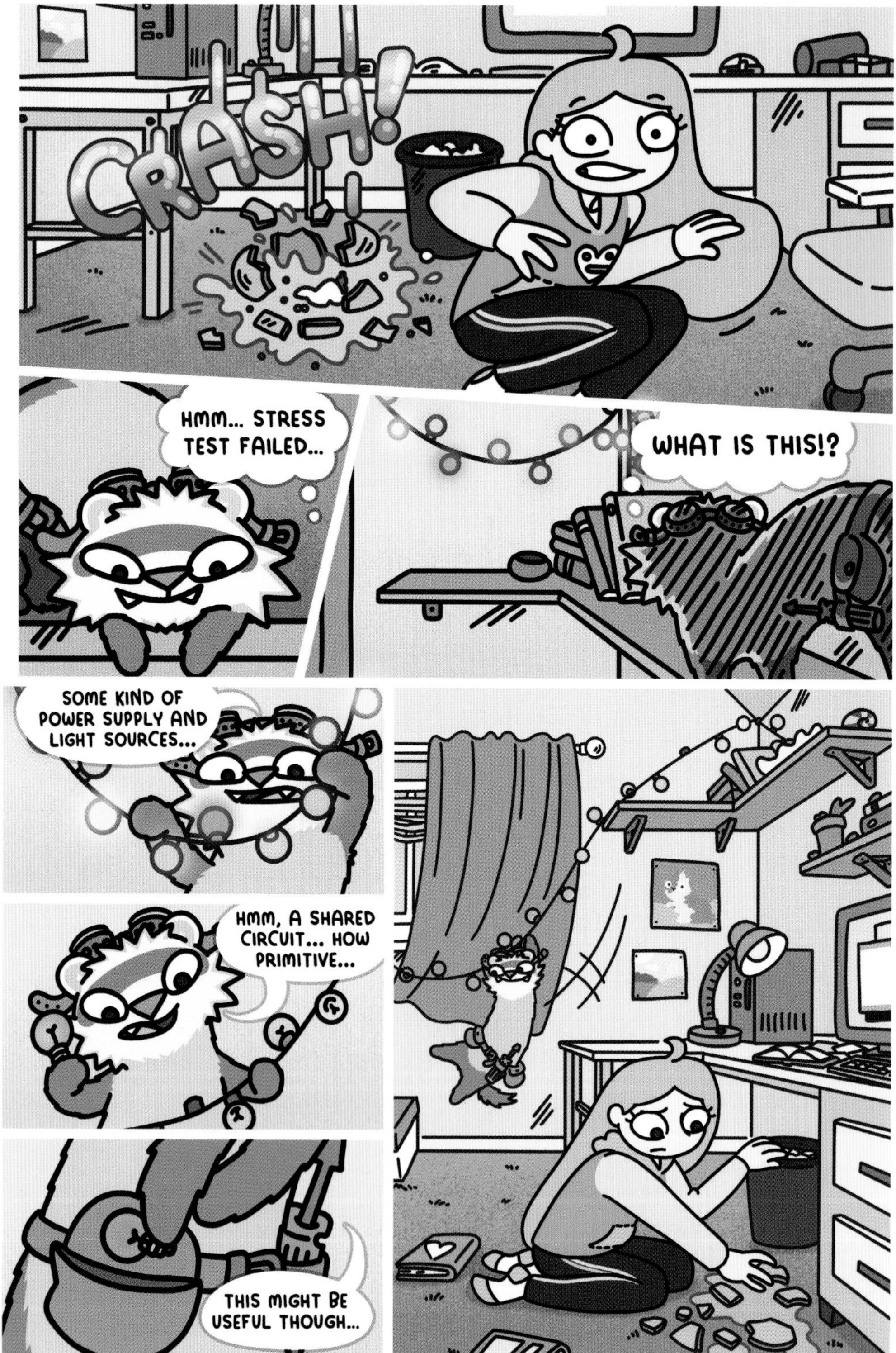
CRASH!
HMM... STRESS TEST FAILED...
WHAT IS THIS!?
SOME KIND OF POWER SUPPLY AND LIGHT SOURCES...
HMM, A SHARED CIRCUIT... HOW PRIMITIVE...
THIS MIGHT BE USEFUL THOUGH...

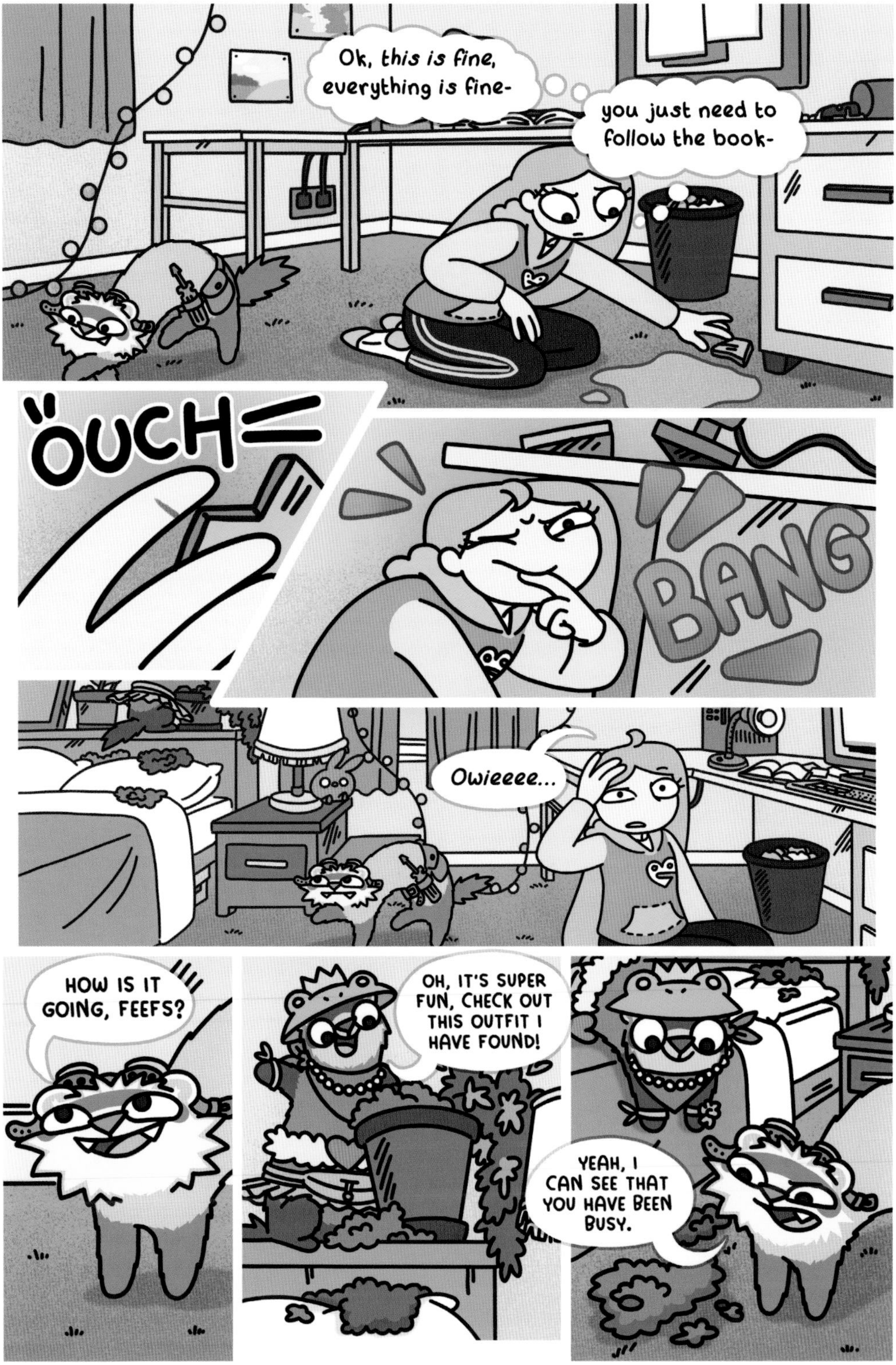
Ok, this is fine, everything is fine-
you just need to follow the book-
"OUCH
BANG
Owieeee...
HOW IS IT GOING, FEEFS?
OH, IT'S SUPER FUN, CHECK OUT THIS OUTFIT I HAVE FOUND!
YEAH, I CAN SEE THAT YOU HAVE BEEN BUSY.

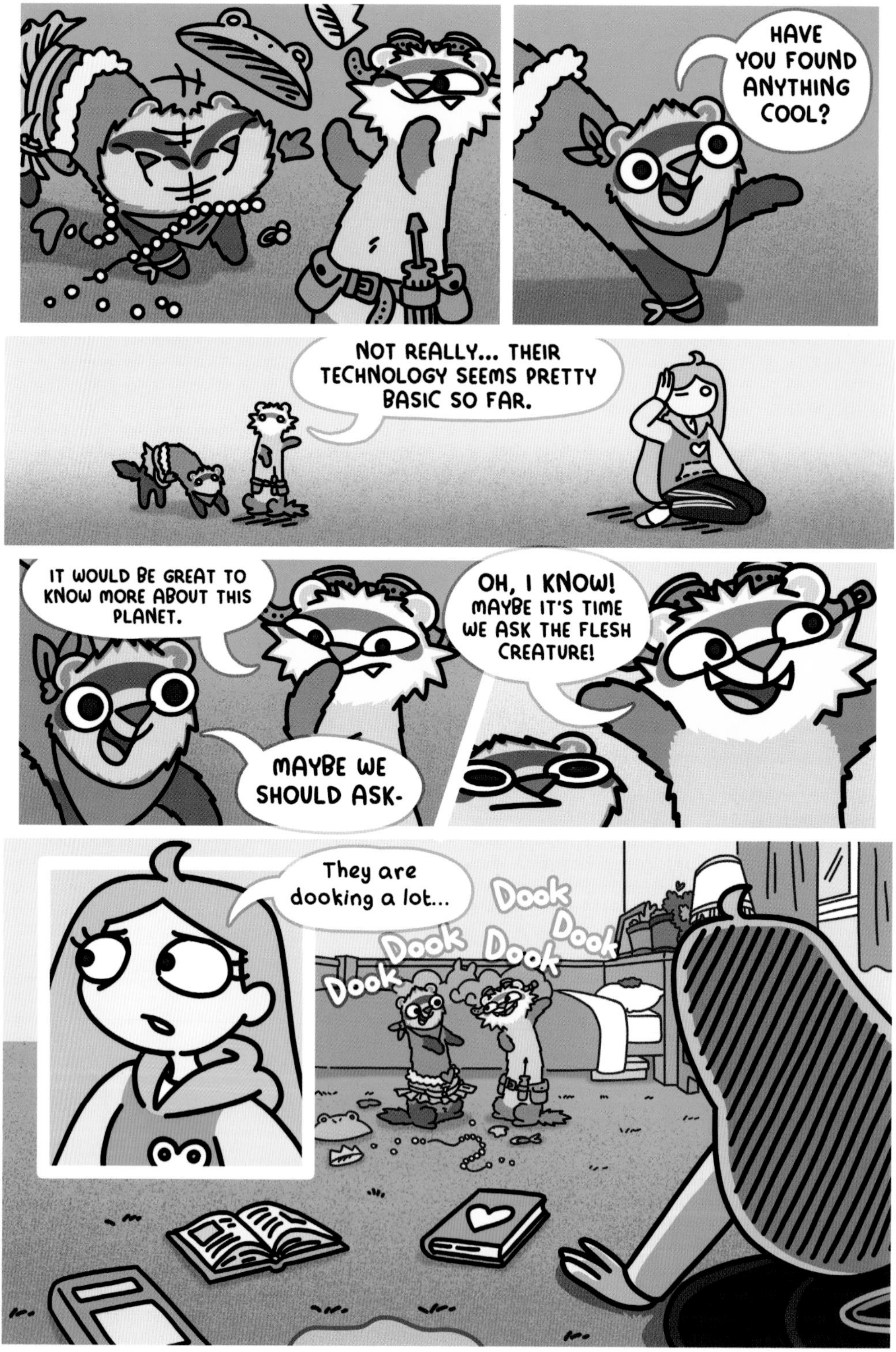
HAVE YOU FOUND ANYTHING COOL?
NOT REALLY... THEIR TECHNOLOGY SEEMS PRETTY BASIC SO FAR.
IT WOULD BE GREAT TO KNOW MORE ABOUT THIS PLANET.
MAYBE WE SHOULD ASK-
OH, I KNOW! MAYBE IT'S TIME WE ASK THE FLESH CREATURE!
They are dooking a lot...
Dook
Dook
Dook
Dook
Dook

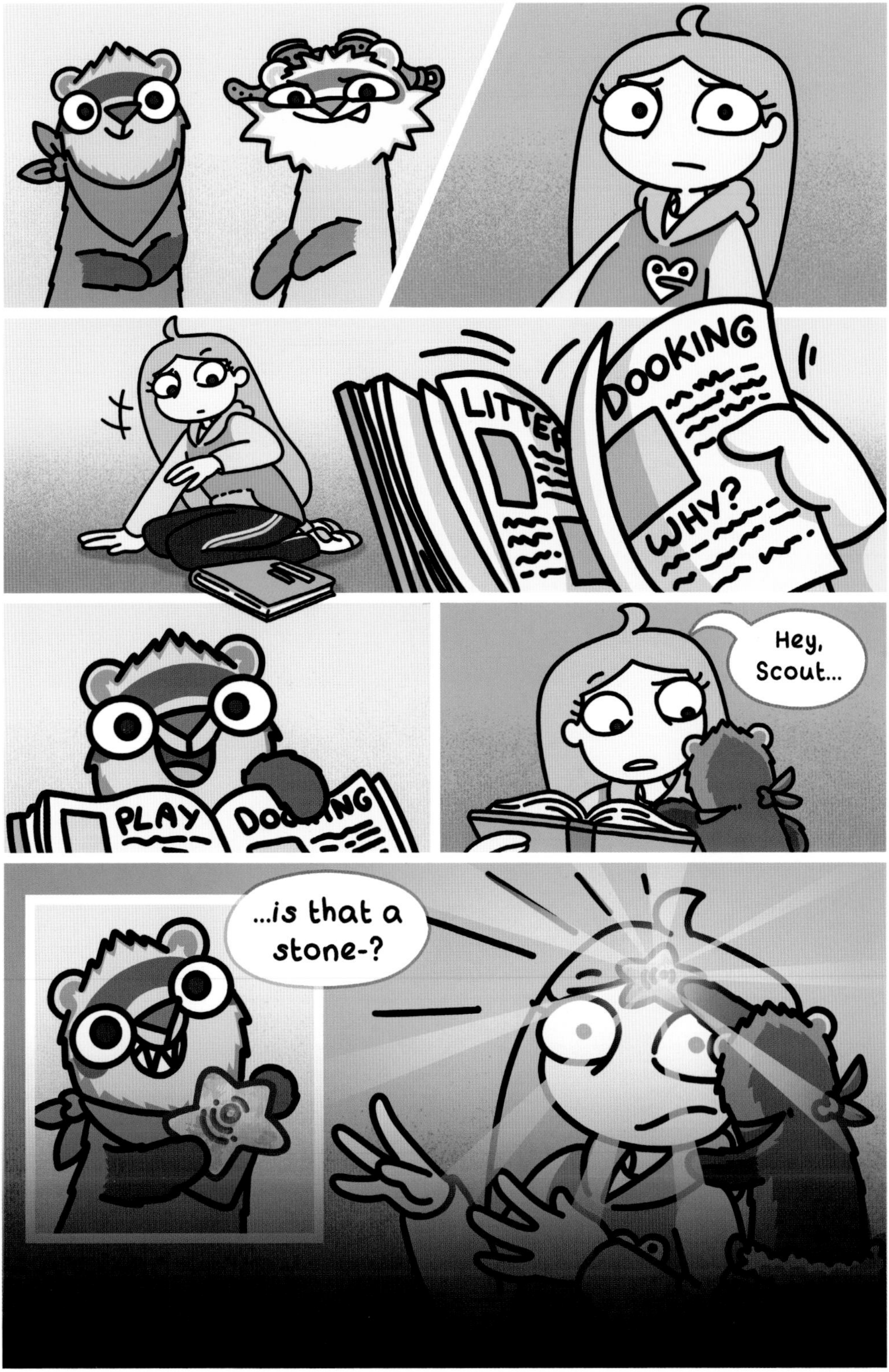
LITTER
DOOKING
WHY?
PLAY
DOOKING
Hey, Scout...
...is that a stone-?

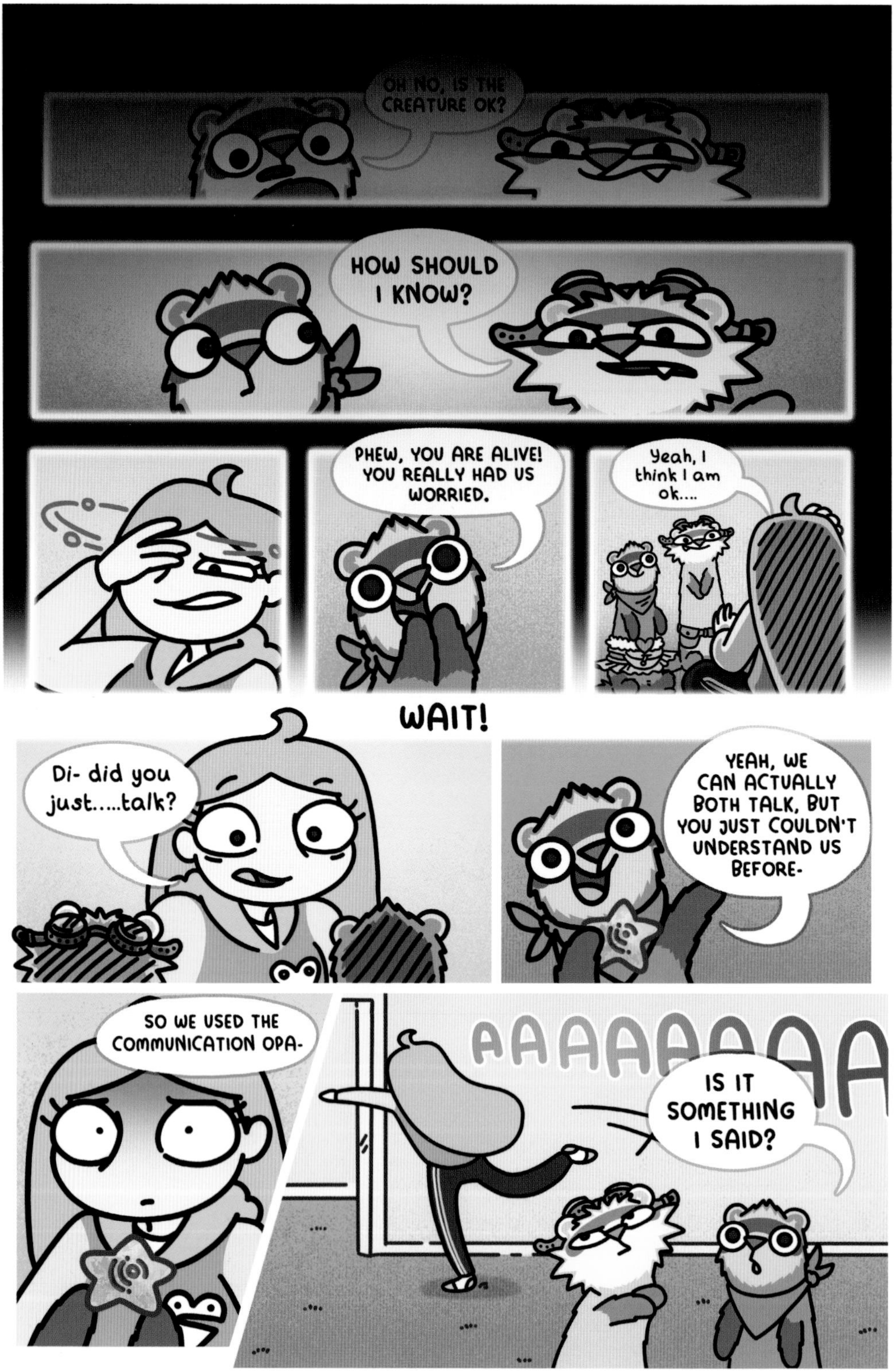
OH NO, IS THE CREATURE OK?
HOW SHOULD I KNOW?
PHEW, YOU ARE ALIVE! YOU REALLY HAD US WORRIED.
Yeah, I think I am ok....
WAIT!
Di- did you just.....talk?
YEAH, WE CAN ACTUALLY BOTH TALK, BUT YOU JUST COULDN'T UNDERSTAND US BEFORE-
SO WE USED THE COMMUNICATION OPA-
AAAAAAAA
IS IT SOMETHING I SAID?

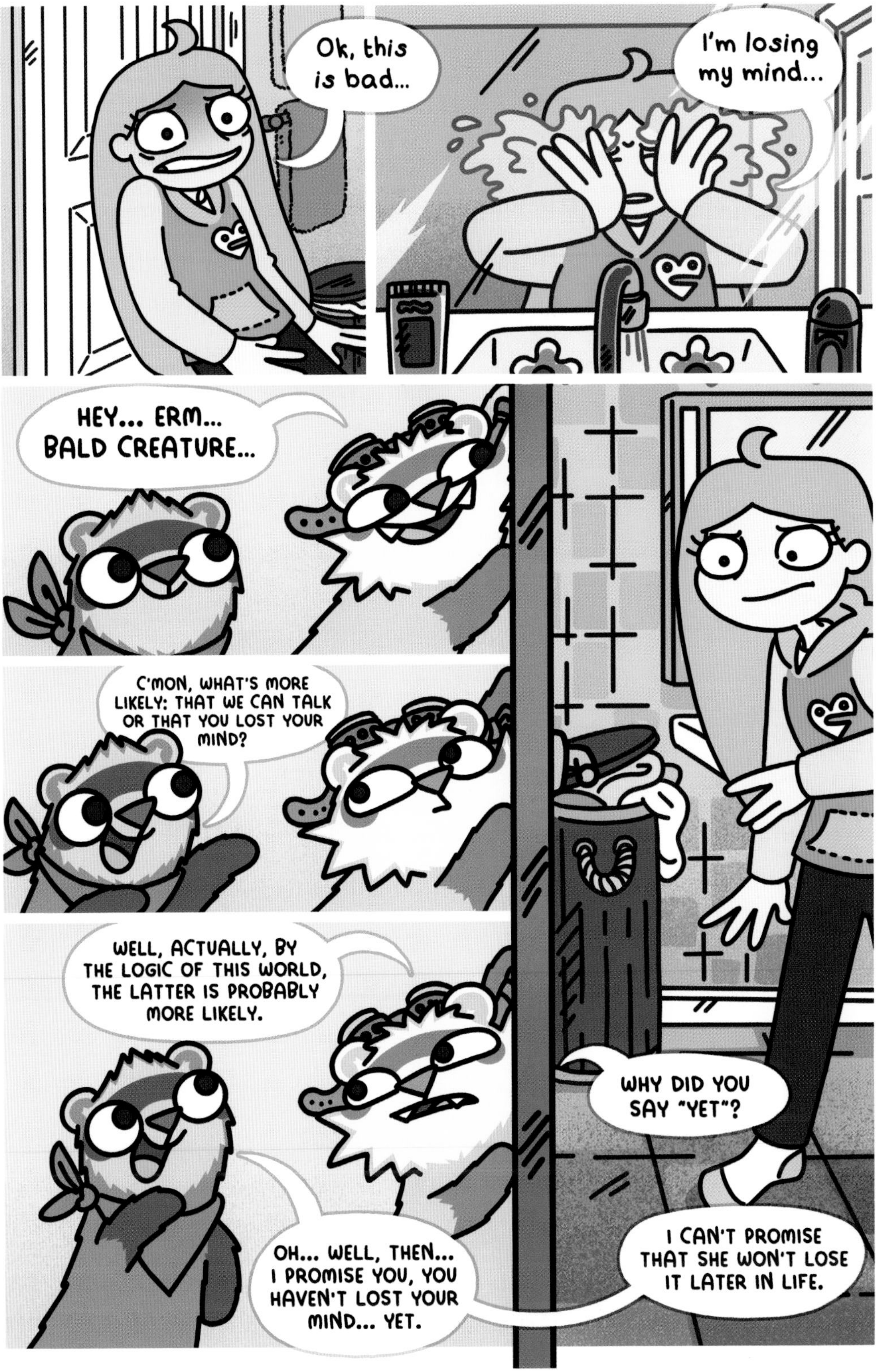
Ok, this is bad...
I'm losing my mind...
HEY... ERM... BALD CREATURE...
C'MON, WHAT'S MORE LIKELY: THAT WE CAN TALK OR THAT YOU LOST YOUR MIND?
WELL, ACTUALLY, BY THE LOGIC OF THIS WORLD, THE LATTER IS PROBABLY MORE LIKELY.
OH... WELL, THEN... I PROMISE YOU, YOU HAVEN'T LOST YOUR MIND... YET.
WHY DID YOU SAY "YET"?
I CAN'T PROMISE THAT SHE WON'T LOSE IT LATER IN LIFE.

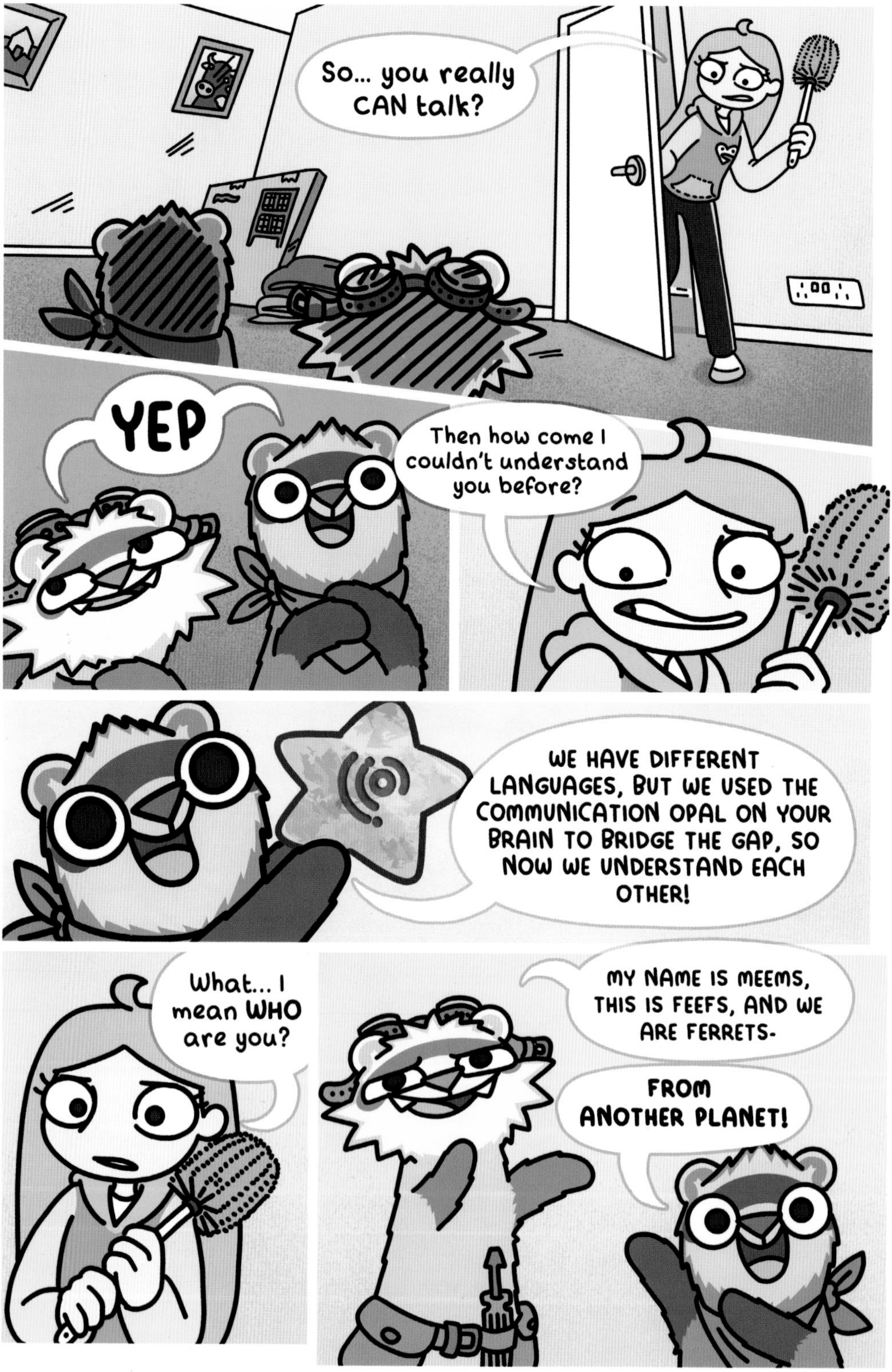
So... you really CAN talk?
YEP
Then how come I couldn't understand you before?
WE HAVE DIFFERENT LANGUAGES, BUT WE USED THE COMMUNICATION OPAL ON YOUR BRAIN TO BRIDGE THE GAP, SO NOW WE UNDERSTAND EACH OTHER!
What... I mean WHO are you?
MY NAME IS MEEMS, THIS IS FEEFS, AND WE ARE FERRETS-
FROM ANOTHER PLANET!

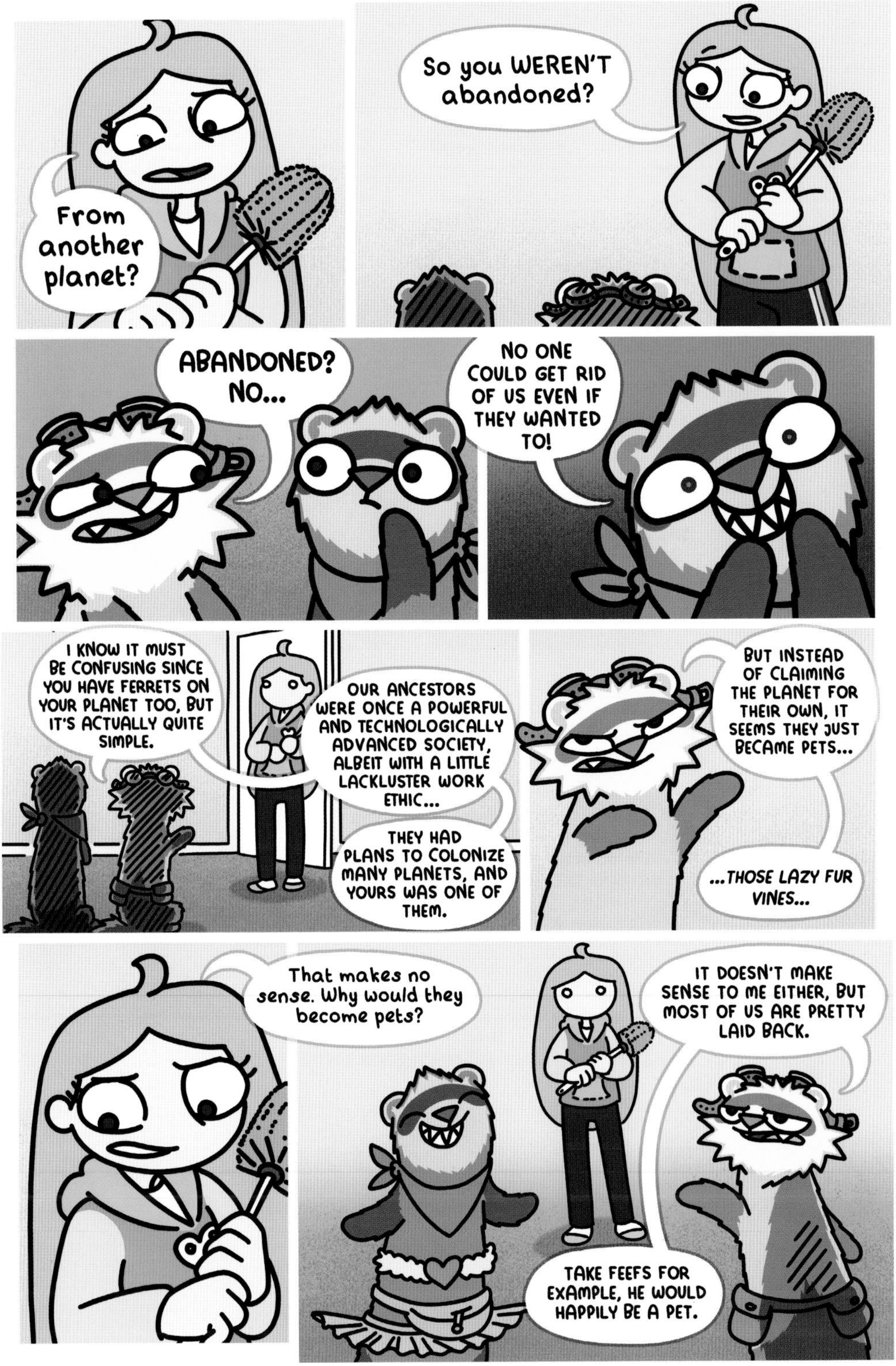
From another planet?
So you WEREN'T abandoned?
ABANDONED? NO...
NO ONE COULD GET RID OF US EVEN IF THEY WANTED TO!
I KNOW IT MUST BE CONFUSING SINCE YOU HAVE FERRETS ON YOUR PLANET TOO, BUT IT'S ACTUALLY QUITE SIMPLE.
OUR ANCESTORS WERE ONCE A POWERFUL AND TECHNOLOGICALLY ADVANCED SOCIETY, ALBEIT WITH A LITTLE LACKLUSTER WORK ETHIC...
THEY HAD PLANS TO COLONIZE MANY PLANETS, AND YOURS WAS ONE OF THEM.
BUT INSTEAD OF CLAIMING THE PLANET FOR THEIR OWN, IT SEEMS THEY JUST BECAME PETS...
...THOSE LAZY FUR VINES...
That makes no sense. Why would they become pets?
IT DOESN'T MAKE SENSE TO ME EITHER, BUT MOST OF US ARE PRETTY LAID BACK.
TAKE FEEFS FOR EXAMPLE, HE WOULD HAPPILY BE A PET.

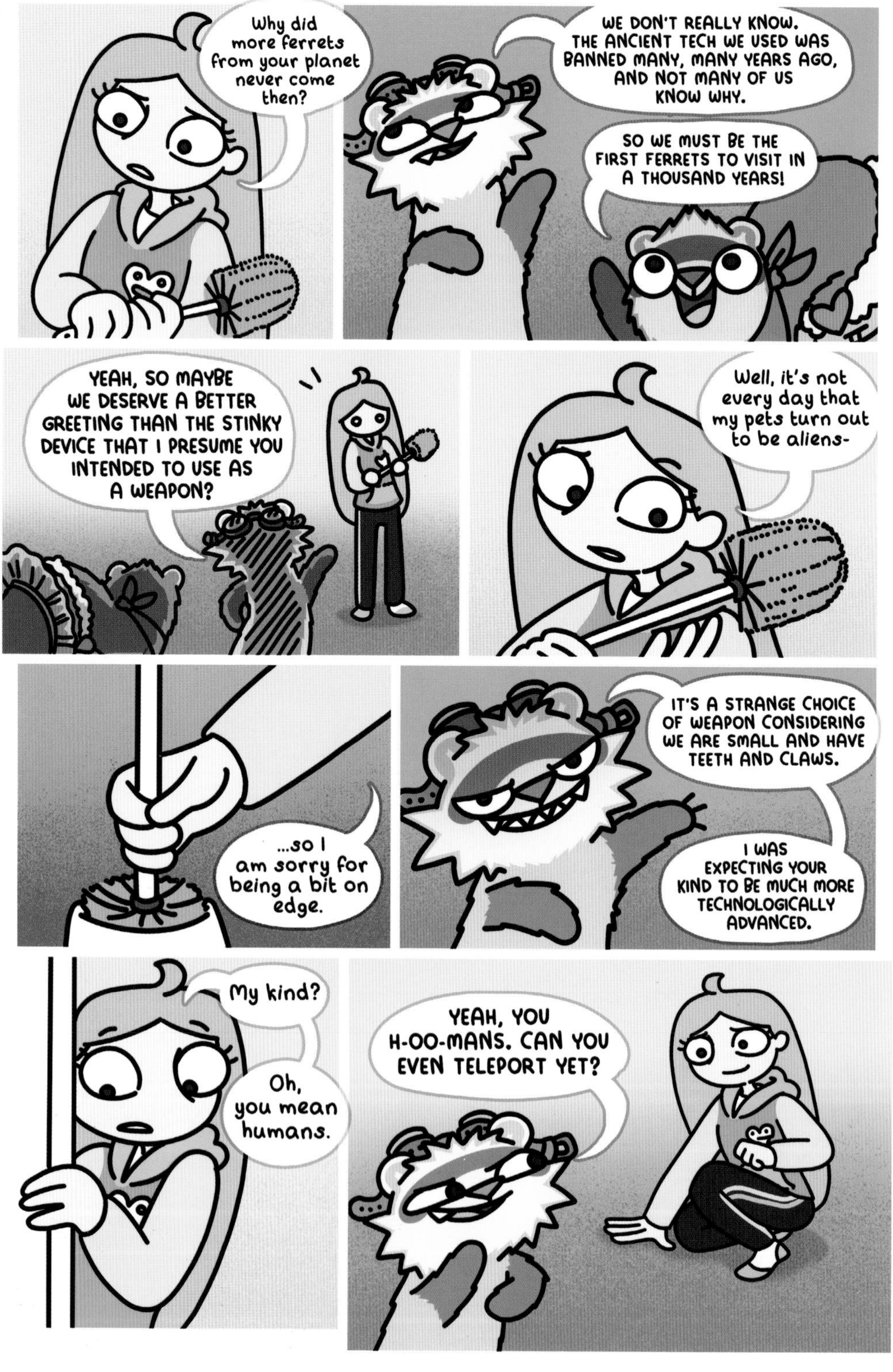
Why did more ferrets from your planet never come then?
WE DON'T REALLY KNOW. THE ANCIENT TECH WE USED WAS BANNED MANY, MANY YEARS AGO, AND NOT MANY OF US KNOW WHY.
SO WE MUST BE THE FIRST FERRETS TO VISIT IN A THOUSAND YEARS!
YEAH, SO MAYBE WE DESERVE A BETTER GREETING THAN THE STINKY DEVICE THAT I PRESUME YOU INTENDED TO USE AS A WEAPON?
Well, it's not every day that my pets turn out to be aliens-
...so I am sorry for being a bit on edge.
IT'S A STRANGE CHOICE OF WEAPON CONSIDERING WE ARE SMALL AND HAVE TEETH AND CLAWS.
I WAS EXPECTING YOUR KIND TO BE MUCH MORE TECHNOLOGICALLY ADVANCED.
My kind?
Oh, you mean humans.
YEAH, YOU H-OO-MANS. CAN YOU EVEN TELEPORT YET?

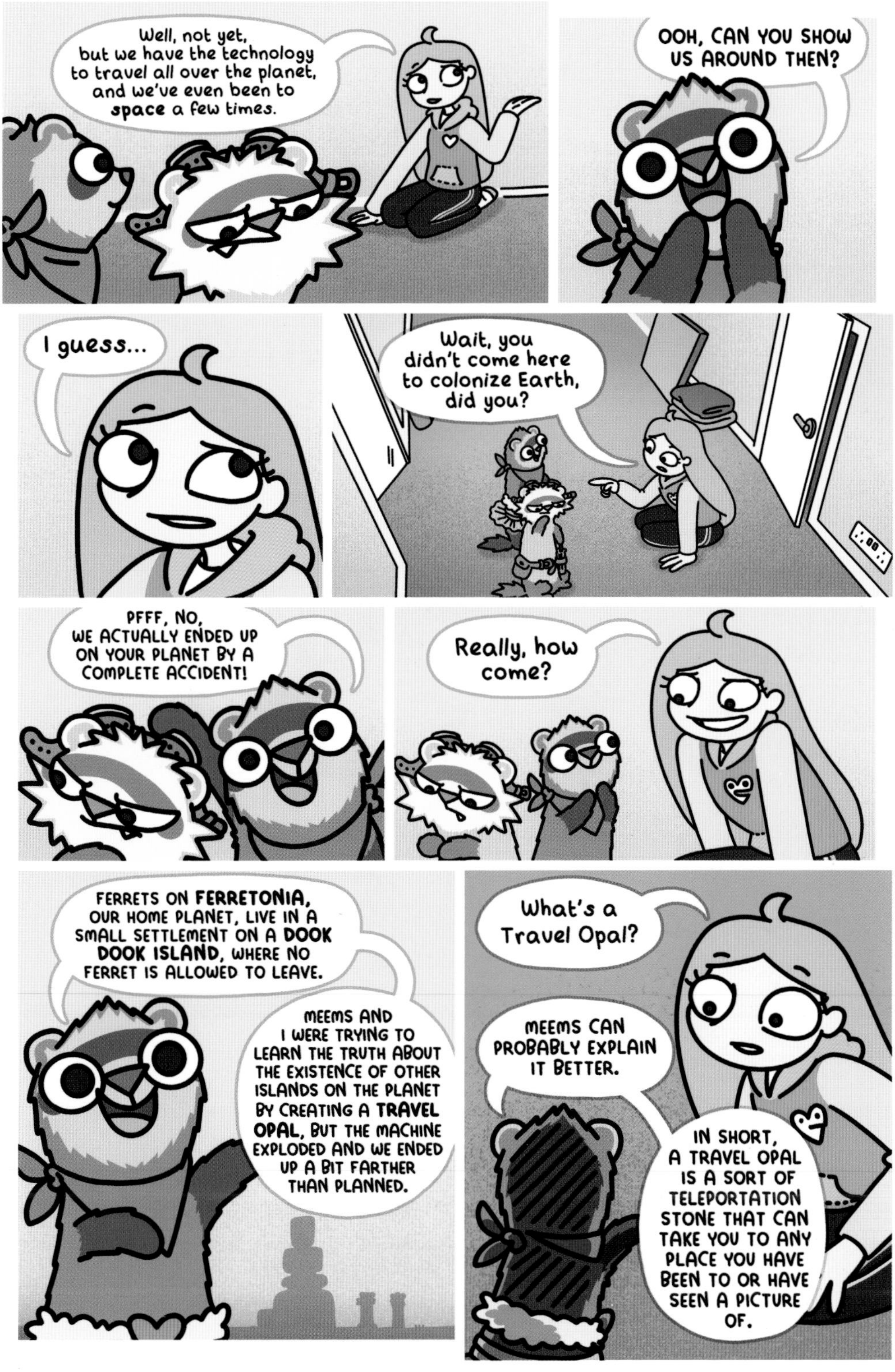
Well, not yet, but we have the technology to travel all over the planet, and we've even been to space a few times.
OOH, CAN YOU SHOW US AROUND THEN?
I guess...
Wait, you didn't come here to colonize Earth, did you?
PFFF, NO, WE ACTUALLY ENDED UP ON YOUR PLANET BY A COMPLETE ACCIDENT!
Really, how come?
FERRETS ON FERRETONIA, OUR HOME PLANET, LIVE IN A SMALL SETTLEMENT ON A DOOK DOOK ISLAND, WHERE NO FERRET IS ALLOWED TO LEAVE.
MEEMS AND I WERE TRYING TO LEARN THE TRUTH ABOUT THE EXISTENCE OF OTHER ISLANDS ON THE PLANET BY CREATING A TRAVEL OPAL, BUT THE MACHINE EXPLODED AND WE ENDED UP A BIT FARTHER THAN PLANNED.
What's a Travel Opal?
MEEMS CAN PROBABLY EXPLAIN IT BETTER.
IN SHORT, A TRAVEL OPAL IS A SORT OF TELEPORTATION STONE THAT CAN TAKE YOU TO ANY PLACE YOU HAVE BEEN TO OR HAVE SEEN A PICTURE OF.

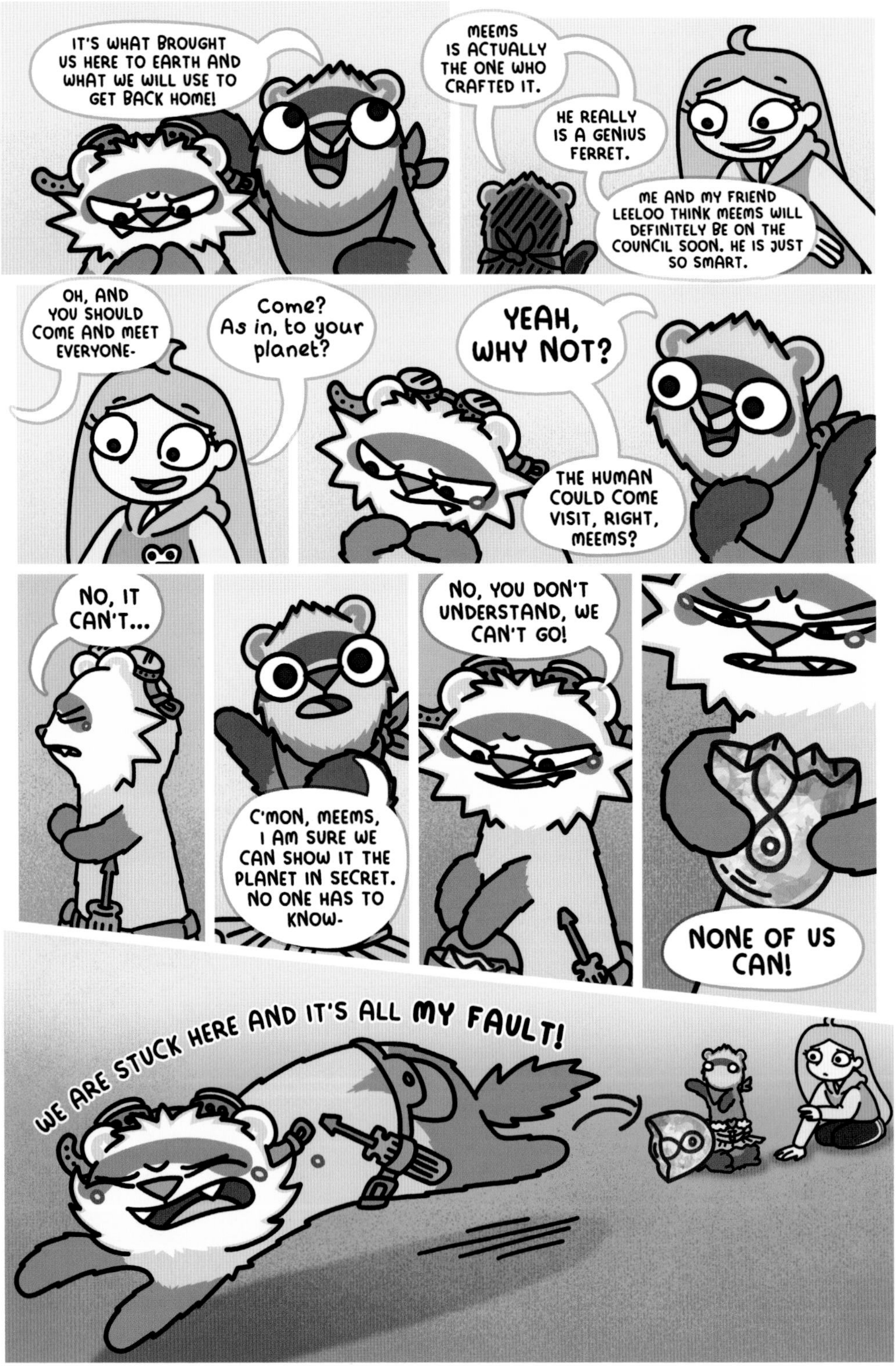

IT'S WHAT BROUGHT US HERE TO EARTH AND WHAT WE WILL USE TO GET BACK HOME!
MEEMS IS ACTUALLY THE ONE WHO CRAFTED IT.
HE REALLY IS A GENIUS FERRET.
ME AND MY FRIEND LEELOO THINK MEEMS WILL DEFINITELY BE ON THE COUNCIL SOON. HE IS JUST SO SMART.
OH, AND YOU SHOULD COME AND MEET EVERYONE-
Come? As in, to your planet?
YEAH, WHY NOT?
THE HUMAN COULD COME VISIT, RIGHT, MEEMS?
NO, IT CAN'T...
C'MON, MEEMS, I AM SURE WE CAN SHOW IT THE PLANET IN SECRET. NO ONE HAS TO KNOW-
NO, YOU DON'T UNDERSTAND, WE CAN'T GO!
NONE OF US CAN!
WE ARE STUCK HERE AND IT'S ALL MY FAULT!

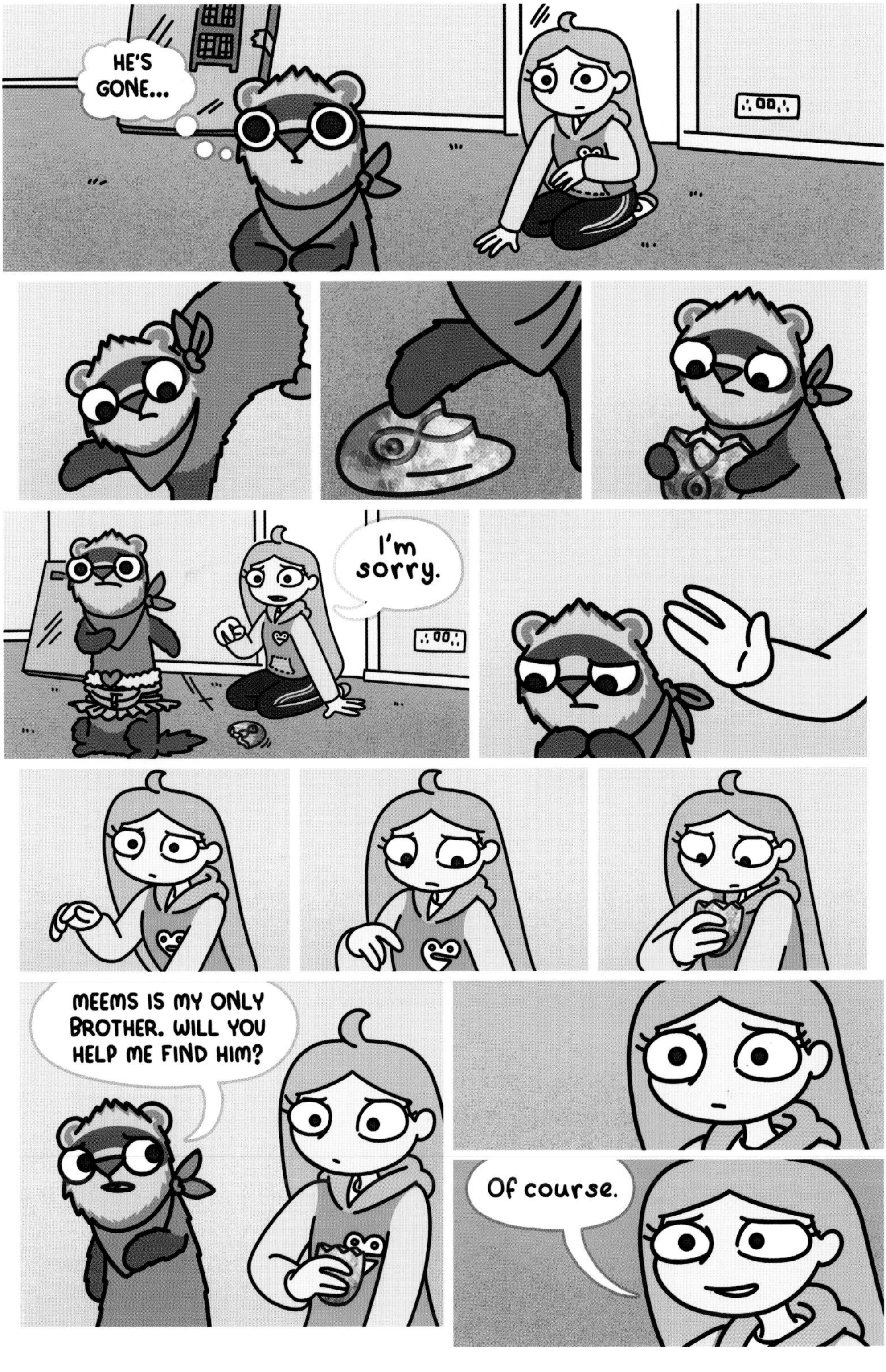
HE'S GONE...
I'm sorry.
MEEMS IS MY ONLY BROTHER. WILL YOU HELP ME FIND HIM?
Of course.

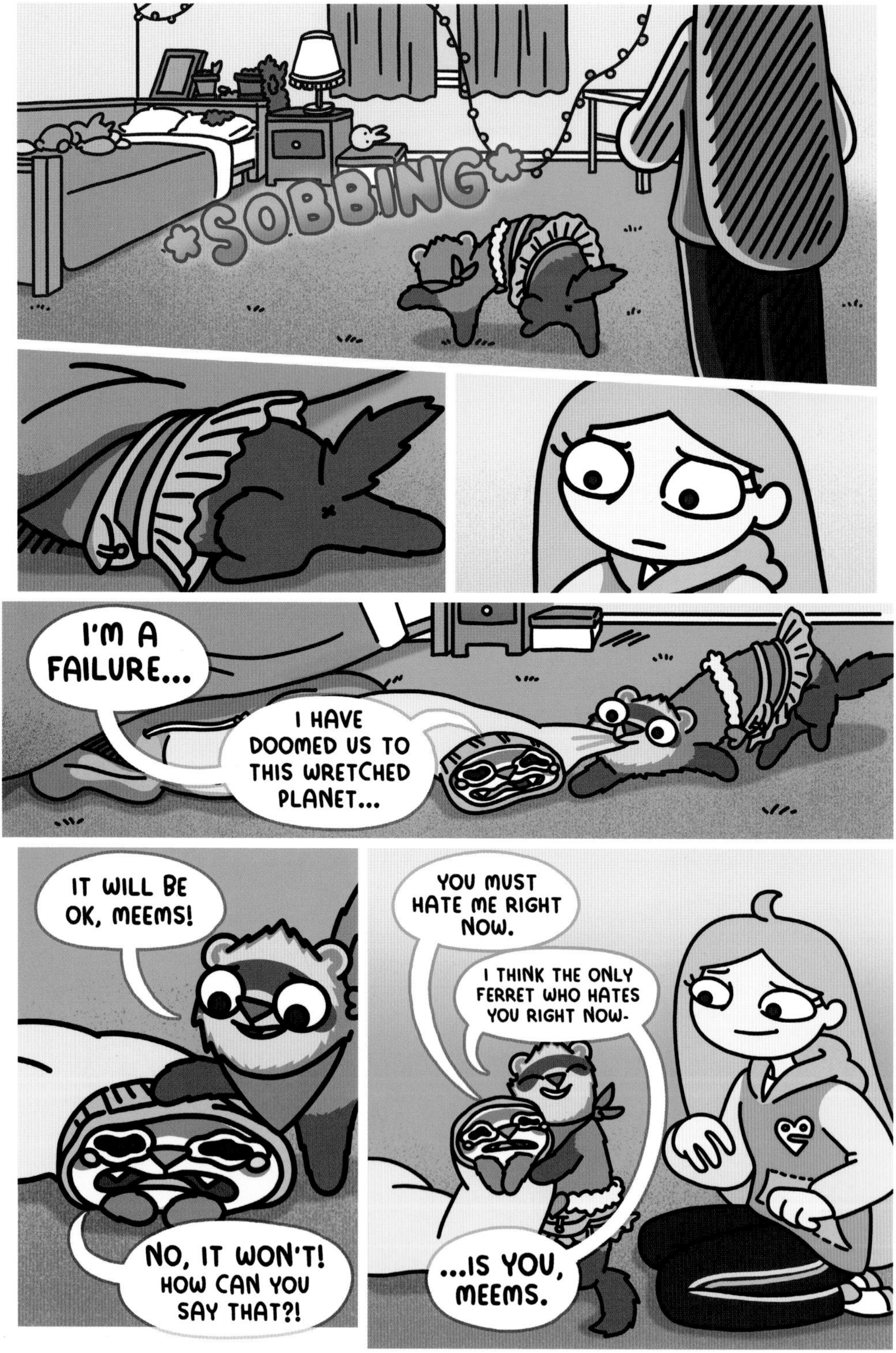
SOBBING
I'M A FAILURE...
I HAVE DOOMED US TO THIS WRETCHED PLANET...
IT WILL BE OK, MEEMS!
NO, IT WON'T! HOW CAN YOU SAY THAT?!
YOU MUST HATE ME RIGHT NOW.
I THINK THE ONLY FERRET WHO HATES YOU RIGHT NOW-
...IS YOU, MEEMS.

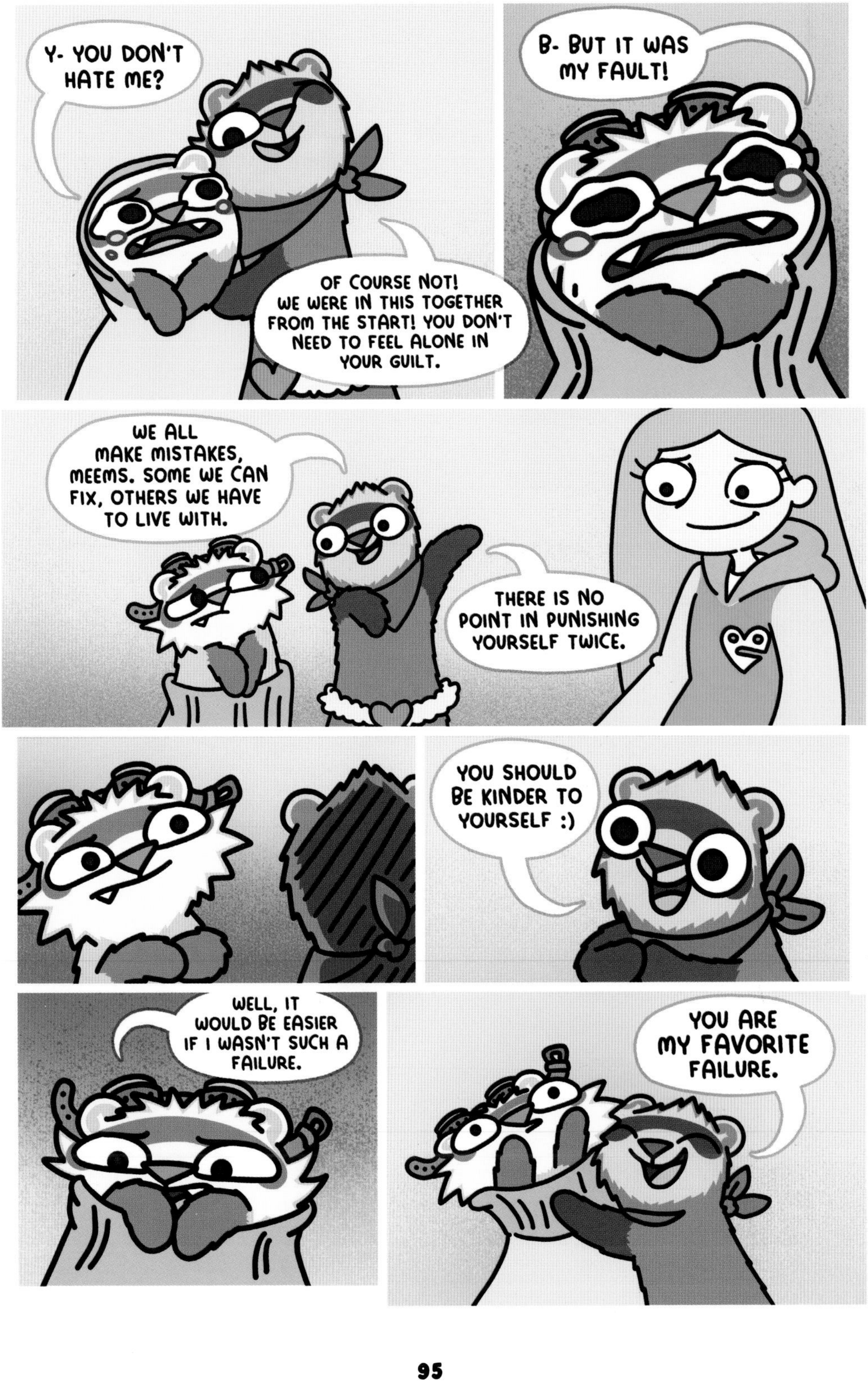
Y- YOU DON'T HATE ME?
OF COURSE NOT! WE WERE IN THIS TOGETHER FROM THE START! YOU DON'T NEED TO FEEL ALONE IN YOUR GUILT.
B- BUT IT WAS MY FAULT!
WE ALL MAKE MISTAKES, MEEMS. SOME WE CAN FIX, OTHERS WE HAVE TO LIVE WITH.
THERE IS NO POINT IN PUNISHING YOURSELF TWICE.
YOU SHOULD BE KINDER TO YOURSELF :)
WELL, IT WOULD BE EASIER IF I WASN'T SUCH A FAILURE.
YOU ARE MY FAVORITE FAILURE.

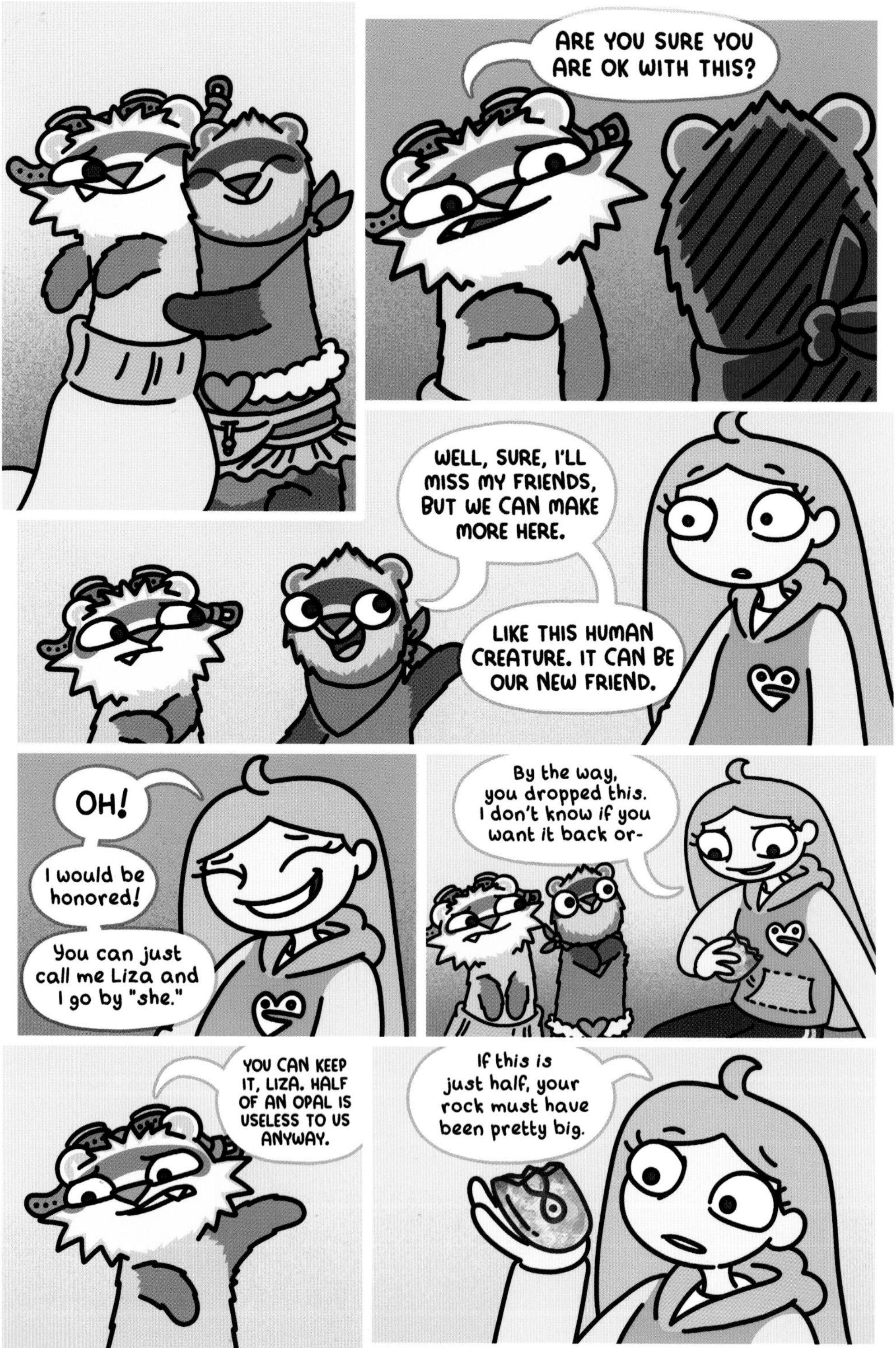
ARE YOU SURE YOU ARE OK WITH THIS?
WELL, SURE, I'LL MISS MY FRIENDS, BUT WE CAN MAKE MORE HERE.
LIKE THIS HUMAN CREATURE. IT CAN BE OUR NEW FRIEND.
OH!
I would be honored!
You can just call me Liza and I go by "she."
By the way, you dropped this. I don't know if you want it back or-
YOU CAN KEEP IT, LIZA. HALF OF AN OPAL IS USELESS TO US ANYWAY.
If this is just half, your rock must have been pretty big.

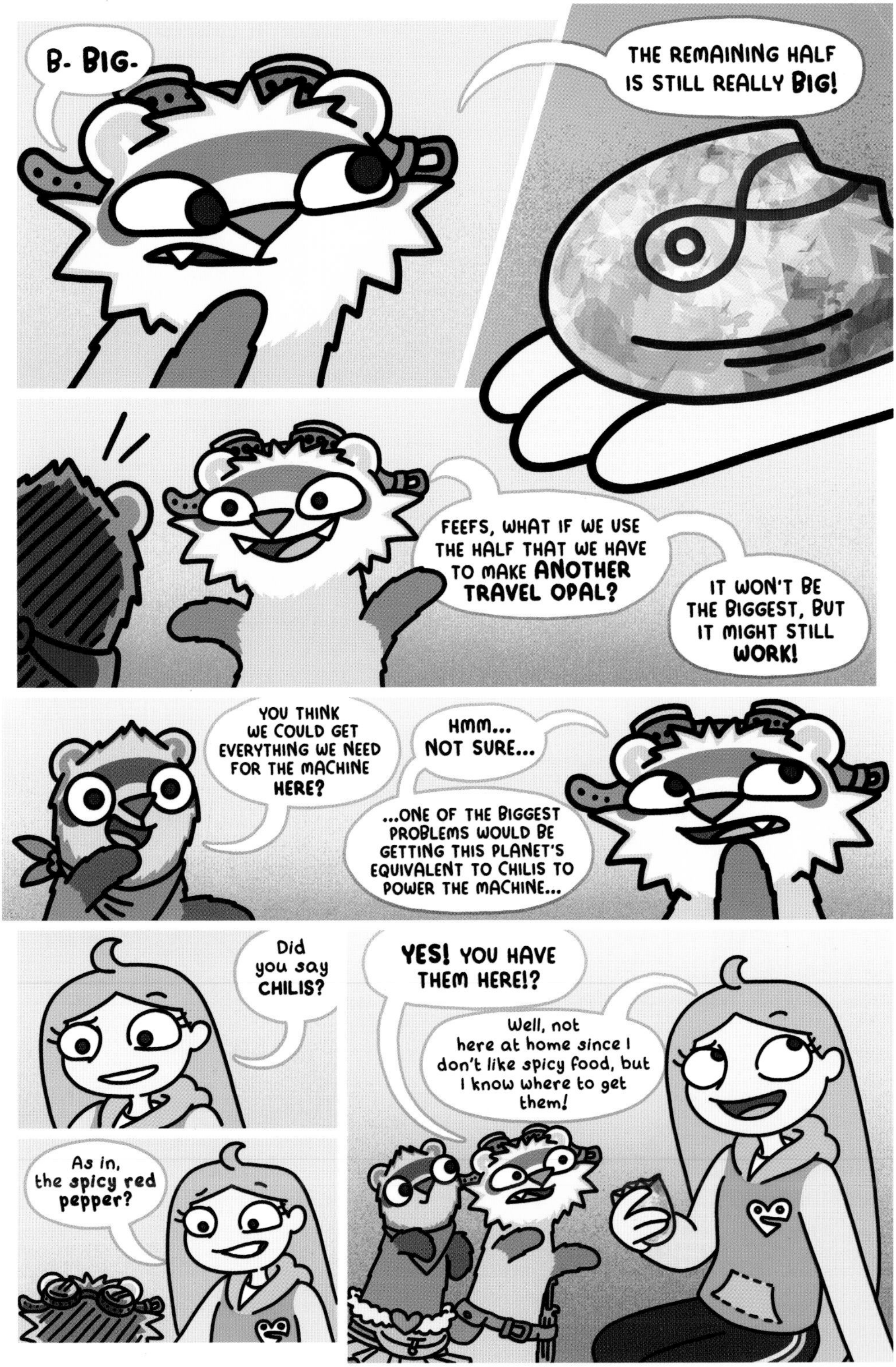
B- BIG-
THE REMAINING HALF IS STILL REALLY BIG!
FEEFS, WHAT IF WE USE THE HALF THAT WE HAVE TO MAKE ANOTHER TRAVEL OPAL?
IT WON'T BE THE BIGGEST, BUT IT MIGHT STILL WORK!
YOU THINK WE COULD GET EVERYTHING WE NEED FOR THE MACHINE HERE?
HMM... NOT SURE...
...ONE OF THE BIGGEST PROBLEMS WOULD BE GETTING THIS PLANET'S EQUIVALENT TO CHILIS TO POWER THE MACHINE...
Did you say CHILIS?
As in, the spicy red pepper?
YES! YOU HAVE THEM HERE!?
Well, not here at home since I don't like spicy food, but I know where to get them!

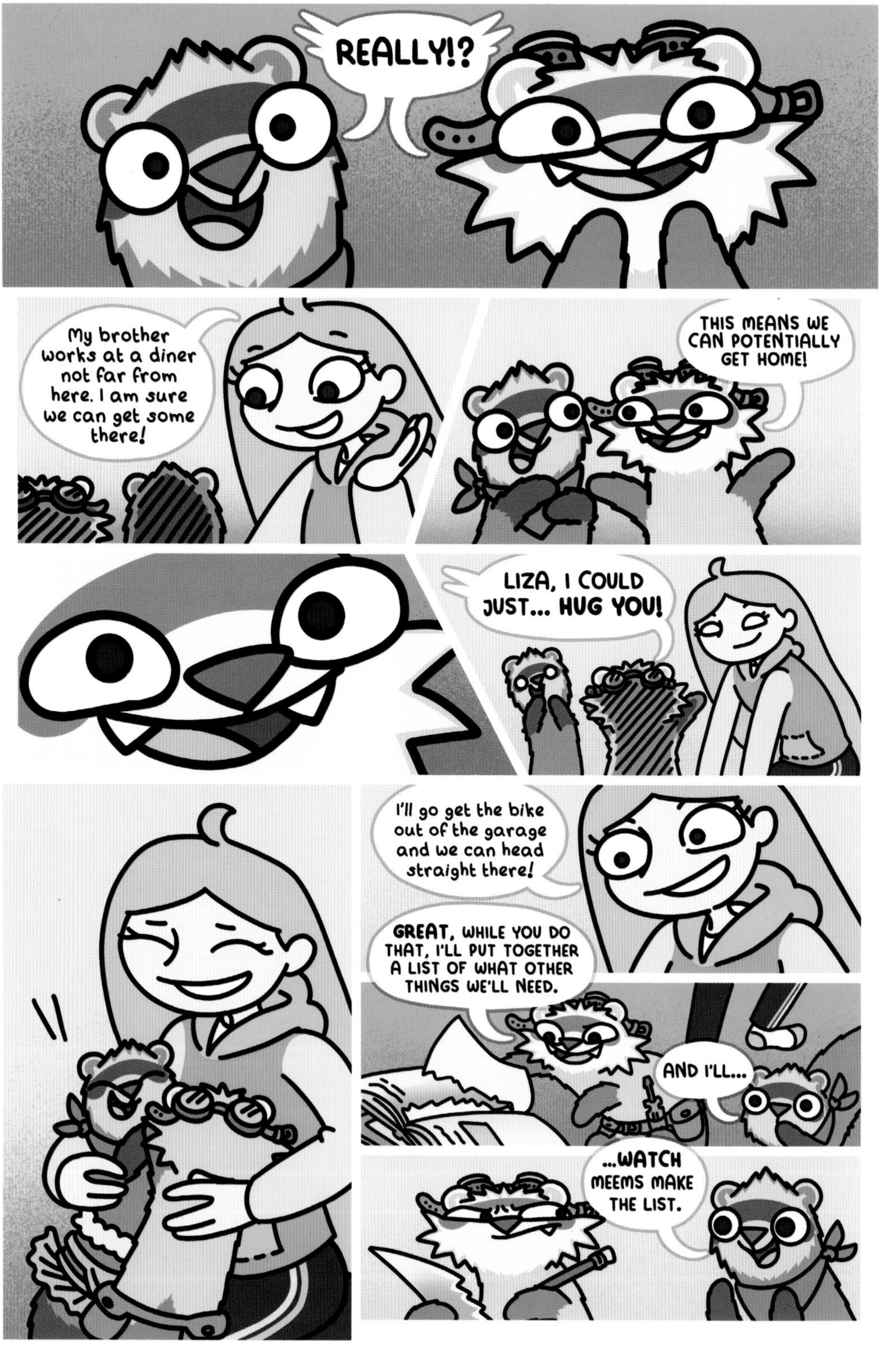
REALLY!?
My brother works at a diner not far from here. I am sure we can get some there!
THIS MEANS WE CAN POTENTIALLY GET HOME!
LIZA, I COULD JUST... HUG YOU!
I'll go get the bike out of the garage and we can head straight there!
GREAT, WHILE YOU DO THAT, I'LL PUT TOGETHER A LIST OF WHAT OTHER THINGS WE'LL NEED.
AND I'LL...
...WATCH MEEMS MAKE THE LIST.

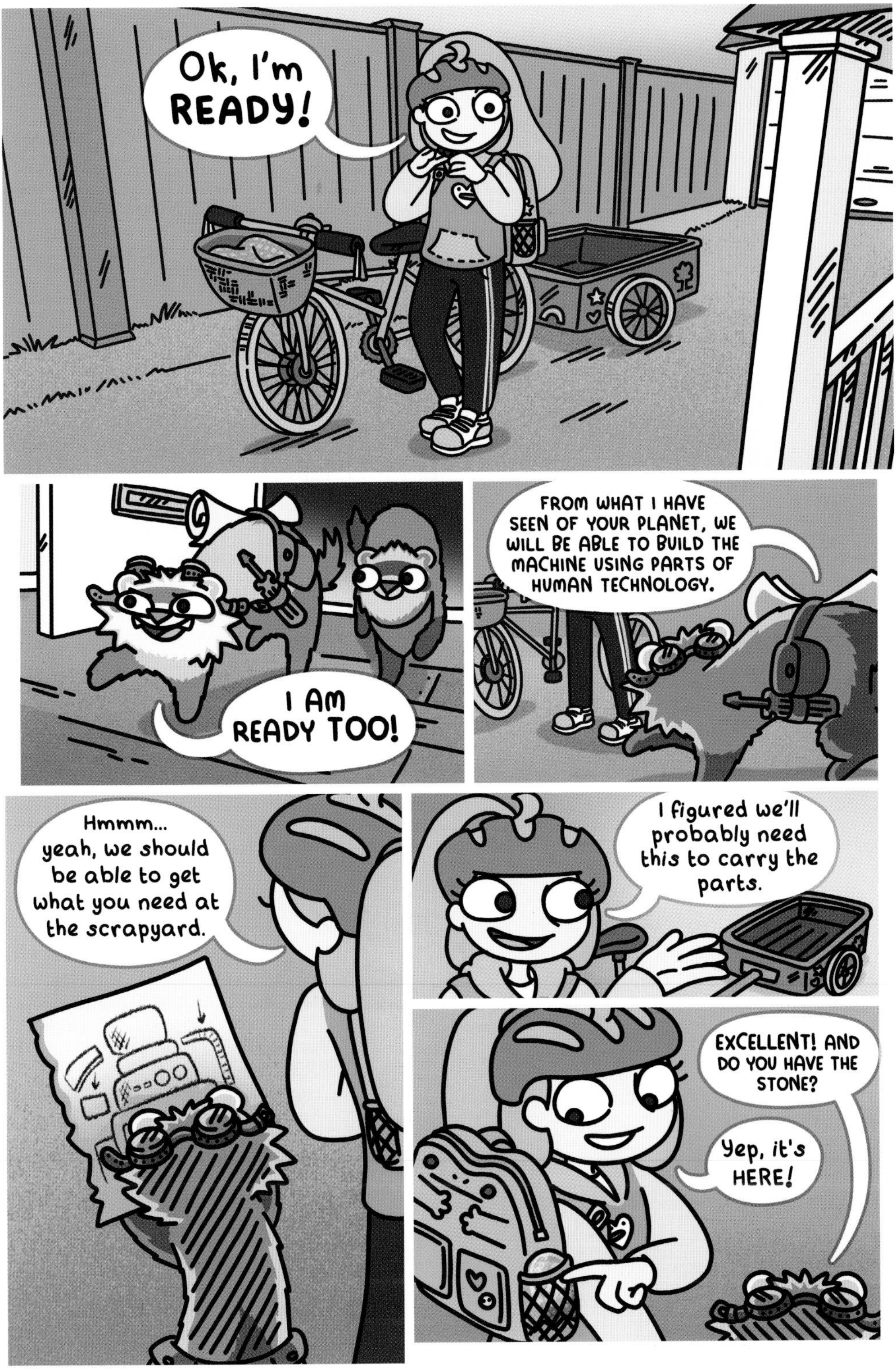
Ok, I'm READY!
I AM READY TOO!
FROM WHAT I HAVE SEEN OF YOUR PLANET, WE WILL BE ABLE TO BUILD THE MACHINE USING PARTS OF HUMAN TECHNOLOGY.
Hmmm... yeah, we should be able to get what you need at the scrapyard.
I figured we'll probably need this to carry the parts.
EXCELLENT! AND DO YOU HAVE THE STONE?
Yep, it's HERE!

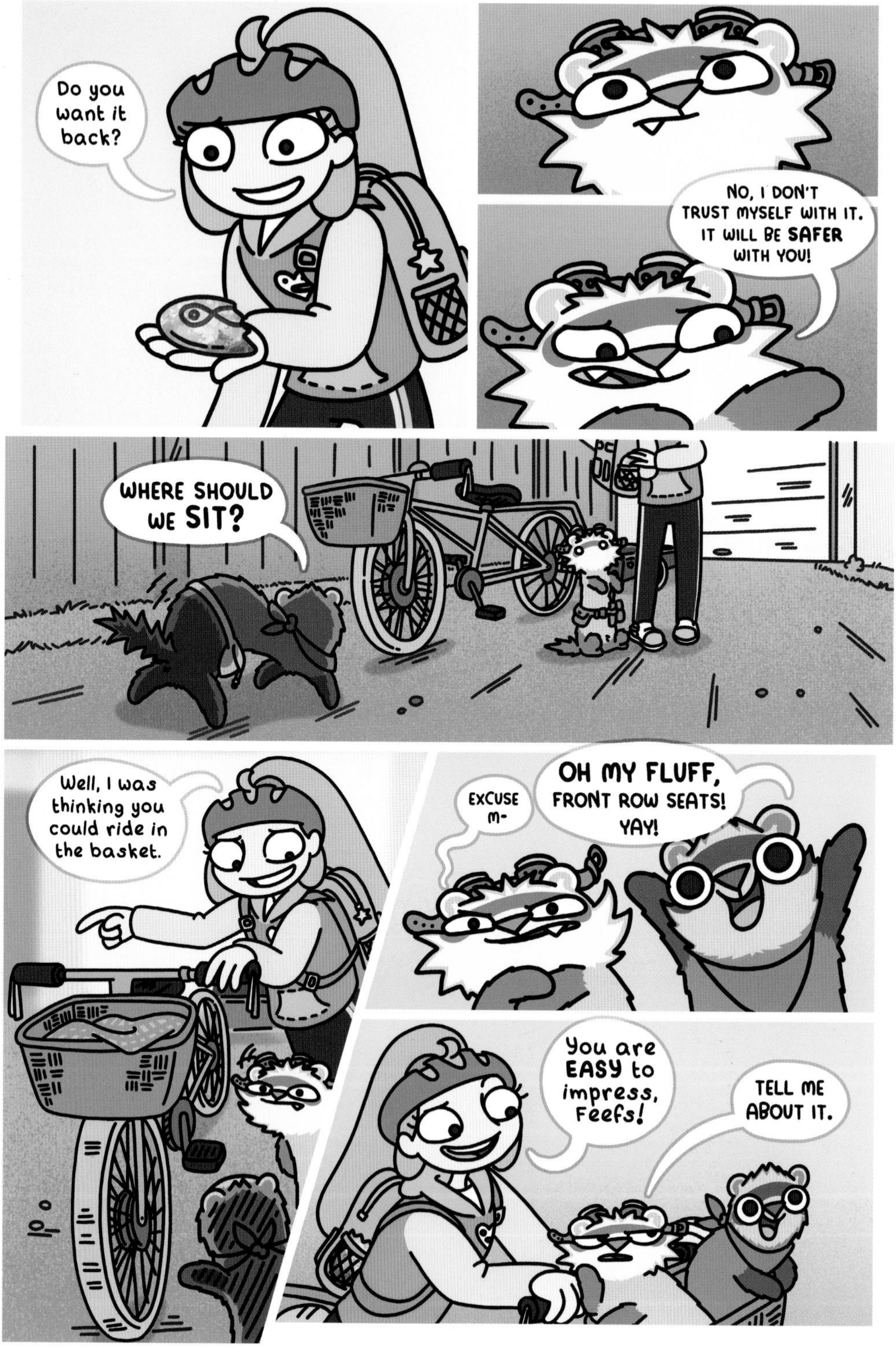
Do you want it back?
NO, I DON'T TRUST MYSELF WITH IT. IT WILL BE SAFER WITH YOU!
WHERE SHOULD WE SIT?
Well, I was thinking you could ride in the basket.
EXCUSE M-
OH MY FLUFF, FRONT ROW SEATS! YAY!
You are EASY to impress, Feefs!
TELL ME ABOUT IT.

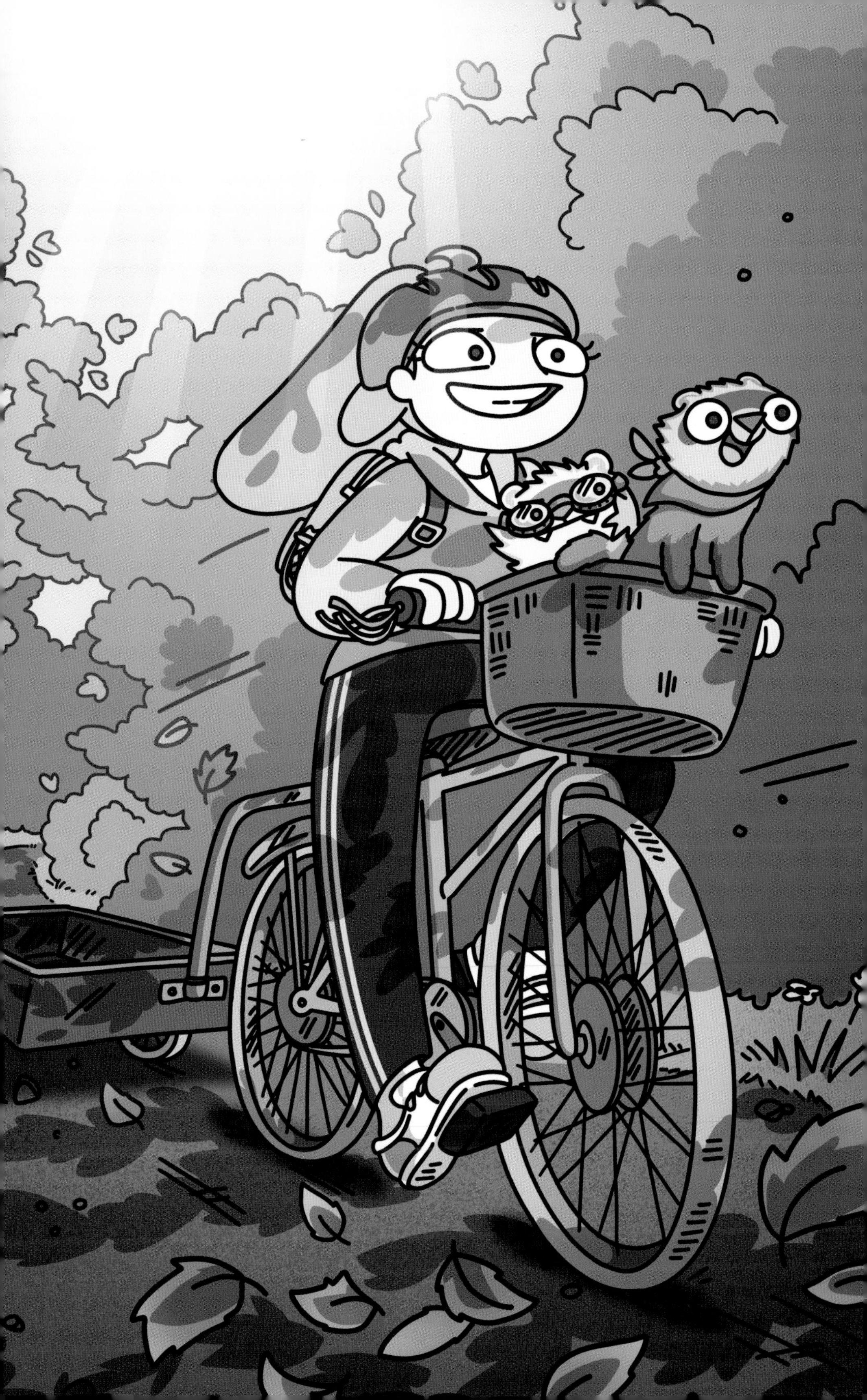

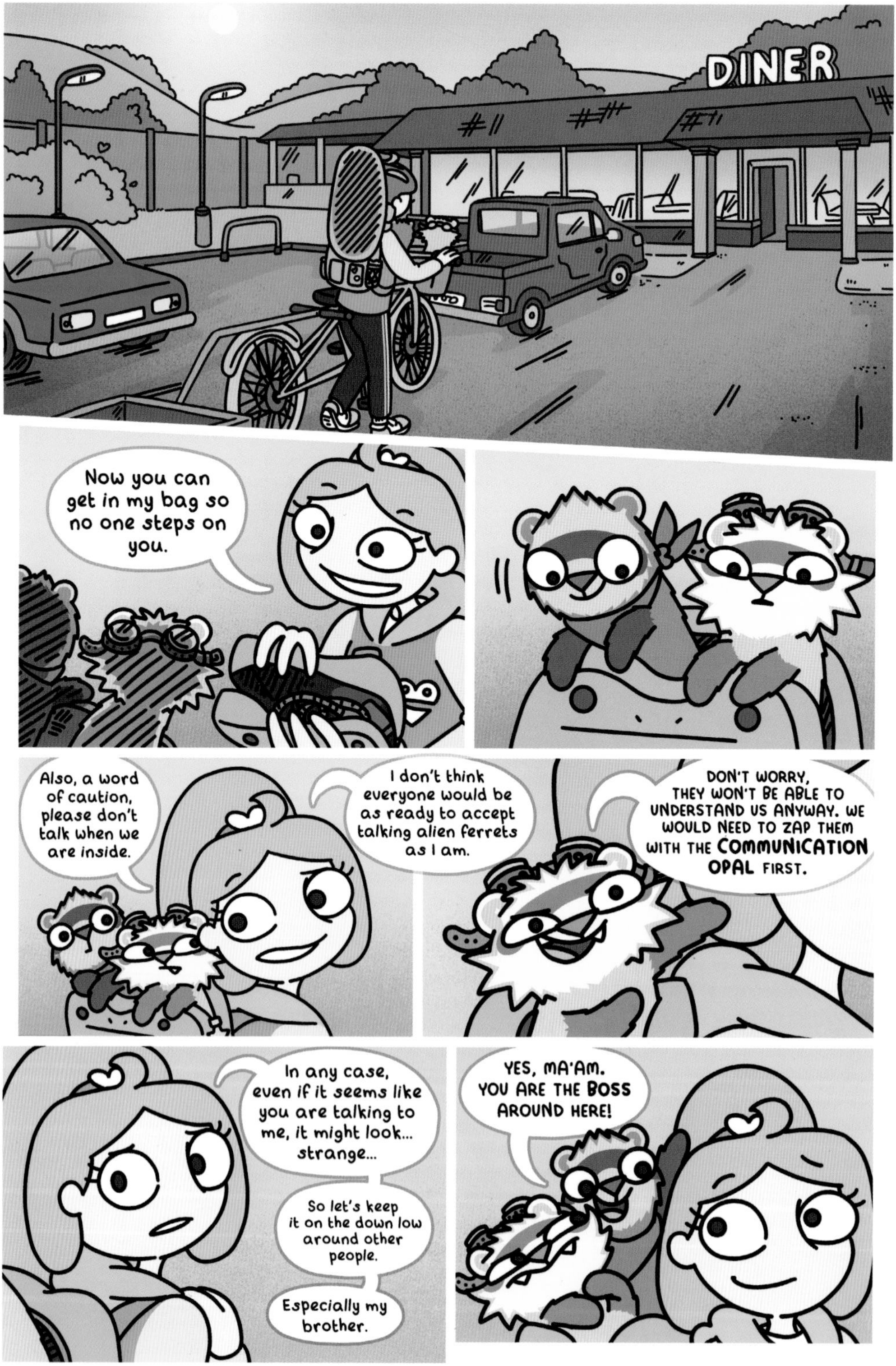
DINER
Now you can get in my bag so no one steps on you.
Also, a word of caution, please don't talk when we are inside.
I don't think everyone would be as ready to accept talking alien ferrets as I am.
DON'T WORRY, THEY WON'T BE ABLE TO UNDERSTAND US ANYWAY. WE WOULD NEED TO ZAP THEM WITH THE COMMUNICATION OPAL FIRST.
In any case, even if it seems like you are talking to me, it might look... strange...
So let's keep it on the down low around other people.
Especially my brother.
YES, MA'AM. YOU ARE THE BOSS AROUND HERE!

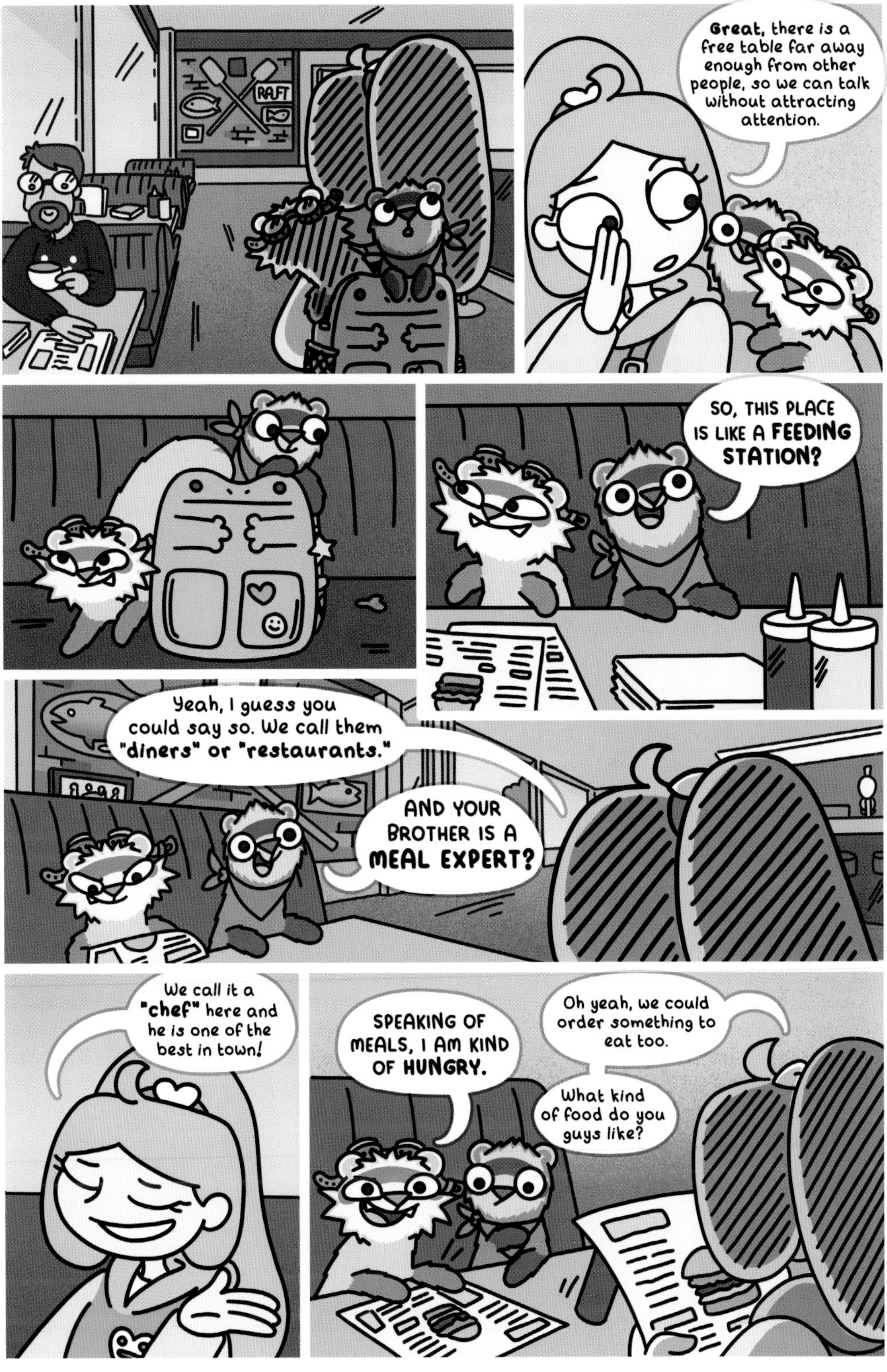
RAFT
Great, there is a free table far away enough from other people, so we can talk without attracting attention.
SO, THIS PLACE IS LIKE A FEEDING STATION?
Yeah, I guess you could say so. We call them "diners" or "restaurants."
AND YOUR BROTHER IS A MEAL EXPERT?
We call it a "chef" here and he is one of the best in town!
SPEAKING OF MEALS, I AM KIND OF HUNGRY.
Oh yeah, we could order something to eat too.
What kind of food do you guys like?

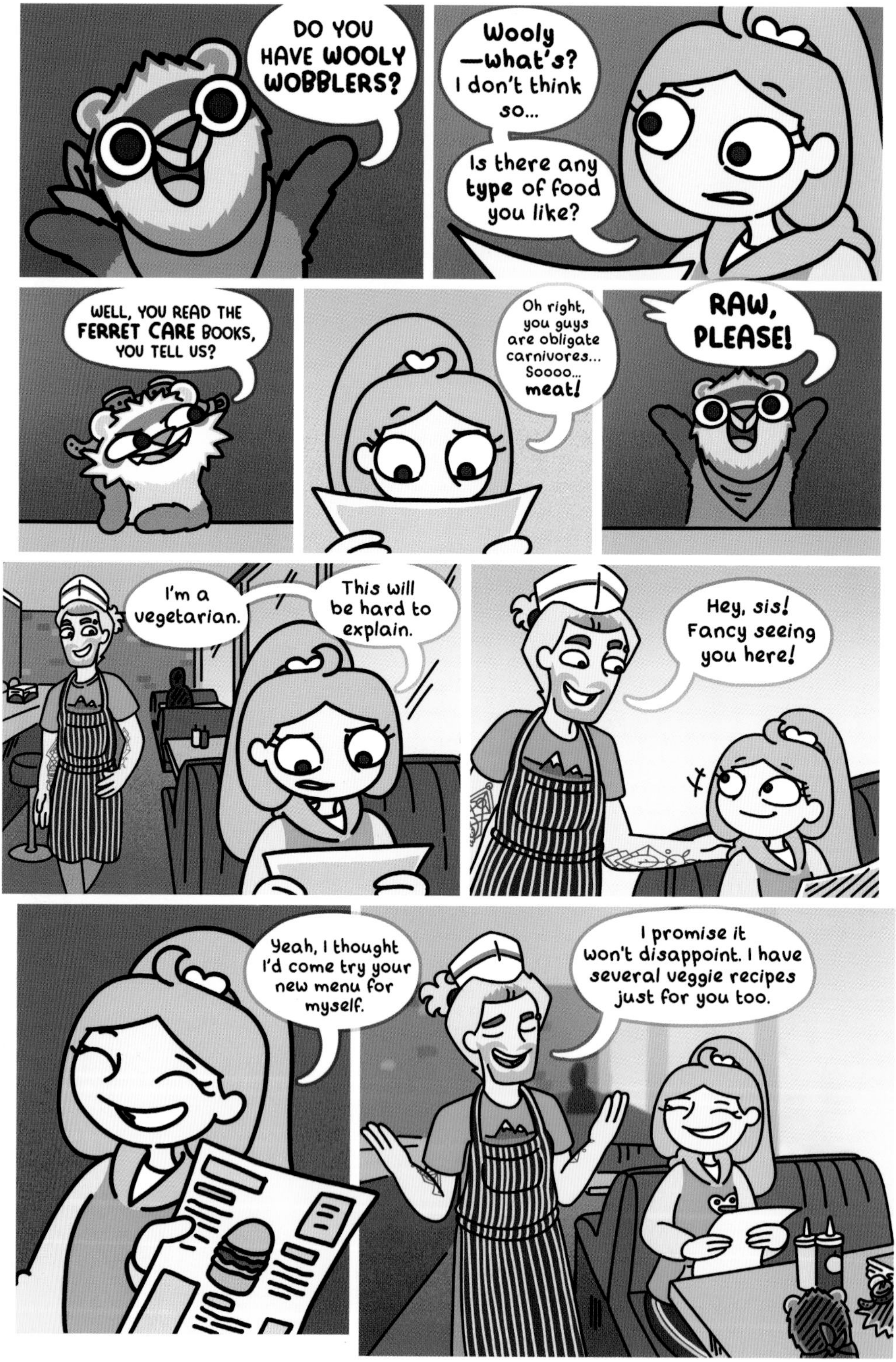
DO YOU HAVE WOOLY WOBBLERS?
Wooly—what's? I don't think so...
Is there any type of food you like?
WELL, YOU READ THE FERRET CARE BOOKS, YOU TELL US?
Oh right, you guys are obligate carnivores... Soooo... meat!
RAW, PLEASE!
I'm a vegetarian.
This will be hard to explain.
Hey, sis! Fancy seeing you here!
Yeah, I thought I'd come try your new menu for myself.
I promise it won't disappoint. I have several veggie recipes just for you too.

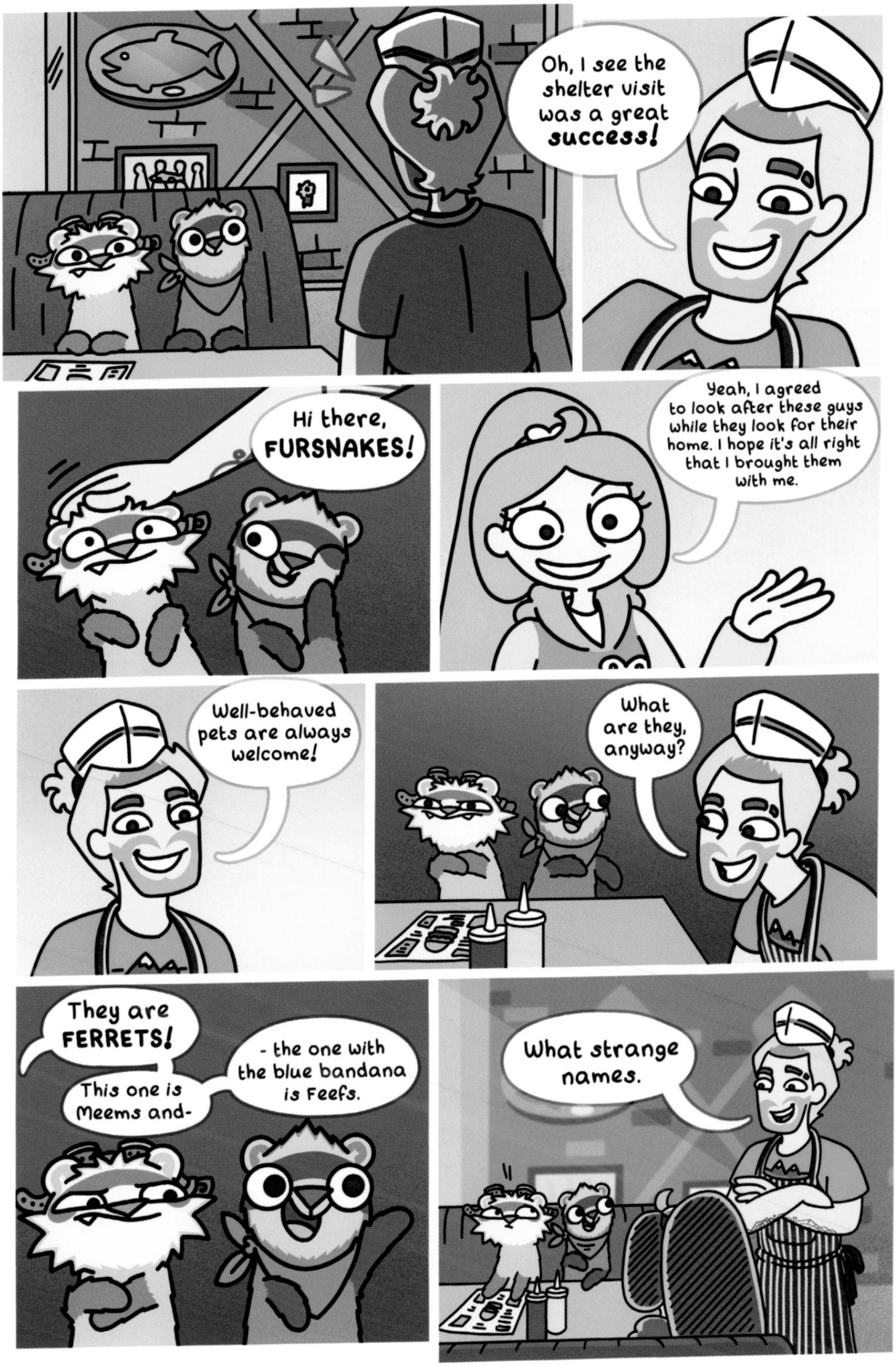
Oh, I see the shelter visit was a great **success!**
Hi there, **FURSNAKES!**
Yeah, I agreed to look after these guys while they look for their home. I hope it's all right that I brought them with me.
Well-behaved pets are always welcome!
What are they, anyway?
They are **FERRETS!**
This one is Meems and-
- the one with the blue bandana is Feefs.
What strange names.

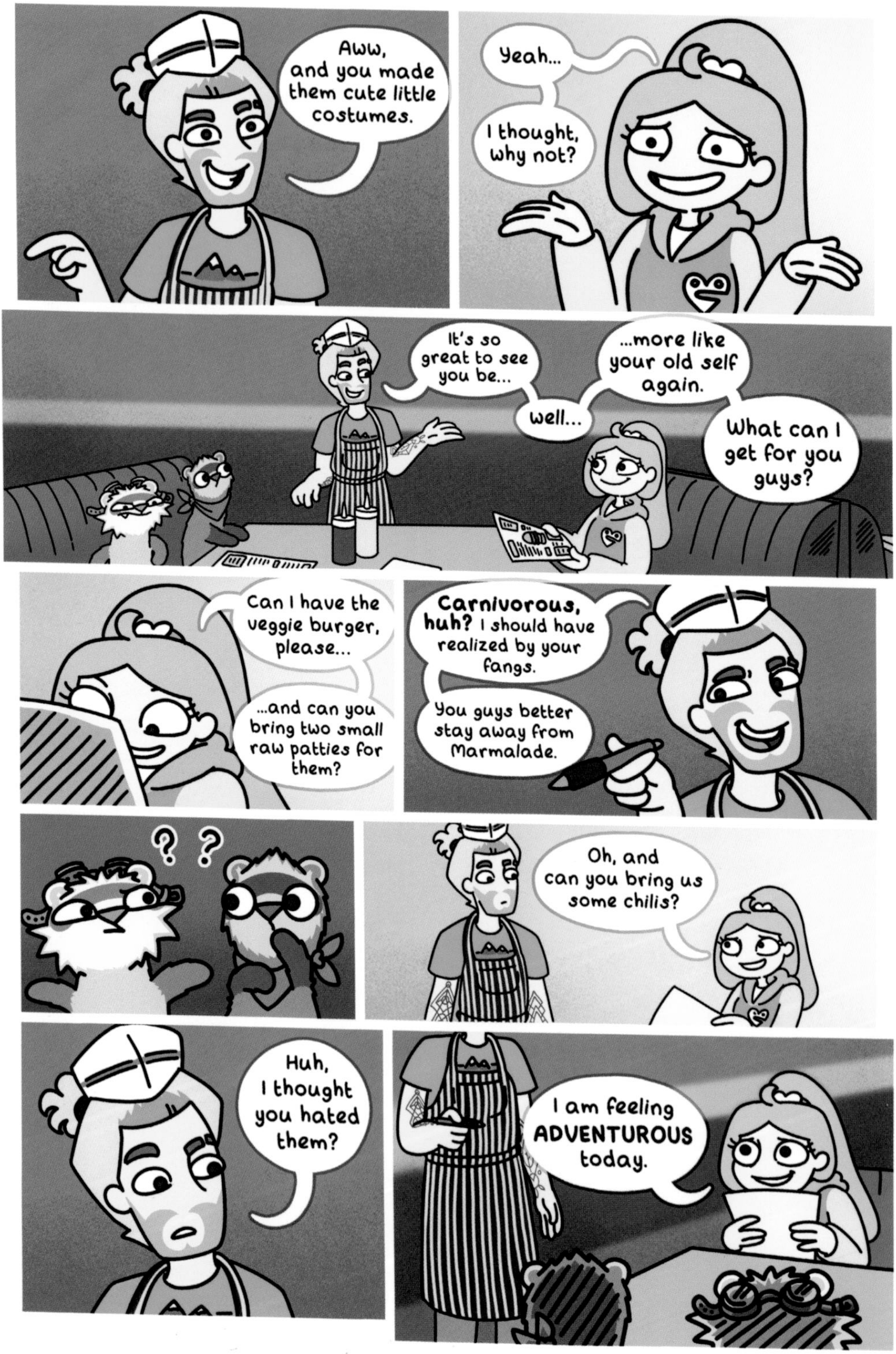
Aww, and you made them cute little costumes.
Yeah...
I thought, why not?
It's so great to see you be...
well...
...more like your old self again.
What can I get for you guys?
Can I have the veggie burger, please...
...and can you bring two small raw patties for them?
Carnivorous, huh? I should have realized by your fangs.
You guys better stay away from Marmalade.
? ?
Oh, and can you bring us some chilis?
Huh, I thought you hated them?
I am feeling **ADVENTUROUS** today.

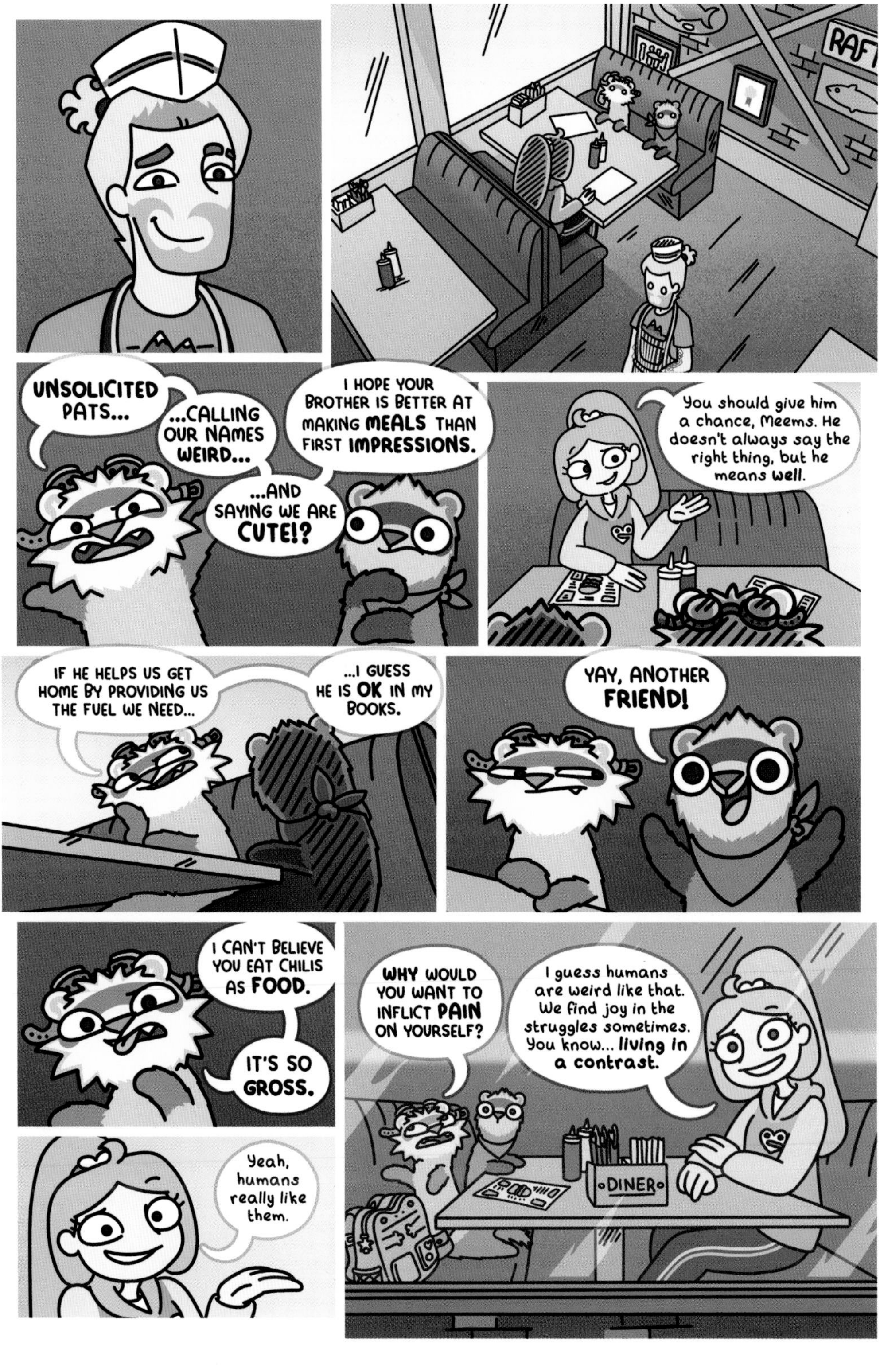
RAFT
UNSOLICITED PATS...
...CALLING OUR NAMES WEIRD...
...AND SAYING WE ARE CUTE!?
I HOPE YOUR BROTHER IS BETTER AT MAKING MEALS THAN FIRST IMPRESSIONS.
You should give him a chance, Meems. He doesn't always say the right thing, but he means well.
IF HE HELPS US GET HOME BY PROVIDING US THE FUEL WE NEED...
...I GUESS HE IS OK IN MY BOOKS.
YAY, ANOTHER FRIEND!
I CAN'T BELIEVE YOU EAT CHILIS AS FOOD.
IT'S SO GROSS.
Yeah, humans really like them.
WHY WOULD YOU WANT TO INFLICT PAIN ON YOURSELF?
I guess humans are weird like that. We find joy in the struggles sometimes. You know... living in a contrast.
DINER

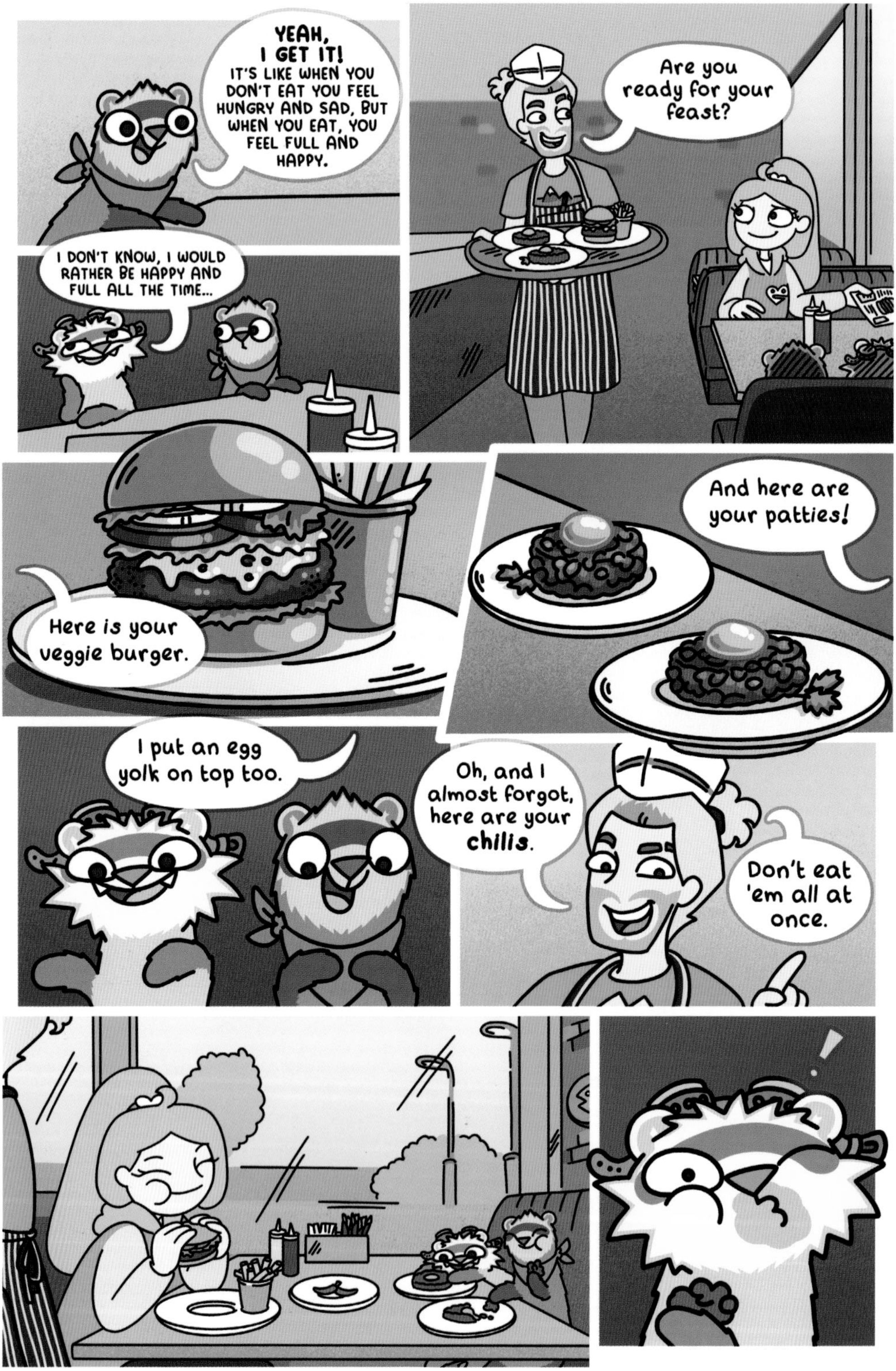
YEAH, I GET IT! IT'S LIKE WHEN YOU DON'T EAT YOU FEEL HUNGRY AND SAD, BUT WHEN YOU EAT, YOU FEEL FULL AND HAPPY.
I DON'T KNOW, I WOULD RATHER BE HAPPY AND FULL ALL THE TIME...
Are you ready for your feast?
Here is your veggie burger.
And here are your patties!
I put an egg yolk on top too.
Oh, and I almost forgot, here are your chilis.
Don't eat 'em all at once.
!

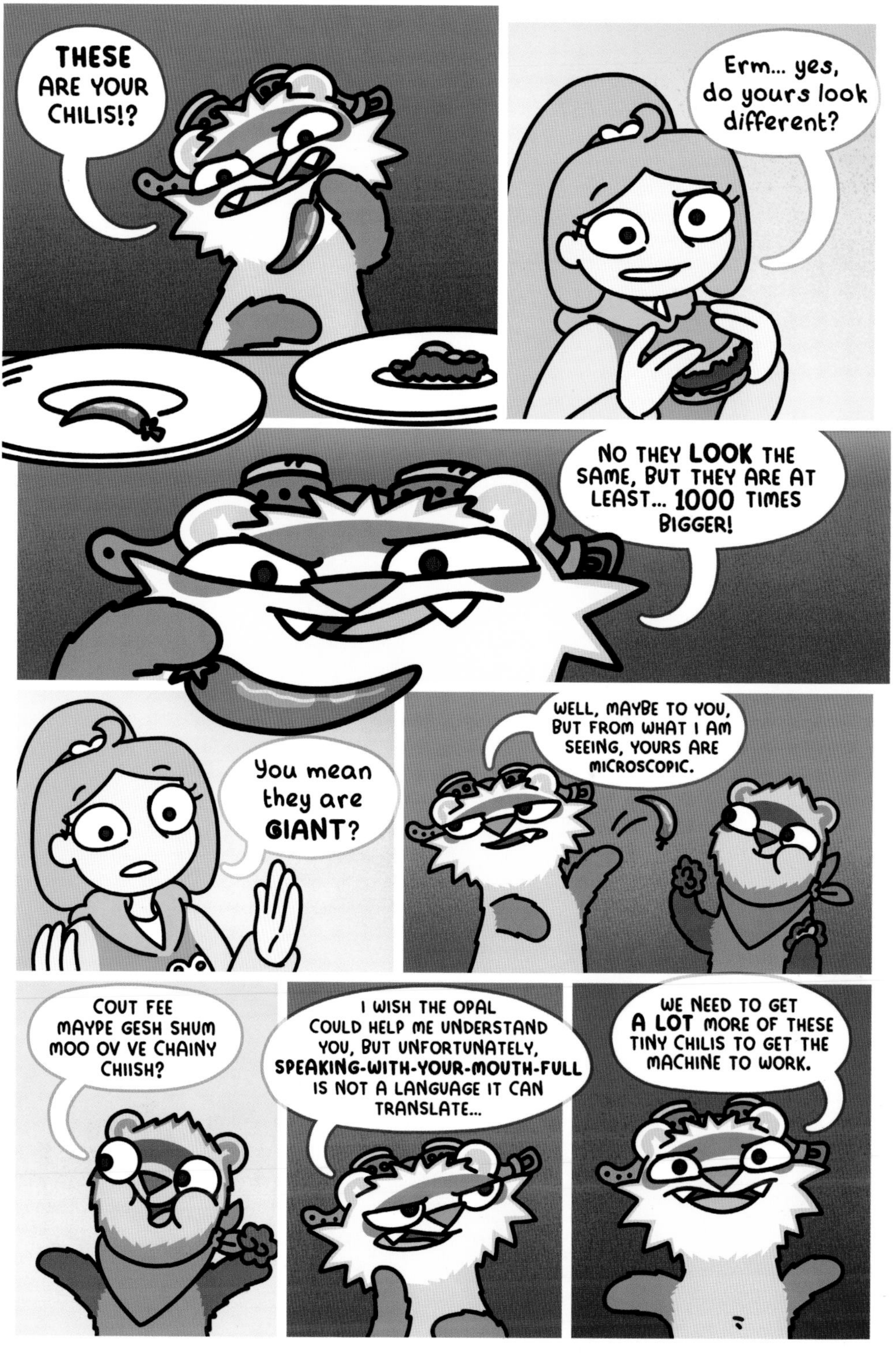
THESE ARE YOUR CHILIS!?
Erm... yes, do yours look different?
NO THEY LOOK THE SAME, BUT THEY ARE AT LEAST... 1000 TIMES BIGGER!
You mean they are GIANT?
WELL, MAYBE TO YOU, BUT FROM WHAT I AM SEEING, YOURS ARE MICROSCOPIC.
COUT FEE MAYPE GESH SHUM MOO OV VE CHAINY CHIISH?
I WISH THE OPAL COULD HELP ME UNDERSTAND YOU, BUT UNFORTUNATELY, SPEAKING-WITH-YOUR-MOUTH-FULL IS NOT A LANGUAGE IT CAN TRANSLATE...
WE NEED TO GET A LOT MORE OF THESE TINY CHILIS TO GET THE MACHINE TO WORK.

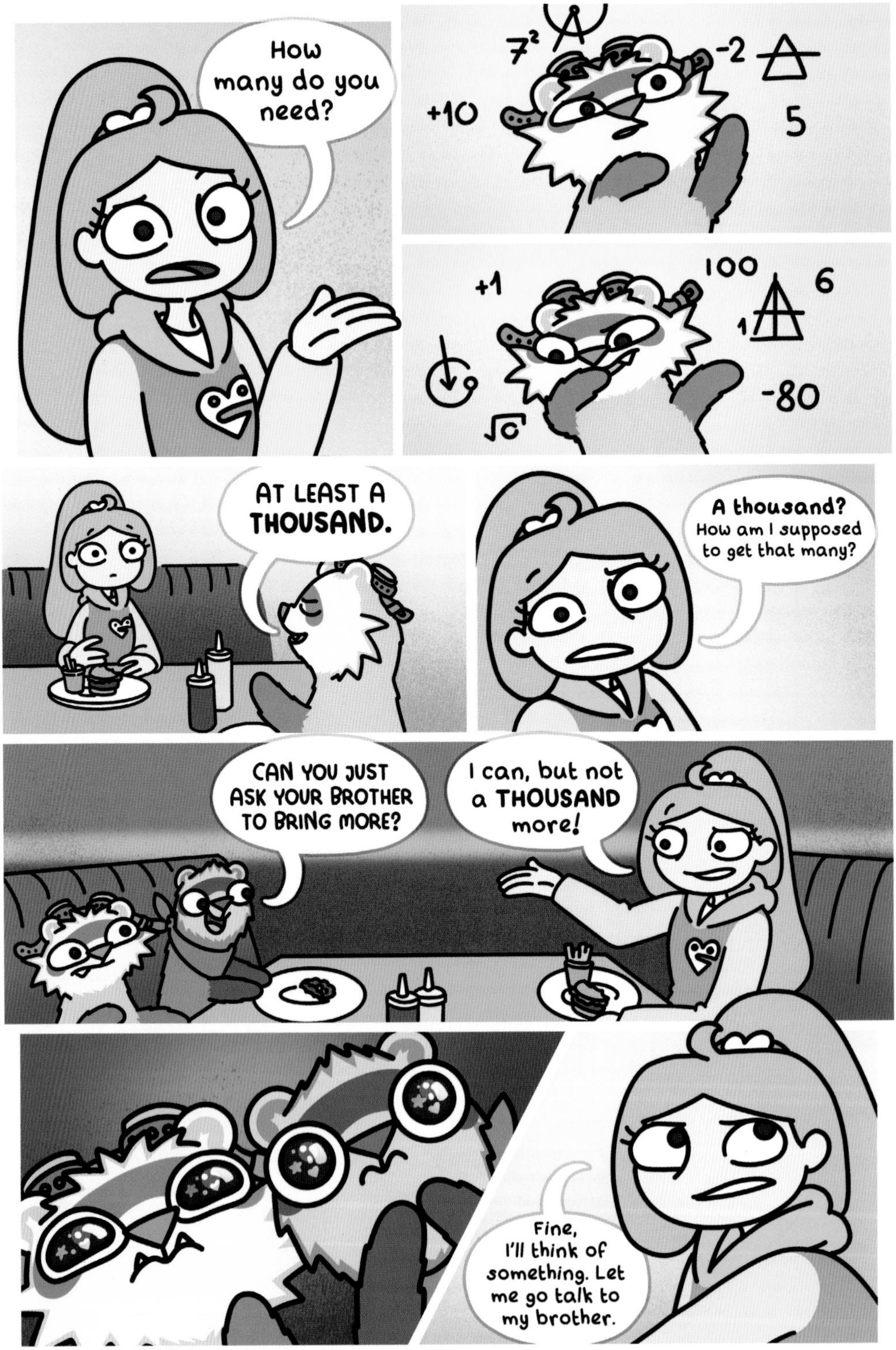
How many do you need?
7²
-2
+10
5
+1
100
6
1
-80
√c
AT LEAST A THOUSAND.
A thousand? How am I supposed to get that many?
CAN YOU JUST ASK YOUR BROTHER TO BRING MORE?
I can, but not a THOUSAND more!
Fine, I'll think of something. Let me go talk to my brother.

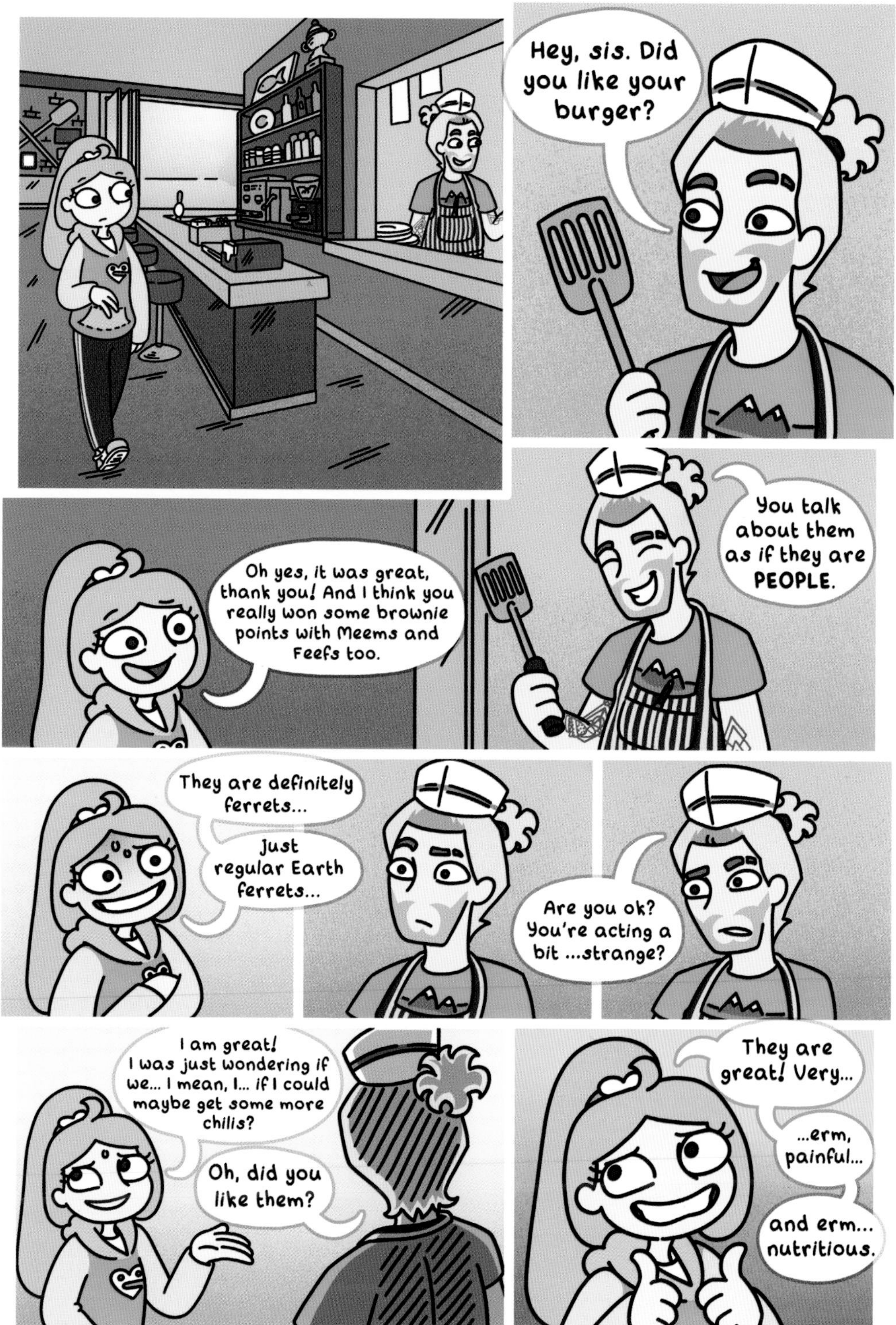
Hey, sis. Did you like your burger?
Oh yes, it was great, thank you! And I think you really won some brownie points with Meems and Feefs too.
You talk about them as if they are PEOPLE.
They are definitely ferrets...
Just regular Earth ferrets...
Are you ok? You're acting a bit ...strange?
I am great! I was just wondering if we... I mean, I... if I could maybe get some more chilis?
Oh, did you like them?
They are great! Very...
...erm, painful...
and erm... nutritious.

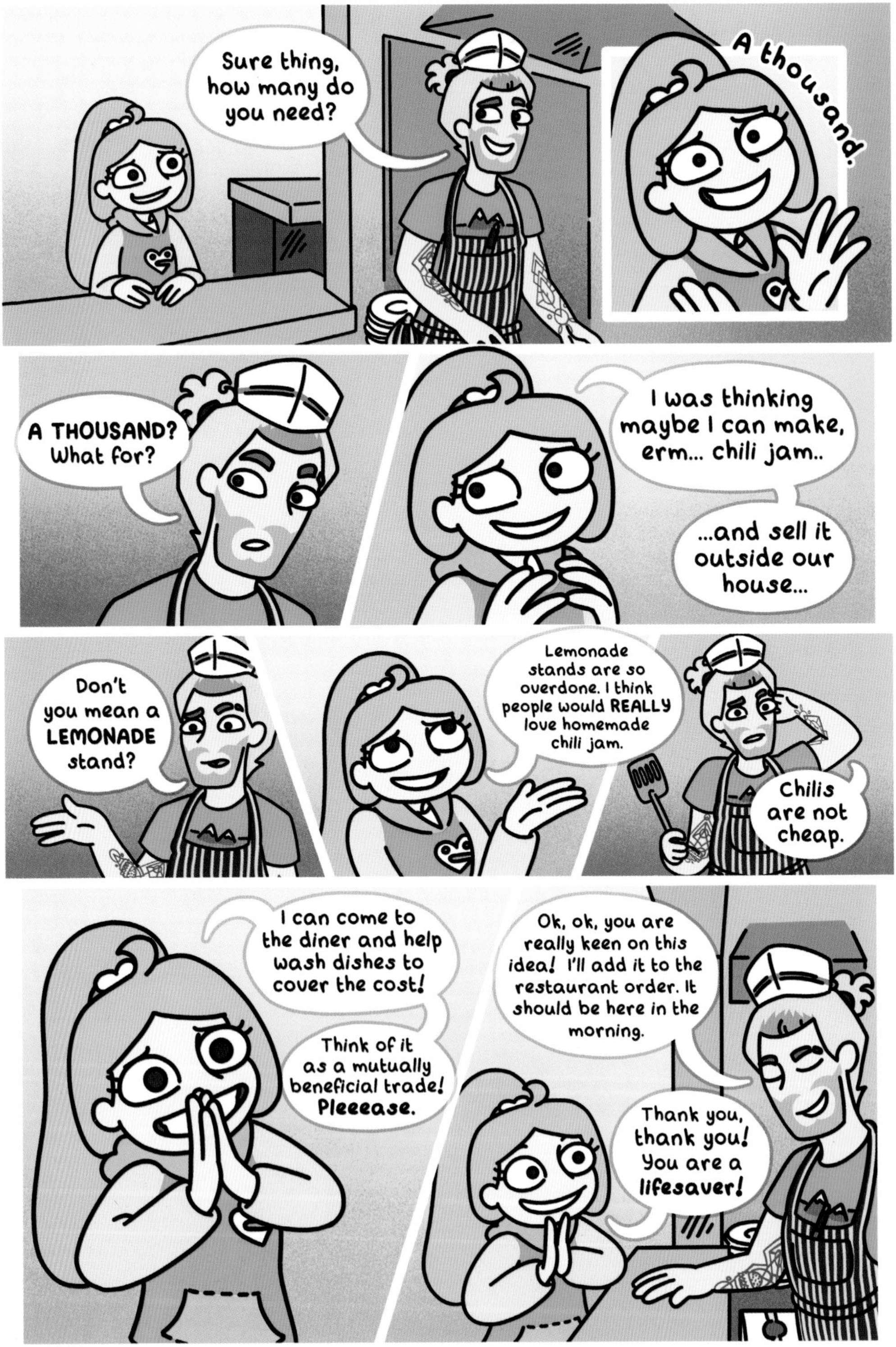
Sure thing, how many do you need?
A thousand.
A THOUSAND? What for?
I was thinking maybe I can make, erm... chili jam..
...and sell it outside our house...
Don't you mean a LEMONADE stand?
Lemonade stands are so overdone. I think people would REALLY love homemade chili jam.
Chilis are not cheap.
I can come to the diner and help wash dishes to cover the cost!
Think of it as a mutually beneficial trade! Pleeease.
Ok, ok, you are really keen on this idea! I'll add it to the restaurant order. It should be here in the morning.
Thank you, thank you! You are a lifesaver!

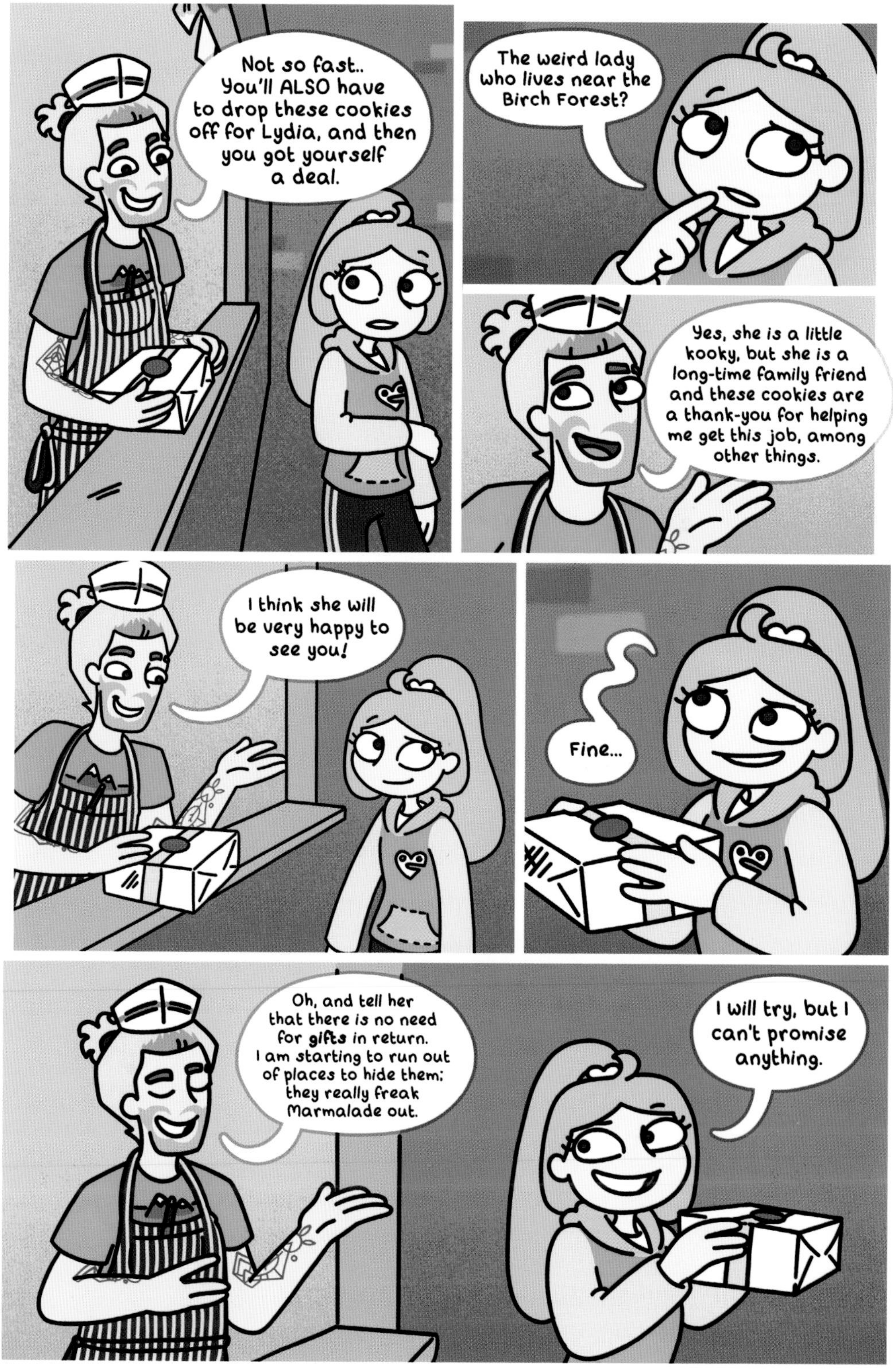
Not so fast..
You'll ALSO have to drop these cookies off for Lydia, and then you got yourself a deal.
The weird lady who lives near the Birch Forest?
Yes, she is a little kooky, but she is a long-time family friend and these cookies are a thank-you for helping me get this job, among other things.
I think she will be very happy to see you!
Fine...
Oh, and tell her that there is no need for gifts in return. I am starting to run out of places to hide them; they really freak Marmalade out.
I will try, but I can't promise anything.

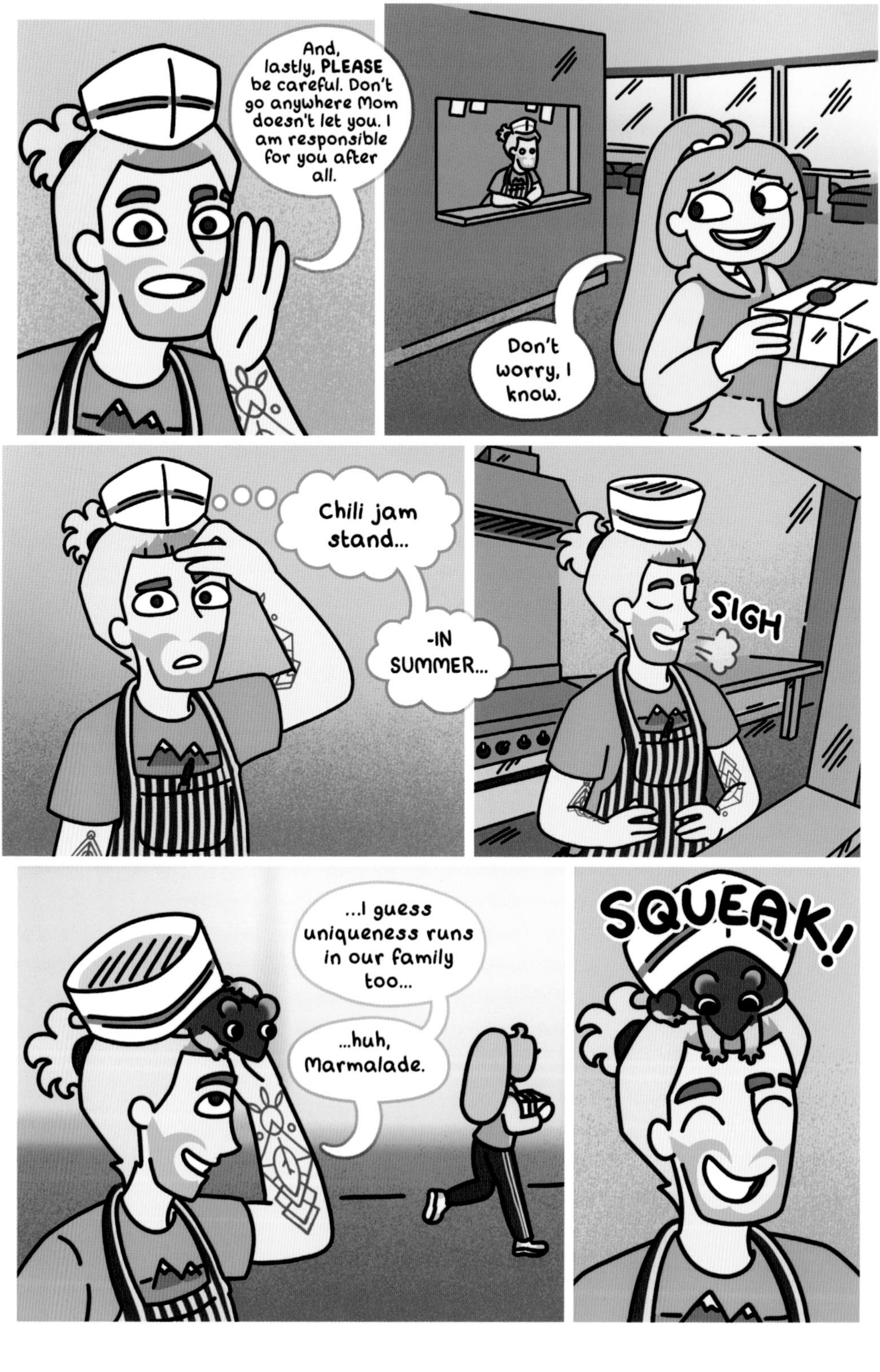
And, lastly, PLEASE be careful. Don't go anywhere Mom doesn't let you. I am responsible for you after all.
Don't worry, I know.
Chili jam stand...
-IN SUMMER...
SIGH
...I guess uniqueness runs in our family too...
...huh, Marmalade.
SQUEAK!

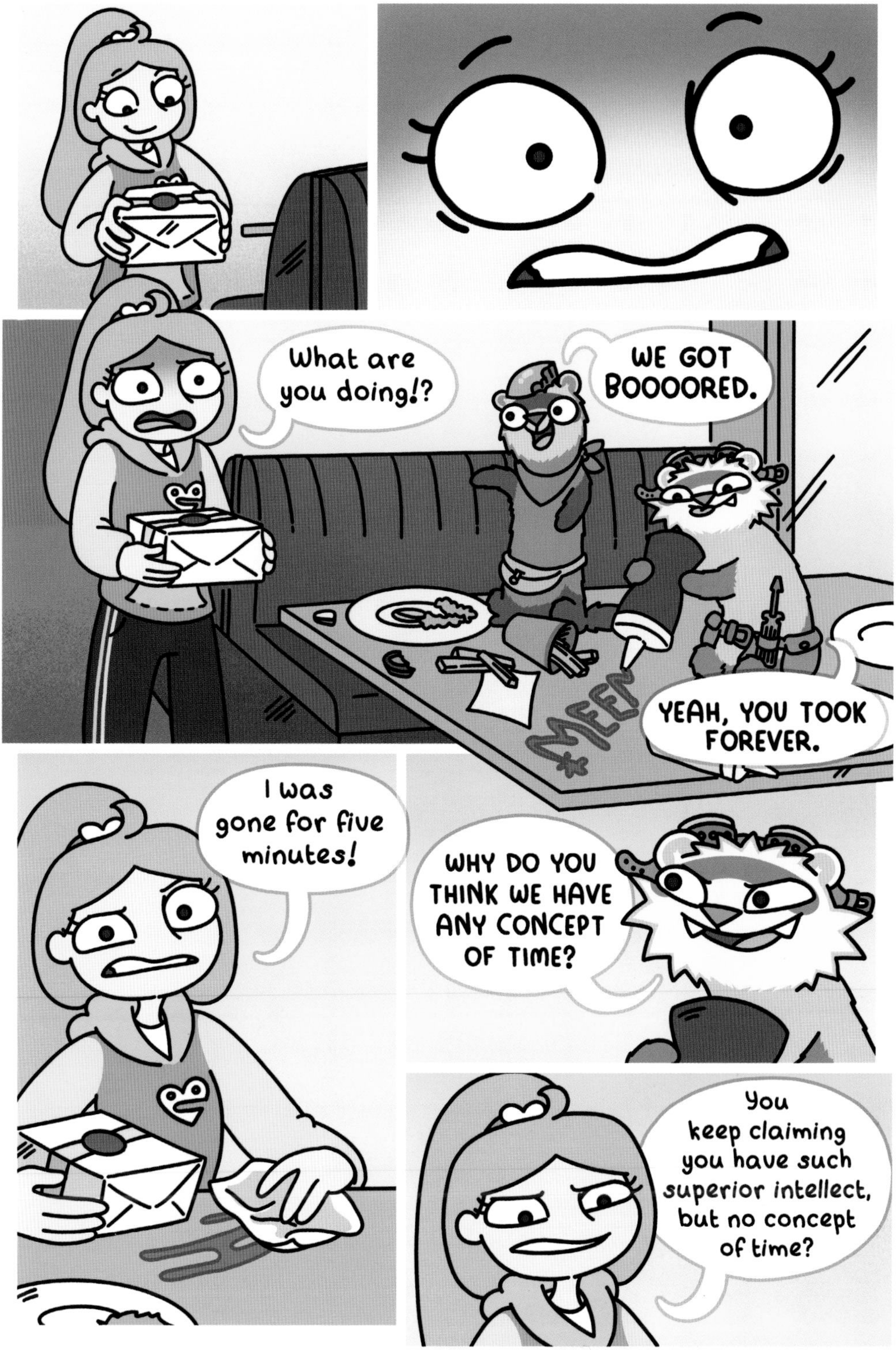
What are you doing!?
WE GOT BOOOORED.
MEEP
YEAH, YOU TOOK FOREVER.
I was gone for five minutes!
WHY DO YOU THINK WE HAVE ANY CONCEPT OF TIME?
You keep claiming you have such superior intellect, but no concept of time?

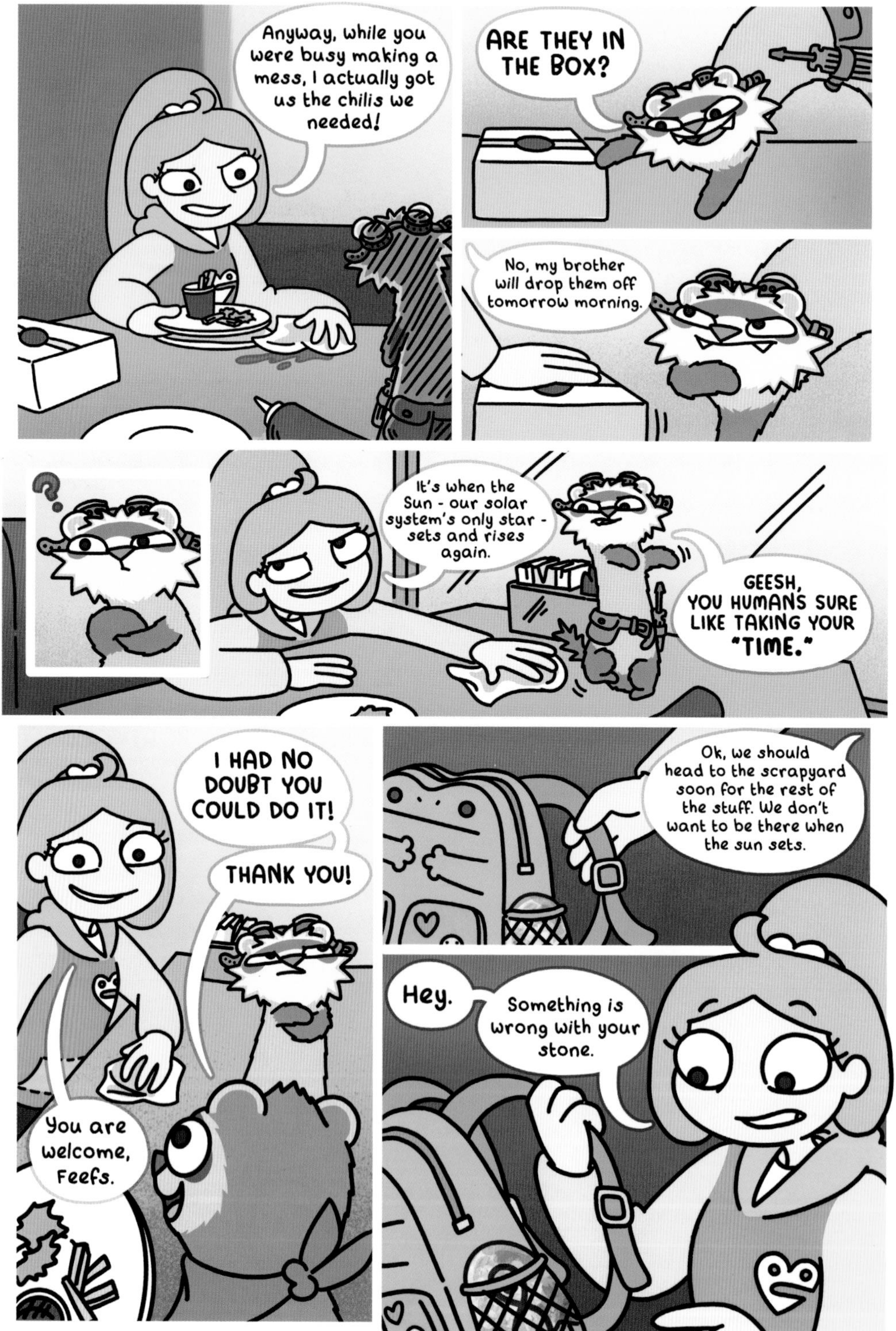

Anyway, while you were busy making a mess, I actually got us the chilis we needed!
ARE THEY IN THE BOX?
No, my brother will drop them off tomorrow morning.
It's when the Sun - our solar system's only star - sets and rises again.
GEESH, YOU HUMANS SURE LIKE TAKING YOUR "TIME."
I HAD NO DOUBT YOU COULD DO IT!
THANK YOU!
You are welcome, Feefs.
Ok, we should head to the scrapyard soon for the rest of the stuff. We don't want to be there when the sun sets.
Hey.
Something is wrong with your stone.

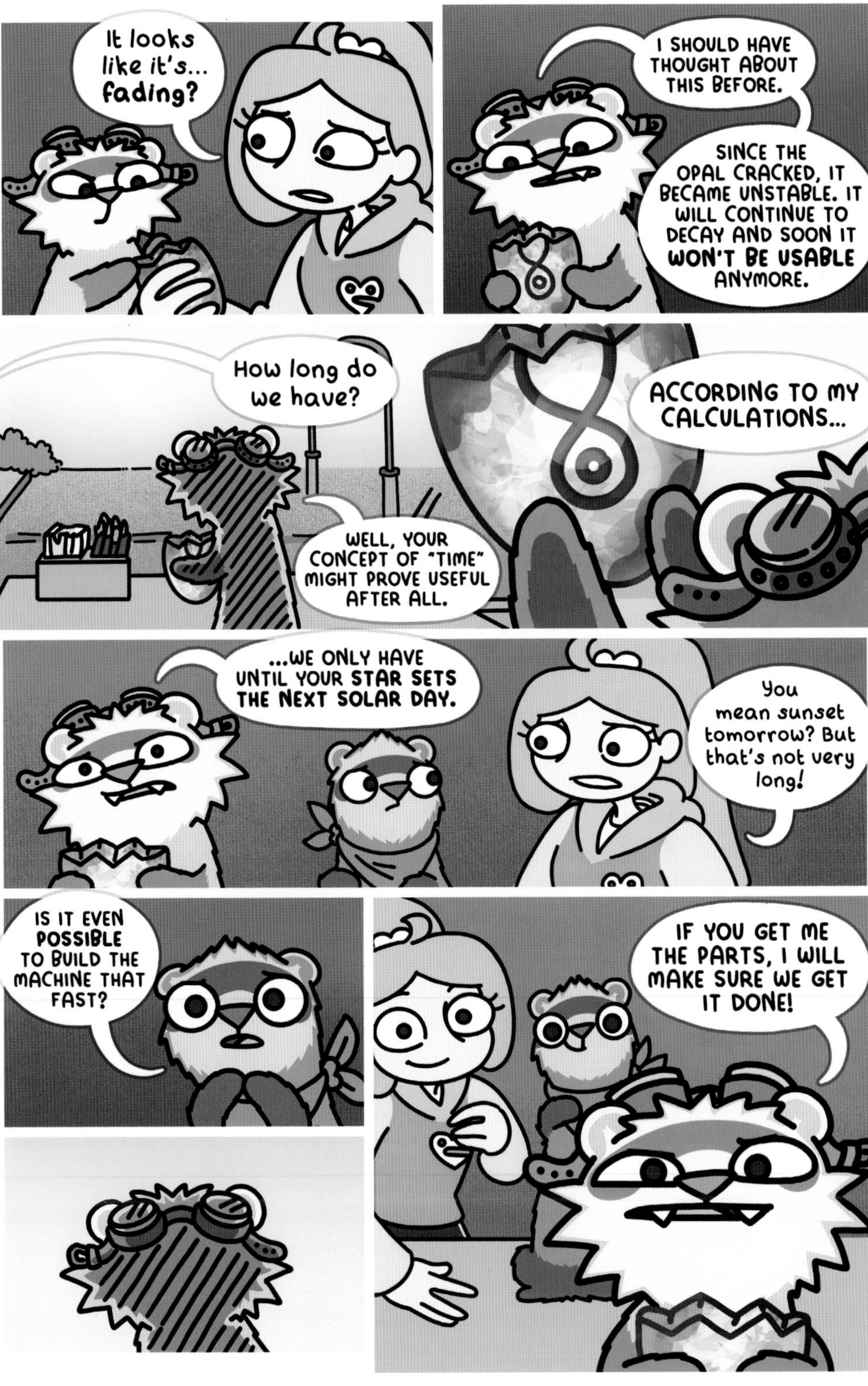
It looks like it's... fading?
I SHOULD HAVE THOUGHT ABOUT THIS BEFORE.
SINCE THE OPAL CRACKED, IT BECAME UNSTABLE. IT WILL CONTINUE TO DECAY AND SOON IT WON'T BE USABLE ANYMORE.
How long do we have?
WELL, YOUR CONCEPT OF "TIME" MIGHT PROVE USEFUL AFTER ALL.
ACCORDING TO MY CALCULATIONS...
...WE ONLY HAVE UNTIL YOUR STAR SETS THE NEXT SOLAR DAY.
You mean sunset tomorrow? But that's not very long!
IS IT EVEN POSSIBLE TO BUILD THE MACHINE THAT FAST?
IF YOU GET ME THE PARTS, I WILL MAKE SURE WE GET IT DONE!

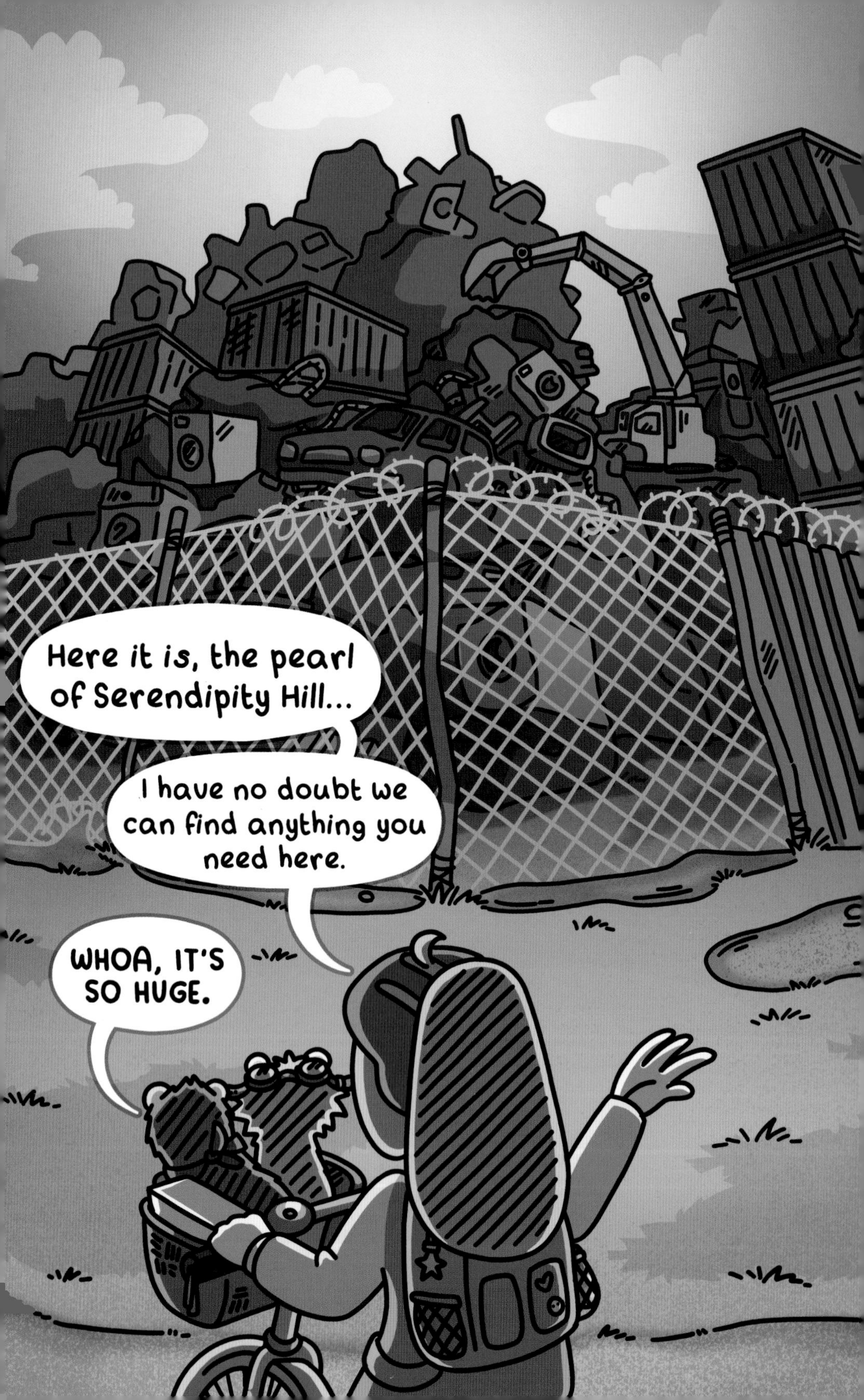
Here it is, the pearl of Serendipity Hill...
I have no doubt we can find anything you need here.
WHOA, IT'S SO HUGE.

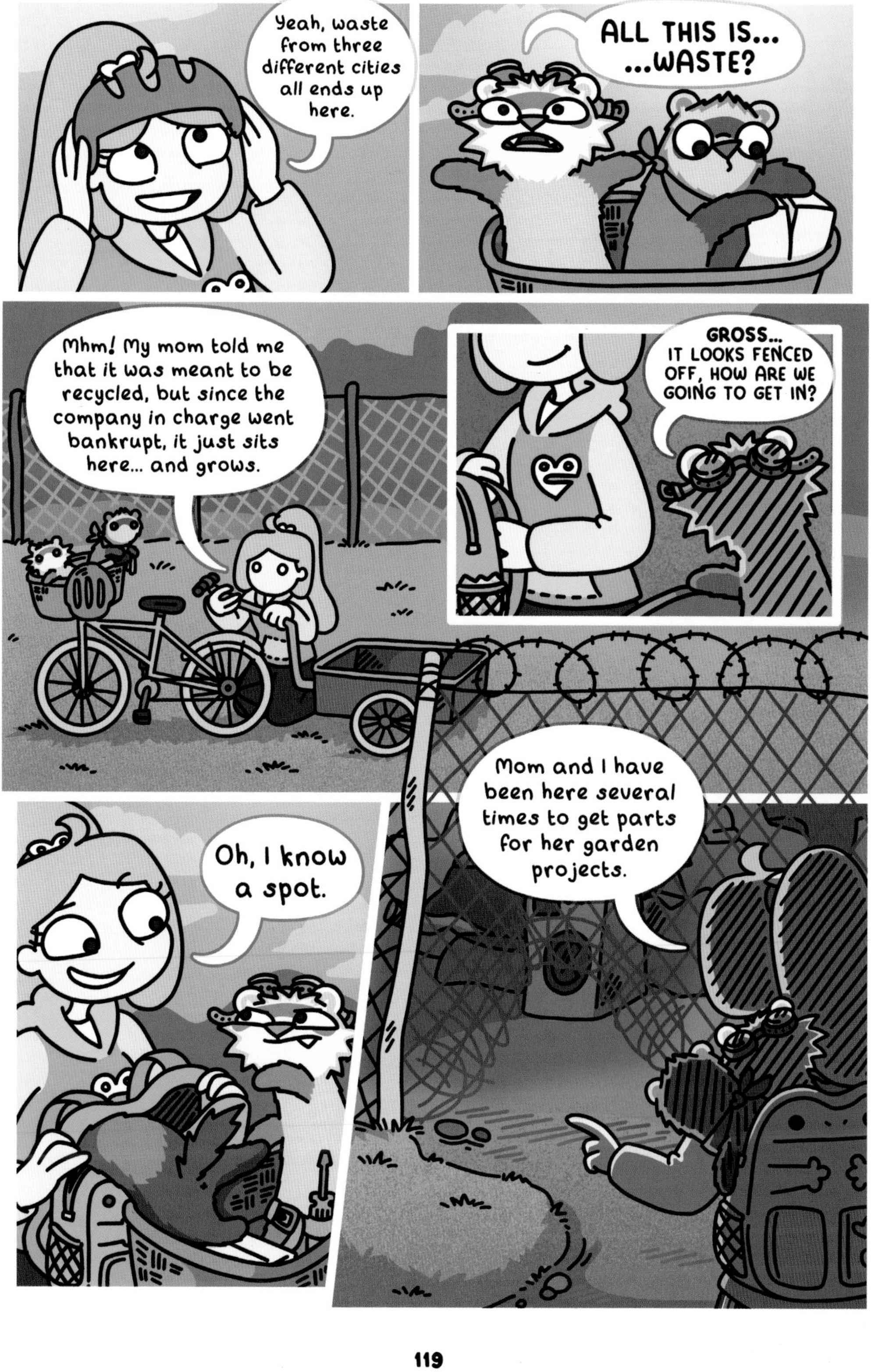
Yeah, waste from three different cities all ends up here.
ALL THIS IS... ...WASTE?
Mhm! My mom told me that it was meant to be recycled, but since the company in charge went bankrupt, it just sits here... and grows.
GROSS... IT LOOKS FENCED OFF, HOW ARE WE GOING TO GET IN?
Oh, I know a spot.
Mom and I have been here several times to get parts for her garden projects.

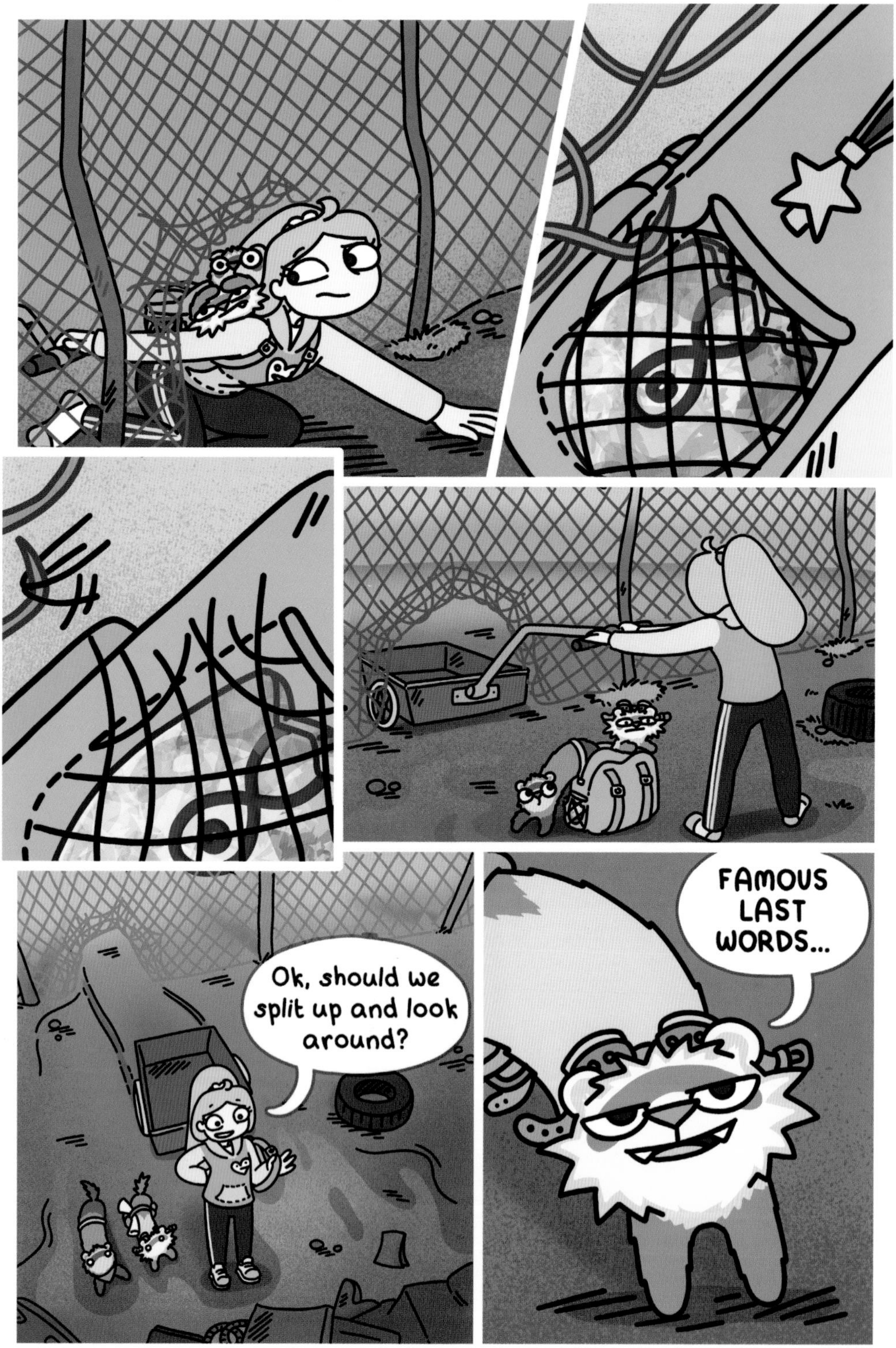
Ok, should we split up and look around?
FAMOUS LAST WORDS...

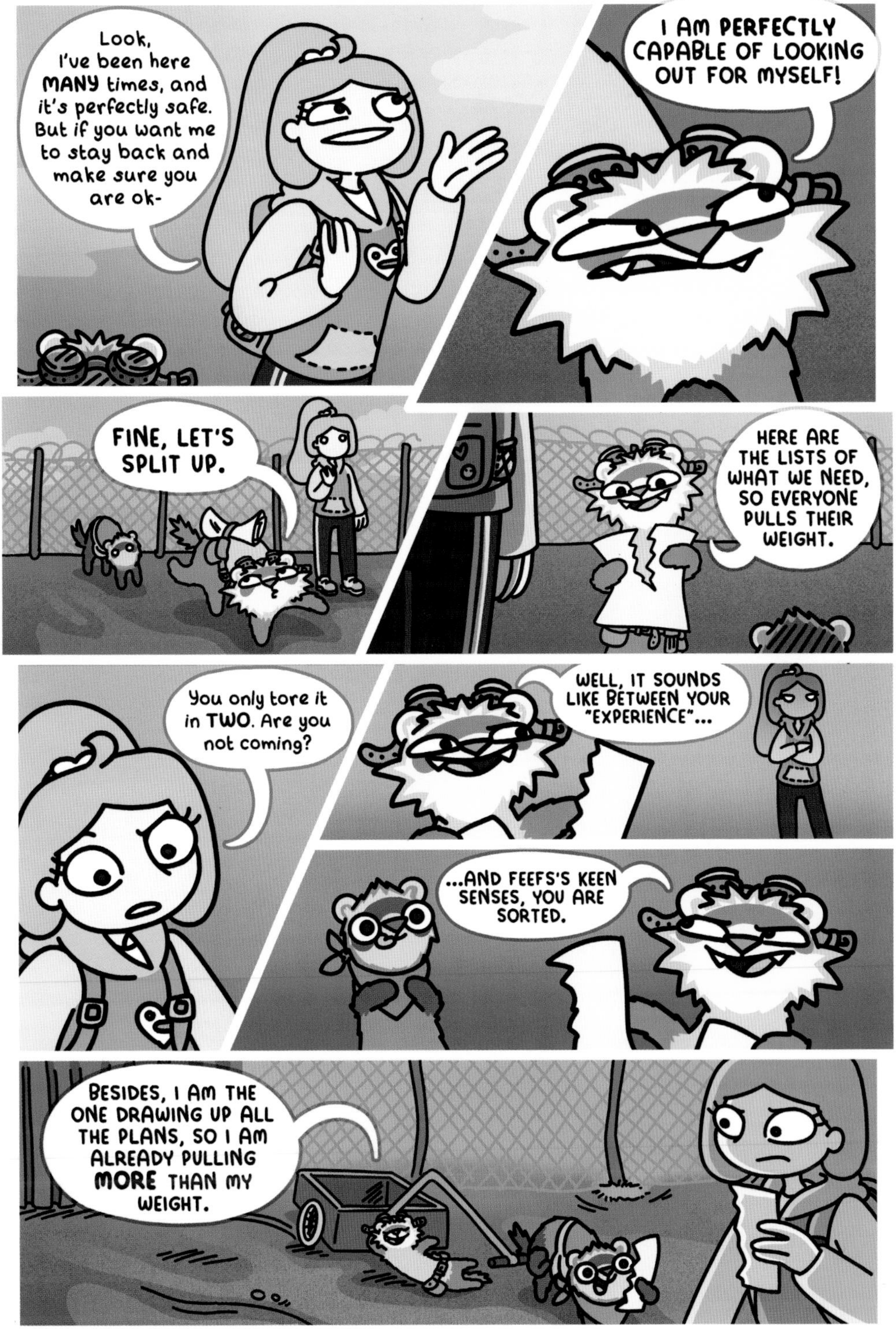
Look, I've been here MANY times, and it's perfectly safe. But if you want me to stay back and make sure you are ok-
I AM PERFECTLY CAPABLE OF LOOKING OUT FOR MYSELF!
FINE, LET'S SPLIT UP.
HERE ARE THE LISTS OF WHAT WE NEED, SO EVERYONE PULLS THEIR WEIGHT.
You only tore it in TWO. Are you not coming?
WELL, IT SOUNDS LIKE BETWEEN YOUR "EXPERIENCE"...
...AND FEEFS'S KEEN SENSES, YOU ARE SORTED.
BESIDES, I AM THE ONE DRAWING UP ALL THE PLANS, SO I AM ALREADY PULLING MORE THAN MY WEIGHT.

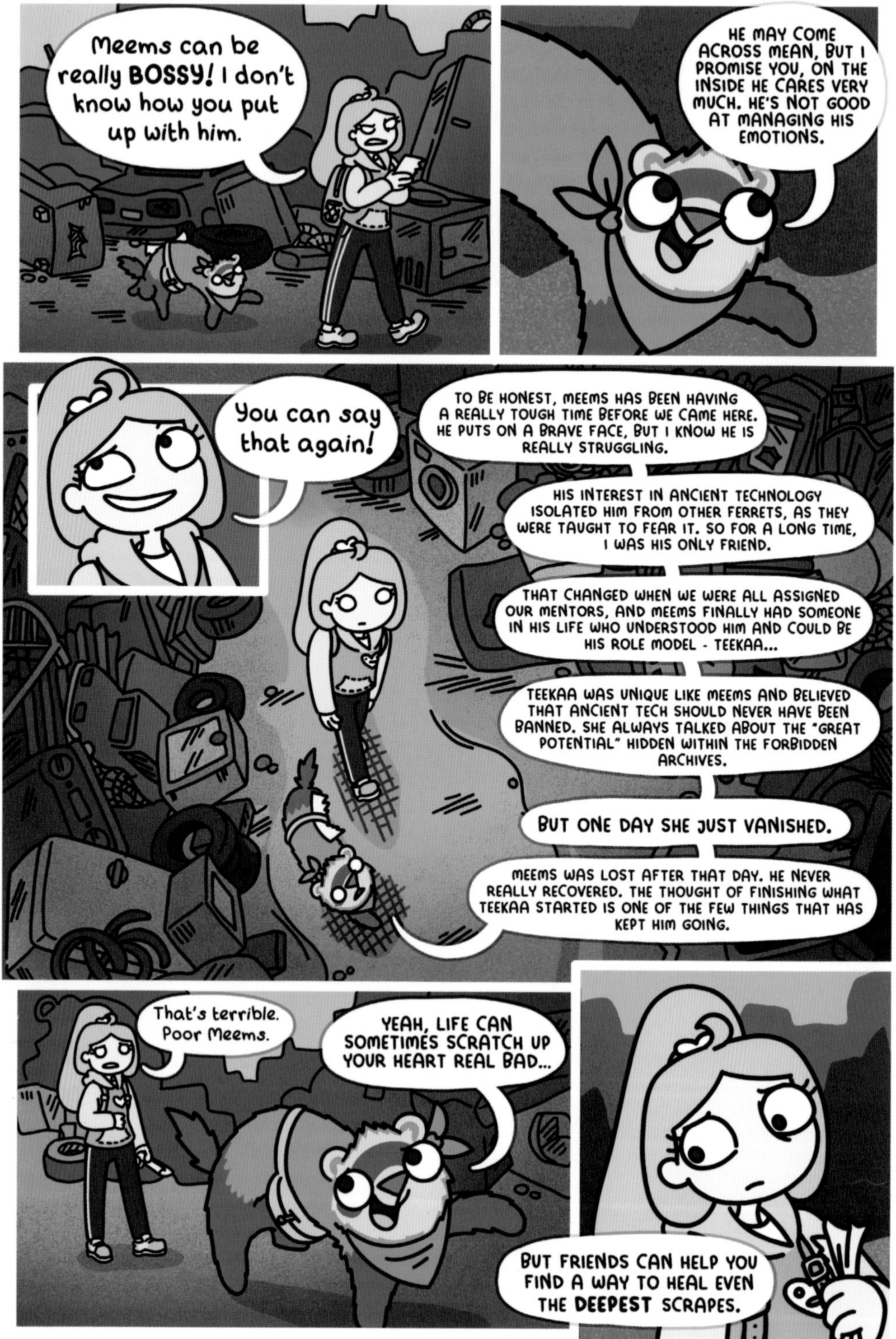

Meems can be really BOSSY! I don't know how you put up with him.
HE MAY COME ACROSS MEAN, BUT I PROMISE YOU, ON THE INSIDE HE CARES VERY MUCH. HE'S NOT GOOD AT MANAGING HIS EMOTIONS.
You can say that again!
TO BE HONEST, MEEMS HAS BEEN HAVING A REALLY TOUGH TIME BEFORE WE CAME HERE. HE PUTS ON A BRAVE FACE, BUT I KNOW HE IS REALLY STRUGGLING.
HIS INTEREST IN ANCIENT TECHNOLOGY ISOLATED HIM FROM OTHER FERRETS, AS THEY WERE TAUGHT TO FEAR IT. SO FOR A LONG TIME, I WAS HIS ONLY FRIEND.
THAT CHANGED WHEN WE WERE ALL ASSIGNED OUR MENTORS, AND MEEMS FINALLY HAD SOMEONE IN HIS LIFE WHO UNDERSTOOD HIM AND COULD BE HIS ROLE MODEL - TEEKAA...
TEEKAA WAS UNIQUE LIKE MEEMS AND BELIEVED THAT ANCIENT TECH SHOULD NEVER HAVE BEEN BANNED. SHE ALWAYS TALKED ABOUT THE "GREAT POTENTIAL" HIDDEN WITHIN THE FORBIDDEN ARCHIVES.
BUT ONE DAY SHE JUST VANISHED.
MEEMS WAS LOST AFTER THAT DAY. HE NEVER REALLY RECOVERED. THE THOUGHT OF FINISHING WHAT TEEKAA STARTED IS ONE OF THE FEW THINGS THAT HAS KEPT HIM GOING.
That's terrible. Poor Meems.
YEAH, LIFE CAN SOMETIMES SCRATCH UP YOUR HEART REAL BAD...
BUT FRIENDS CAN HELP YOU FIND A WAY TO HEAL EVEN THE DEEPEST SCRAPES.

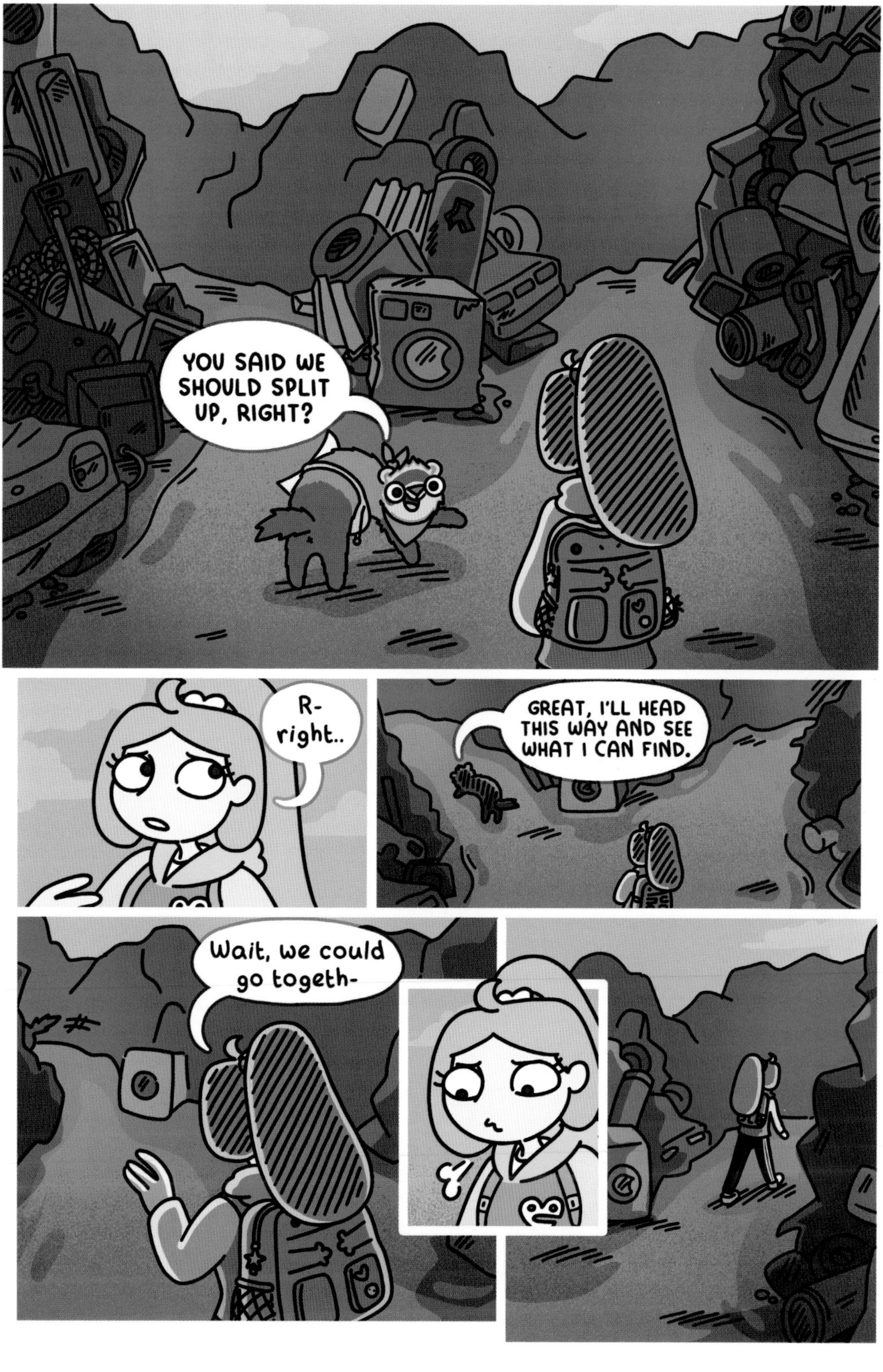
YOU SAID WE SHOULD SPLIT UP, RIGHT?
R- right..
GREAT, I'LL HEAD THIS WAY AND SEE WHAT I CAN FIND.
Wait, we could go togeth-

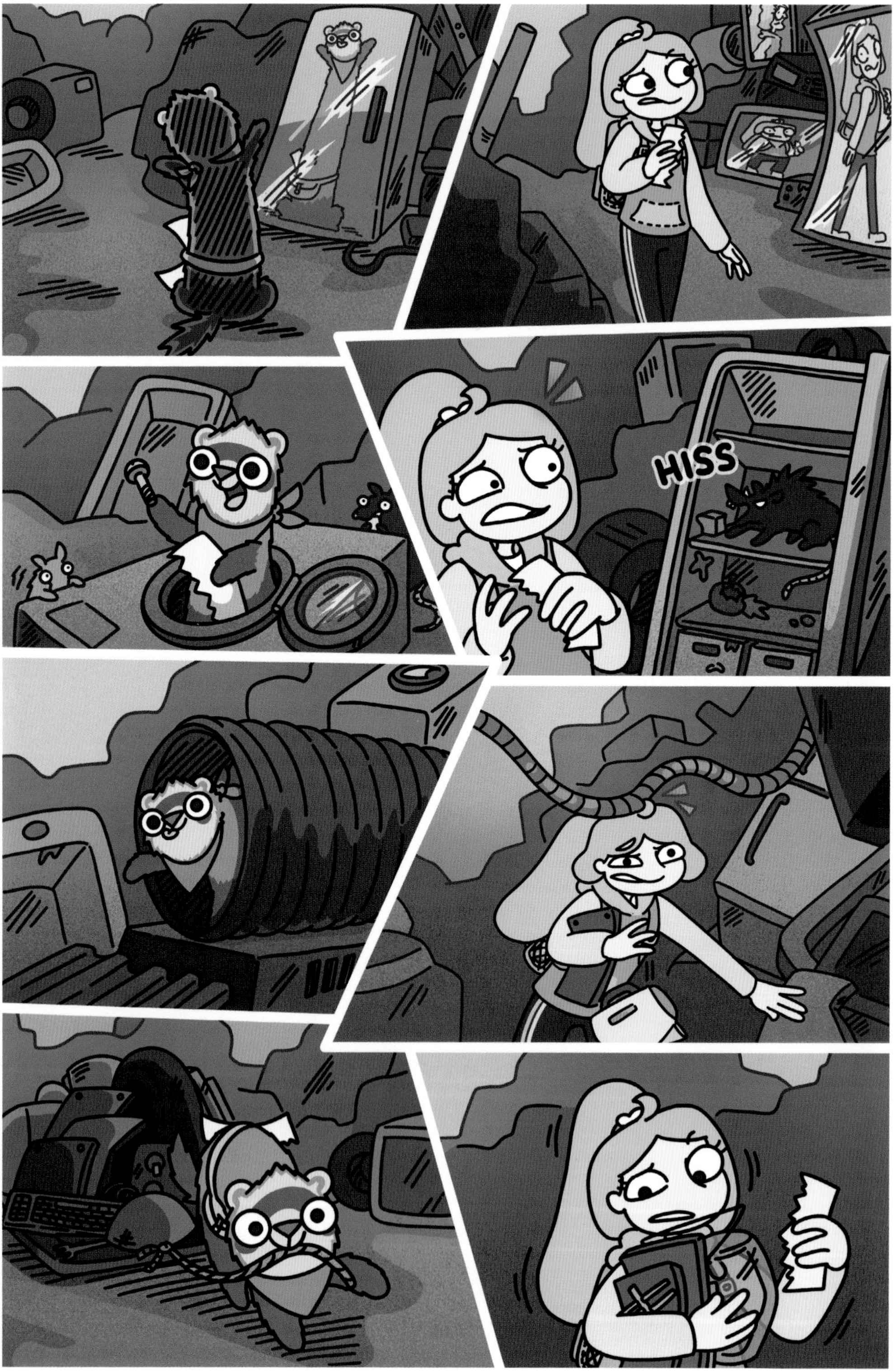
HISS

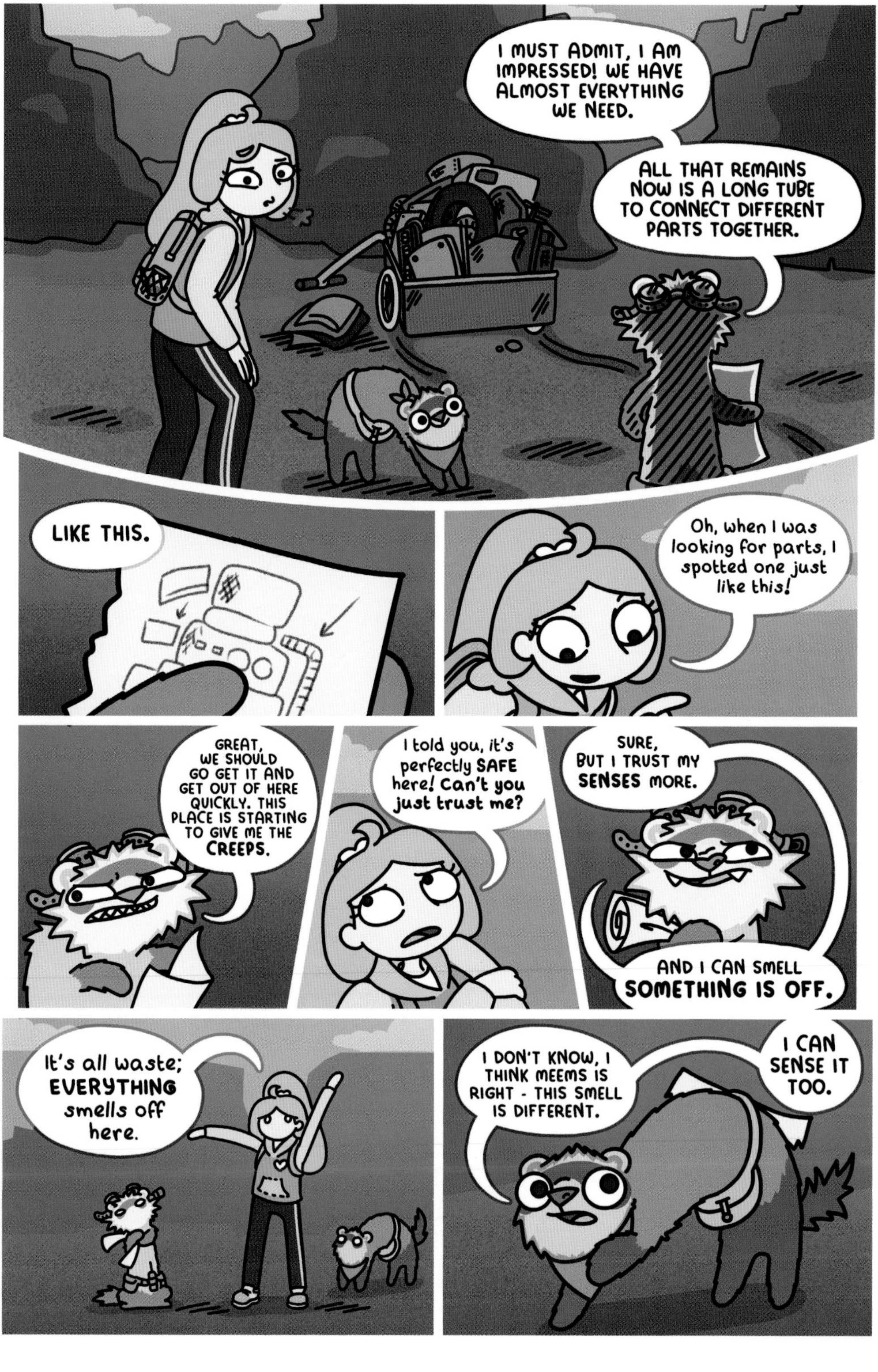
I MUST ADMIT, I AM IMPRESSED! WE HAVE ALMOST EVERYTHING WE NEED.
ALL THAT REMAINS NOW IS A LONG TUBE TO CONNECT DIFFERENT PARTS TOGETHER.
LIKE THIS.
Oh, when I was looking for parts, I spotted one just like this!
GREAT, WE SHOULD GO GET IT AND GET OUT OF HERE QUICKLY. THIS PLACE IS STARTING TO GIVE ME THE CREEPS.
I told you, it's perfectly SAFE here! Can't you just trust me?
SURE, BUT I TRUST MY SENSES MORE.
AND I CAN SMELL SOMETHING IS OFF.
It's all waste; EVERYTHING smells off here.
I DON'T KNOW, I THINK MEEMS IS RIGHT - THIS SMELL IS DIFFERENT.
I CAN SENSE IT TOO.

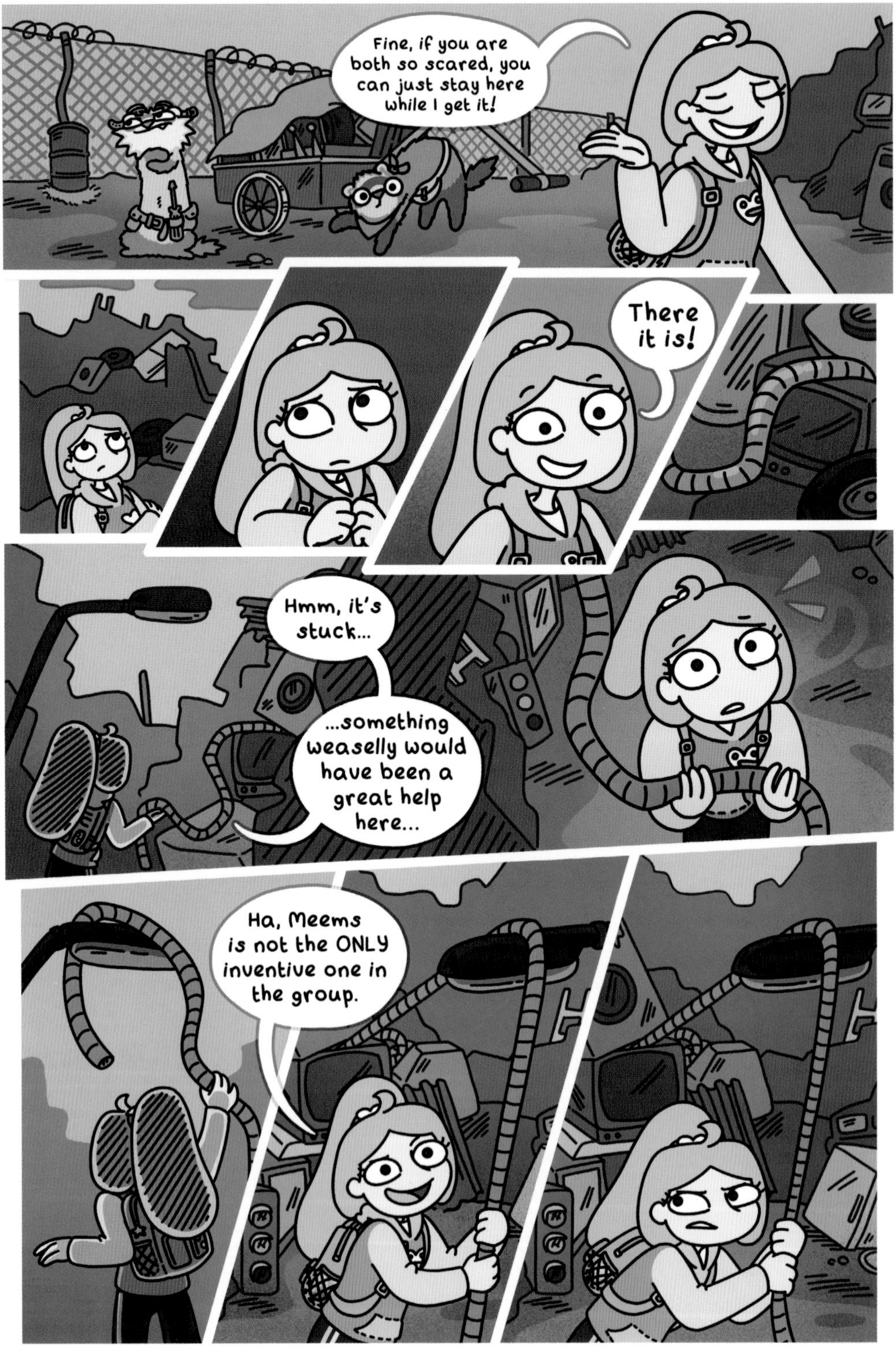

Fine, if you are both so scared, you can just stay here while I get it!
There it is!
Hmm, it's stuck...
...something weaselly would have been a great help here...
Ha, Meems is not the ONLY inventive one in the group.

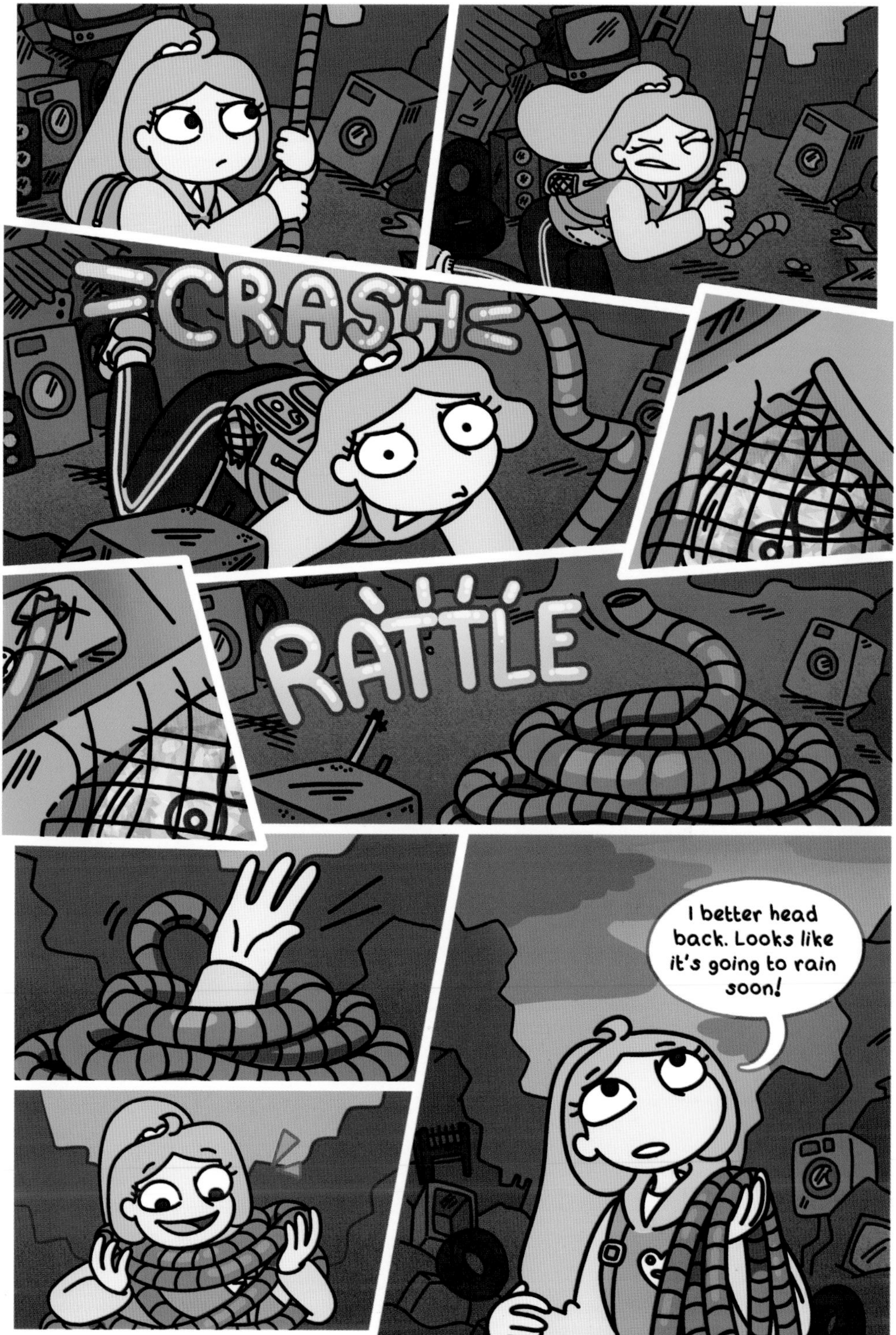
CRASH
RATTLE
I better head back. Looks like it's going to rain soon!

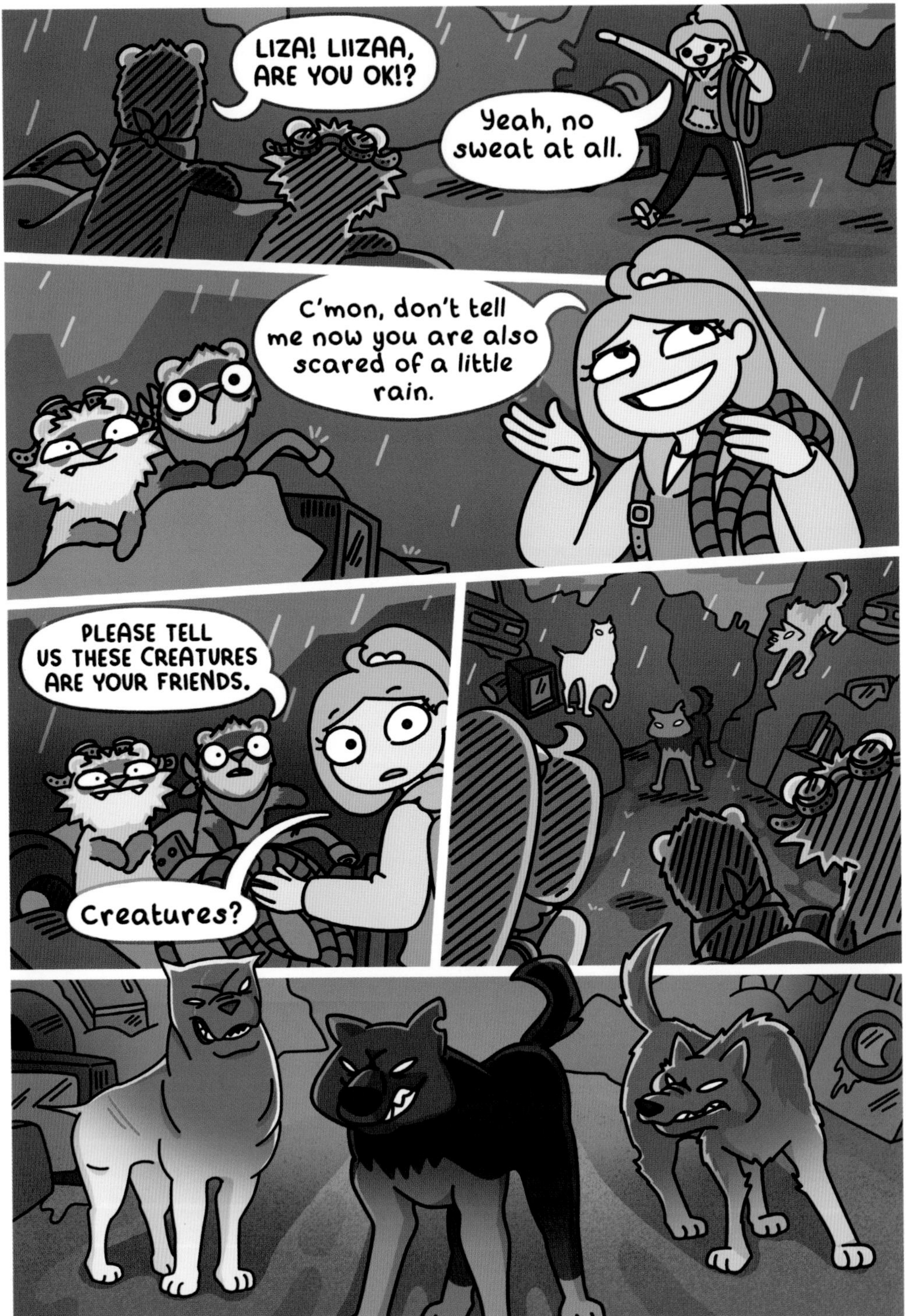
LIZA! LIIZAA, ARE YOU OK!?
Yeah, no sweat at all.
C'mon, don't tell me now you are also scared of a little rain.
PLEASE TELL US THESE CREATURES ARE YOUR FRIENDS.
Creatures?
....HOLD ON!

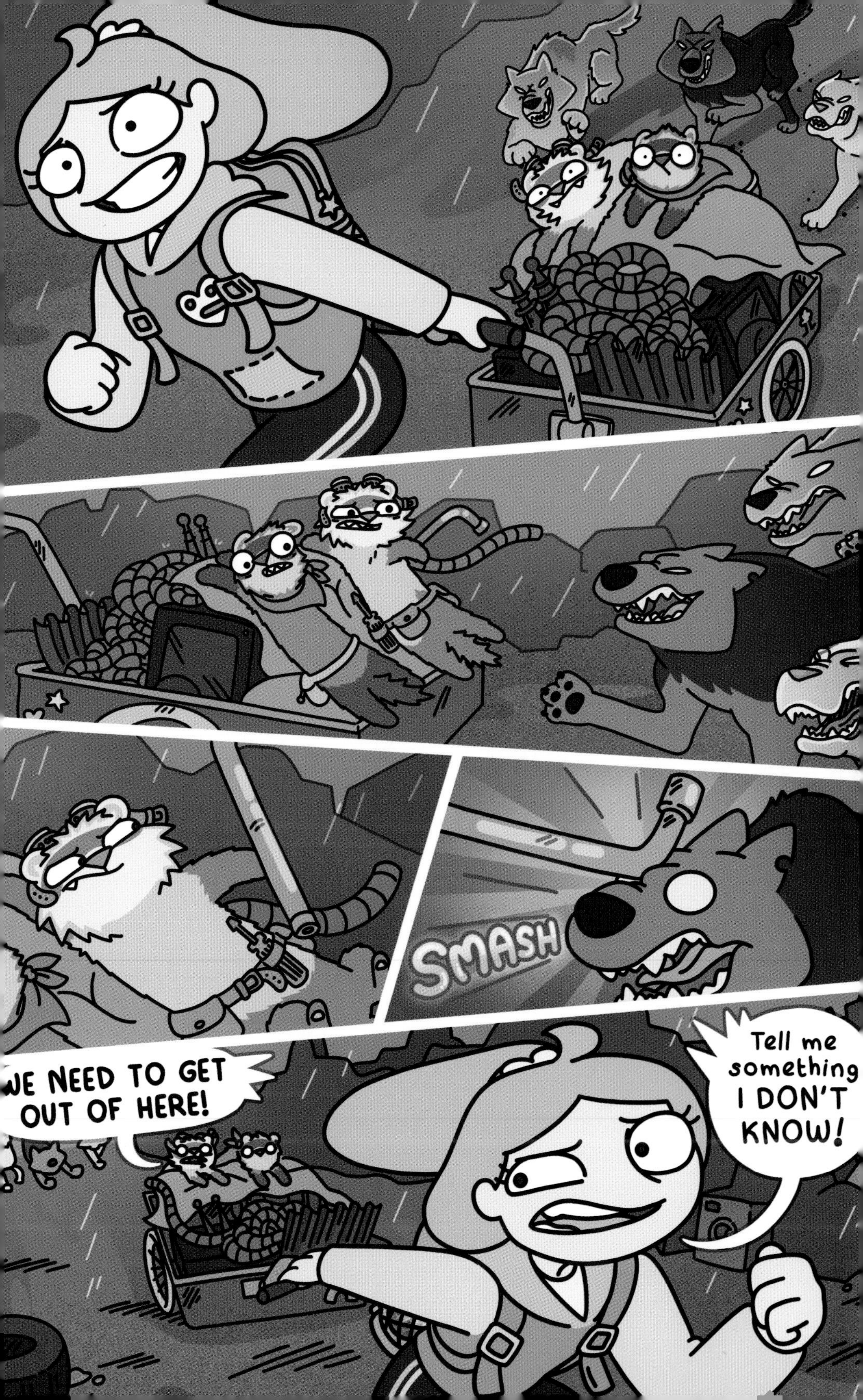
SMASH
WE NEED TO GET OUT OF HERE!
Tell me something I DON'T KNOW!

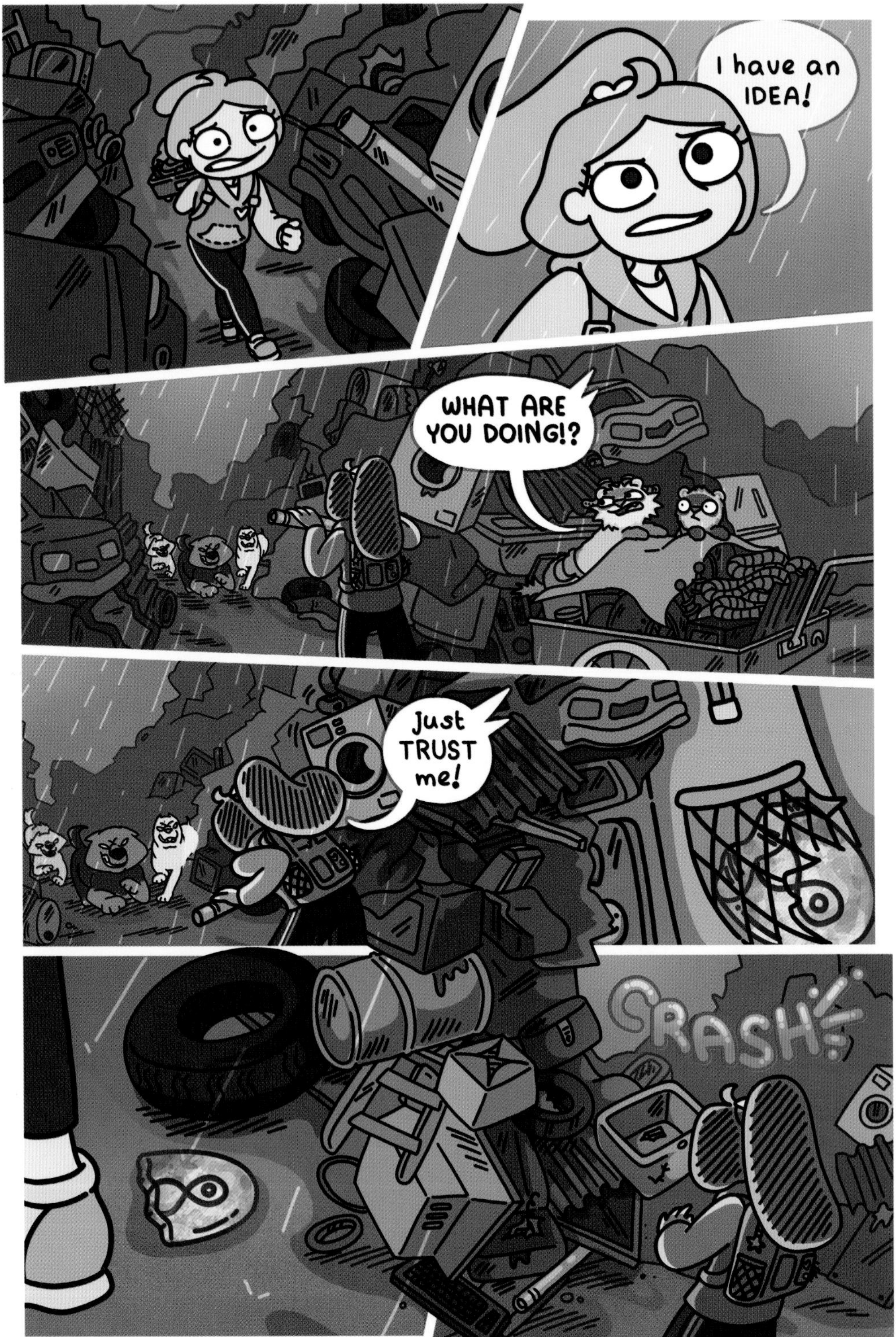
I have an IDEA!
WHAT ARE YOU DOING!?
Just TRUST me!
CRASH

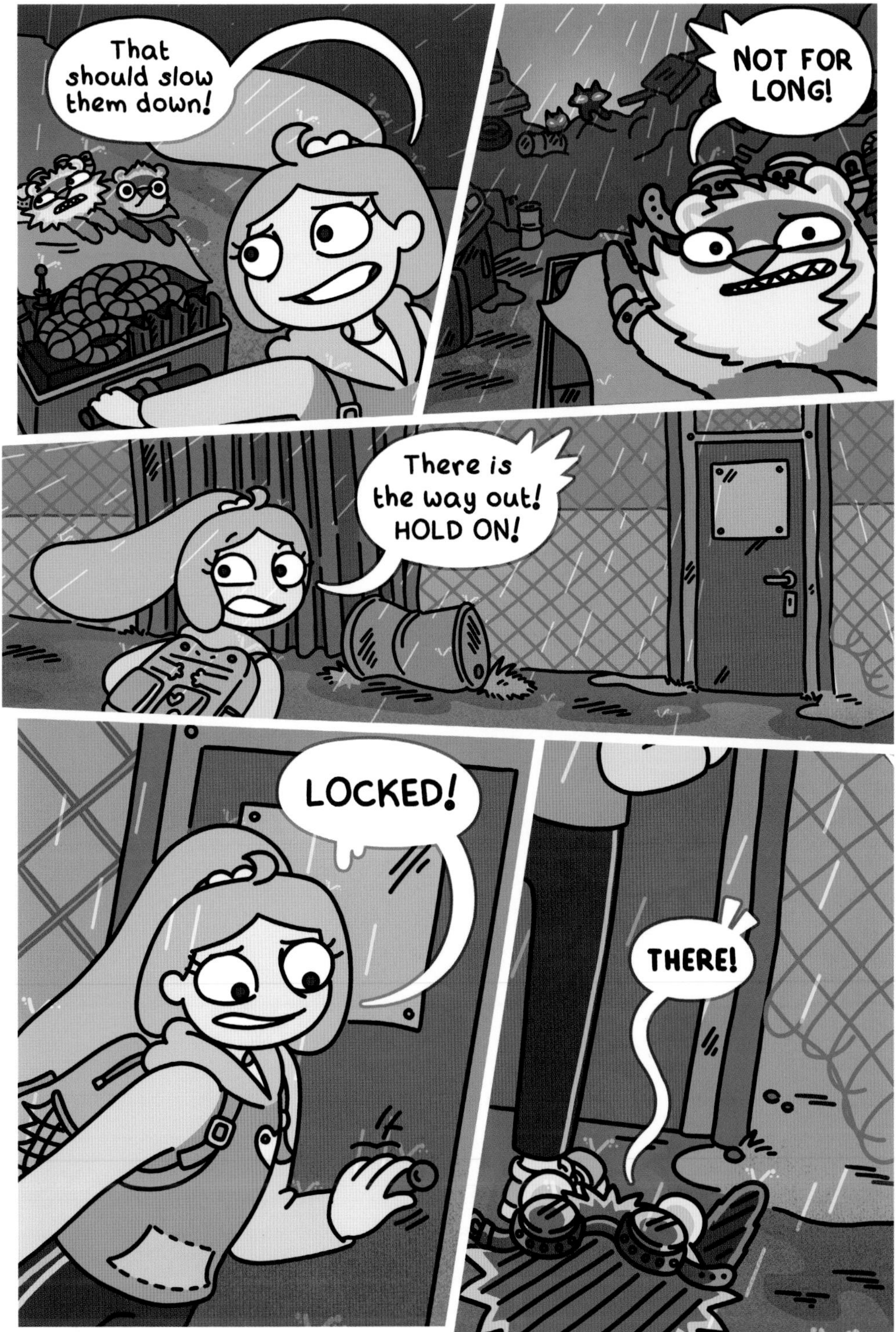
That should slow them down!
NOT FOR LONG!
There is the way out! HOLD ON!
LOCKED!
THERE!

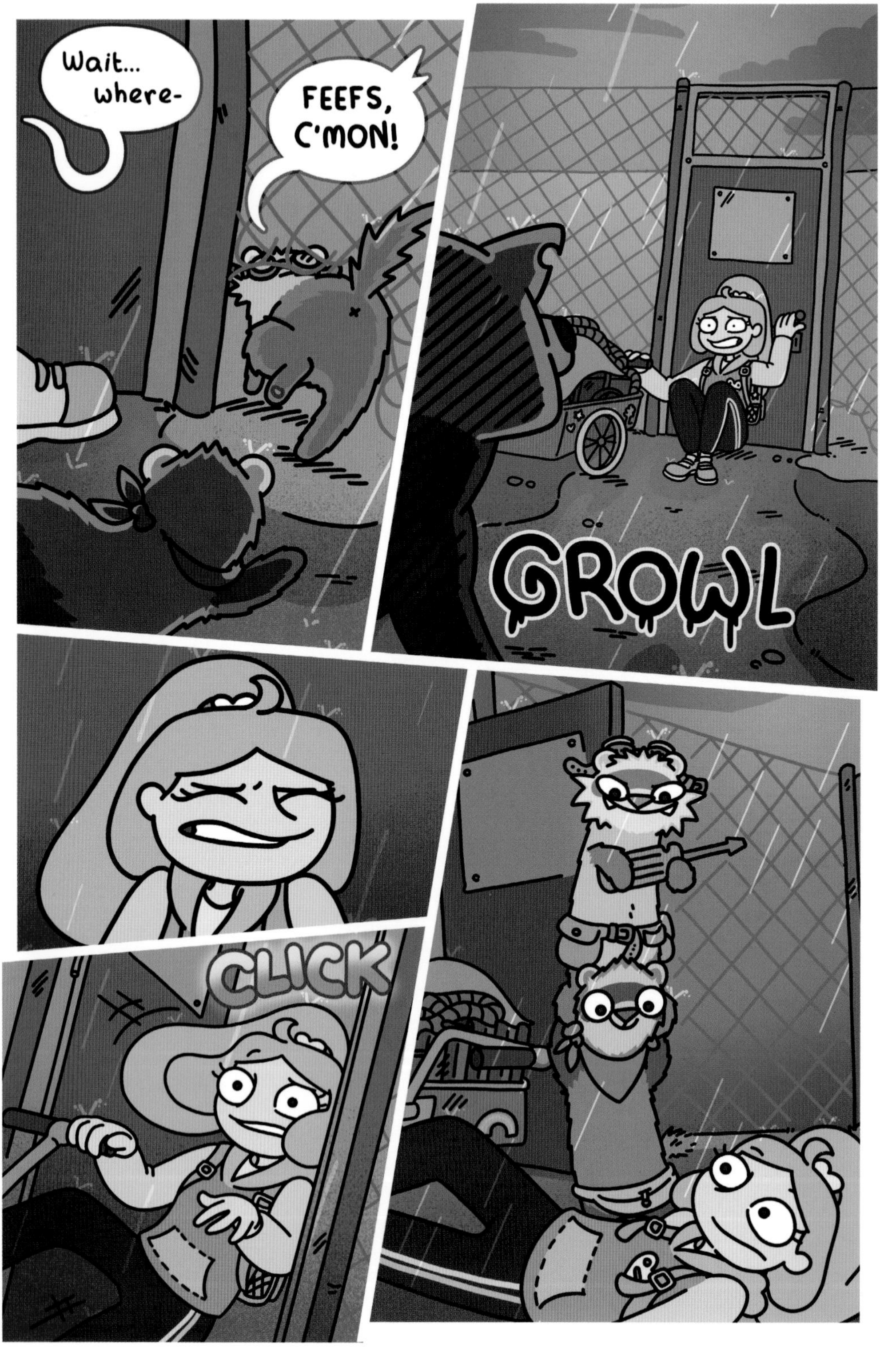
Wait... where-
FEEFS, C'MON!
GROWL
CLICK

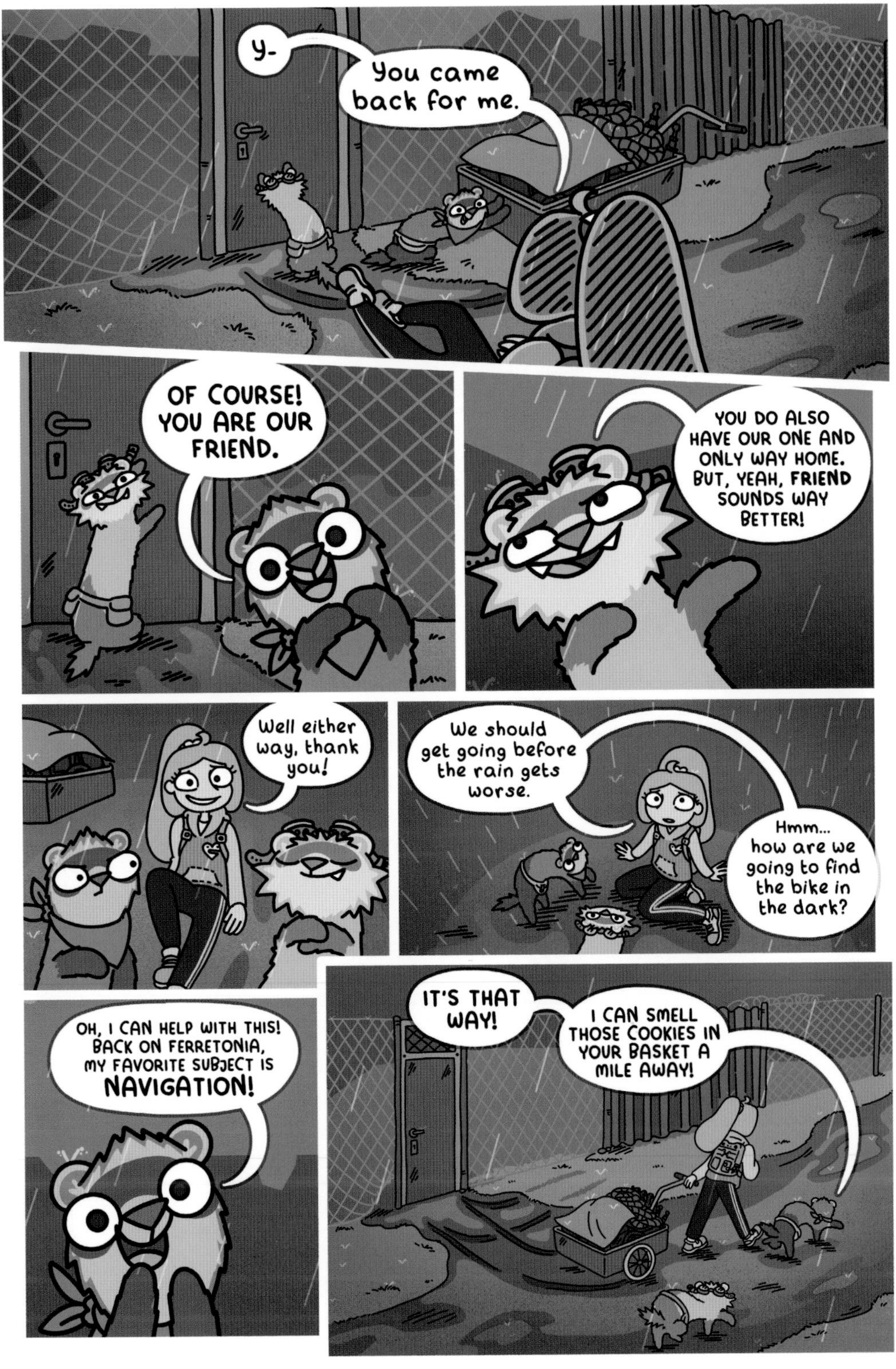
Y-
You came back for me.
OF COURSE! YOU ARE OUR FRIEND.
YOU DO ALSO HAVE OUR ONE AND ONLY WAY HOME. BUT, YEAH, FRIEND SOUNDS WAY BETTER!
Well either way, thank you!
We should get going before the rain gets worse.
Hmm... how are we going to find the bike in the dark?
OH, I CAN HELP WITH THIS! BACK ON FERRETONIA, MY FAVORITE SUBJECT IS NAVIGATION!
IT'S THAT WAY!
I CAN SMELL THOSE COOKIES IN YOUR BASKET A MILE AWAY!

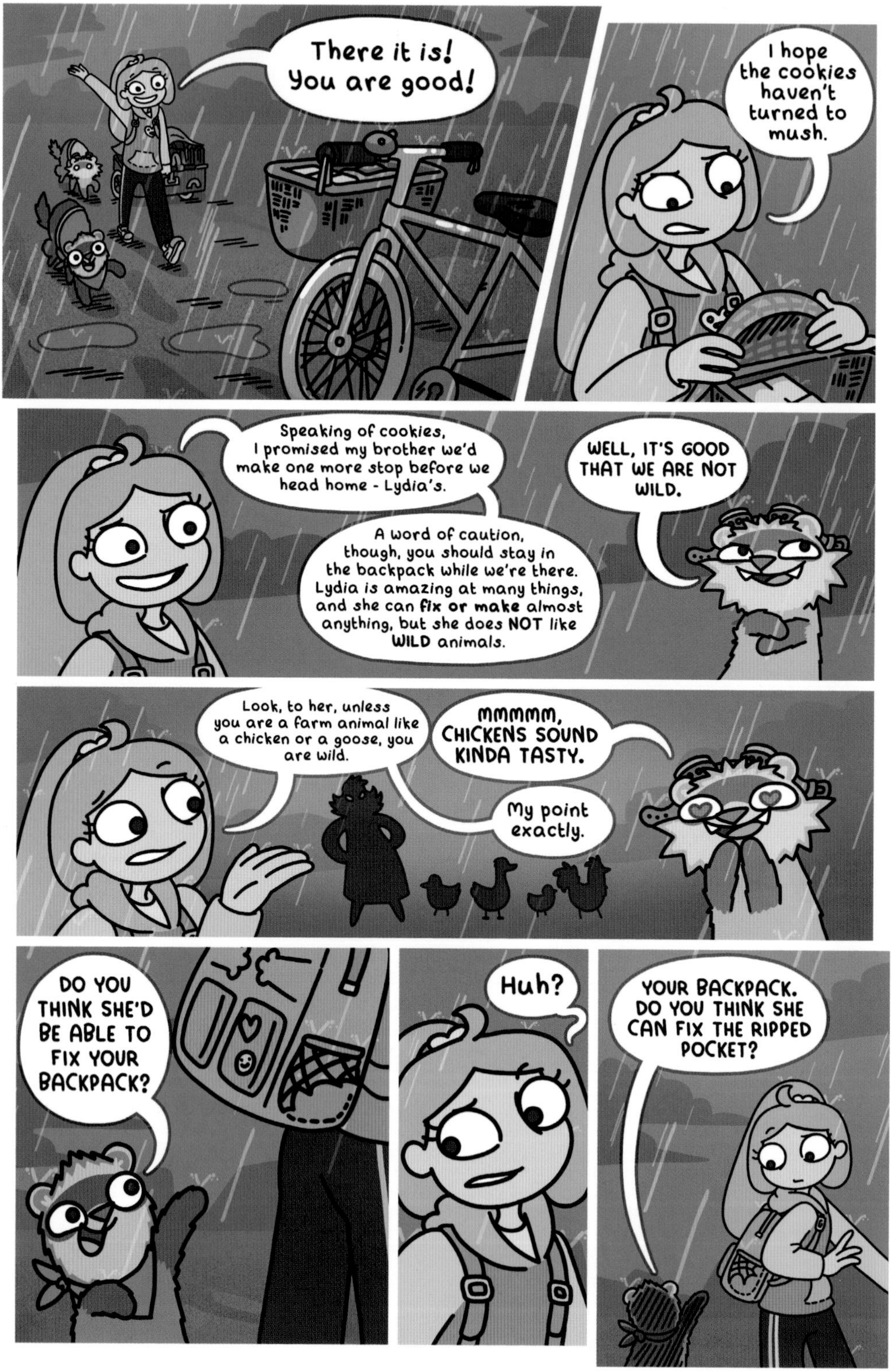
There it is! You are good!
I hope the cookies haven't turned to mush.
Speaking of cookies, I promised my brother we'd make one more stop before we head home - Lydia's.
A word of caution, though, you should stay in the backpack while we're there. Lydia is amazing at many things, and she can fix or make almost anything, but she does NOT like WILD animals.
WELL, IT'S GOOD THAT WE ARE NOT WILD.
Look, to her, unless you are a farm animal like a chicken or a goose, you are wild.
MMMMM, CHICKENS SOUND KINDA TASTY.
My point exactly.
DO YOU THINK SHE'D BE ABLE TO FIX YOUR BACKPACK?
Huh?
YOUR BACKPACK. DO YOU THINK SHE CAN FIX THE RIPPED POCKET?

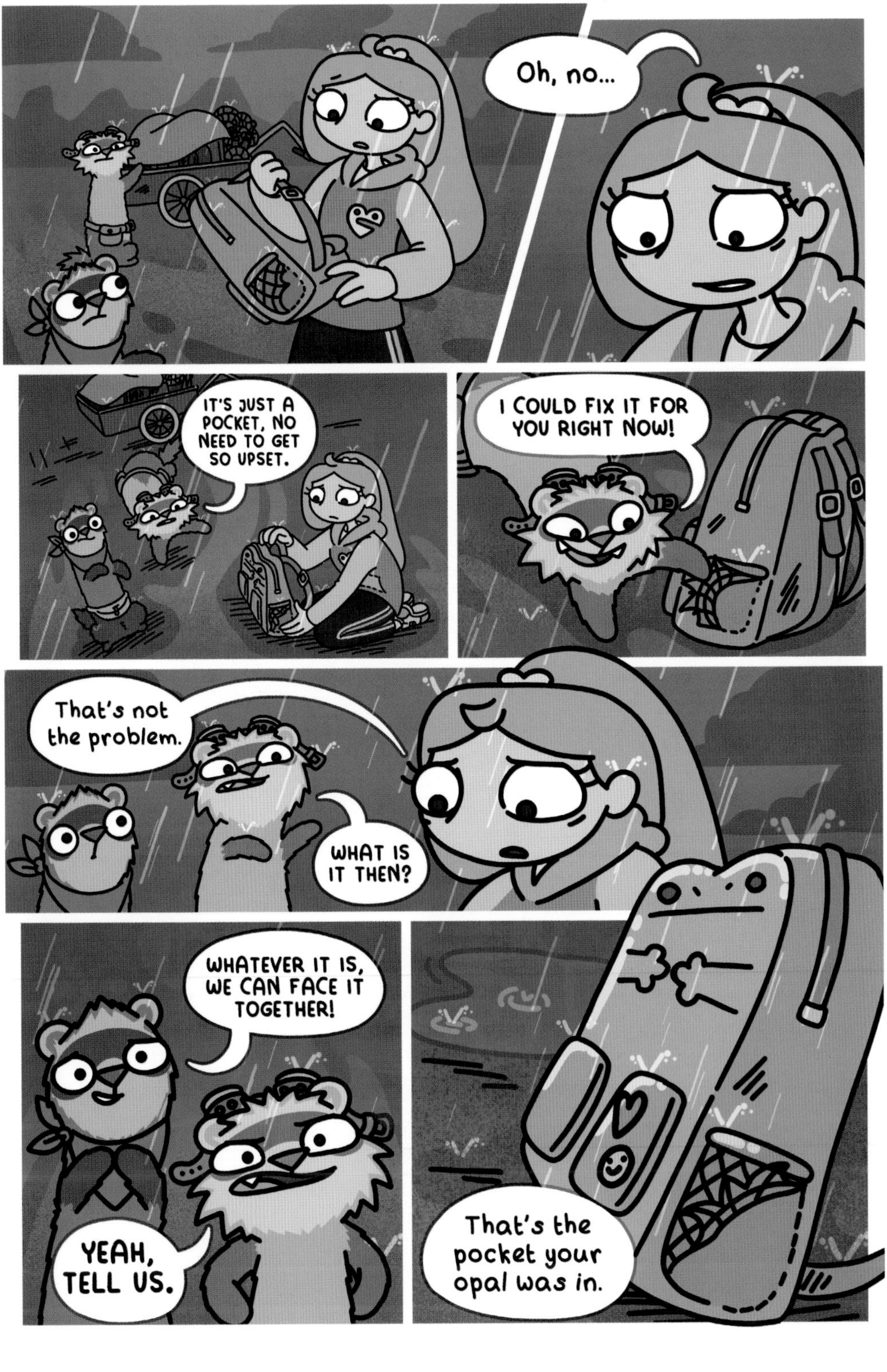
Oh, no...
IT'S JUST A POCKET, NO NEED TO GET SO UPSET.
I COULD FIX IT FOR YOU RIGHT NOW!
That's not the problem.
WHAT IS IT THEN?
WHATEVER IT IS, WE CAN FACE IT TOGETHER!
YEAH, TELL US.
That's the pocket your opal was in.

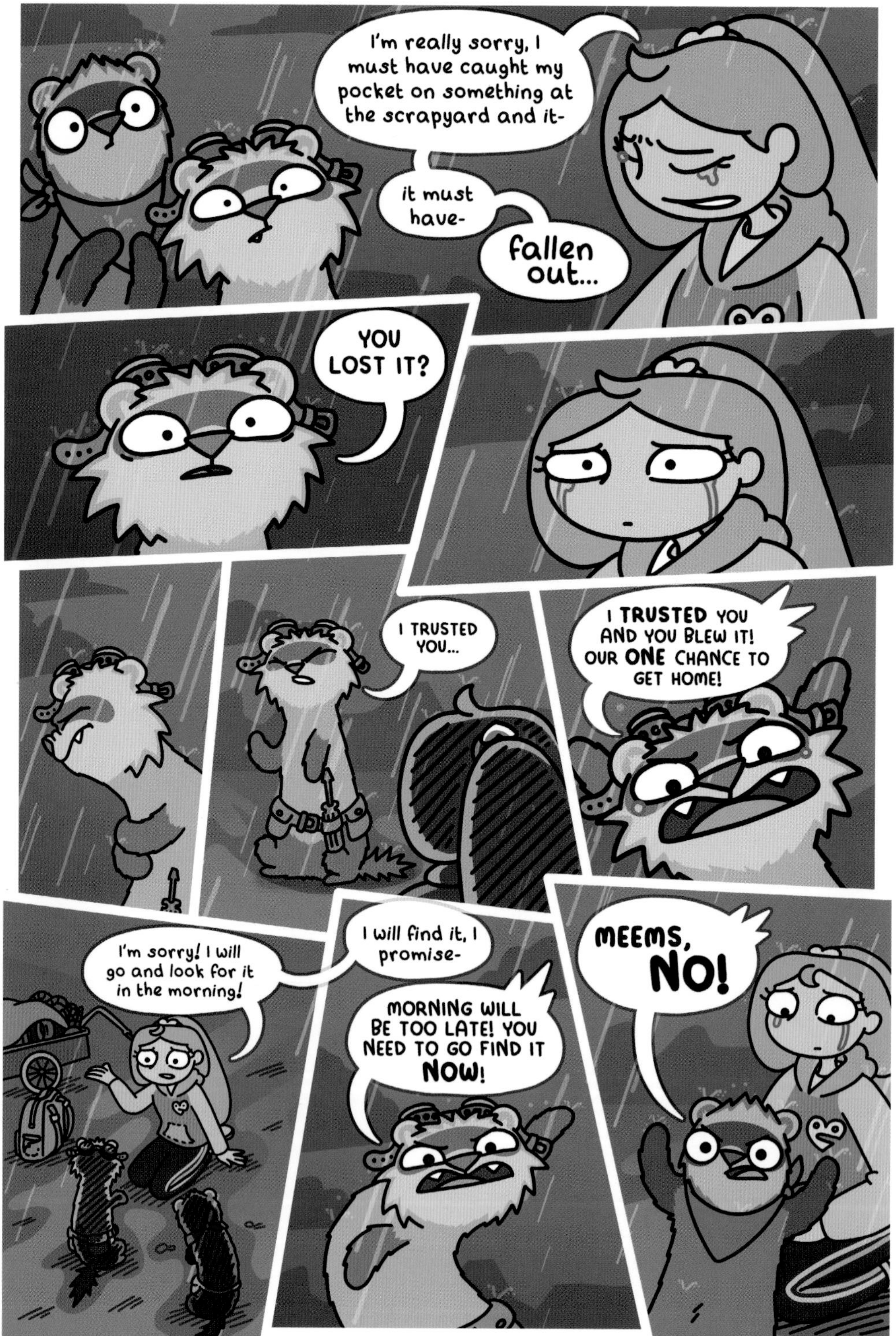
I'm really sorry, I must have caught my pocket on something at the scrapyard and it-
it must have-
fallen out...
YOU LOST IT?
I TRUSTED YOU...
I TRUSTED YOU AND YOU BLEW IT! OUR ONE CHANCE TO GET HOME!
I'm sorry! I will go and look for it in the morning!
I will find it, I promise-
MORNING WILL BE TOO LATE! YOU NEED TO GO FIND IT NOW!
MEEMS, NO!

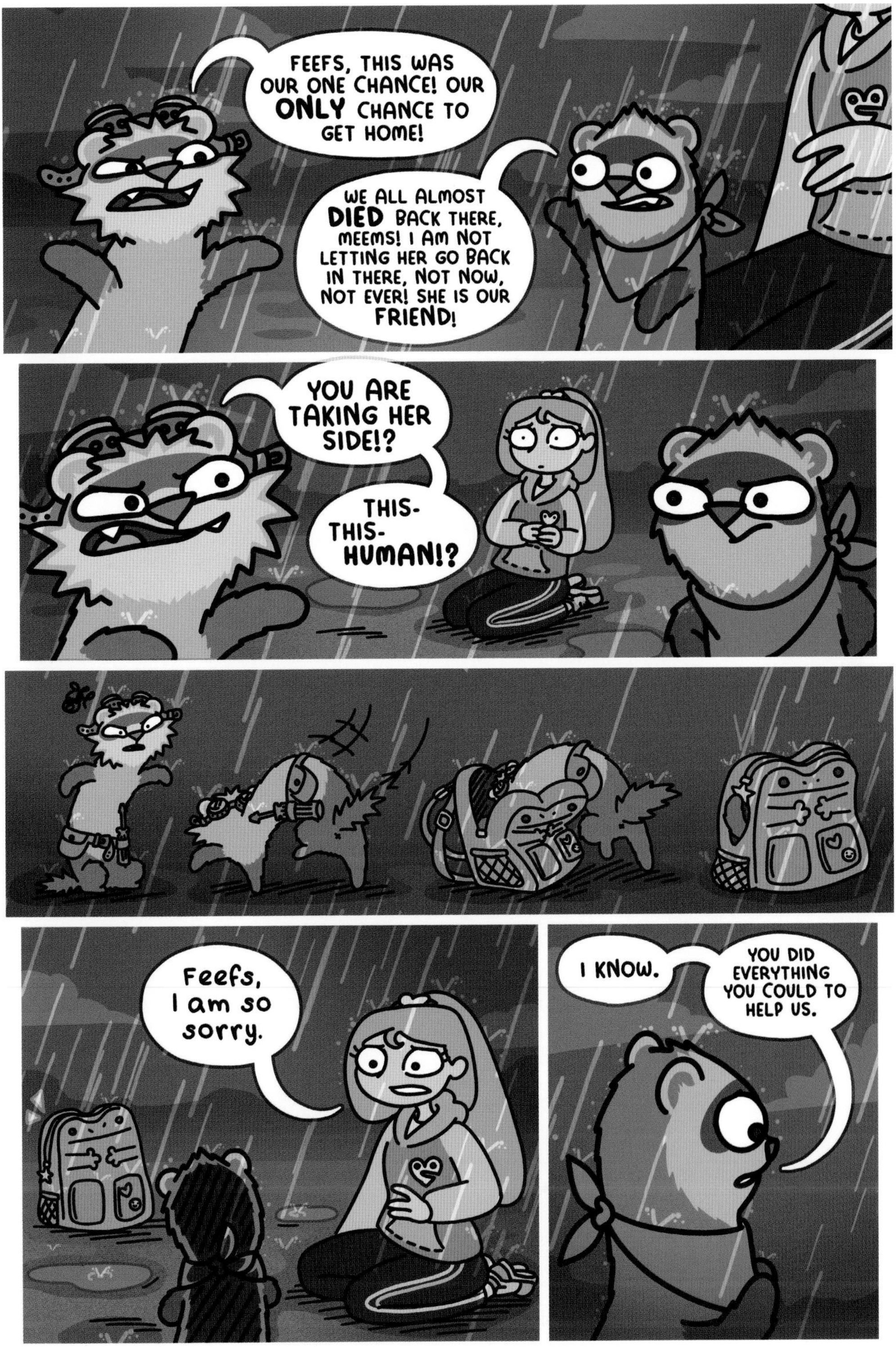
FEEFS, THIS WAS OUR ONE CHANCE! OUR ONLY CHANCE TO GET HOME!
WE ALL ALMOST DIED BACK THERE, MEEMS! I AM NOT LETTING HER GO BACK IN THERE, NOT NOW, NOT EVER! SHE IS OUR FRIEND!
YOU ARE TAKING HER SIDE!?
THIS- THIS- HUMAN!?
Feefs, I am so sorry.
I KNOW.
YOU DID EVERYTHING YOU COULD TO HELP US.

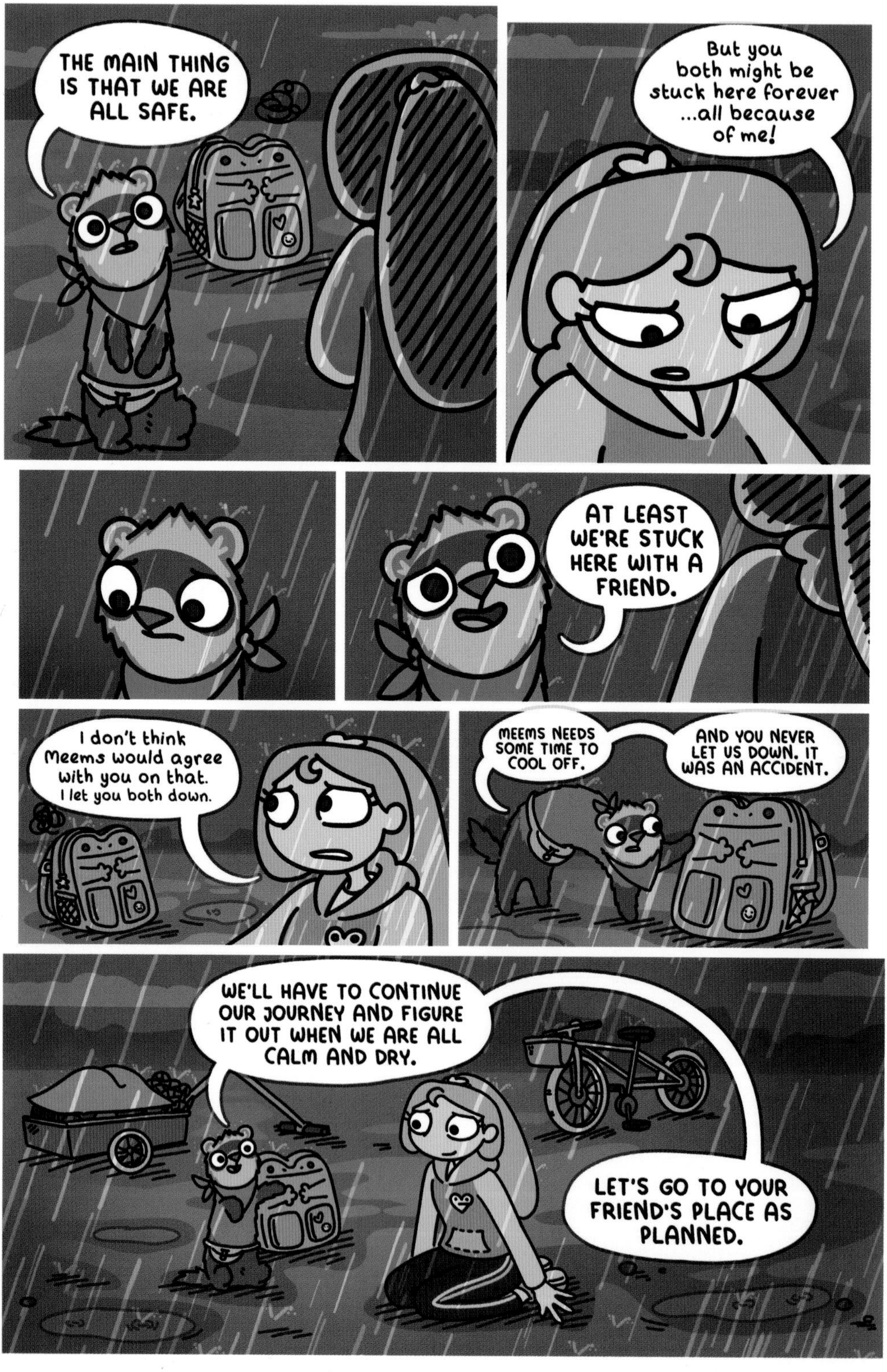
THE MAIN THING IS THAT WE ARE ALL SAFE.
But you both might be stuck here forever ...all because of me!
AT LEAST WE'RE STUCK HERE WITH A FRIEND.
I don't think Meems would agree with you on that. I let you both down.
MEEMS NEEDS SOME TIME TO COOL OFF.
AND YOU NEVER LET US DOWN. IT WAS AN ACCIDENT.
WE'LL HAVE TO CONTINUE OUR JOURNEY AND FIGURE IT OUT WHEN WE ARE ALL CALM AND DRY.
LET'S GO TO YOUR FRIEND'S PLACE AS PLANNED.

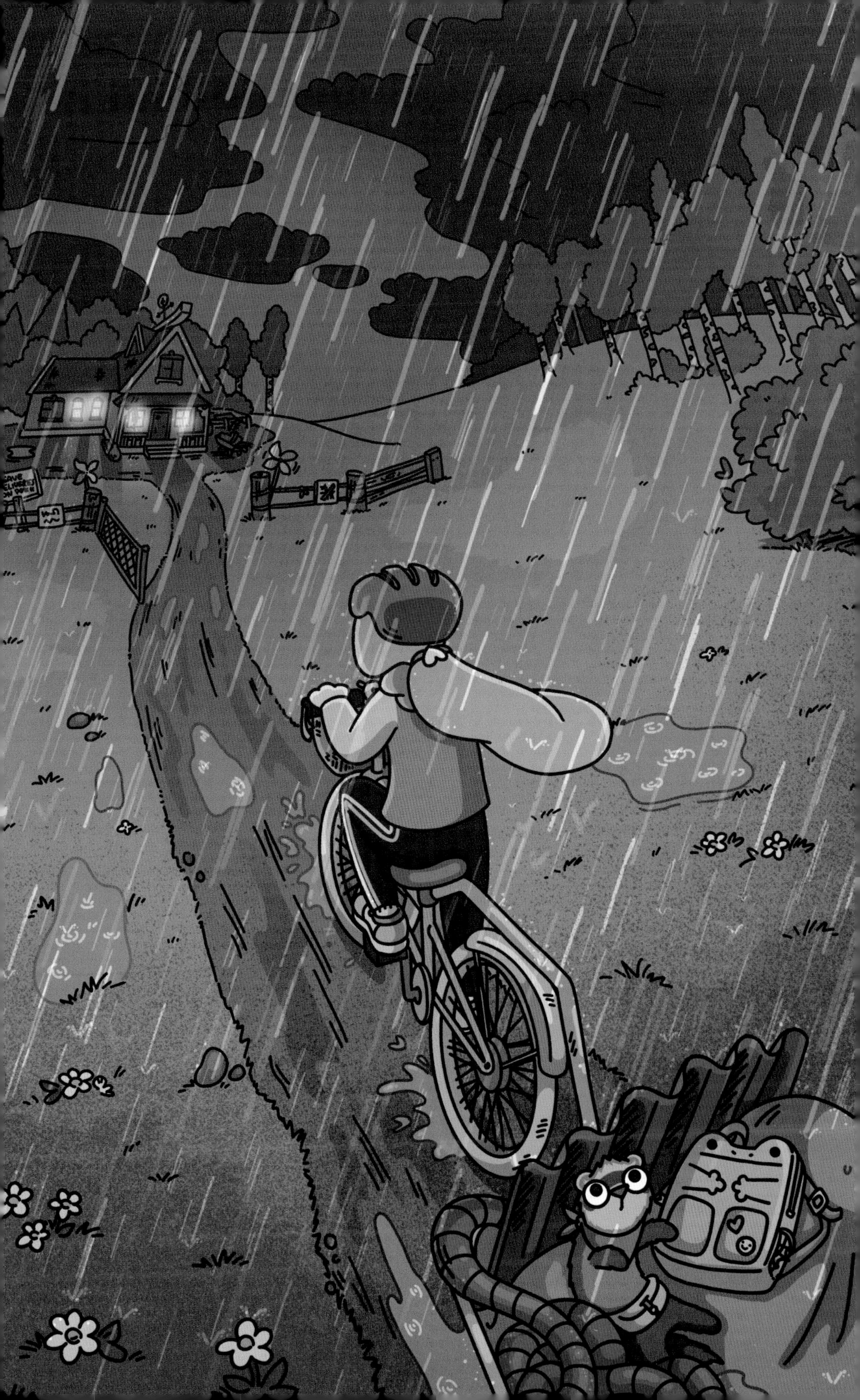

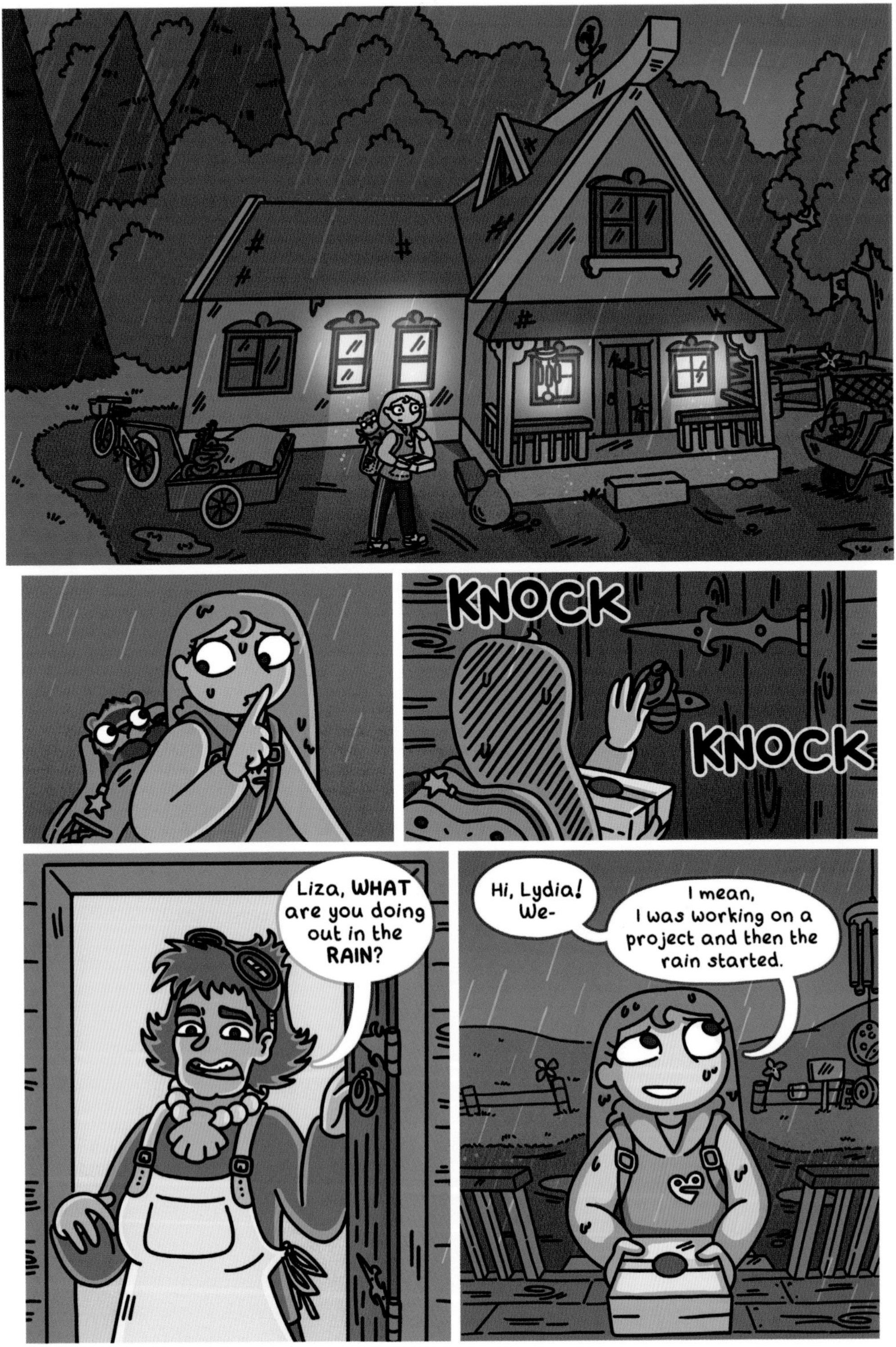

KNOCK
KNOCK
Liza, WHAT are you doing out in the RAIN?
Hi, Lydia! We-
I mean, I was working on a project and then the rain started.

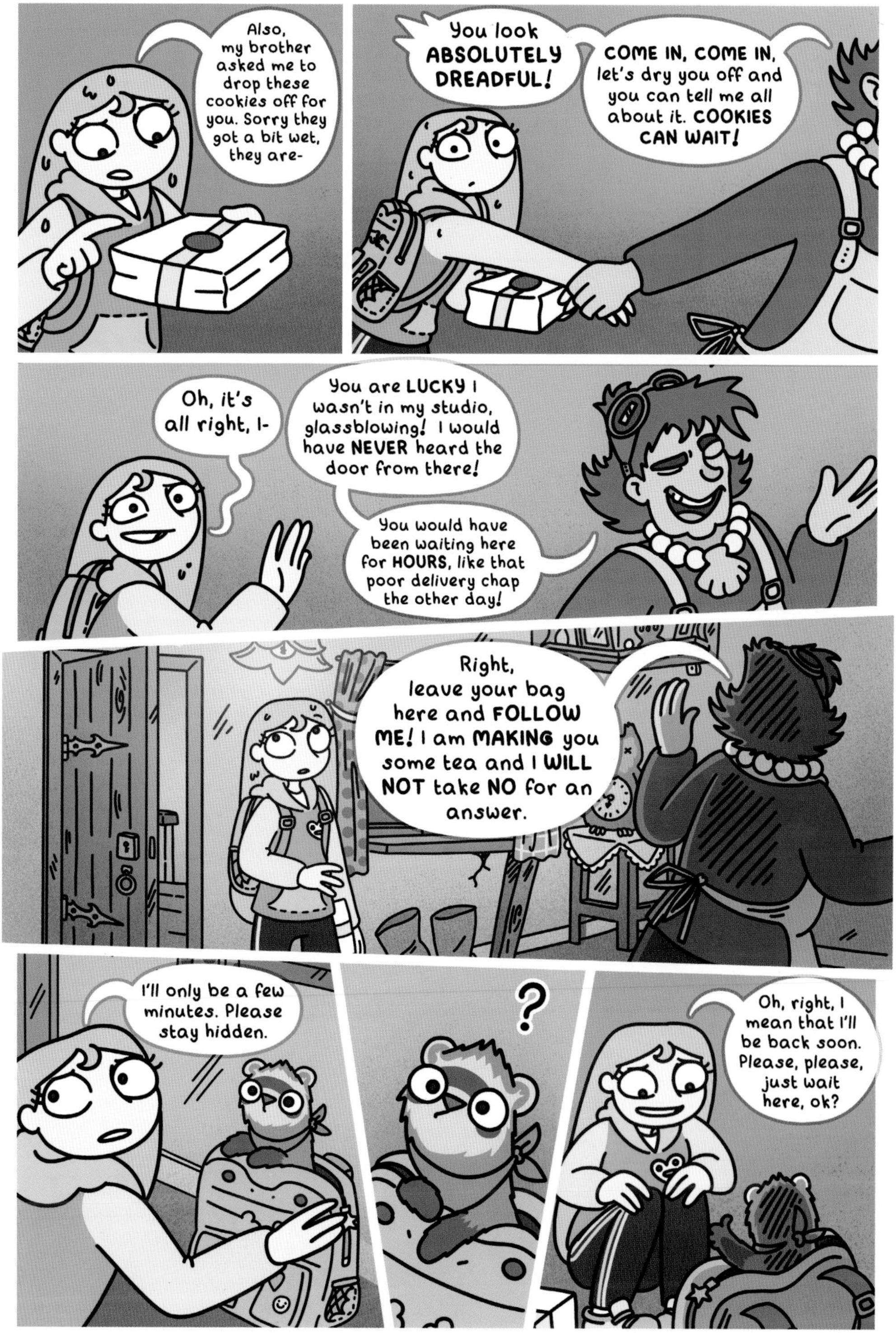
Also, my brother asked me to drop these cookies off for you. Sorry they got a bit wet, they are-
You look ABSOLUTELY DREADFUL!
COME IN, COME IN, let's dry you off and you can tell me all about it. COOKIES CAN WAIT!
Oh, it's all right, I-
You are LUCKY I wasn't in my studio, glassblowing! I would have NEVER heard the door from there!
You would have been waiting here for HOURS, like that poor delivery chap the other day!
Right, leave your bag here and FOLLOW ME! I am MAKING you some tea and I WILL NOT take NO for an answer.
I'll only be a few minutes. Please stay hidden.
?
Oh, right, I mean that I'll be back soon. Please, please, just wait here, ok?

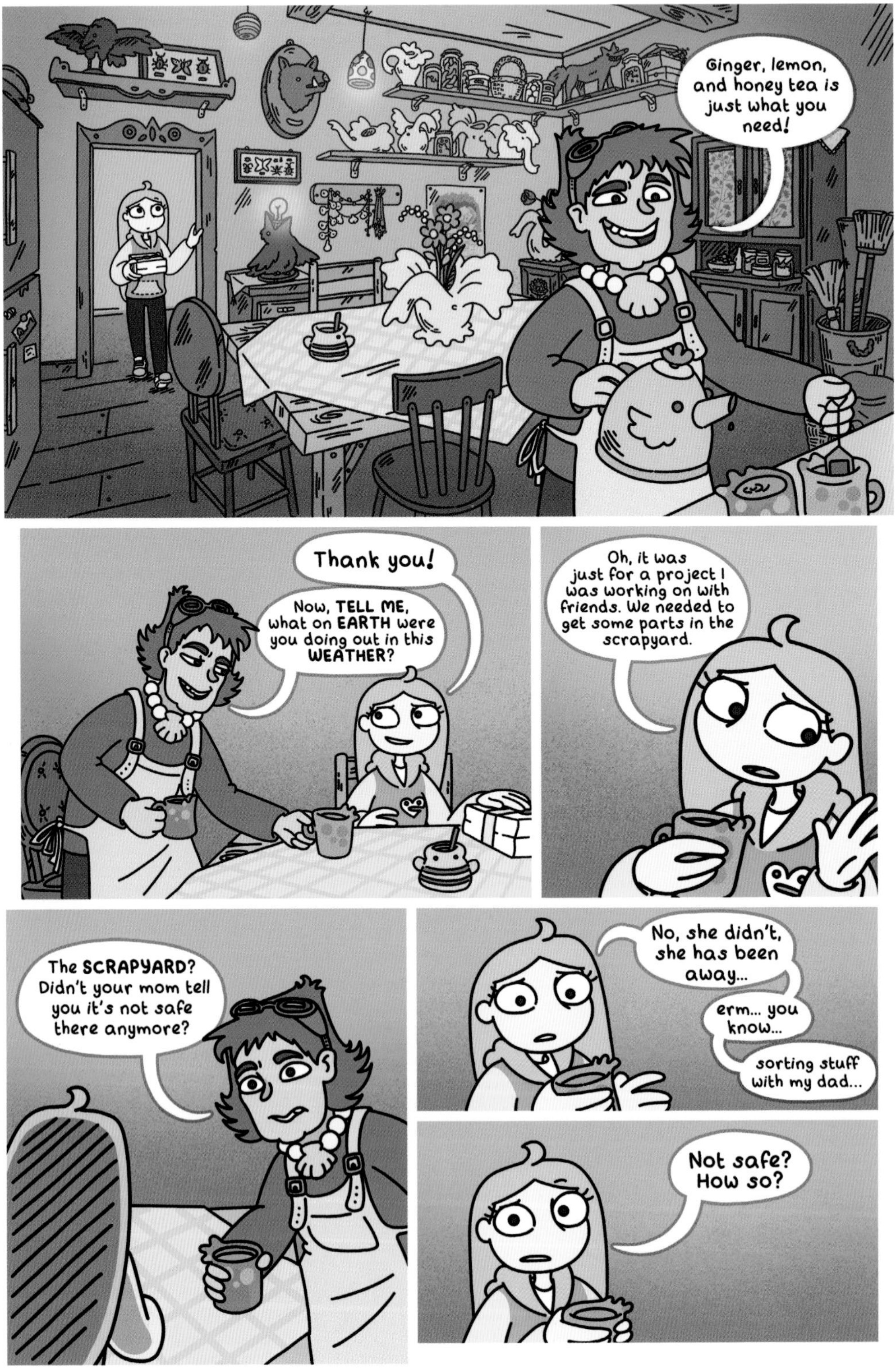
Ginger, lemon, and honey tea is just what you need!
Thank you!
Now, TELL ME, what on EARTH were you doing out in this WEATHER?
Oh, it was just for a project I was working on with friends. We needed to get some parts in the scrapyard.
The SCRAPYARD? Didn't your mom tell you it's not safe there anymore?
No, she didn't, she has been away...
erm... you know...
sorting stuff with my dad...
Not safe? How so?

WELL, the place changed owners not long ago, and now they released a bunch of **RABID HOUNDS** to run around that place **UNCONTROLLED**...

...those filthy furry fiends....

You should **STAY AWAY** from the Scrapyard from now on.

Thank you, I will keep that in mind...

I am glad you didn't run into them already. Those things will chase **ANYTHING** that moves.

Just remember this: **NEVER** make the mistake of running away from a dog pack.

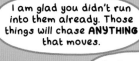

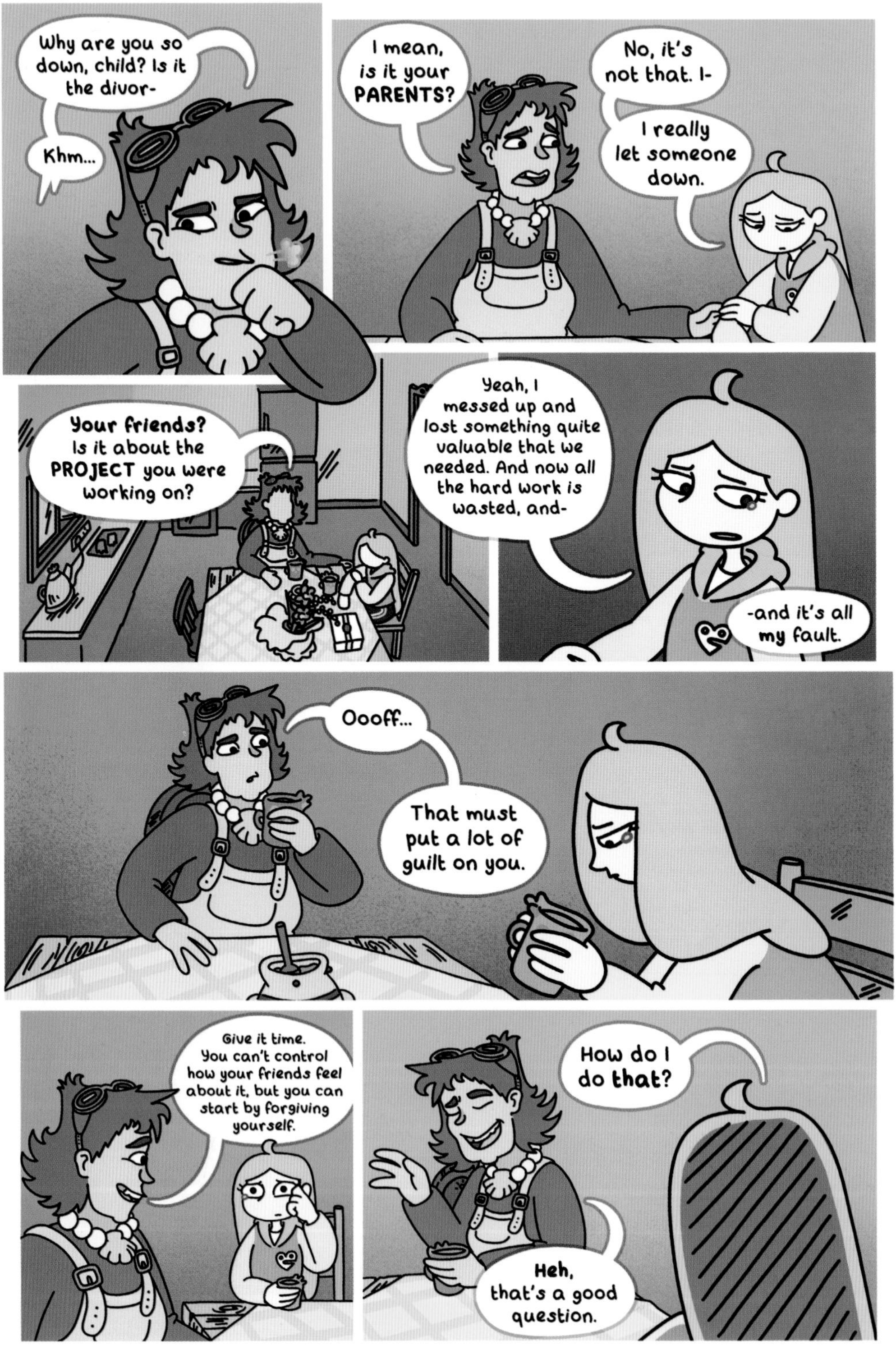
Why are you so down, child? Is it the divor-
Khm...
I mean, is it your PARENTS?
No, it's not that. I-
I really let someone down.
Your friends? Is it about the PROJECT you were working on?
Yeah, I messed up and lost something quite valuable that we needed. And now all the hard work is wasted, and-
-and it's all my fault.
Oooff...
That must put a lot of guilt on you.
Give it time. You can't control how your friends feel about it, but you can start by forgiving yourself.
How do I do that?
Heh, that's a good question.

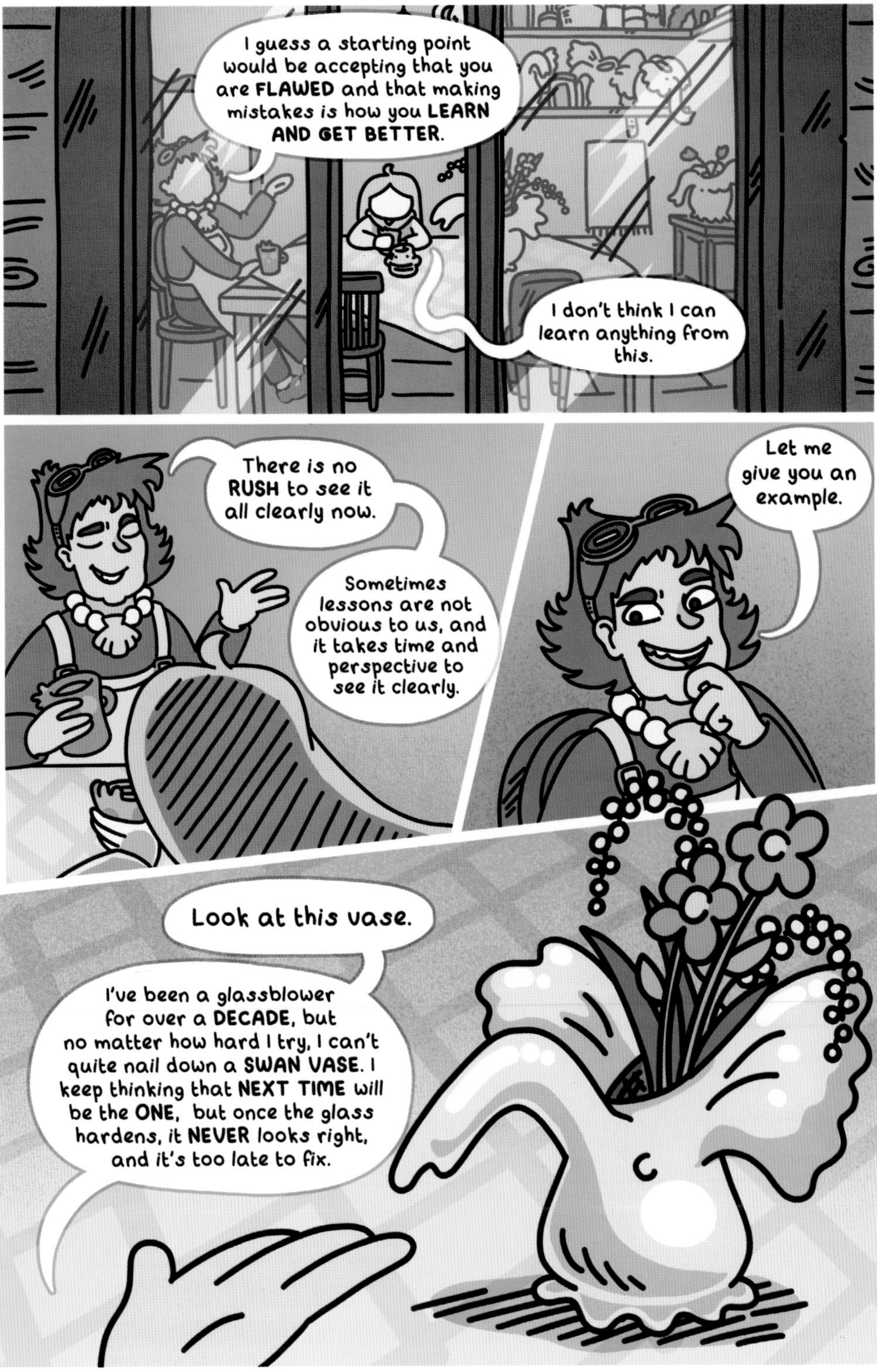

I guess a starting point would be accepting that you are FLAWED and that making mistakes is how you LEARN AND GET BETTER.
I don't think I can learn anything from this.
There is no RUSH to see it all clearly now.
Sometimes lessons are not obvious to us, and it takes time and perspective to see it clearly.
Let me give you an example.
Look at this vase.
I've been a glassblower for over a DECADE, but no matter how hard I try, I can't quite nail down a SWAN VASE. I keep thinking that NEXT TIME will be the ONE, but once the glass hardens, it NEVER looks right, and it's too late to fix.

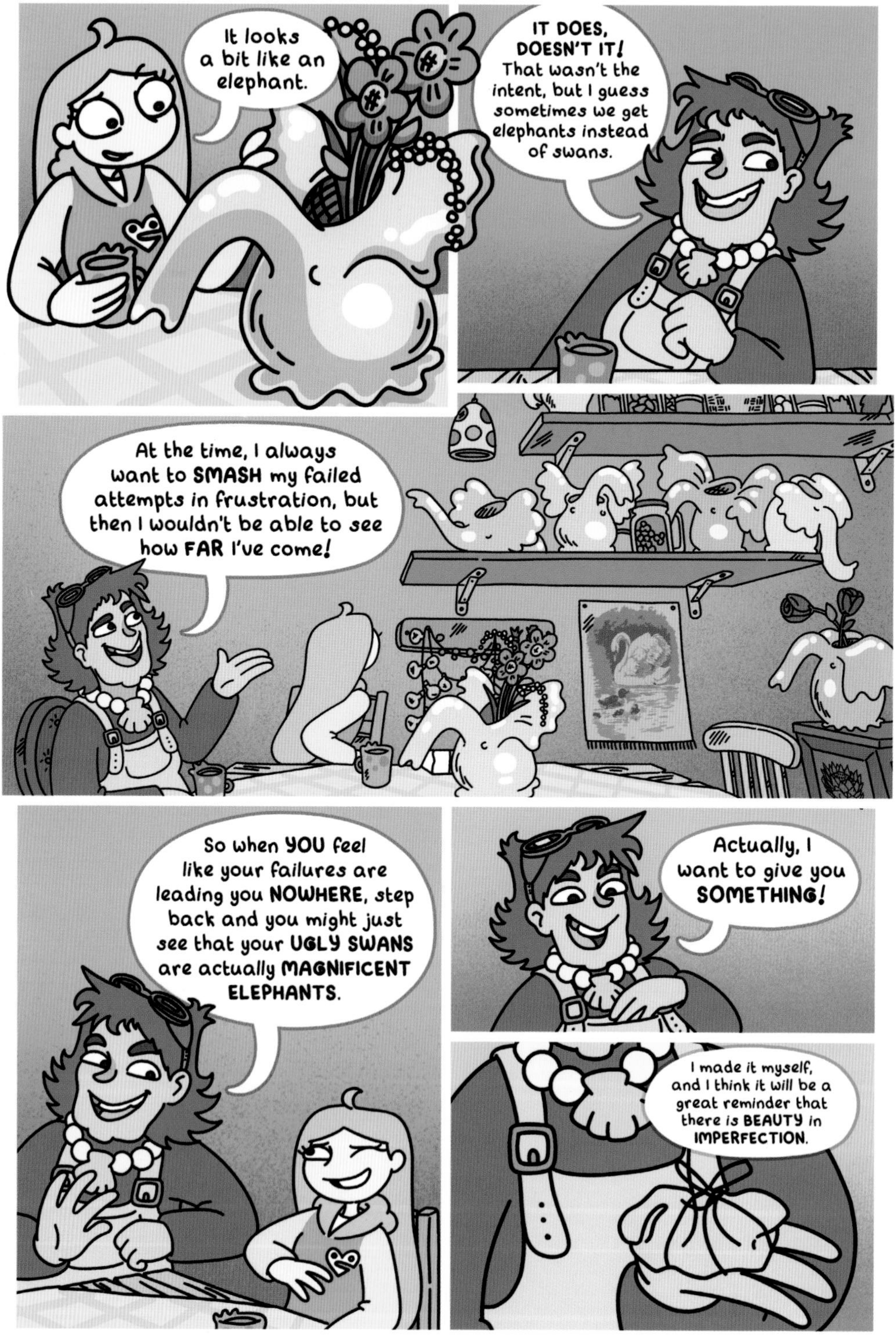
It looks a bit like an elephant.
IT DOES, DOESN'T IT! That wasn't the intent, but I guess sometimes we get elephants instead of swans.
At the time, I always want to SMASH my failed attempts in frustration, but then I wouldn't be able to see how FAR I've come!
So when YOU feel like your failures are leading you NOWHERE, step back and you might just see that your UGLY SWANS are actually MAGNIFICENT ELEPHANTS.
Actually, I want to give you SOMETHING!
I made it myself, and I think it will be a great reminder that there is BEAUTY in IMPERFECTION.

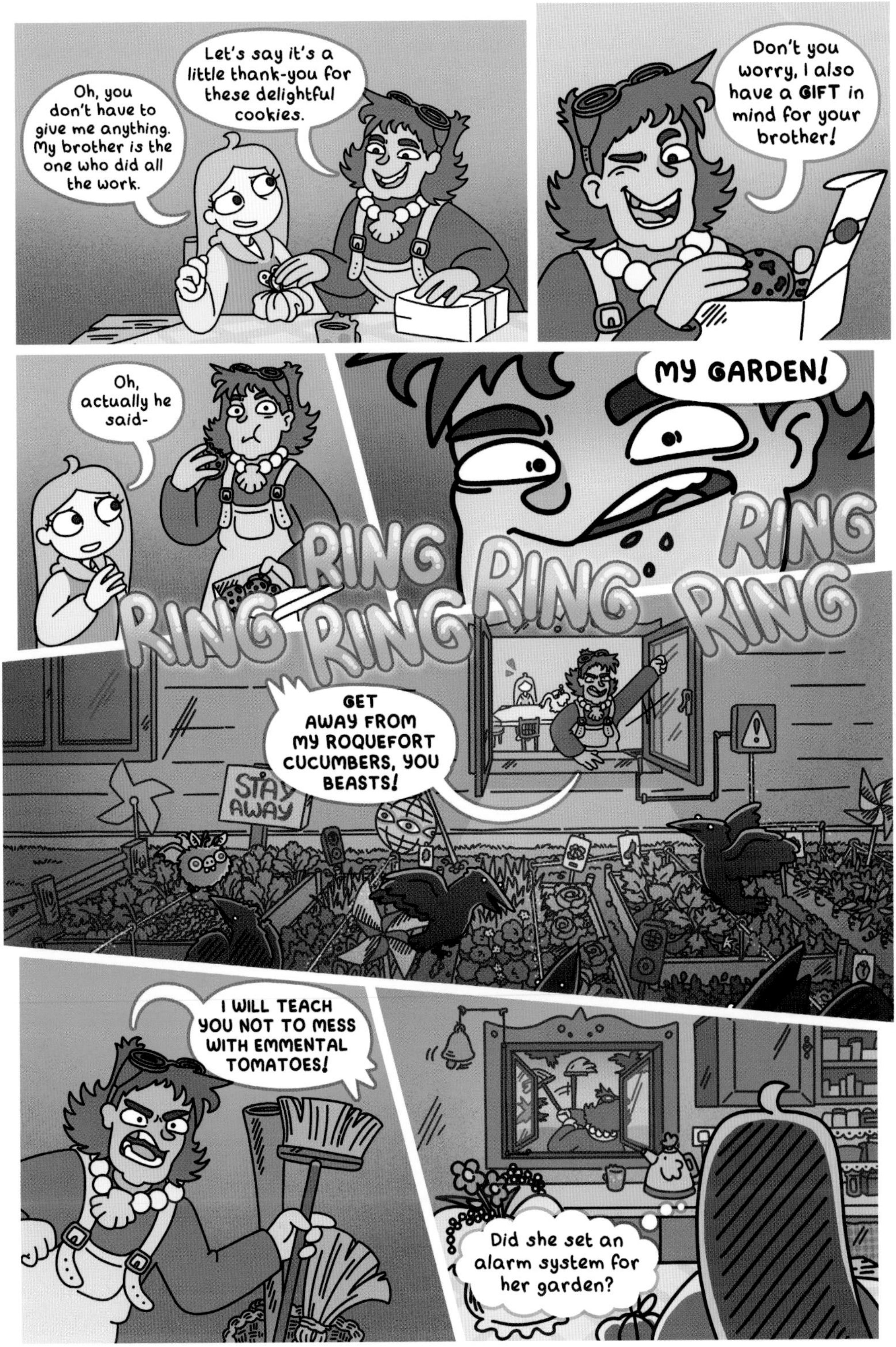
Oh, you don't have to give me anything. My brother is the one who did all the work.
Let's say it's a little thank-you for these delightful cookies.
Don't you worry, I also have a GIFT in mind for your brother!
Oh, actually he said-
MY GARDEN!
RING RING RING RING RING RING
GET AWAY FROM MY ROQUEFORT CUCUMBERS, YOU BEASTS!
STAY AWAY
I WILL TEACH YOU NOT TO MESS WITH EMMENTAL TOMATOES!
Did she set an alarm system for her garden?

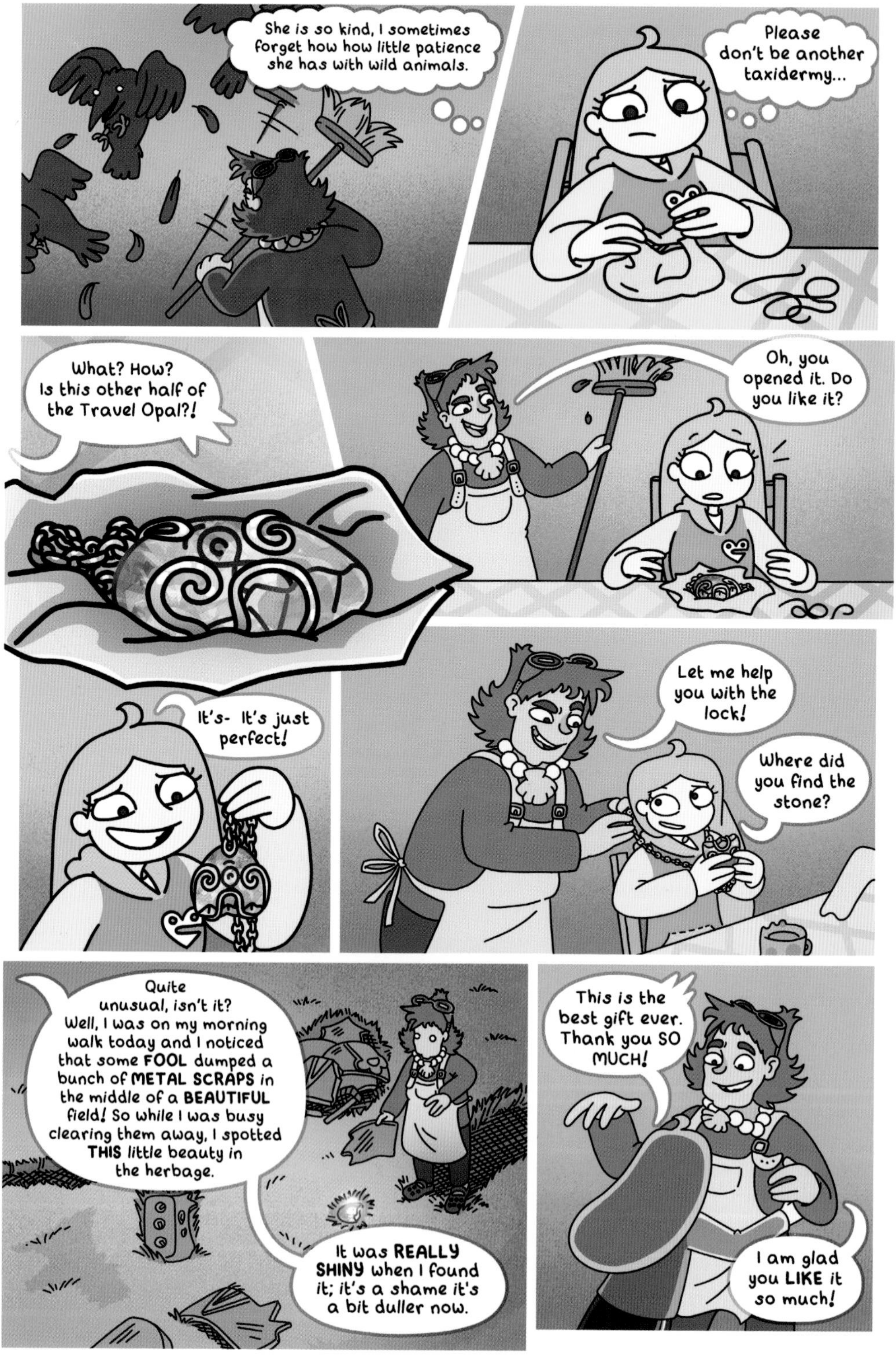
She is so kind, I sometimes forget how how little patience she has with wild animals.
Please don't be another taxidermy...
What? How? Is this other half of the Travel Opal?!
Oh, you opened it. Do you like it?
It's- It's just perfect!
Let me help you with the lock!
Where did you find the stone?
Quite unusual, isn't it? Well, I was on my morning walk today and I noticed that some FOOL dumped a bunch of METAL SCRAPS in the middle of a BEAUTIFUL field! So while I was busy clearing them away, I spotted THIS little beauty in the herbage.
It was REALLY SHINY when I found it; it's a shame it's a bit duller now.
This is the best gift ever. Thank you SO MUCH!
I am glad you LIKE it so much!

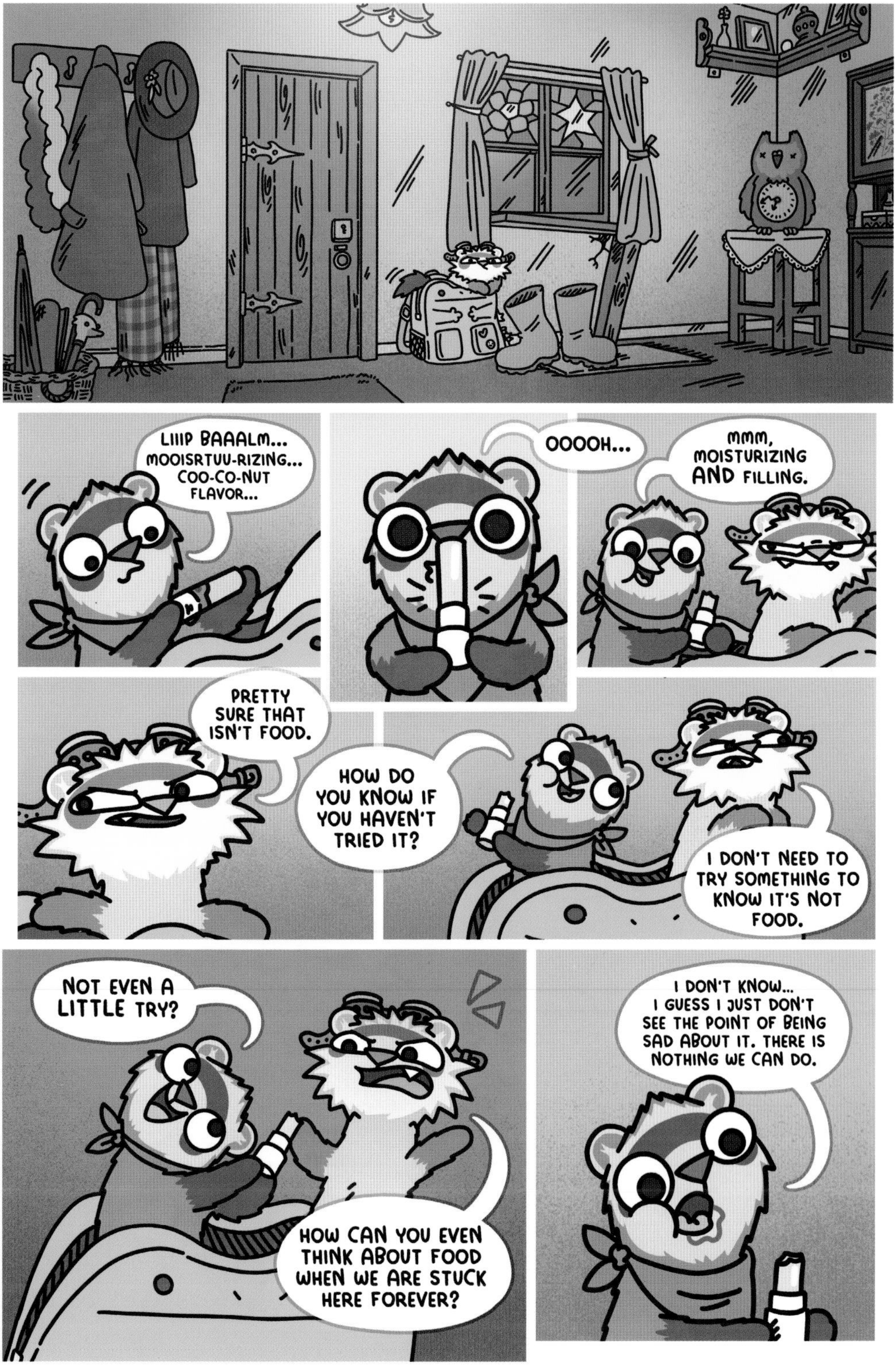
LIIIP BAAALM... MOOISRTUU-RIZING... COO-CO-NUT FLAVOR...
OOOOH...
MMM, MOISTURIZING AND FILLING.
PRETTY SURE THAT ISN'T FOOD.
HOW DO YOU KNOW IF YOU HAVEN'T TRIED IT?
I DON'T NEED TO TRY SOMETHING TO KNOW IT'S NOT FOOD.
NOT EVEN A LITTLE TRY?
HOW CAN YOU EVEN THINK ABOUT FOOD WHEN WE ARE STUCK HERE FOREVER?
I DON'T KNOW... I GUESS I JUST DON'T SEE THE POINT OF BEING SAD ABOUT IT. THERE IS NOTHING WE CAN DO.

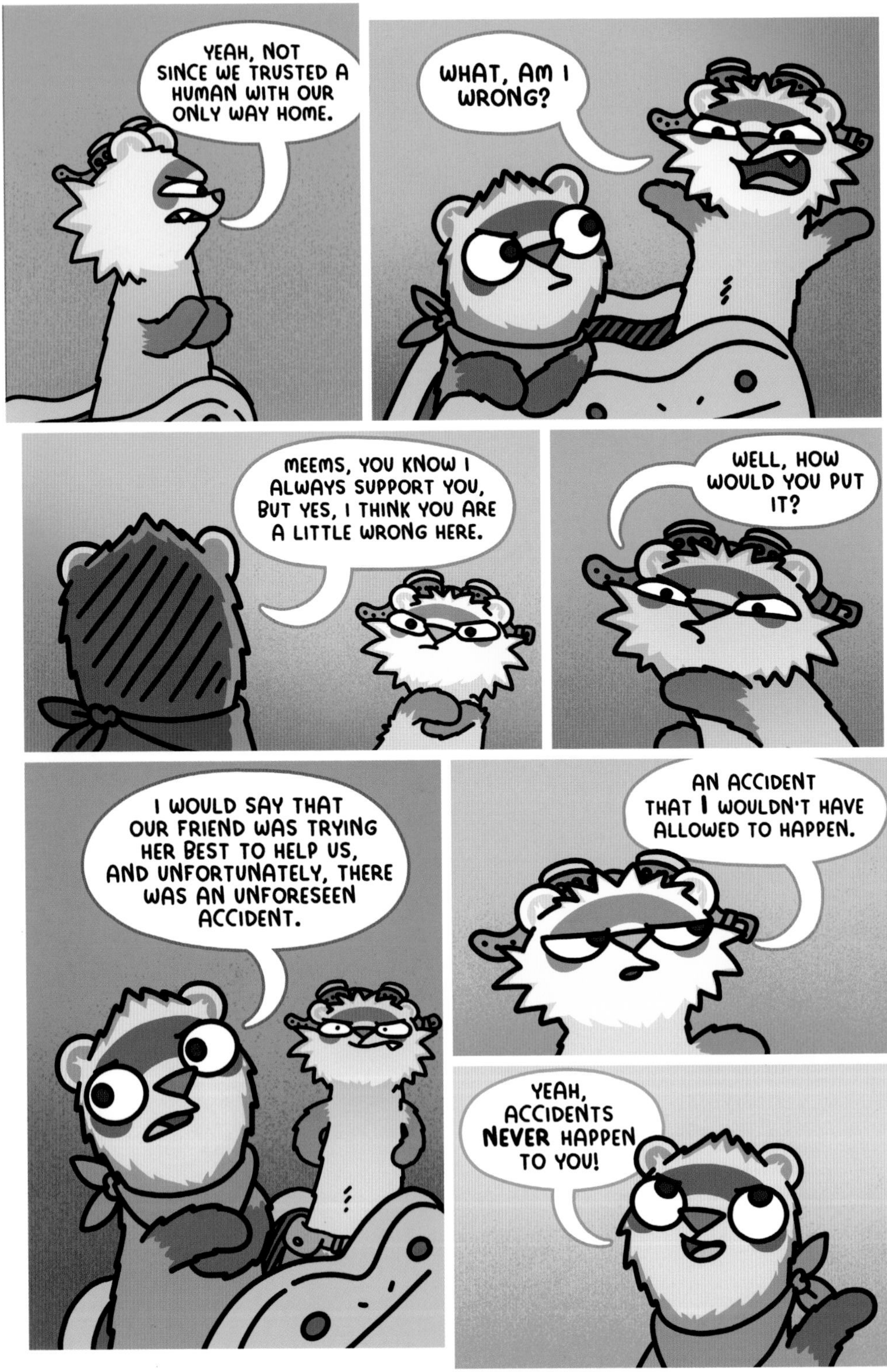
YEAH, NOT SINCE WE TRUSTED A HUMAN WITH OUR ONLY WAY HOME.
WHAT, AM I WRONG?
MEEMS, YOU KNOW I ALWAYS SUPPORT YOU, BUT YES, I THINK YOU ARE A LITTLE WRONG HERE.
WELL, HOW WOULD YOU PUT IT?
I WOULD SAY THAT OUR FRIEND WAS TRYING HER BEST TO HELP US, AND UNFORTUNATELY, THERE WAS AN UNFORESEEN ACCIDENT.
AN ACCIDENT THAT I WOULDN'T HAVE ALLOWED TO HAPPEN.
YEAH, ACCIDENTS NEVER HAPPEN TO YOU!

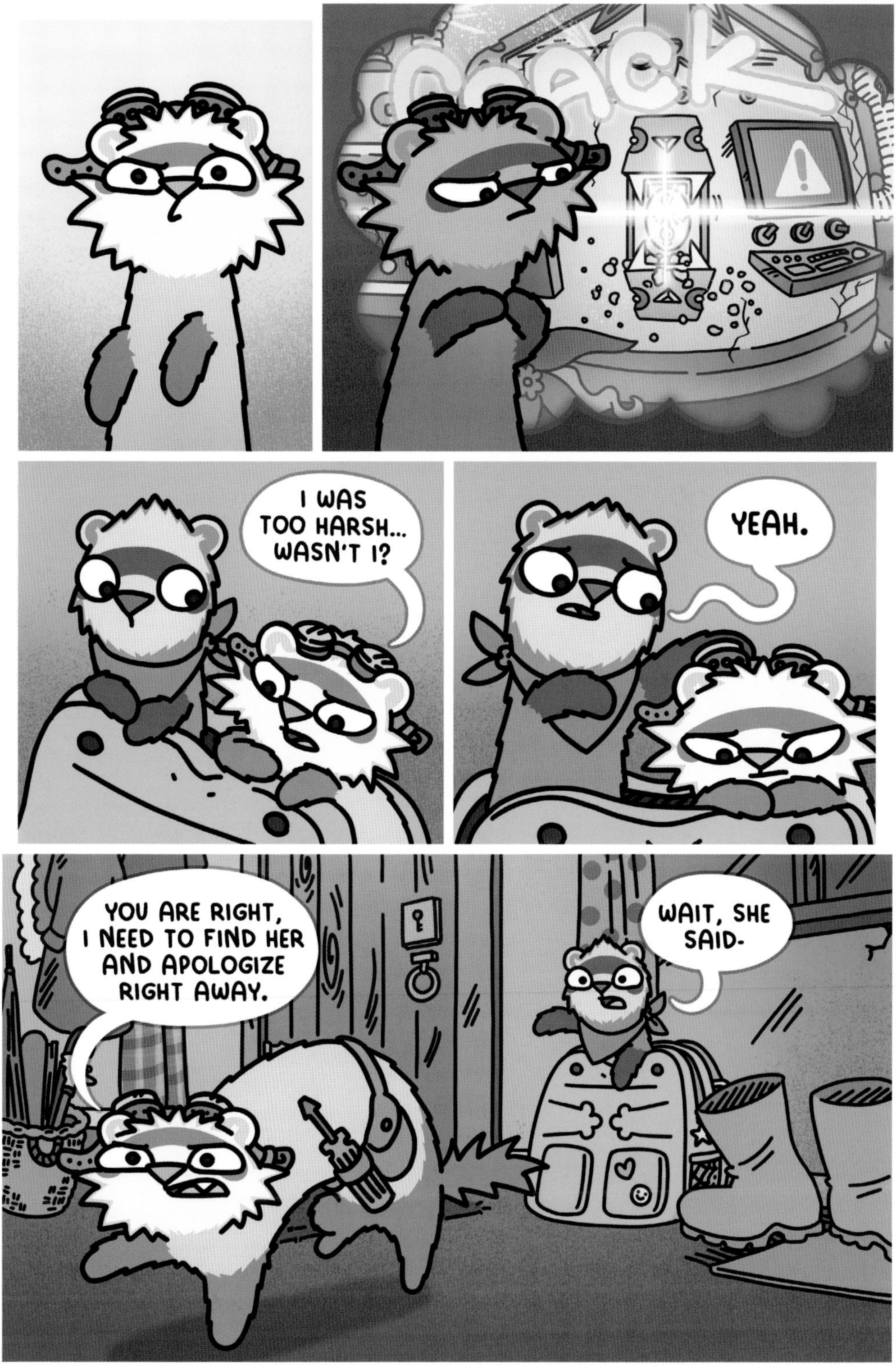
I WAS TOO HARSH... WASN'T I?
YEAH.
YOU ARE RIGHT, I NEED TO FIND HER AND APOLOGIZE RIGHT AWAY.
WAIT, SHE SAID-

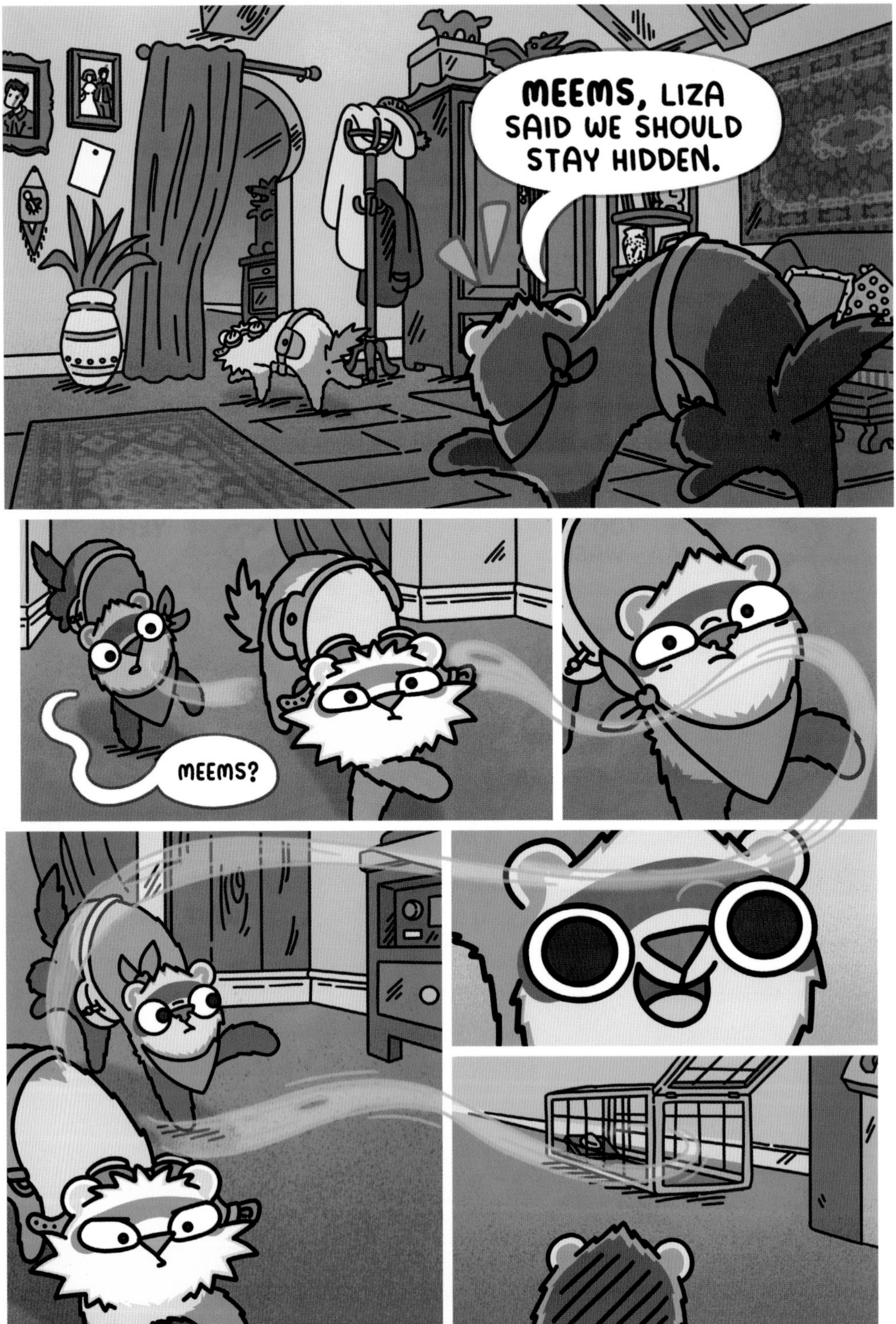
MEEMS, LIZA SAID WE SHOULD STAY HIDDEN.
MEEMS?

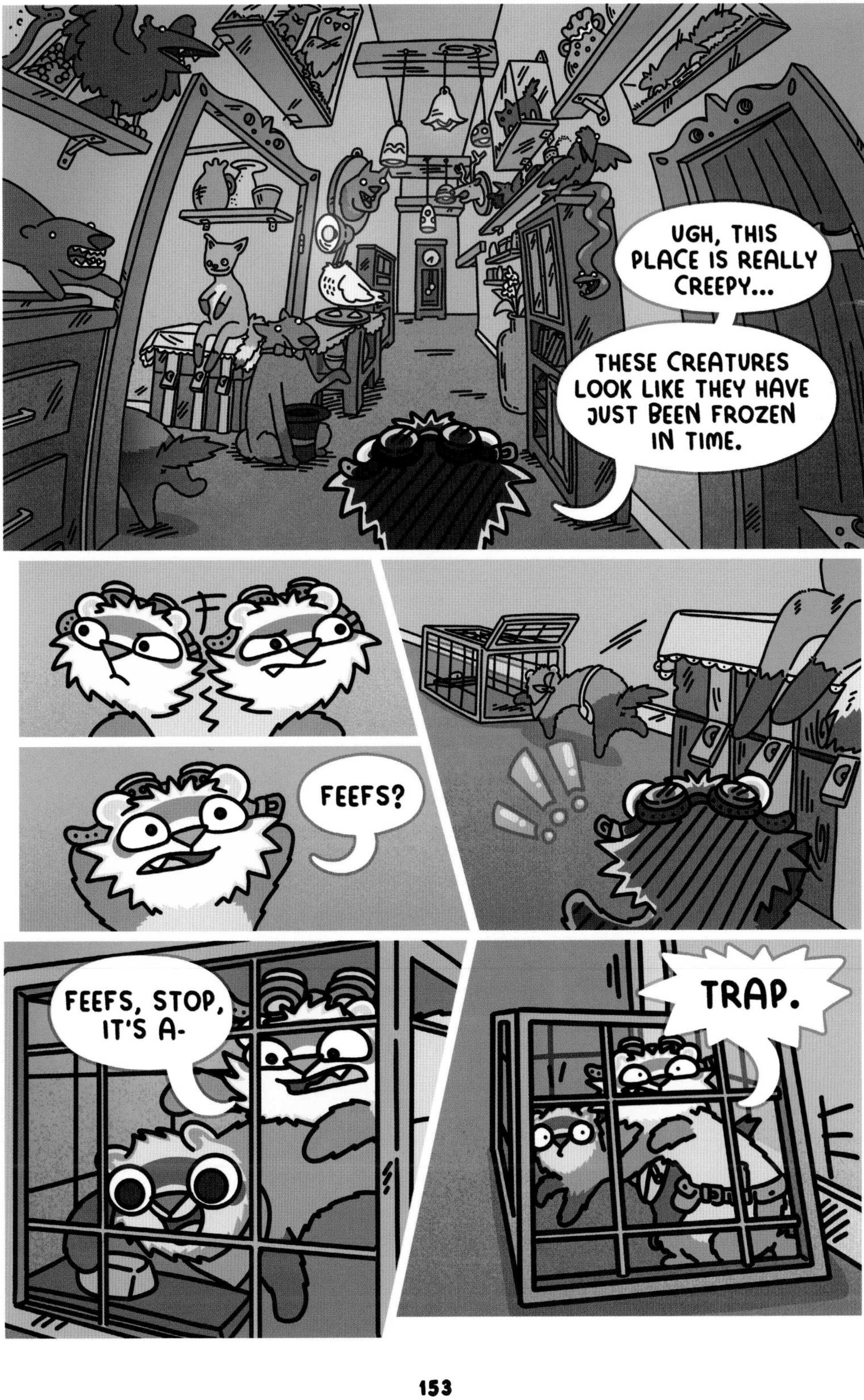
UGH, THIS PLACE IS REALLY CREEPY...
THESE CREATURES LOOK LIKE THEY HAVE JUST BEEN FROZEN IN TIME.
FEEFS?
FEEFS, STOP, IT'S A-
TRAP.

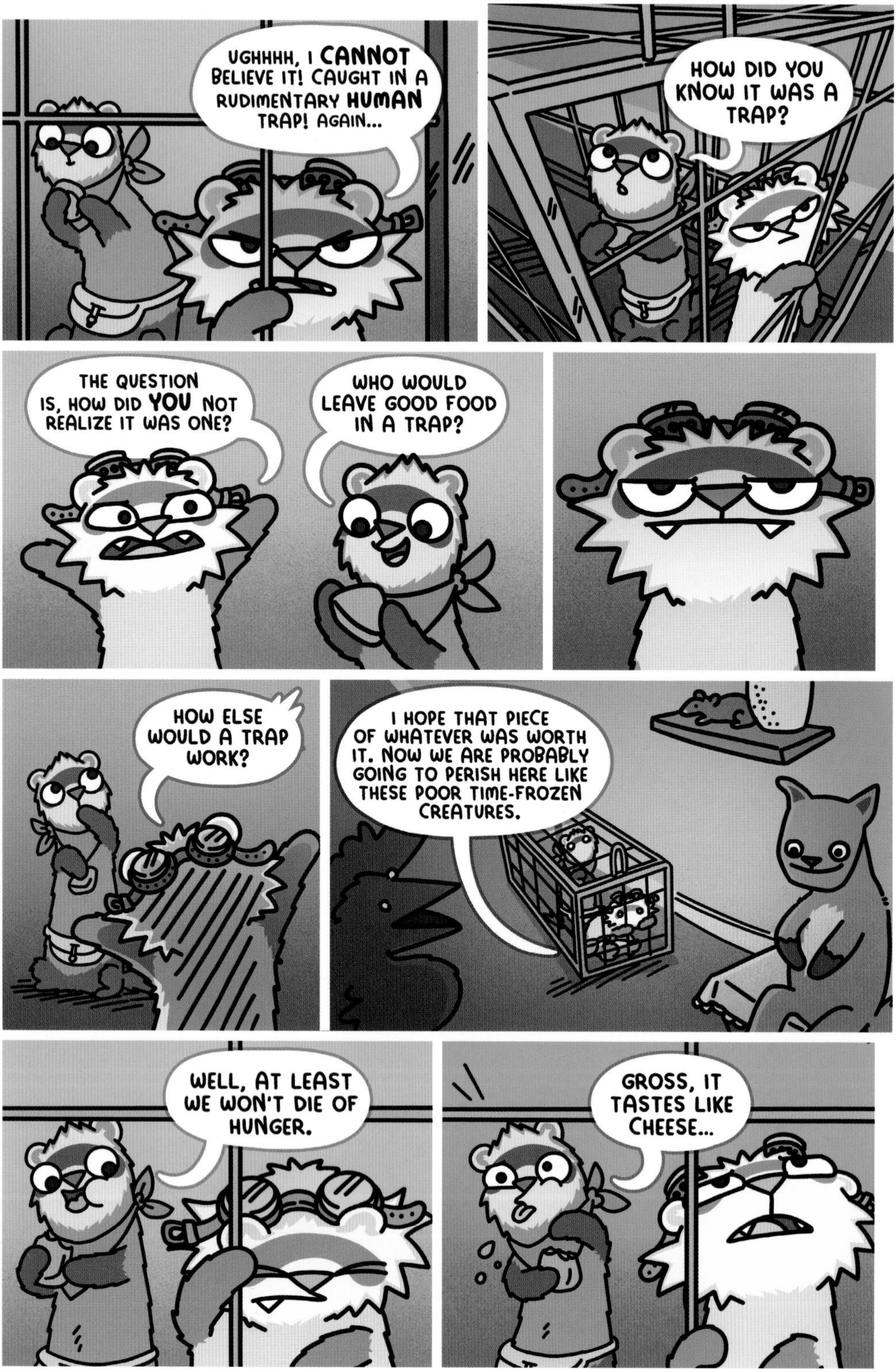
UGHHHH, I CANNOT BELIEVE IT! CAUGHT IN A RUDIMENTARY HUMAN TRAP! AGAIN...
HOW DID YOU KNOW IT WAS A TRAP?
THE QUESTION IS, HOW DID YOU NOT REALIZE IT WAS ONE?
WHO WOULD LEAVE GOOD FOOD IN A TRAP?
HOW ELSE WOULD A TRAP WORK?
I HOPE THAT PIECE OF WHATEVER WAS WORTH IT. NOW WE ARE PROBABLY GOING TO PERISH HERE LIKE THESE POOR TIME-FROZEN CREATURES.
WELL, AT LEAST WE WON'T DIE OF HUNGER.
GROSS, IT TASTES LIKE CHEESE...

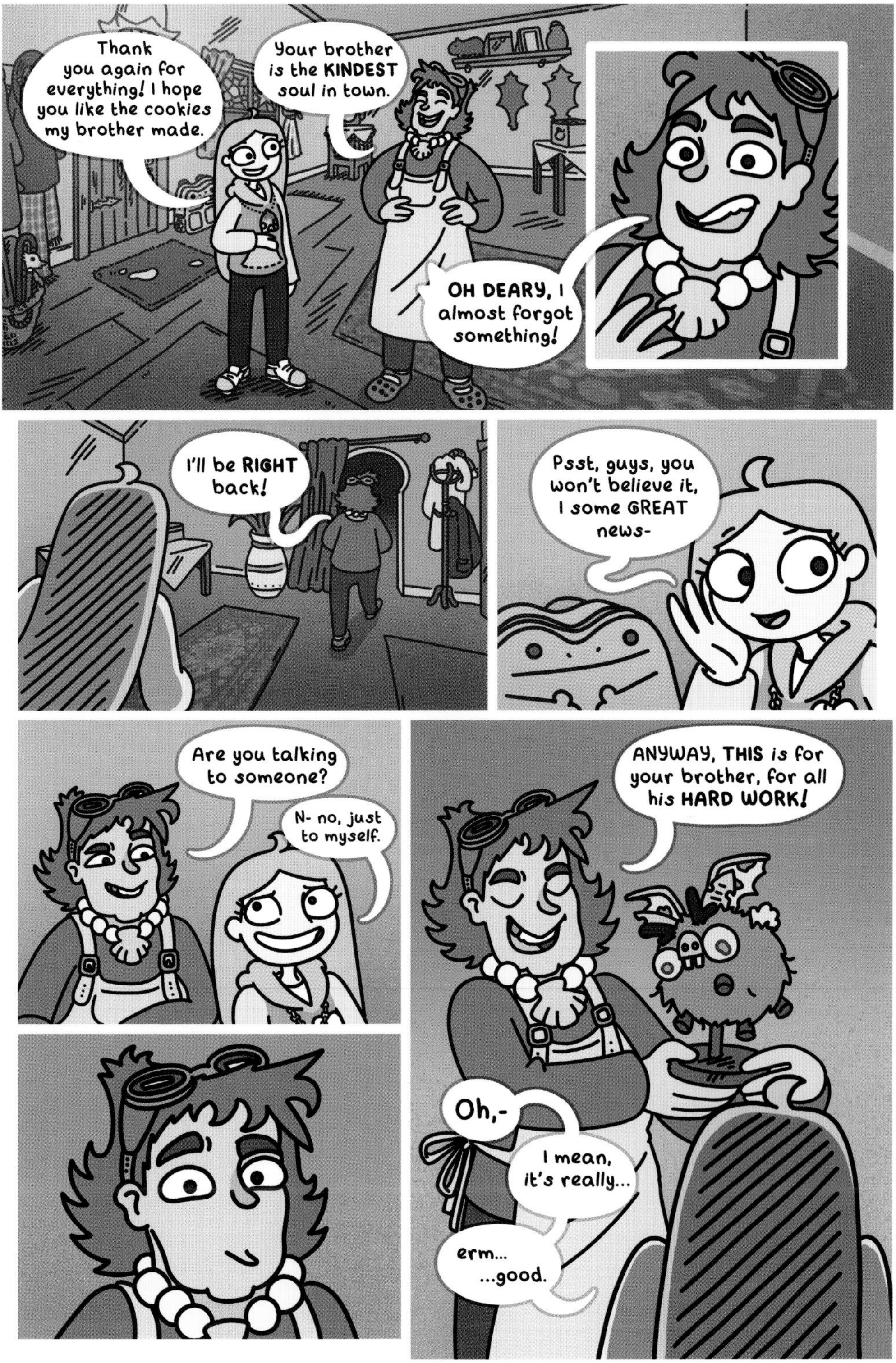
Thank you again for everything! I hope you like the cookies my brother made.
Your brother is the KINDEST soul in town.
OH DEARY, I almost forgot something!
I'll be RIGHT back!
Psst, guys, you won't believe it, I some GREAT news-
Are you talking to someone?
N- no, just to myself.
ANYWAY, THIS is for your brother, for all his HARD WORK!
Oh,-
I mean, it's really...
erm...
...good.

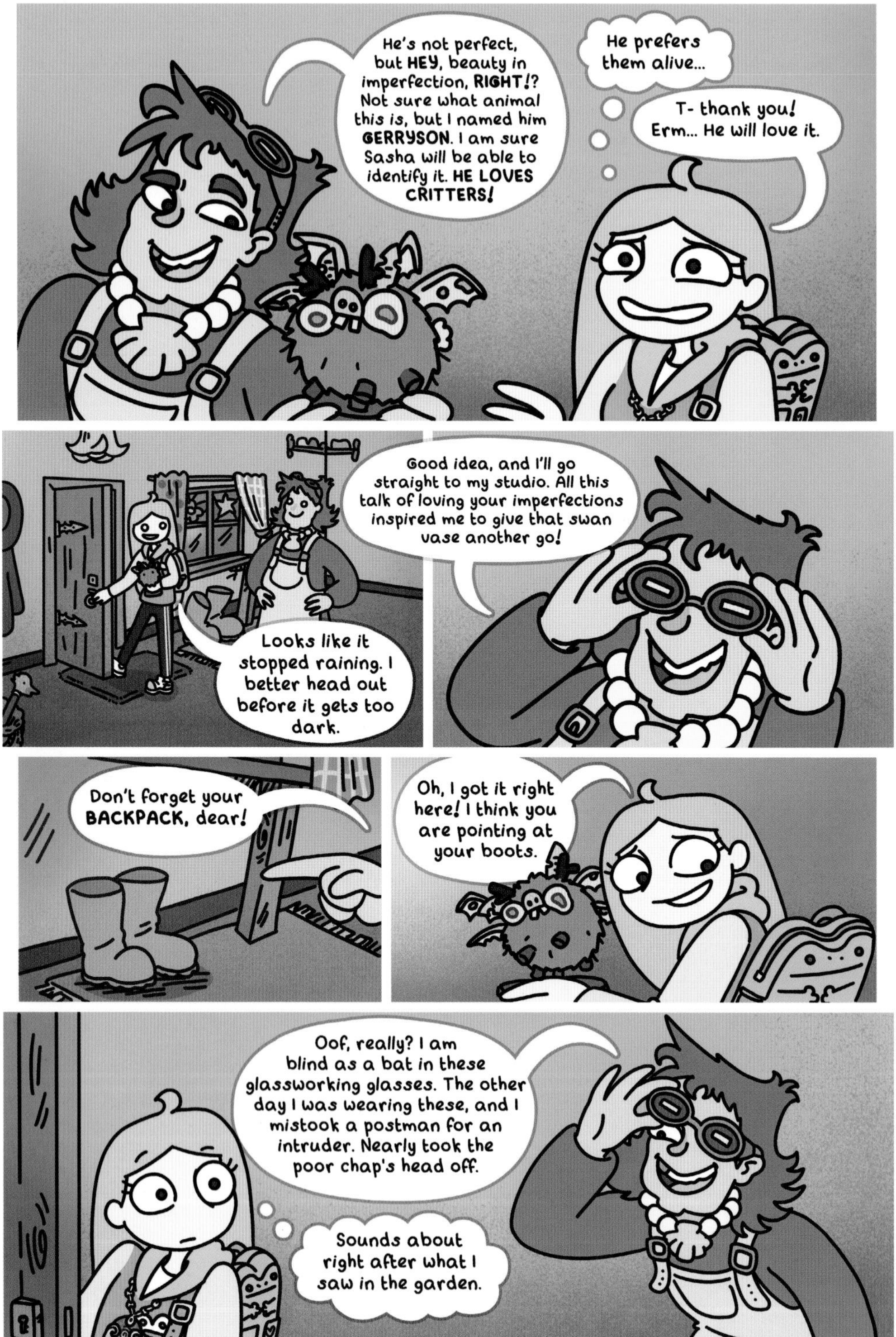
He's not perfect, but HEY, beauty in imperfection, RIGHT!? Not sure what animal this is, but I named him GERRYSON. I am sure Sasha will be able to identify it. HE LOVES CRITTERS!
He prefers them alive...
T- thank you! Erm... He will love it.
Looks like it stopped raining. I better head out before it gets too dark.
Good idea, and I'll go straight to my studio. All this talk of loving your imperfections inspired me to give that swan vase another go!
Don't forget your BACKPACK, dear!
Oh, I got it right here! I think you are pointing at your boots.
Oof, really? I am blind as a bat in these glassworking glasses. The other day I was wearing these, and I mistook a postman for an intruder. Nearly took the poor chap's head off.
Sounds about right after what I saw in the garden.

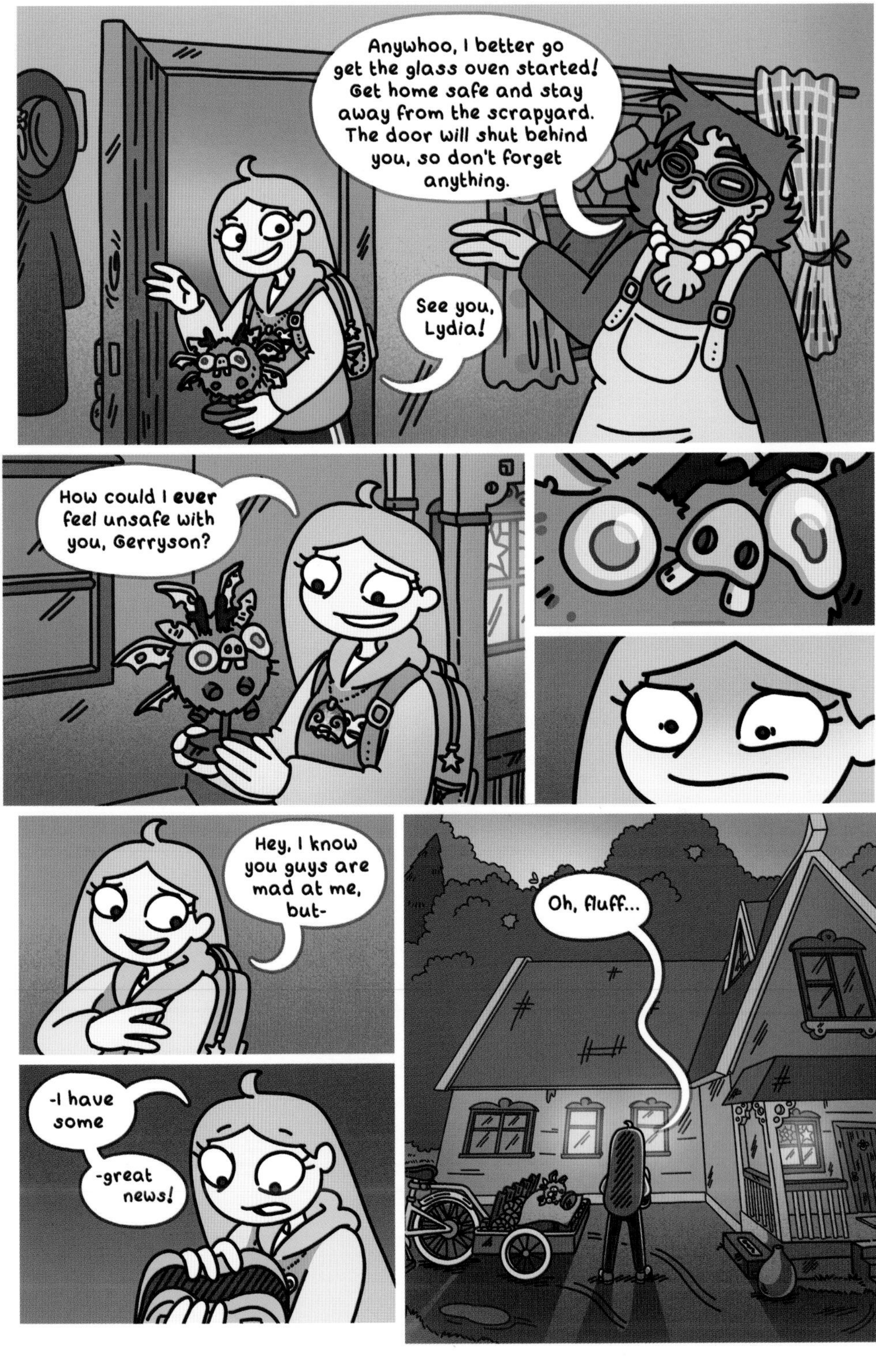
Anywhoo, I better go get the glass oven started! Get home safe and stay away from the scrapyard. The door will shut behind you, so don't forget anything.
See you, Lydia!
How could I ever feel unsafe with you, Gerryson?
Hey, I know you guys are mad at me, but-
-I have some
-great news!
Oh, fluff...

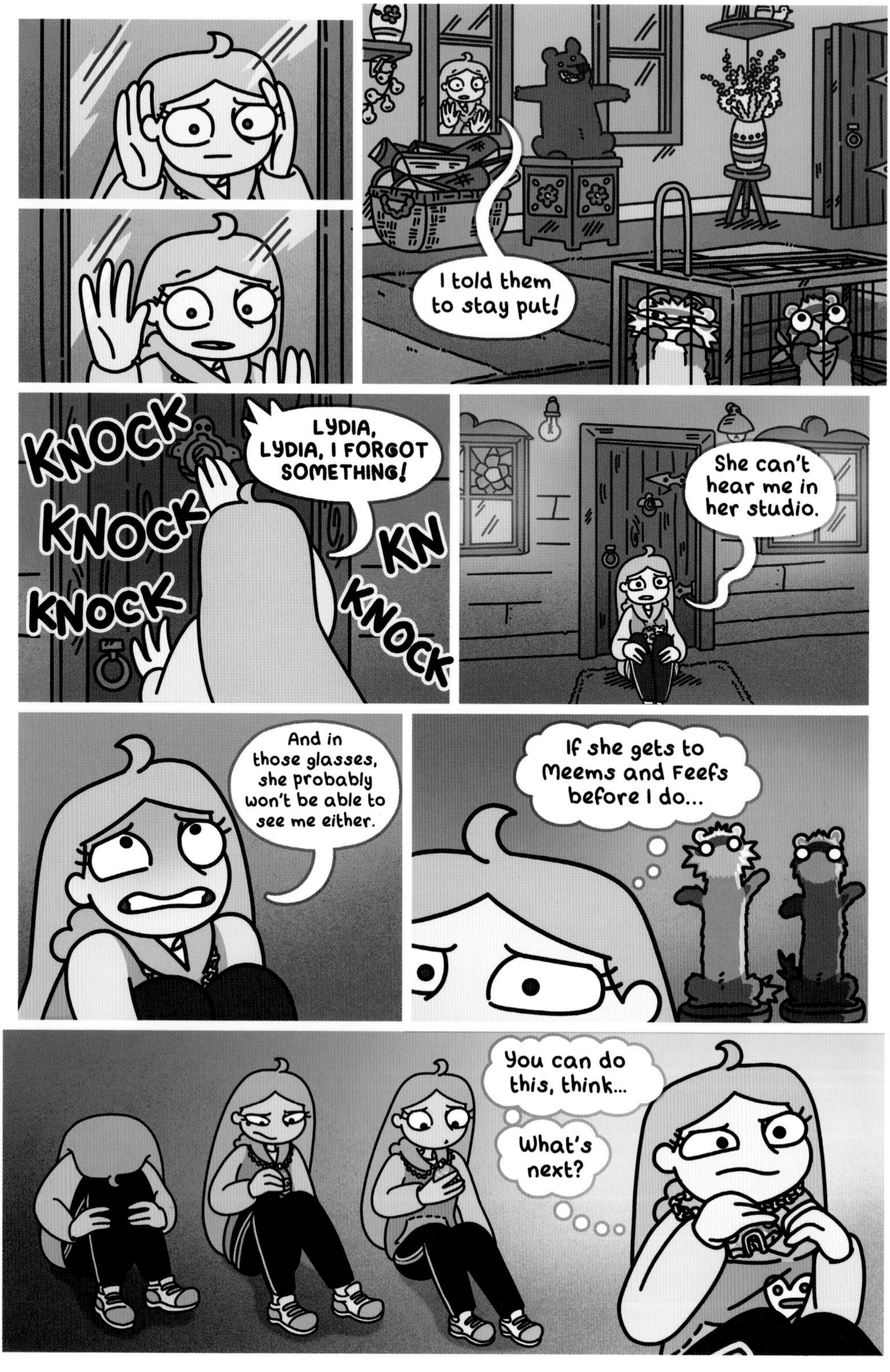
I told them to stay put!
KNOCK KNOCK KNOCK
LYDIA, LYDIA, I FORGOT SOMETHING!
KN KNOCK
She can't hear me in her studio.
And in those glasses, she probably won't be able to see me either.
If she gets to Meems and Feefs before I do...
You can do this, think...
What's next?

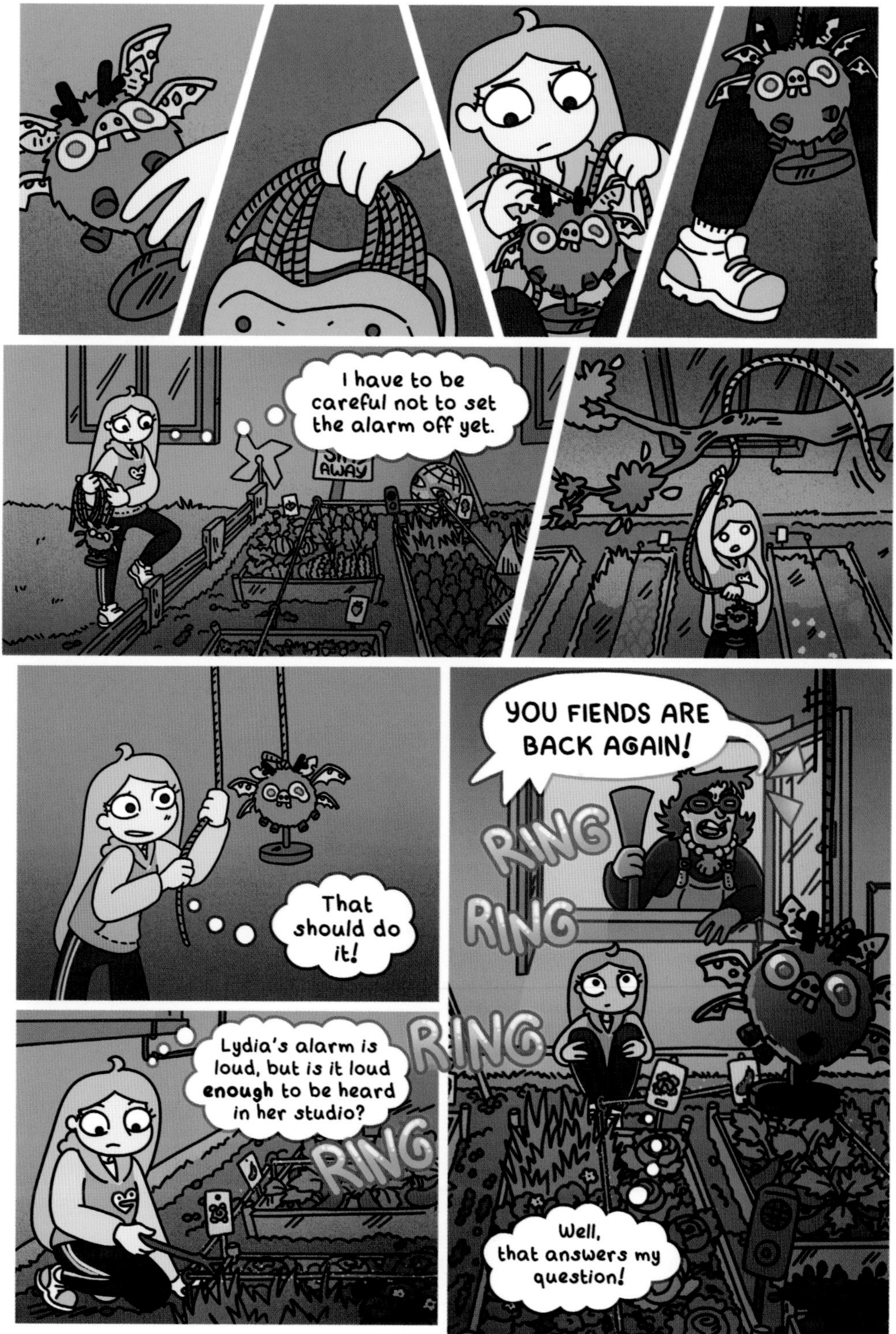
I have to be careful not to set the alarm off yet.
AWAY
That should do it!
Lydia's alarm is loud, but is it loud enough to be heard in her studio?
RING
RING
YOU FIENDS ARE BACK AGAIN!
RING
RING
Well, that answers my question!

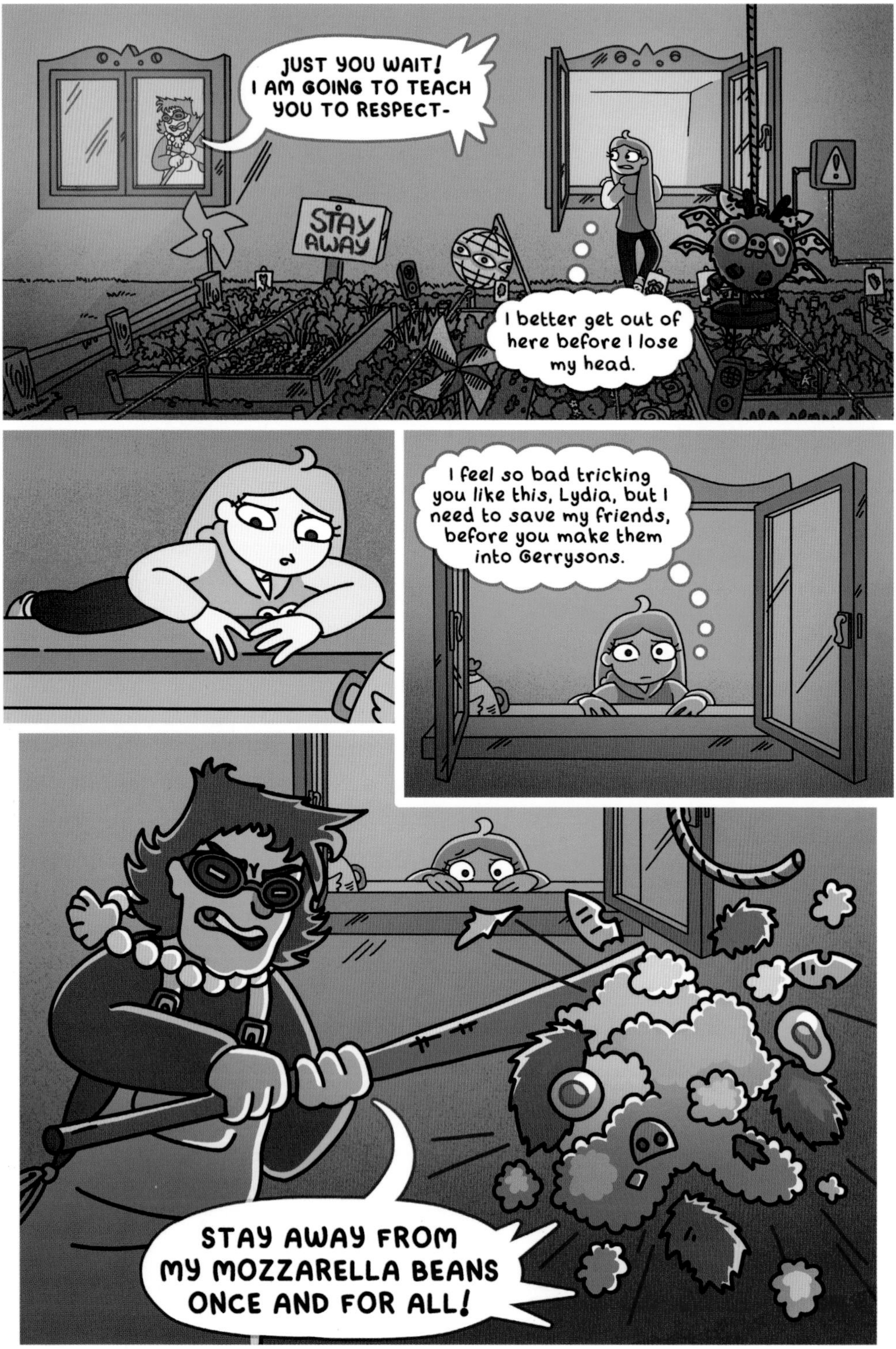
JUST YOU WAIT! I AM GOING TO TEACH YOU TO RESPECT-
STAY AWAY
I better get out of here before I lose my head.
I feel so bad tricking you like this, Lydia, but I need to save my friends, before you make them into Gerrysons.
STAY AWAY FROM MY MOZZARELLA BEANS ONCE AND FOR ALL!

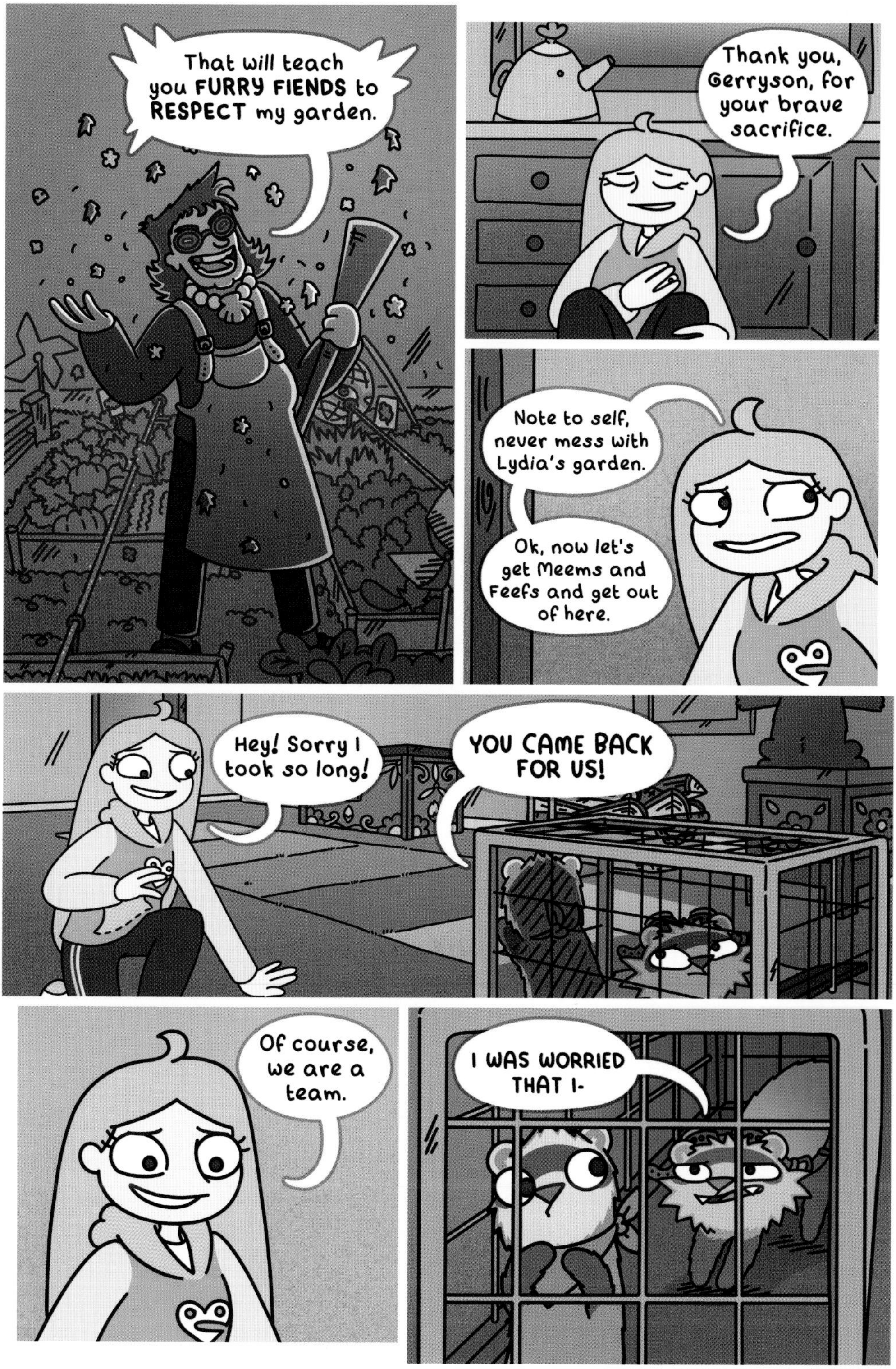
That will teach you FURRY FIENDS to RESPECT my garden.
Thank you, Gerryson, for your brave sacrifice.
Note to self, never mess with Lydia's garden.
Ok, now let's get Meems and Feefs and get out of here.
Hey! Sorry I took so long!
YOU CAME BACK FOR US!
Of course, we are a team.
I WAS WORRIED THAT I-

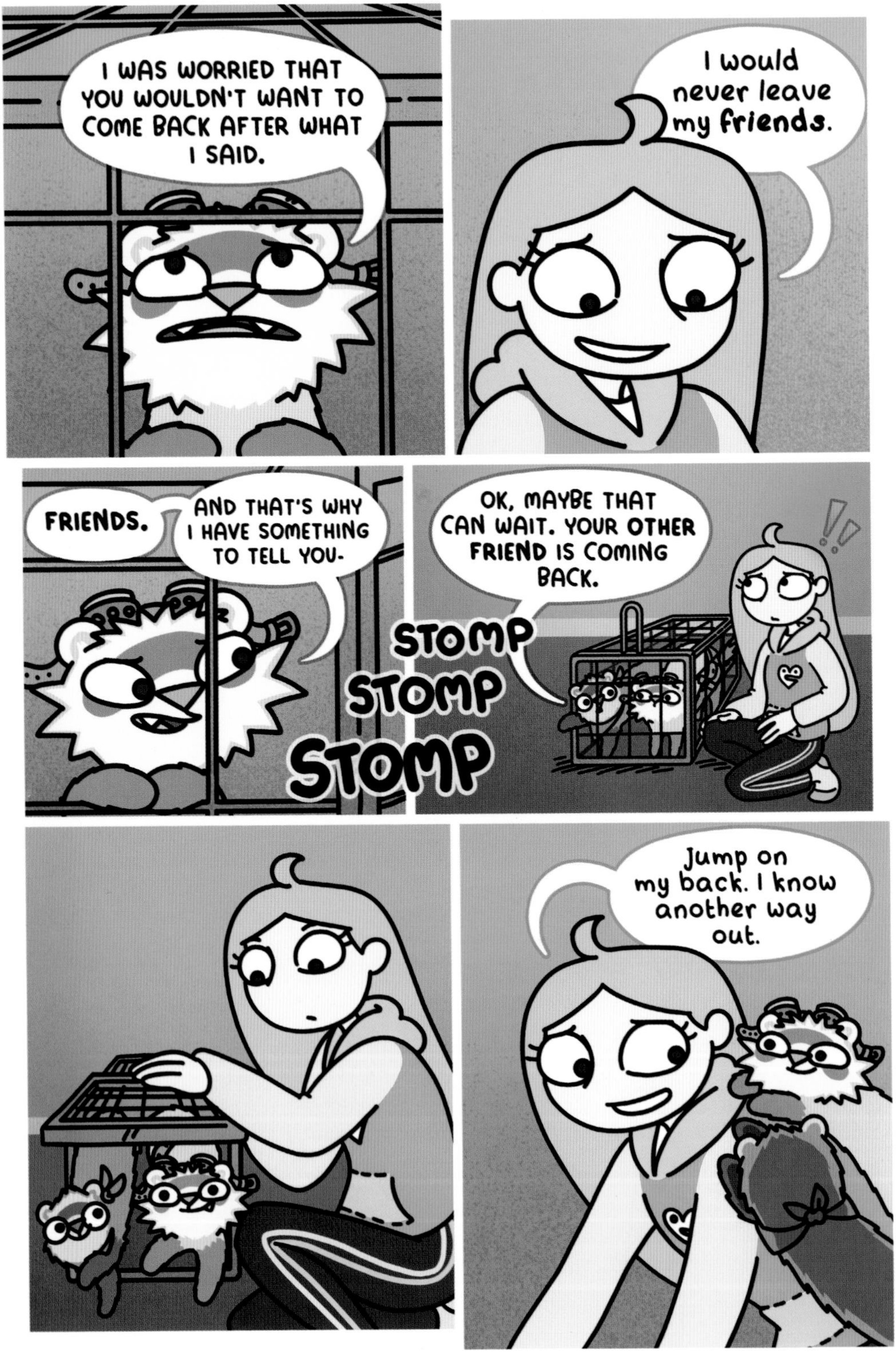
I WAS WORRIED THAT YOU WOULDN'T WANT TO COME BACK AFTER WHAT I SAID.
I would never leave my friends.
FRIENDS.
AND THAT'S WHY I HAVE SOMETHING TO TELL YOU-
OK, MAYBE THAT CAN WAIT. YOUR OTHER FRIEND IS COMING BACK.
!!
STOMP
STOMP
STOMP
Jump on my back. I know another way out.

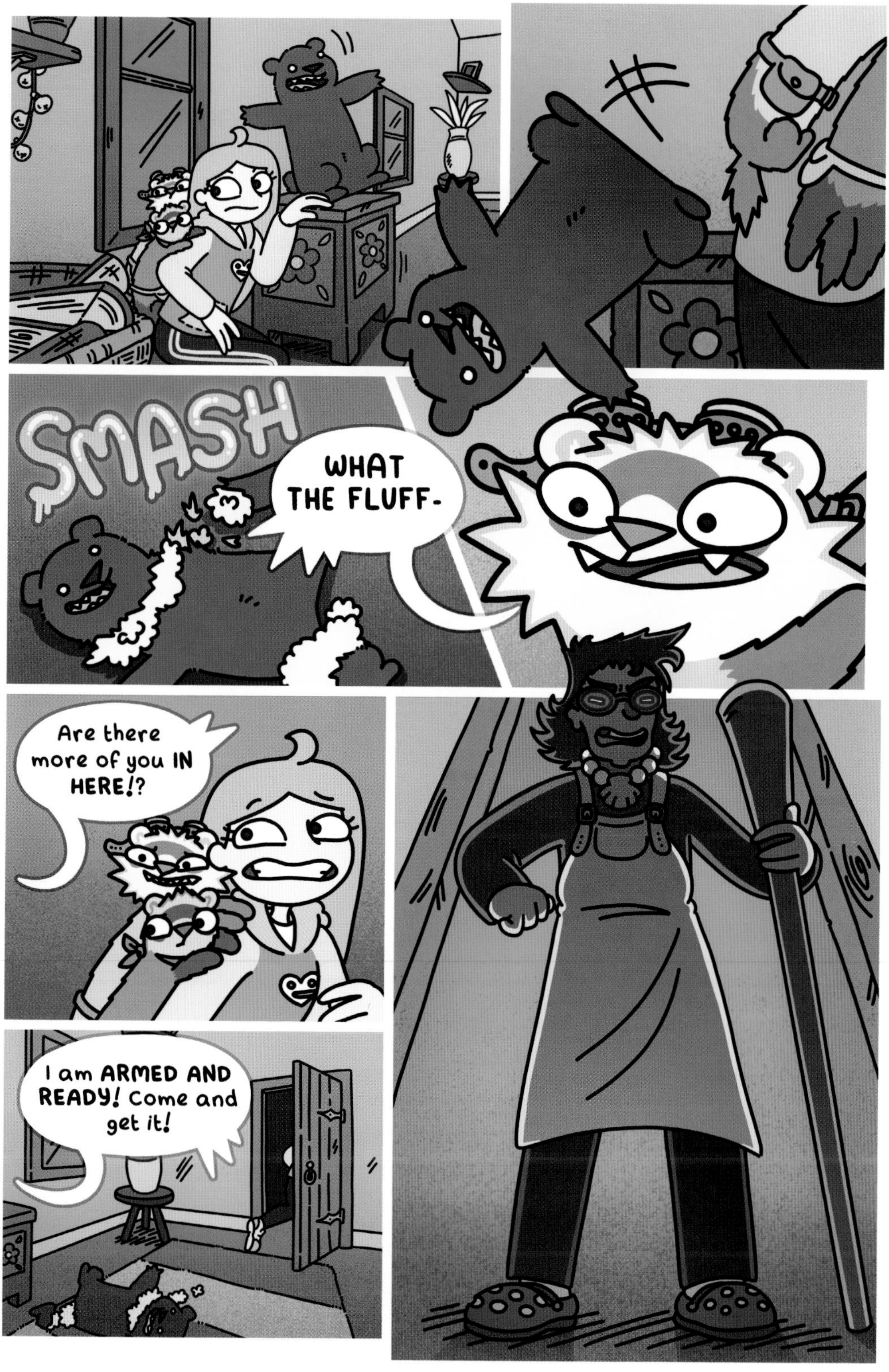
SMASH
WHAT THE FLUFF-
Are there more of you IN HERE!?
I am ARMED AND READY! Come and get it!

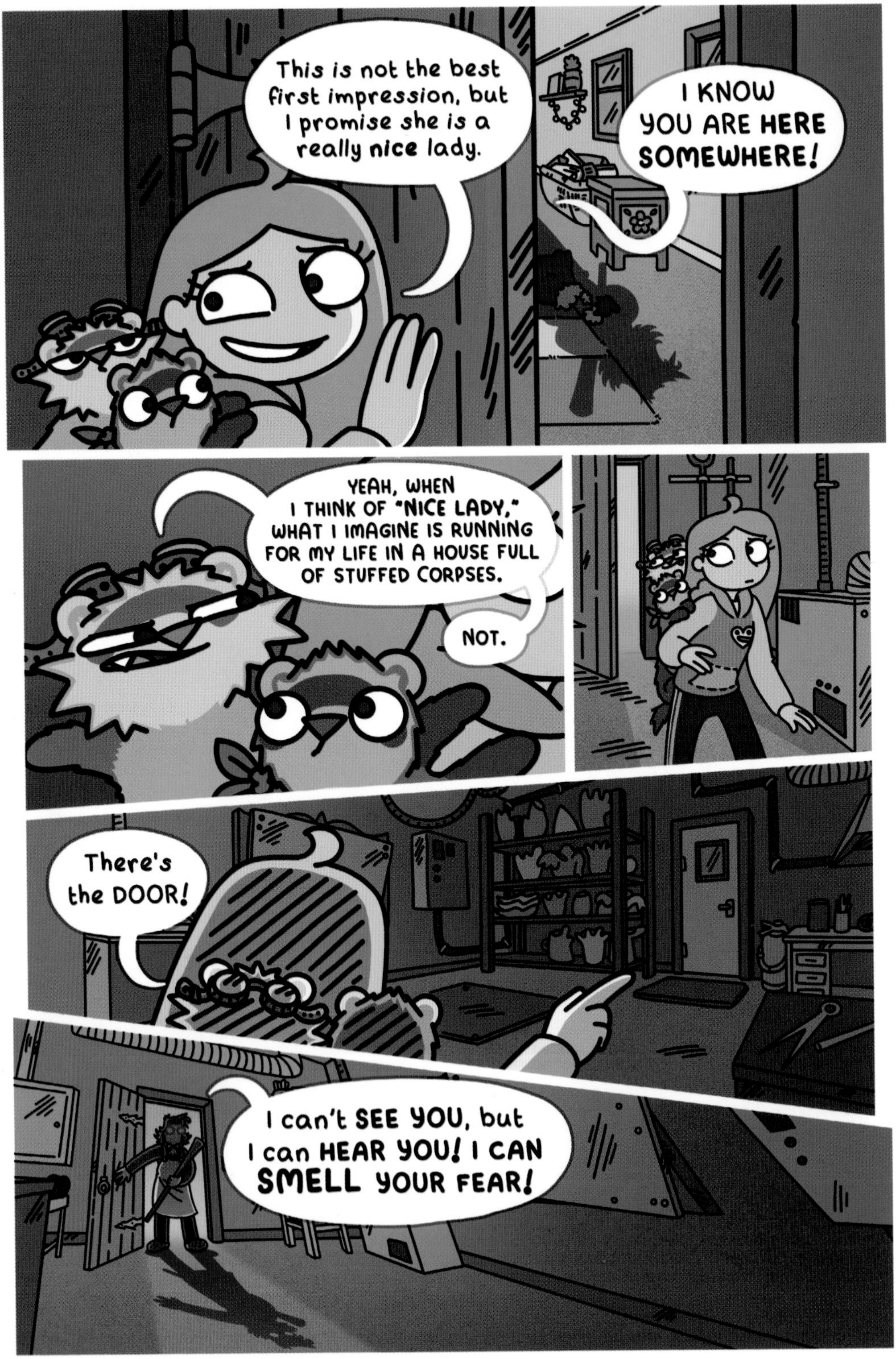
This is not the best first impression, but I promise she is a really nice lady.
I KNOW YOU ARE HERE SOMEWHERE!
YEAH, WHEN I THINK OF "NICE LADY," WHAT I IMAGINE IS RUNNING FOR MY LIFE IN A HOUSE FULL OF STUFFED CORPSES.
NOT.
There's the DOOR!
I can't SEE YOU, but I can HEAR YOU! I CAN SMELL YOUR FEAR!

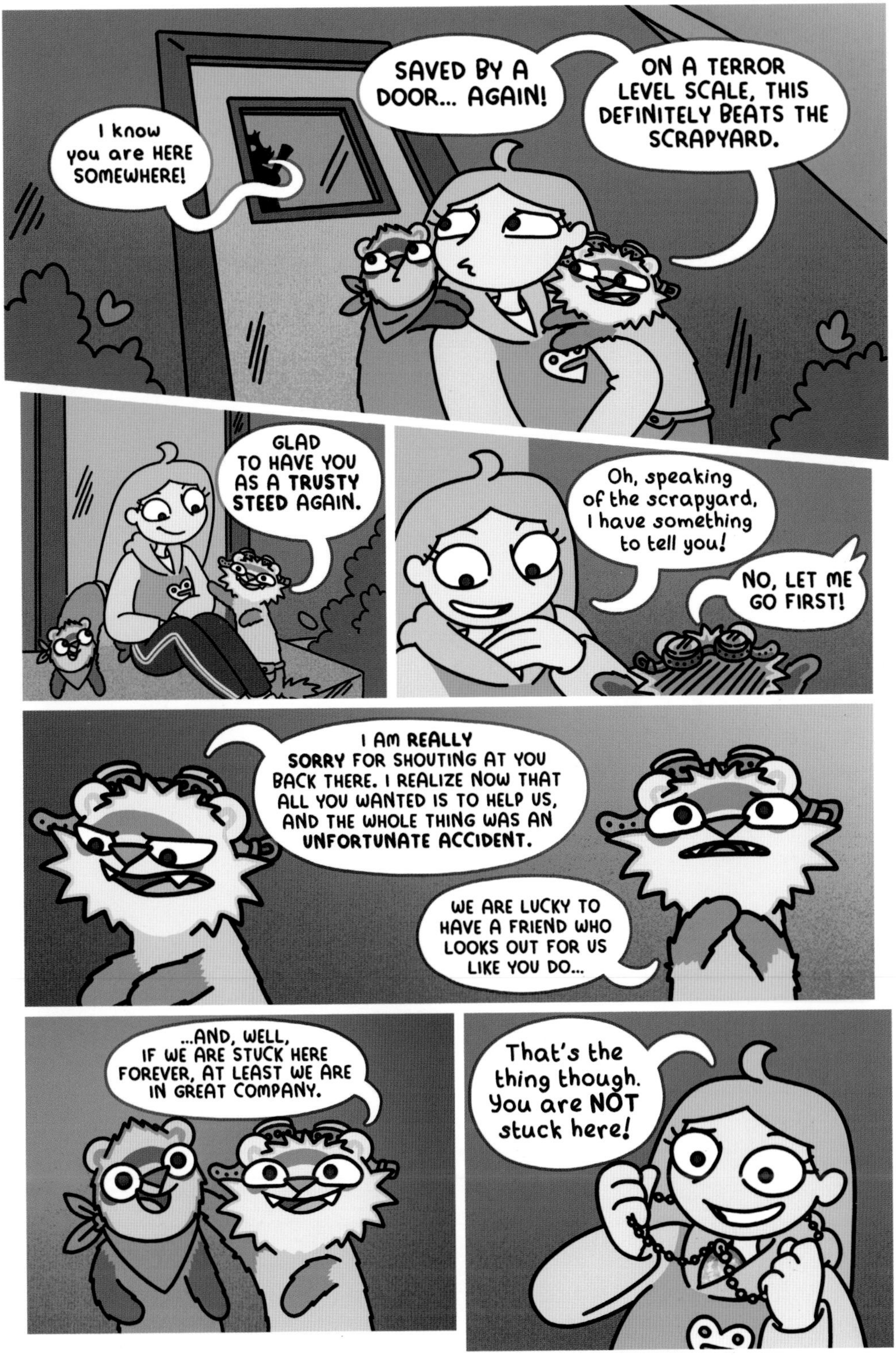
I know you are HERE SOMEWHERE!
SAVED BY A DOOR... AGAIN!
ON A TERROR LEVEL SCALE, THIS DEFINITELY BEATS THE SCRAPYARD.
GLAD TO HAVE YOU AS A TRUSTY STEED AGAIN.
Oh, speaking of the scrapyard, I have something to tell you!
NO, LET ME GO FIRST!
I AM REALLY SORRY FOR SHOUTING AT YOU BACK THERE. I REALIZE NOW THAT ALL YOU WANTED IS TO HELP US, AND THE WHOLE THING WAS AN UNFORTUNATE ACCIDENT.
WE ARE LUCKY TO HAVE A FRIEND WHO LOOKS OUT FOR US LIKE YOU DO...
...AND, WELL, IF WE ARE STUCK HERE FOREVER, AT LEAST WE ARE IN GREAT COMPANY.
That's the thing though. You are NOT stuck here!

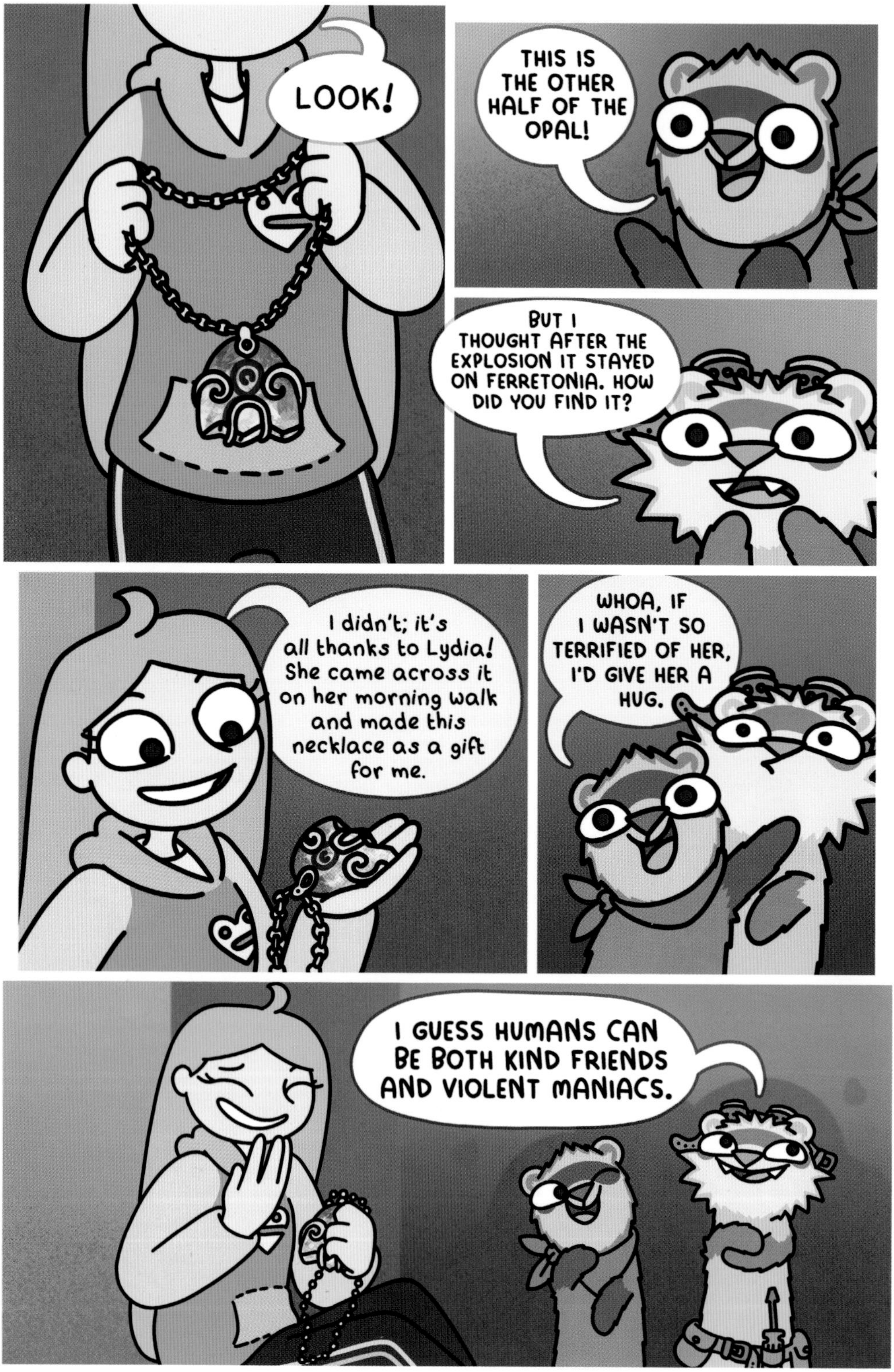
LOOK!
THIS IS THE OTHER HALF OF THE OPAL!
BUT I THOUGHT AFTER THE EXPLOSION IT STAYED ON FERRETONIA. HOW DID YOU FIND IT?
I didn't; it's all thanks to Lydia! She came across it on her morning walk and made this necklace as a gift for me.
WHOA, IF I WASN'T SO TERRIFIED OF HER, I'D GIVE HER A HUG.
I GUESS HUMANS CAN BE BOTH KIND FRIENDS AND VIOLENT MANIACS.

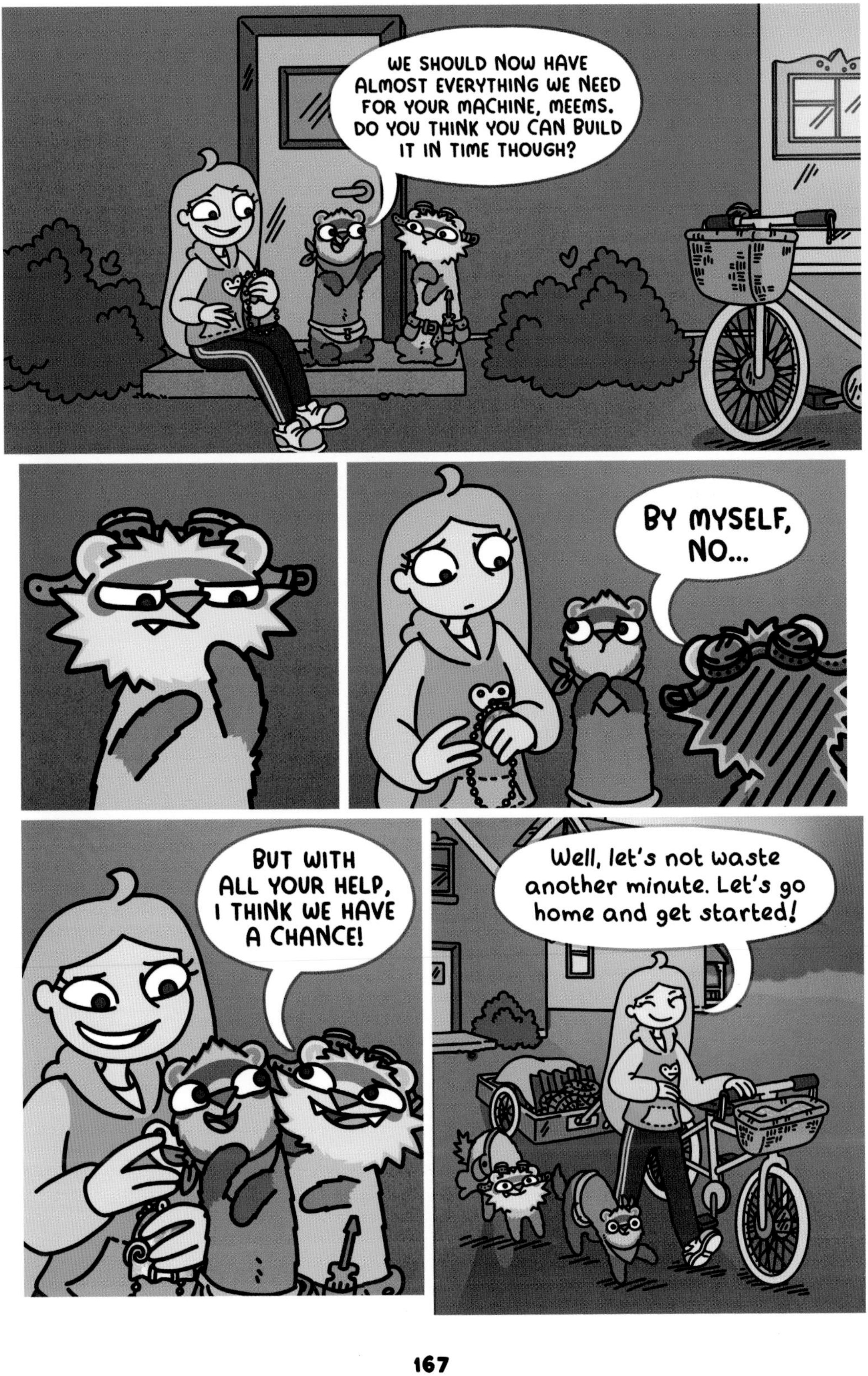
WE SHOULD NOW HAVE ALMOST EVERYTHING WE NEED FOR YOUR MACHINE, MEEMS. DO YOU THINK YOU CAN BUILD IT IN TIME THOUGH?
BY MYSELF, NO...
BUT WITH ALL YOUR HELP, I THINK WE HAVE A CHANCE!
Well, let's not waste another minute. Let's go home and get started!

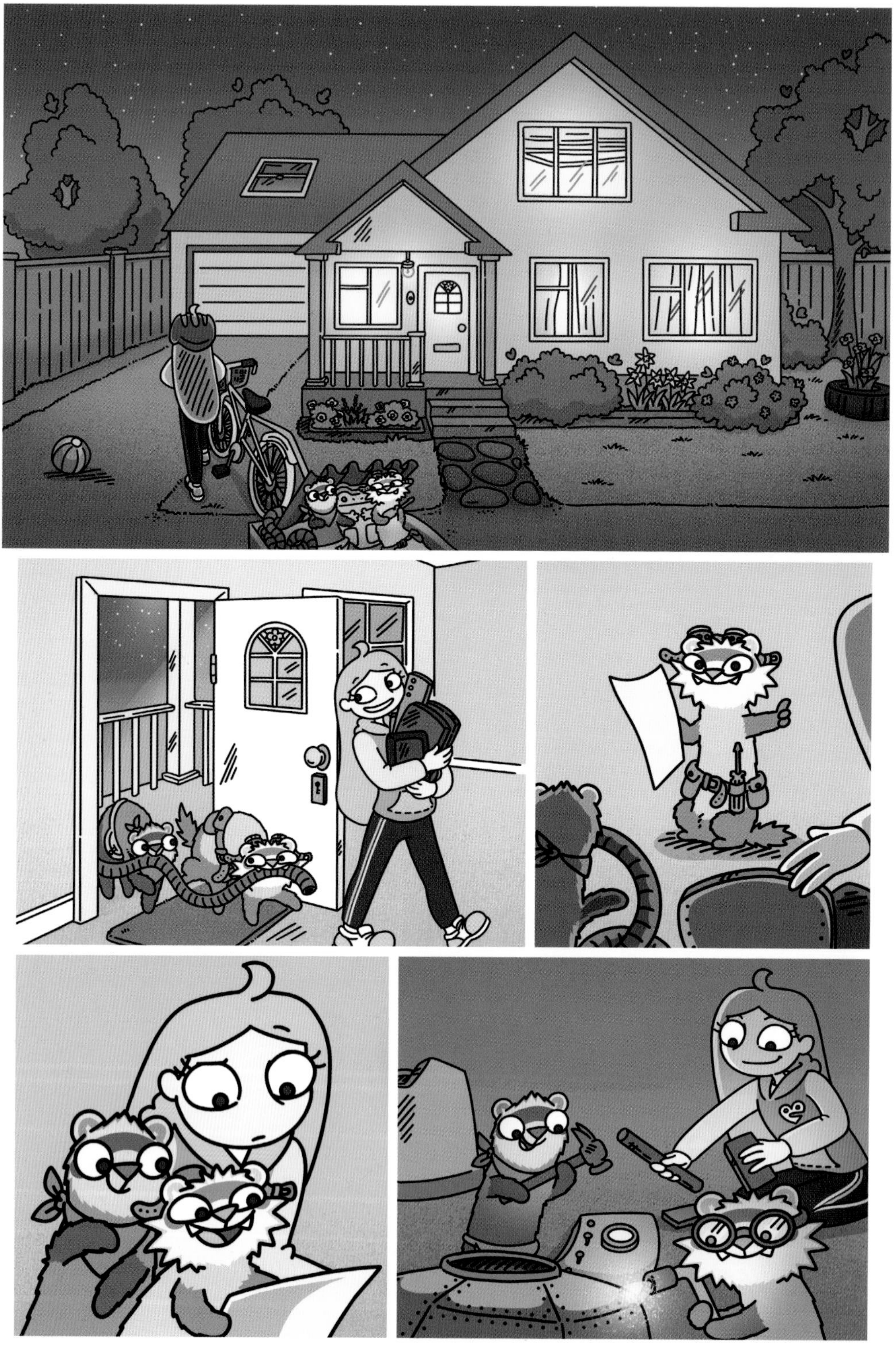

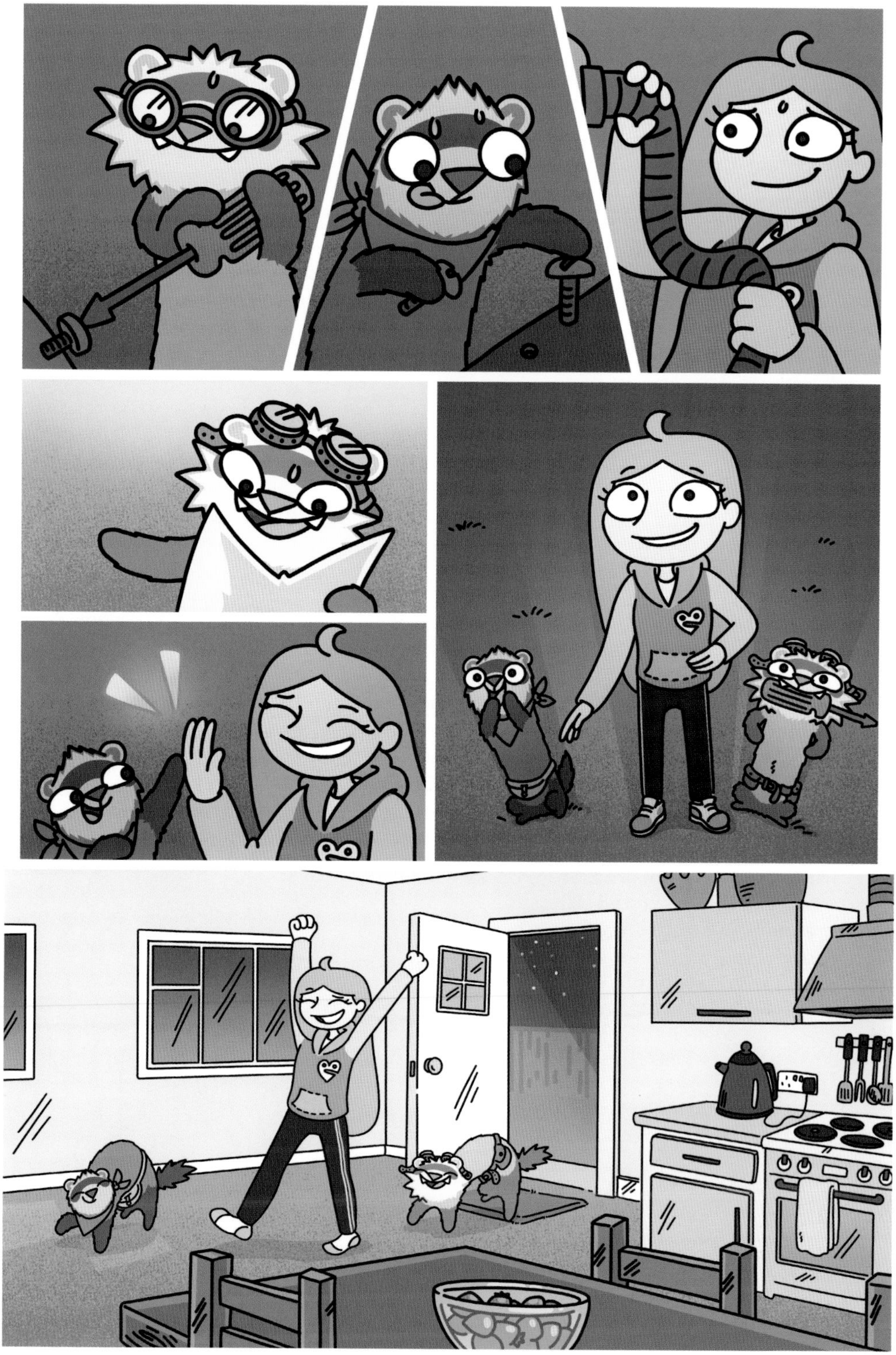

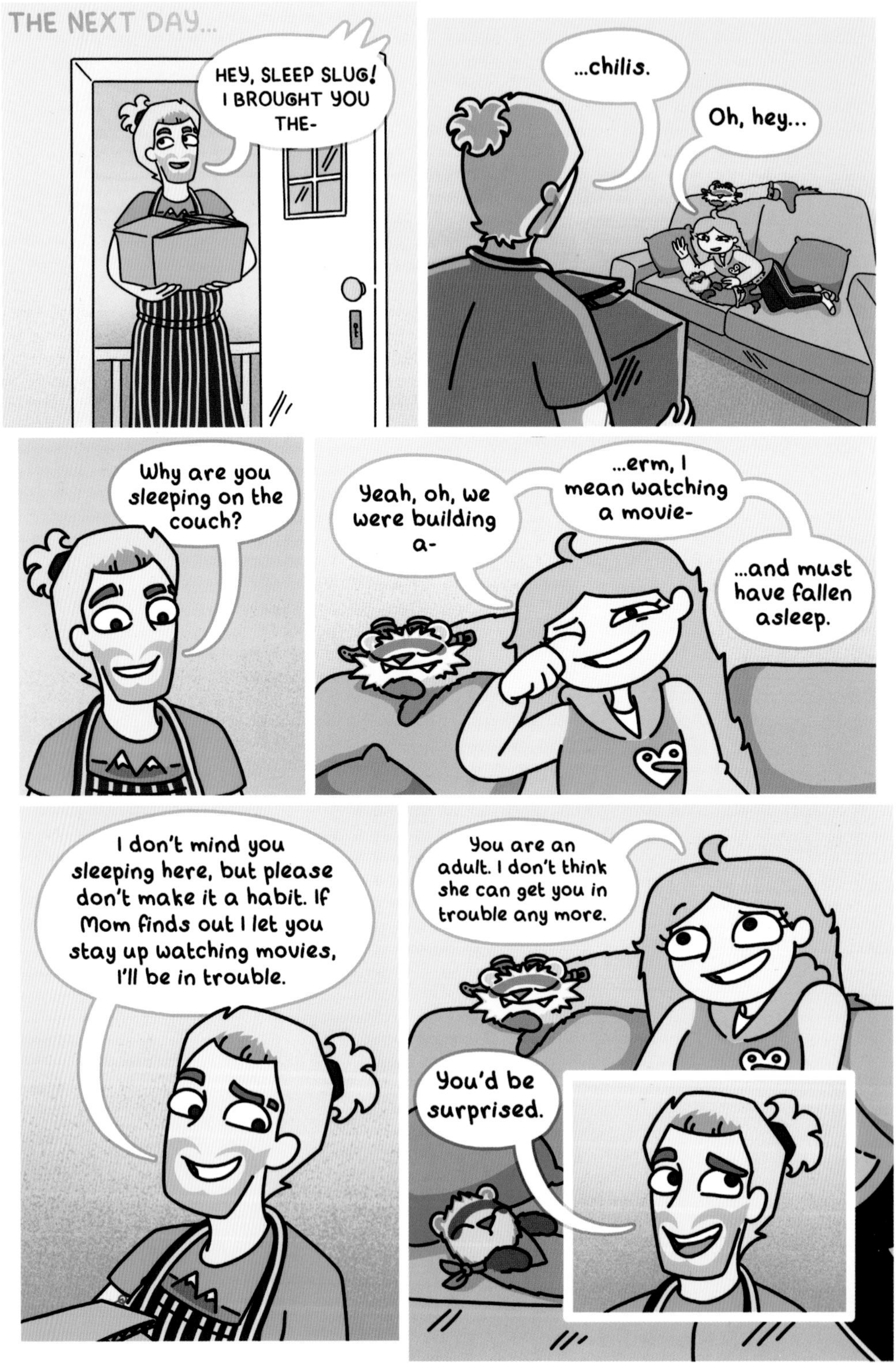
THE NEXT DAY...
HEY, SLEEP SLUG! I BROUGHT YOU THE-
...chilis.
Oh, hey...
Why are you sleeping on the couch?
Yeah, oh, we were building a-
...erm, I mean watching a movie-
...and must have fallen asleep.
I don't mind you sleeping here, but please don't make it a habit. If Mom finds out I let you stay up watching movies, I'll be in trouble.
You are an adult. I don't think she can get you in trouble any more.
You'd be surprised.

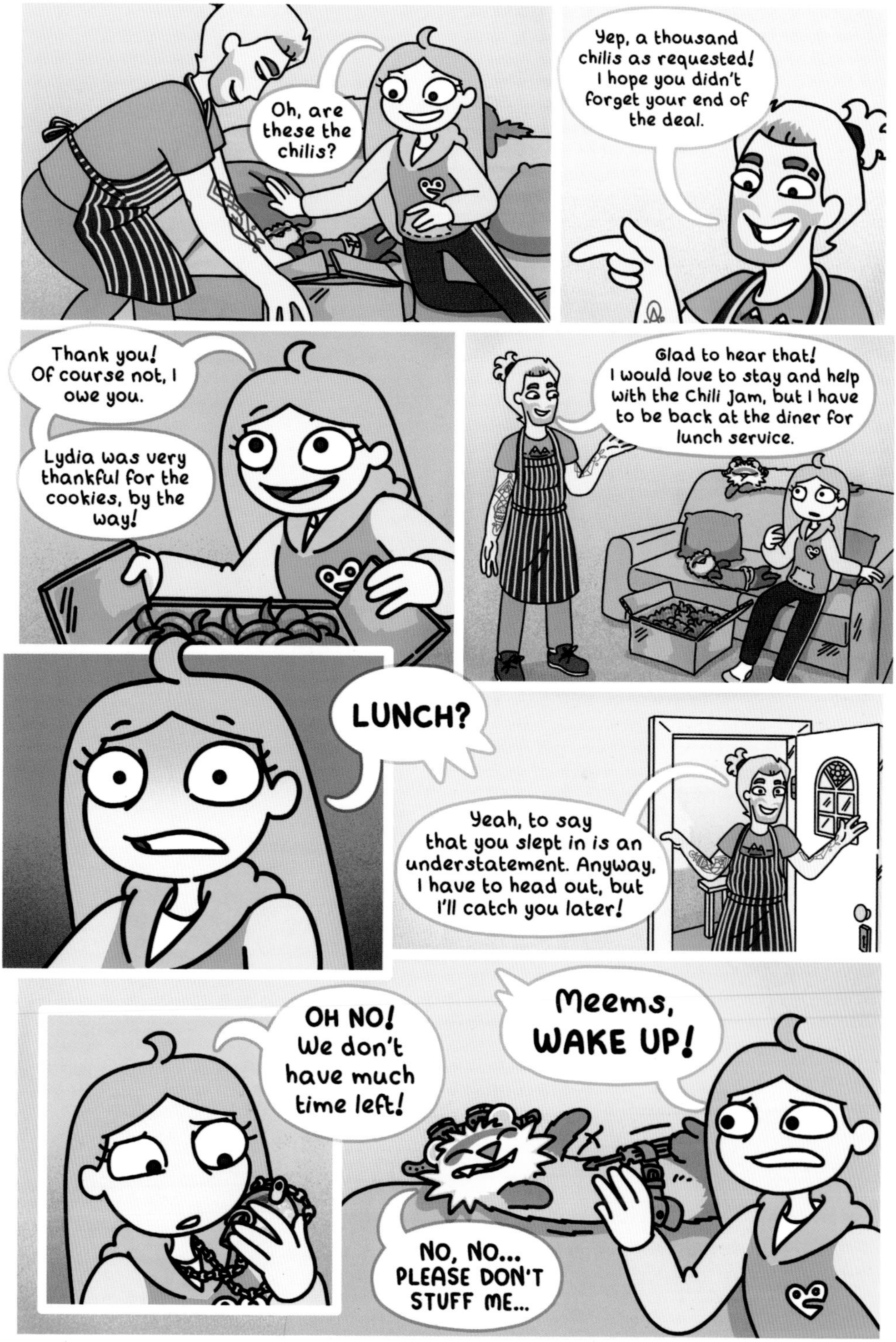

Oh, are these the chilis?
Yep, a thousand chilis as requested! I hope you didn't forget your end of the deal.
Thank you! Of course not, I owe you.
Lydia was very thankful for the cookies, by the way!
Glad to hear that! I would love to stay and help with the Chili Jam, but I have to be back at the diner for lunch service.
LUNCH?
Yeah, to say that you slept in is an understatement. Anyway, I have to head out, but I'll catch you later!
OH NO! We don't have much time left!
Meems, WAKE UP!
NO, NO... PLEASE DON'T STUFF ME...

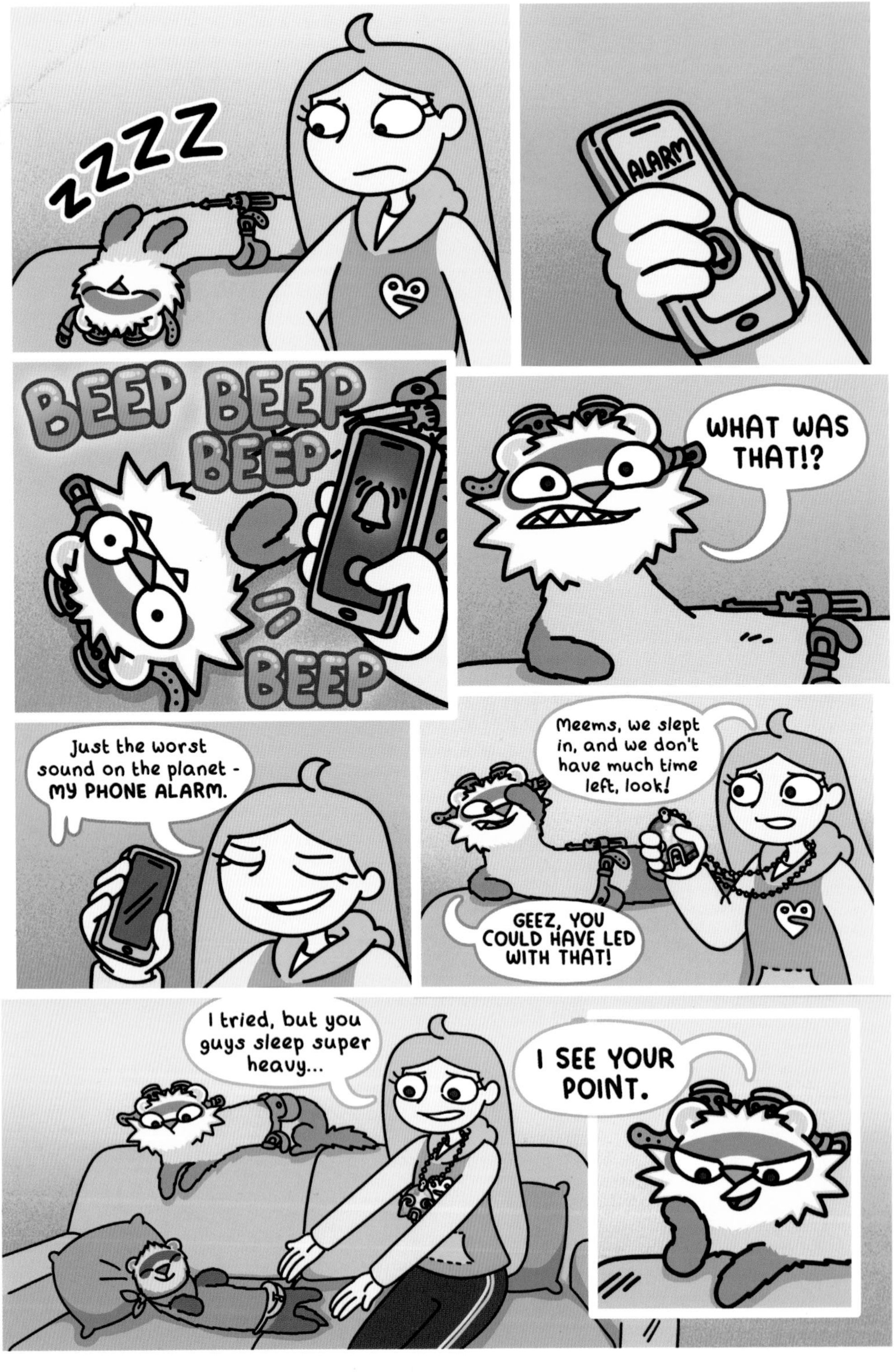
zZZZ
ALARM
BEEP BEEP
BEEP
BEEP
WHAT WAS THAT!?
Just the worst sound on the planet - MY PHONE ALARM.
Meems, we slept in, and we don't have much time left, look!
GEEZ, YOU COULD HAVE LED WITH THAT!
I tried, but you guys sleep super heavy...
I SEE YOUR POINT.

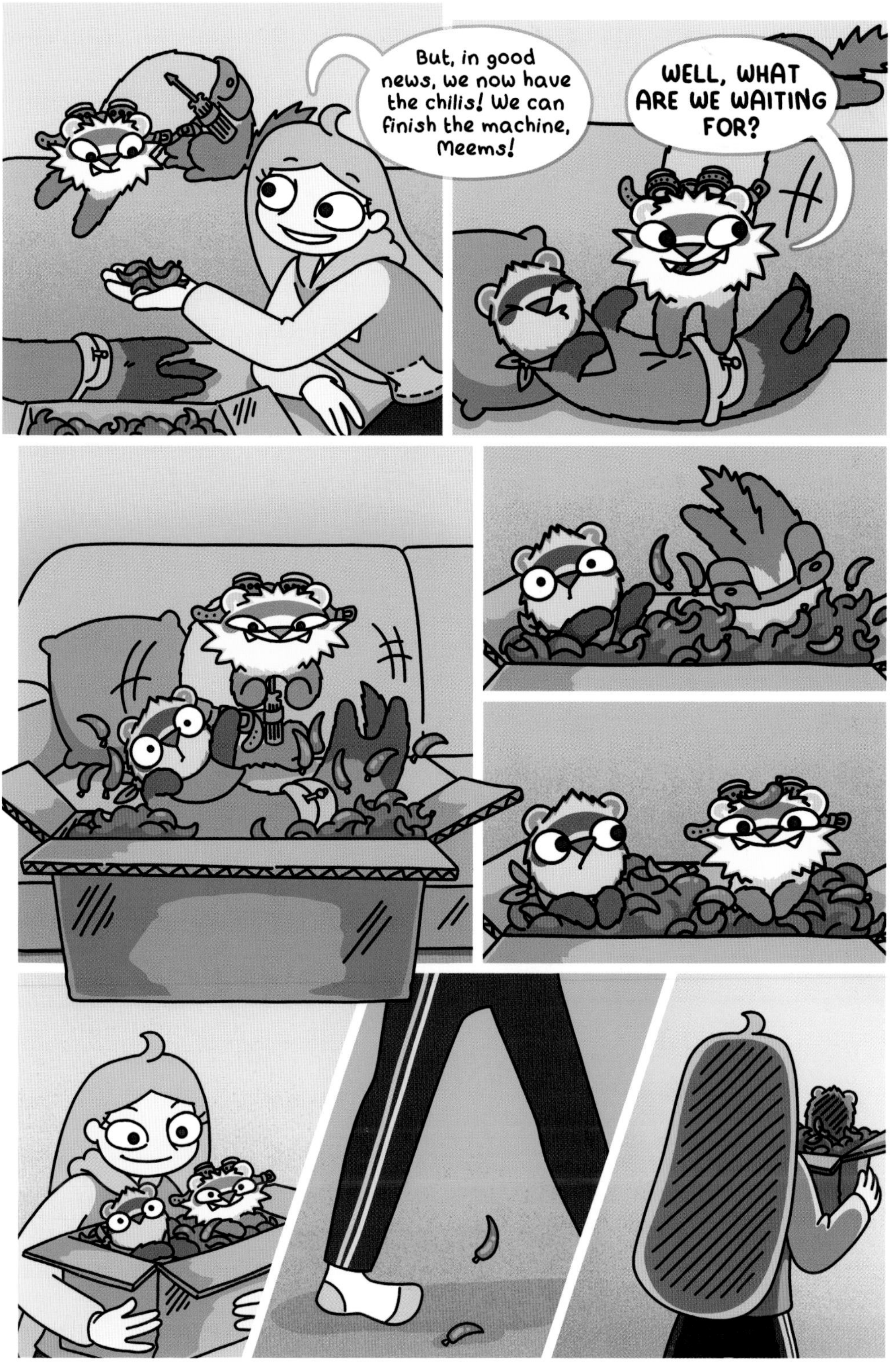
But, in good news, we now have the chilis! We can finish the machine, Meems!
WELL, WHAT ARE WE WAITING FOR?

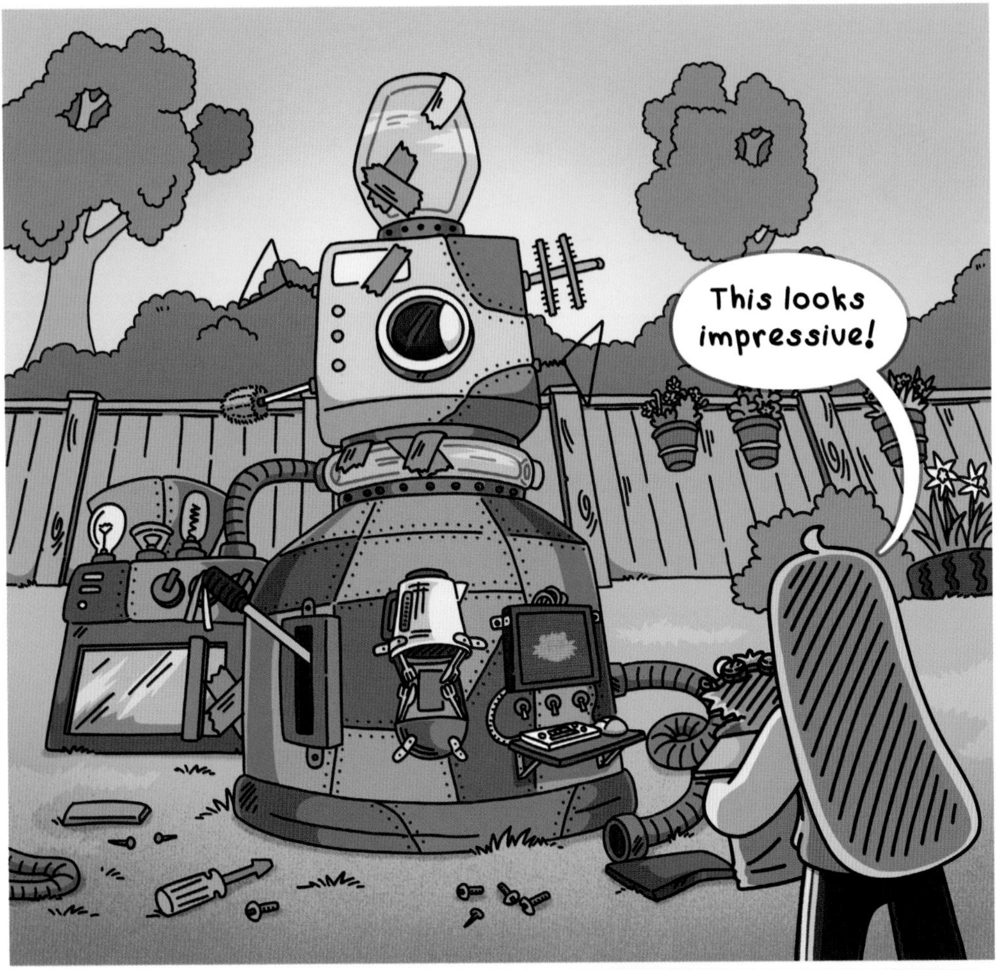
This looks impressive!

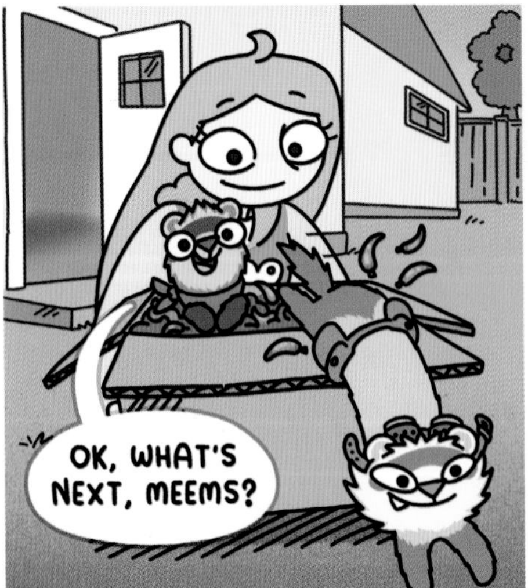
OK, WHAT'S NEXT, MEEMS?

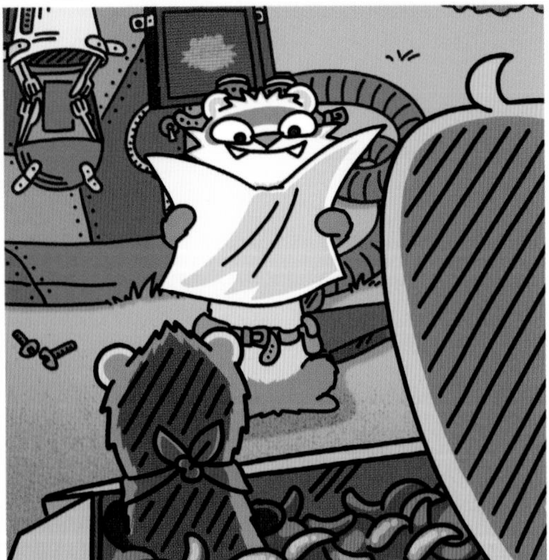

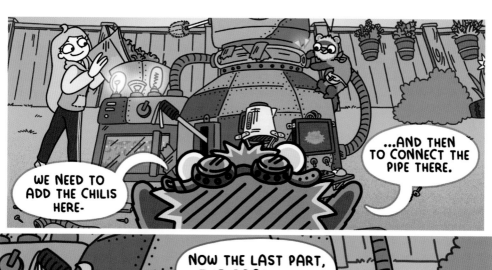

...AND THEN TO CONNECT THE PIPE THERE.

WE NEED TO ADD THE CHILIS HERE-

NOW THE LAST PART, THE OPAL—GOES RIGHT HERE.

IT'S – IT'S READY!!

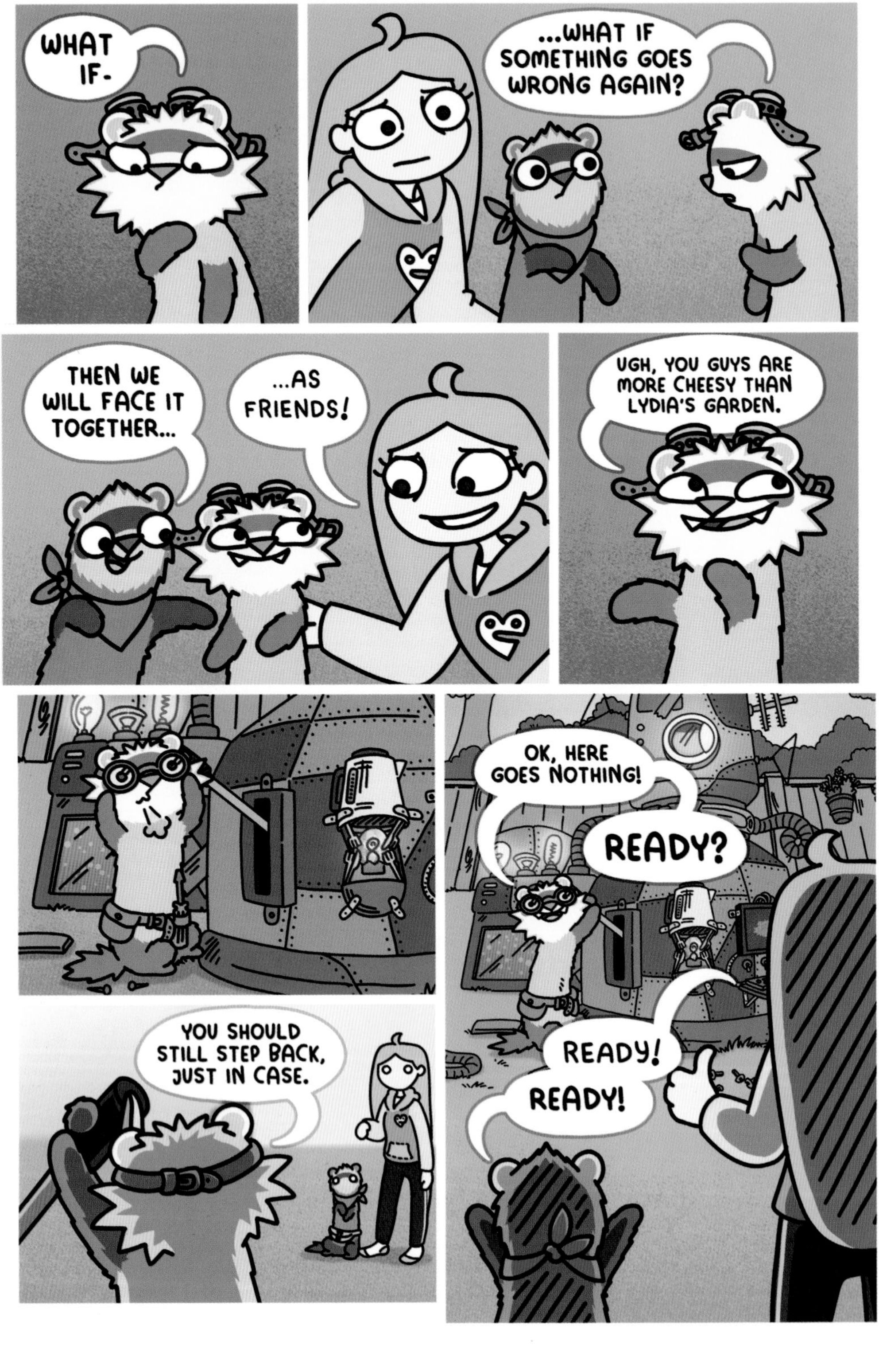
WHAT IF-
...WHAT IF SOMETHING GOES WRONG AGAIN?
THEN WE WILL FACE IT TOGETHER...
...AS FRIENDS!
UGH, YOU GUYS ARE MORE CHEESY THAN LYDIA'S GARDEN.
OK, HERE GOES NOTHING!
READY?
READY!
READY!
YOU SHOULD STILL STEP BACK, JUST IN CASE.

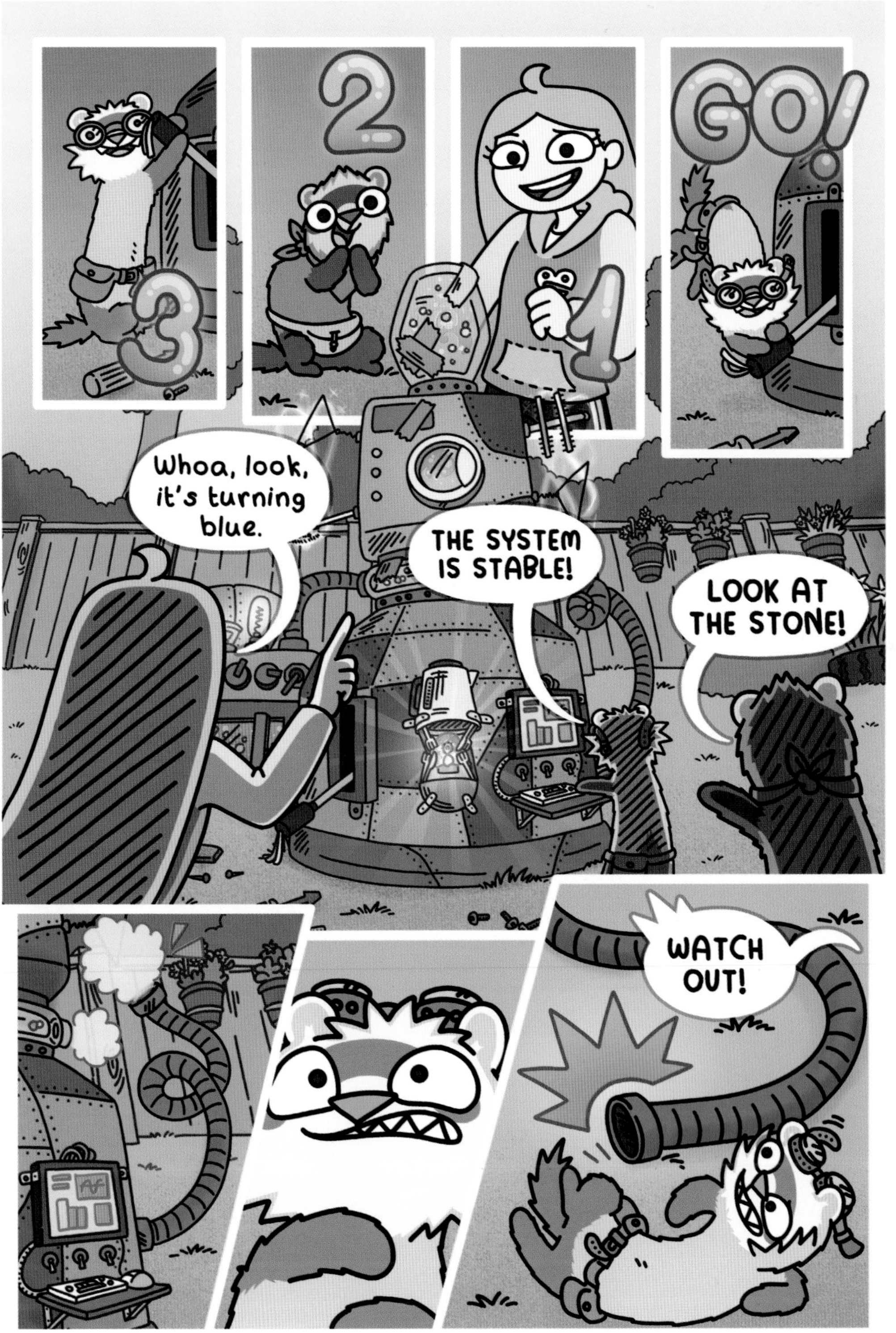
3
2
1
GO!
Whoa, look, it's turning blue.
THE SYSTEM IS STABLE!
LOOK AT THE STONE!
WATCH OUT!

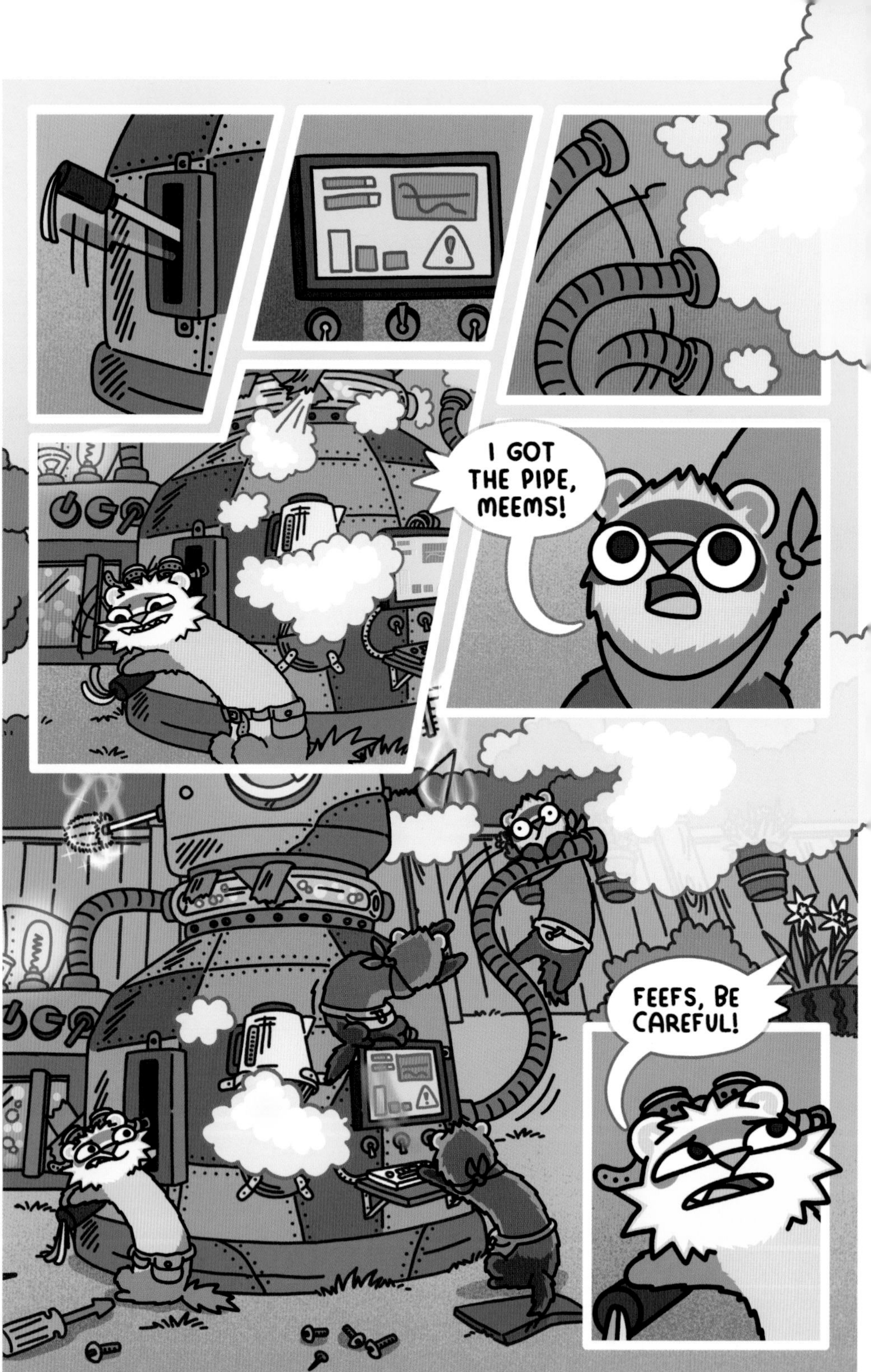
I GOT THE PIPE, MEEMS!
FEEFS, BE CAREFUL!

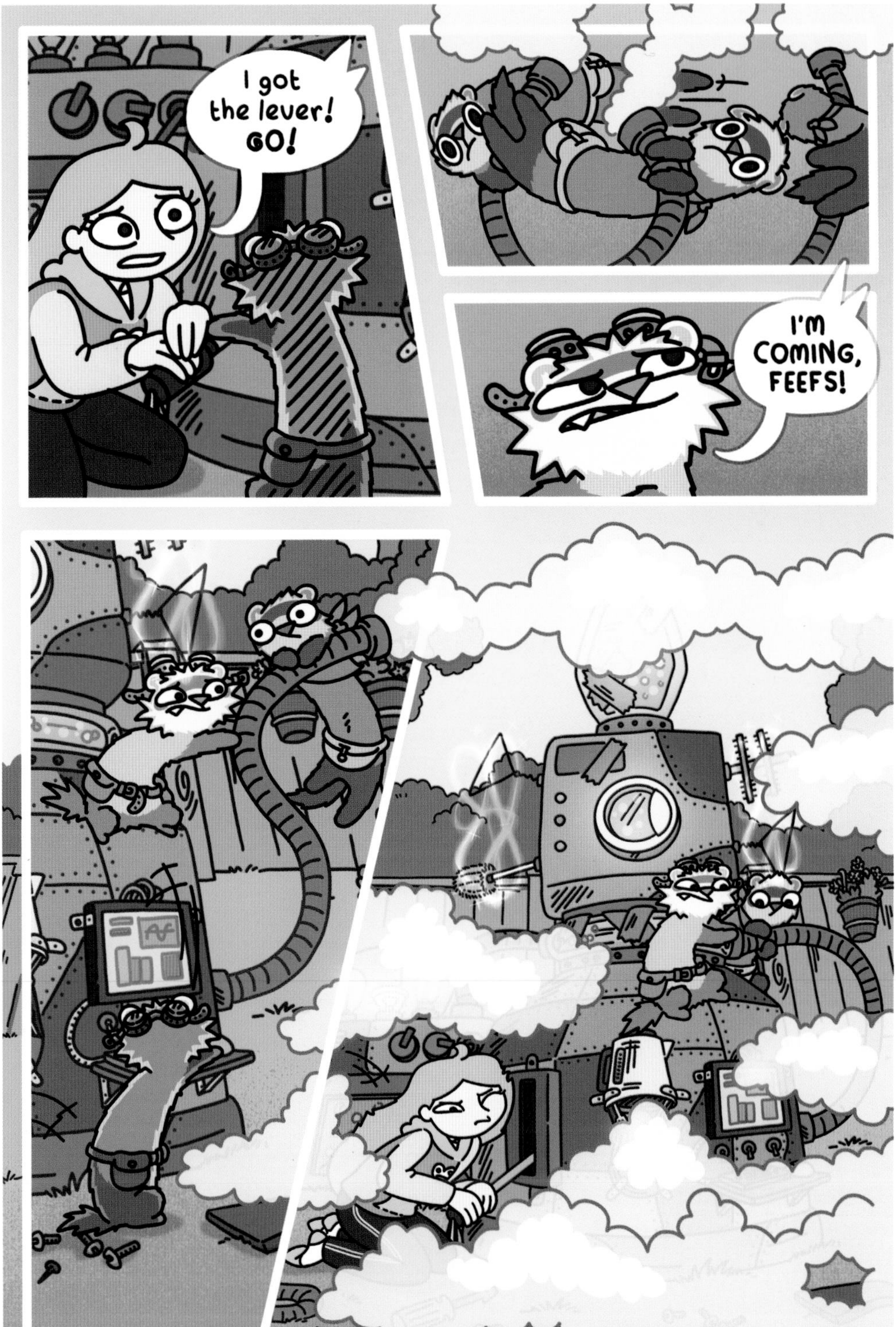
I got the lever! GO!
I'M COMING, FEEFS!

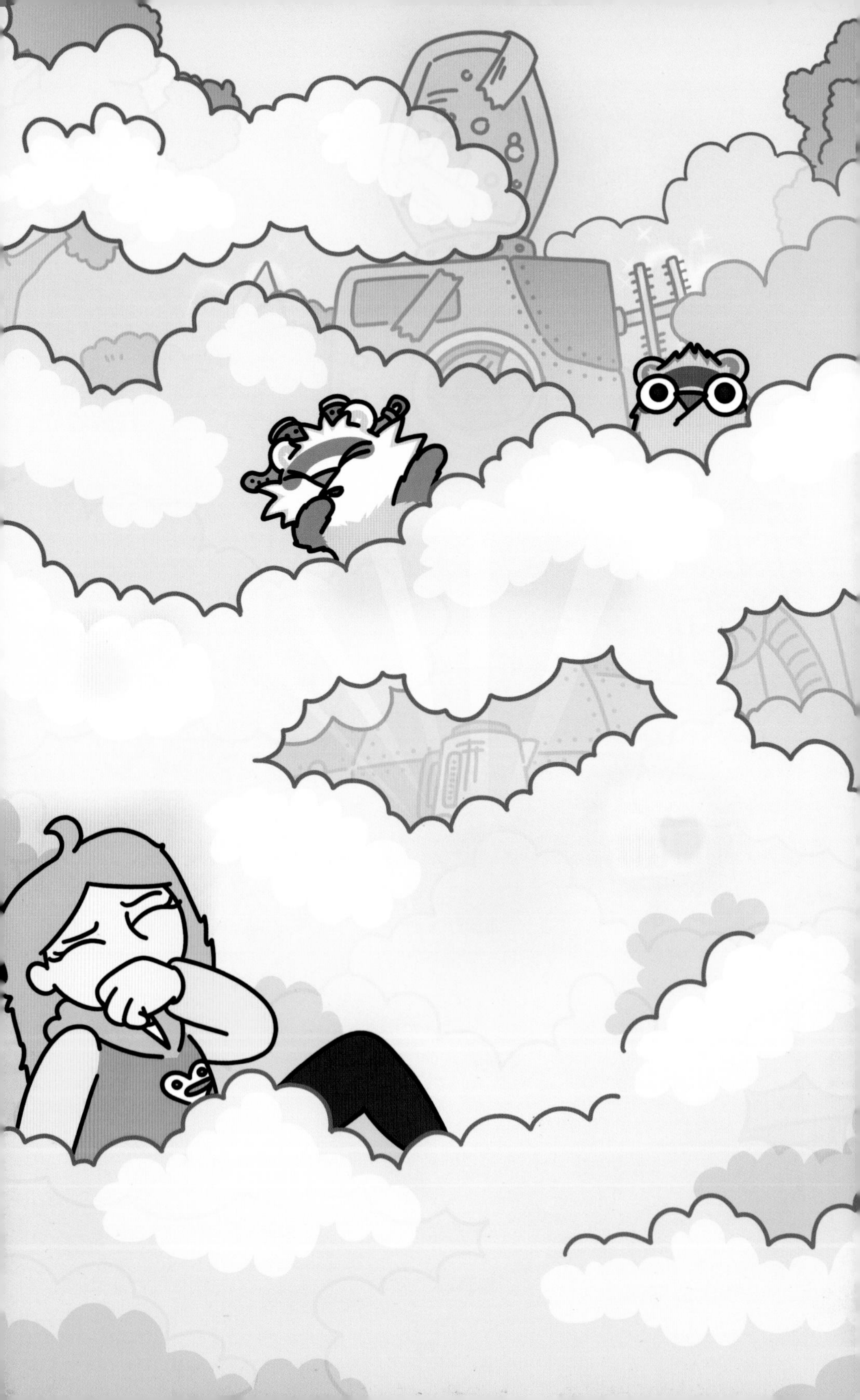

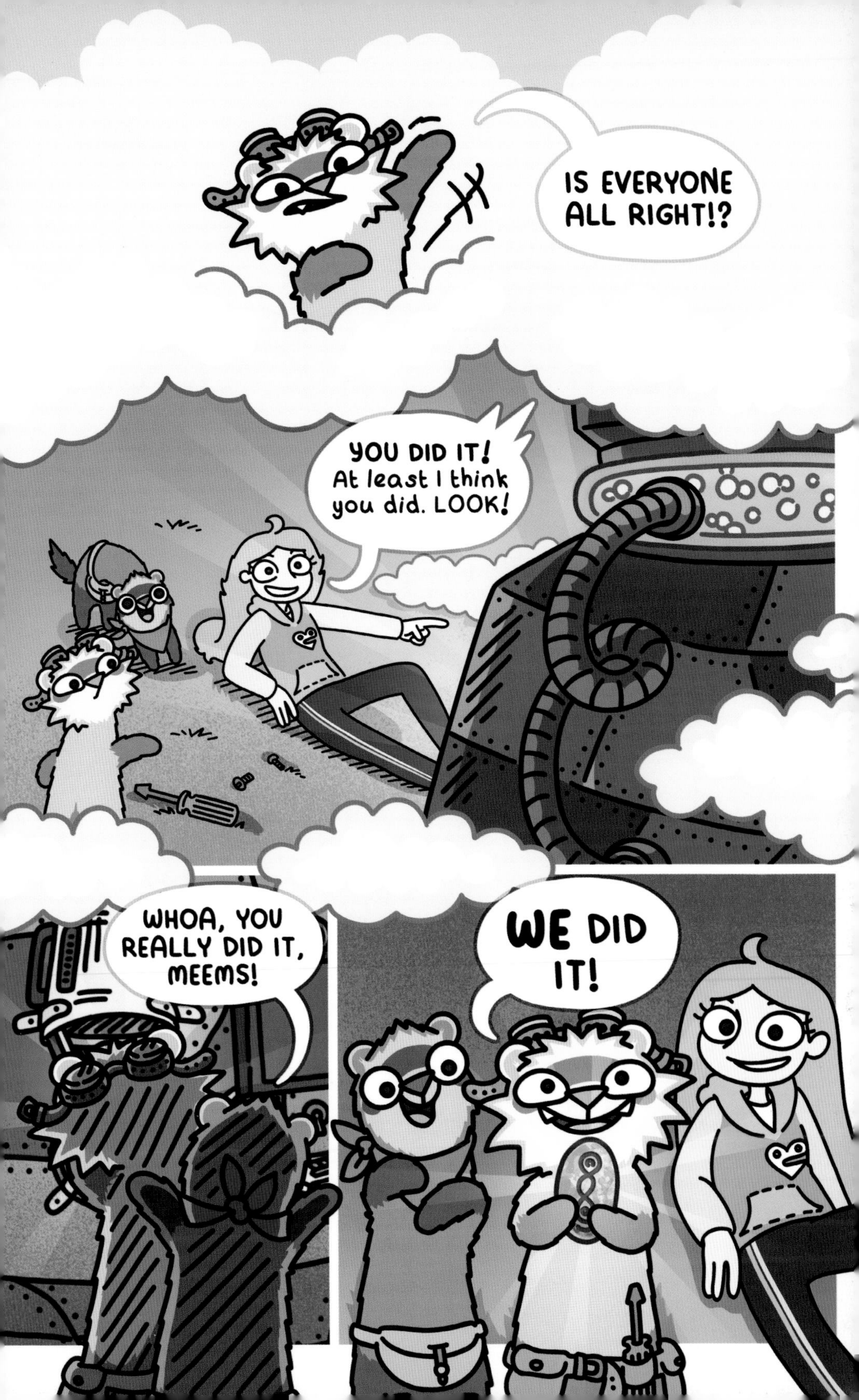
IS EVERYONE ALL RIGHT!?
YOU DID IT! At least I think you did. LOOK!
WHOA, YOU REALLY DID IT, MEEMS!
WE DID IT!

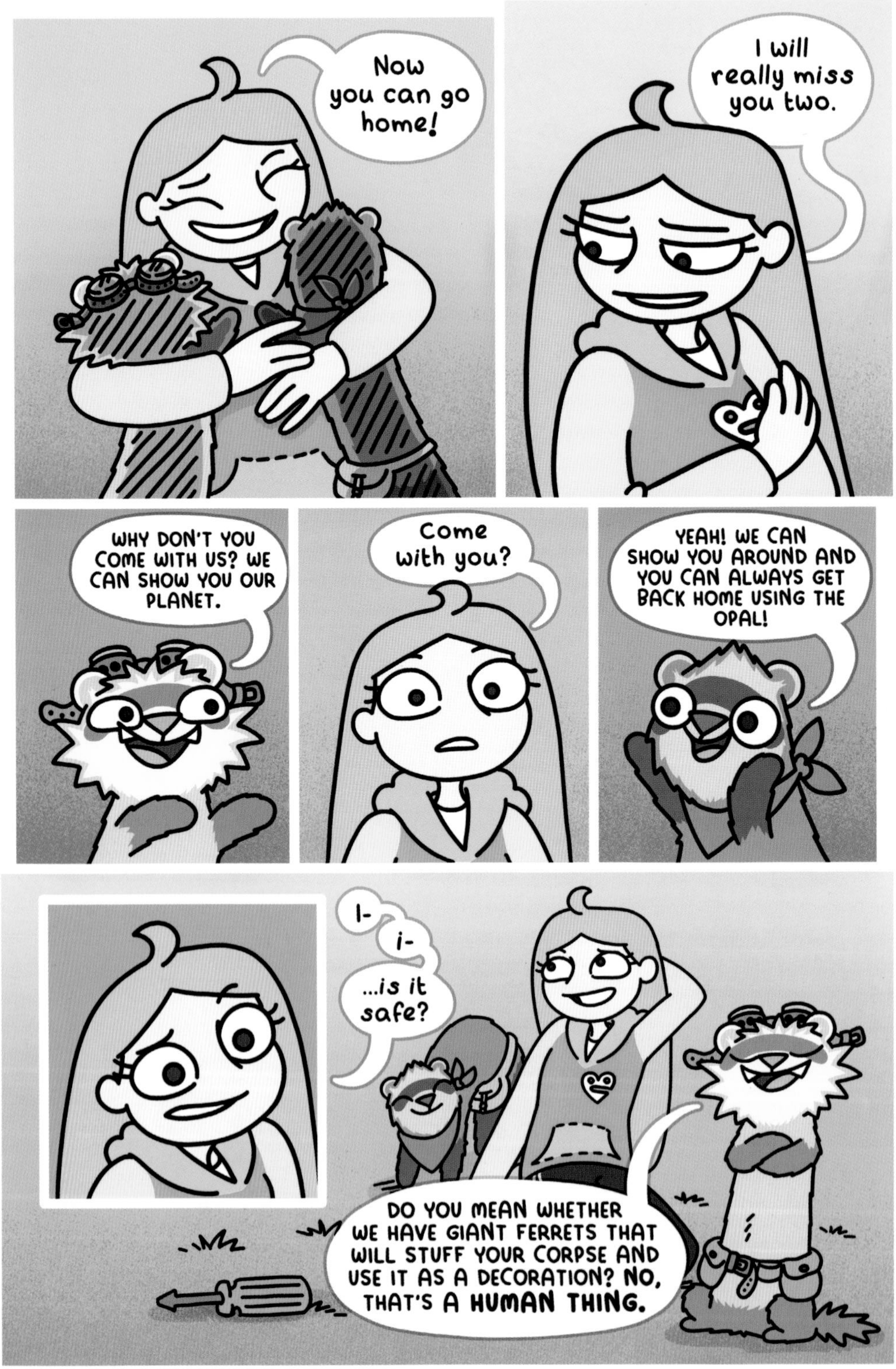
Now you can go home!
I will really miss you two.
WHY DON'T YOU COME WITH US? WE CAN SHOW YOU OUR PLANET.
Come with you?
YEAH! WE CAN SHOW YOU AROUND AND YOU CAN ALWAYS GET BACK HOME USING THE OPAL!
I-
i-
...is it safe?
DO YOU MEAN WHETHER WE HAVE GIANT FERRETS THAT WILL STUFF YOUR CORPSE AND USE IT AS A DECORATION? NO, THAT'S A HUMAN THING.

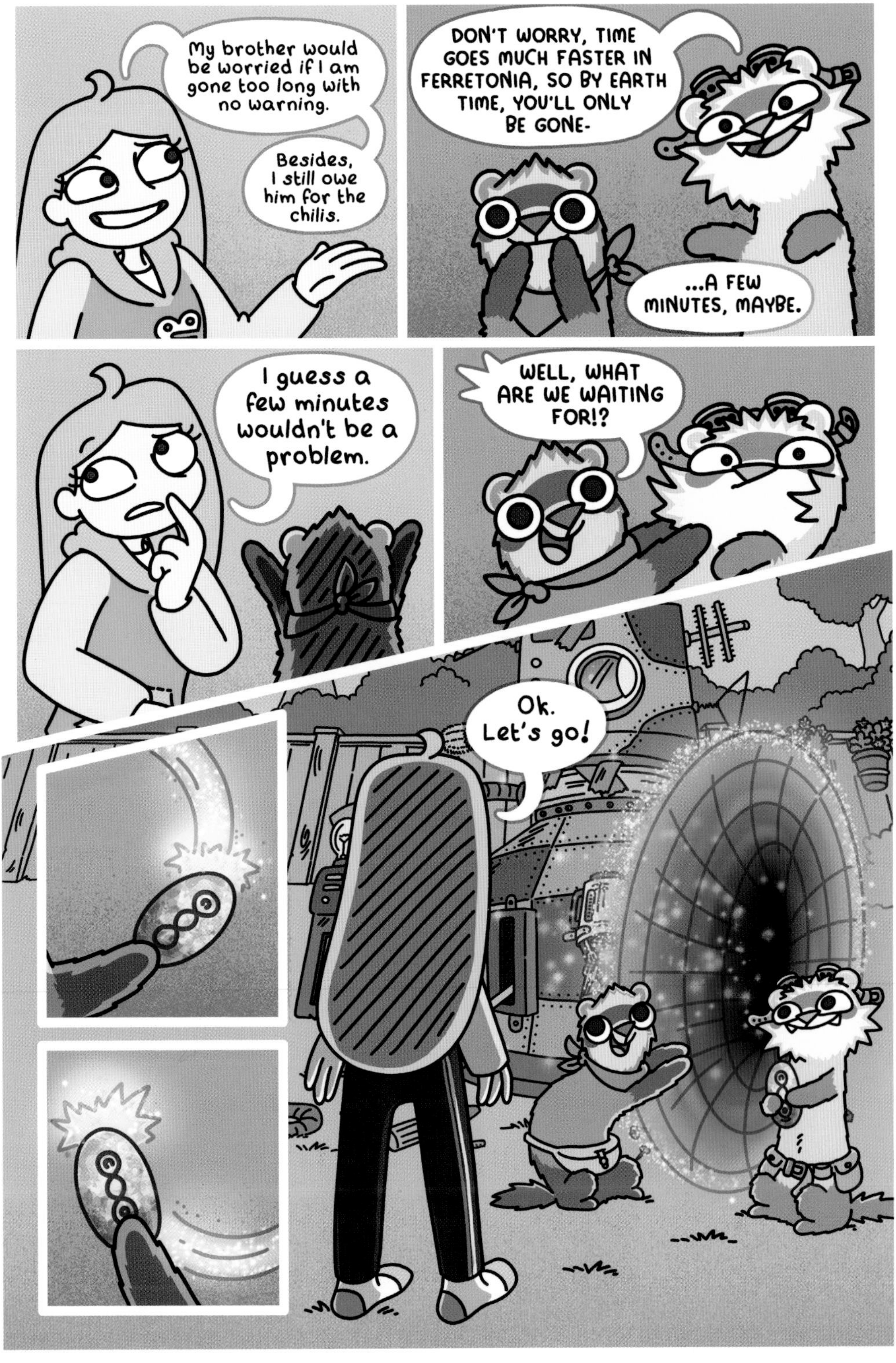

My brother would be worried if I am gone too long with no warning.
Besides, I still owe him for the chilis.
DON'T WORRY, TIME GOES MUCH FASTER IN FERRETONIA, SO BY EARTH TIME, YOU'LL ONLY BE GONE-
...A FEW MINUTES, MAYBE.
I guess a few minutes wouldn't be a problem.
WELL, WHAT ARE WE WAITING FOR!?
Ok. Let's go!

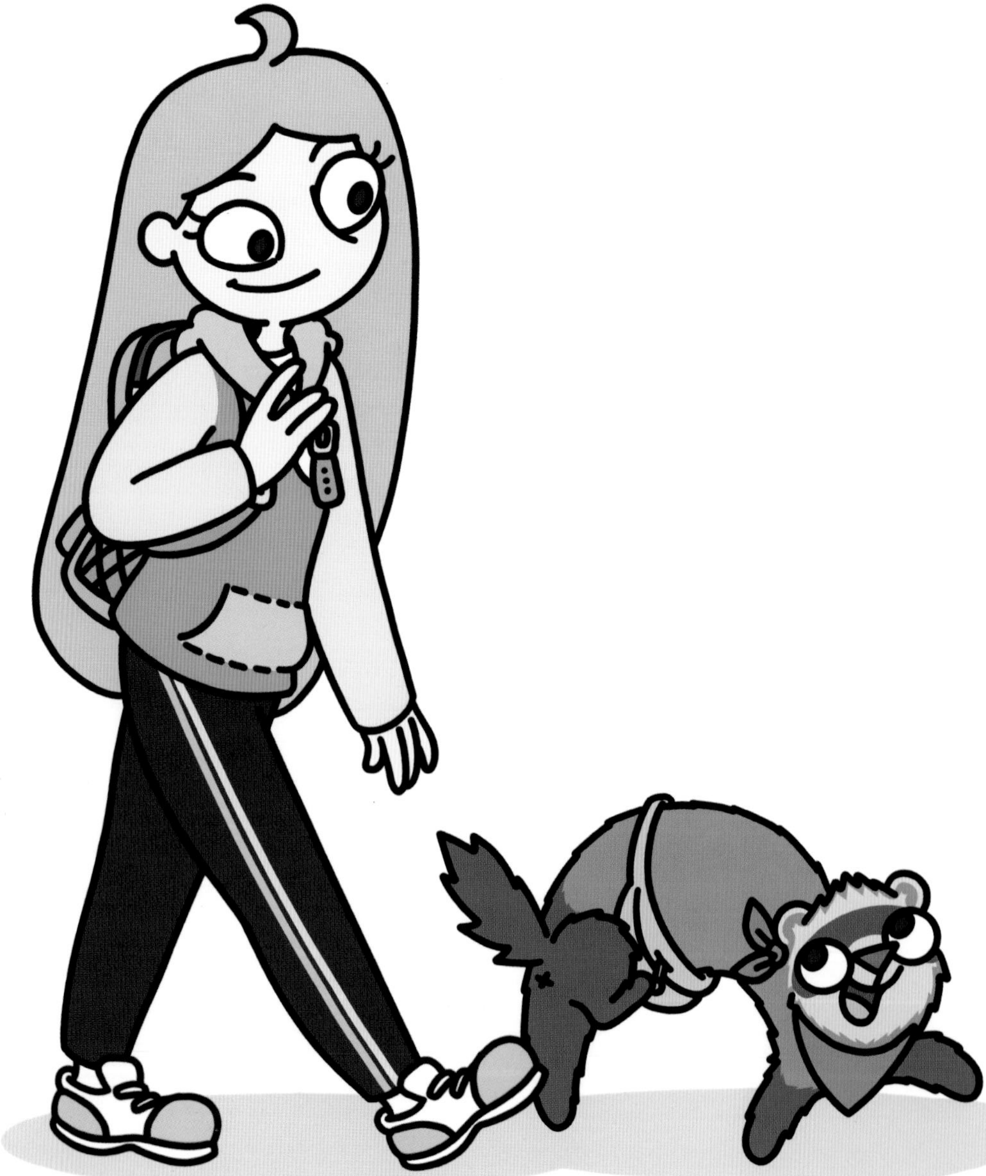

ADVENTURE WILL CONTINUE IN BOOK TWO!

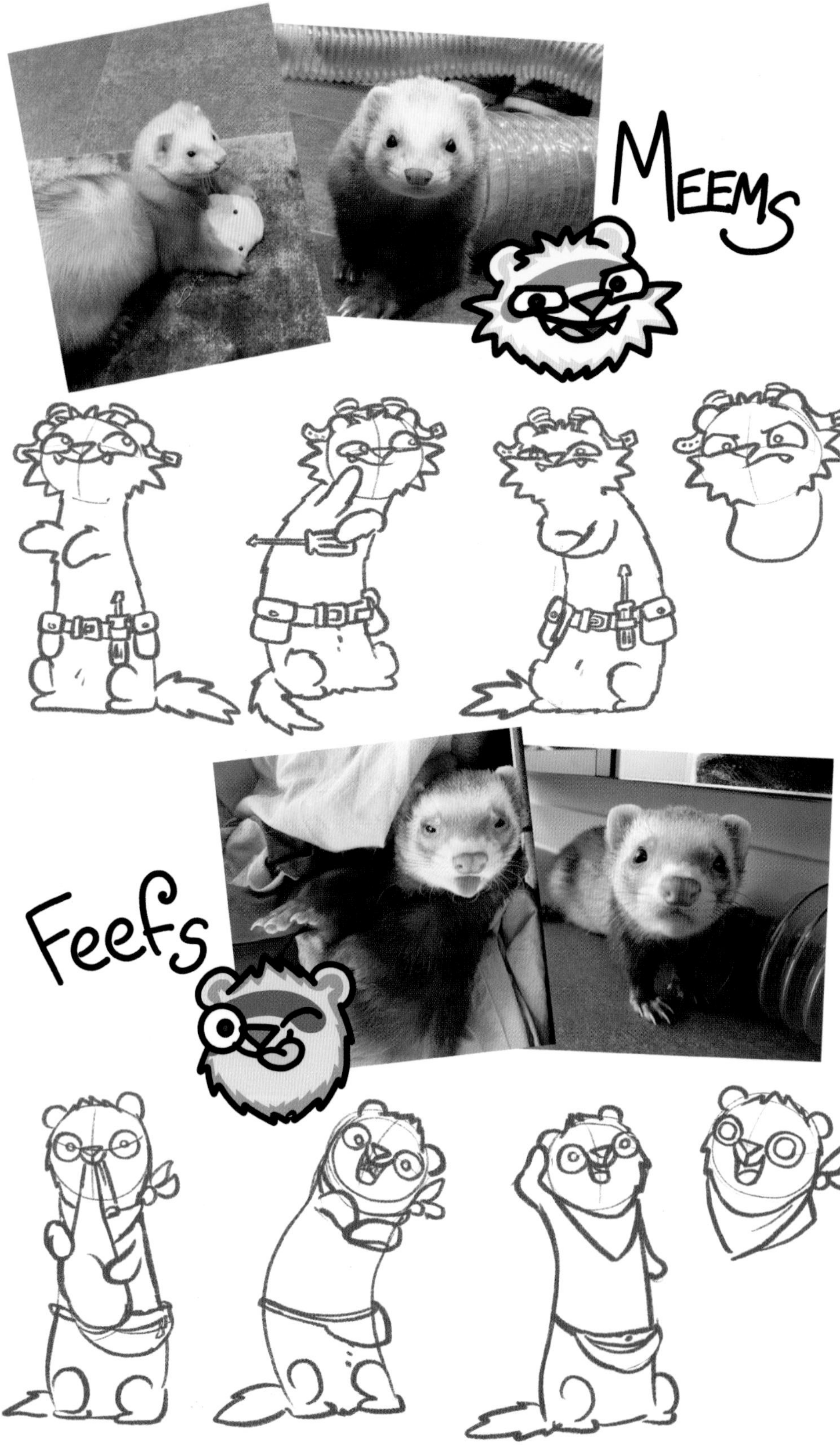
MEEMS
Feefs

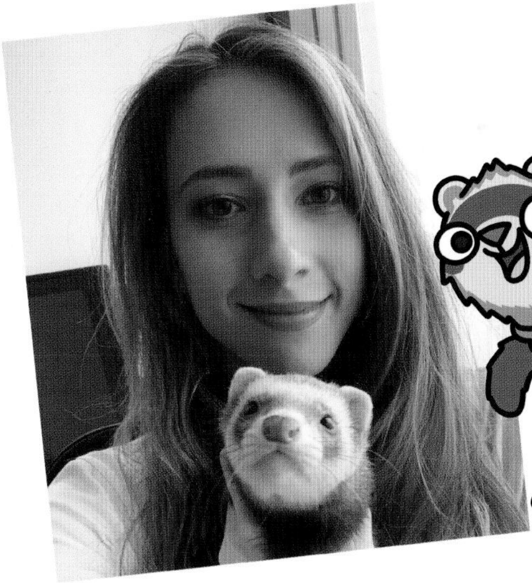

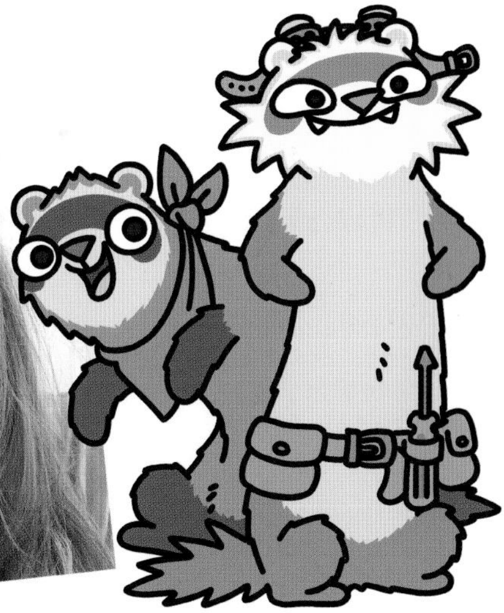

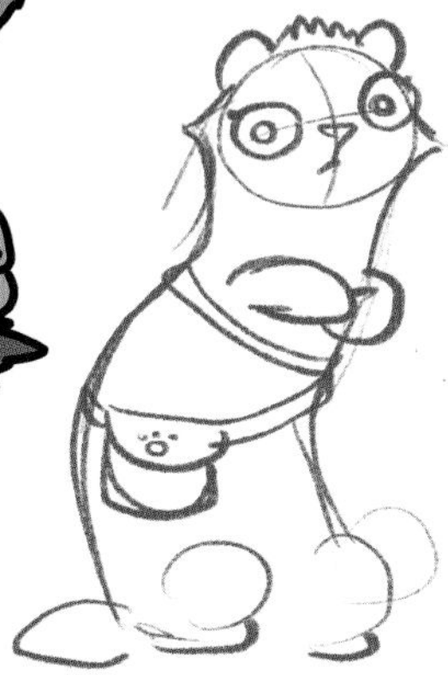

ABOUT THE AUTHOR :)

Liza N. Cooper is an artist and digital content creator who goes by the pen name Siberian Lizard online. Originally born in the wild and frosty Siberia, she has since settled down in a much warmer (and wetter) London, where she lives with her two naughty ferrets and a Pomeranian pup.

As a curious and outgoing child with a vivid imagination, she spent most of her summers in the countryside accompanied by her doting, but eccentric gran. Together they explored the wilderness, foraged for mushrooms, told stories, and painted every day.

Liza set her heart on being an artist early on, but it wasn't a straight forward journey. After graduating highschool, she was convinced that she had to have a conventional career and went on to study business at King's College London.

Flipping through the lecture notes at the end of her first year however, it was clear that she made a big mistake, as they were filled to the brim with drawings.

Liza got a chance to change course, and eventually she graduated from Central Saint Martins in London receiving a BA in Graphic Design specializing in Illustration and Animation.

Before branching out on her own, Liza worked as an Art Director for the viral hit animated series—Simon's Cat.

This is her debut graphic novel series and the beginning of something very exciting!

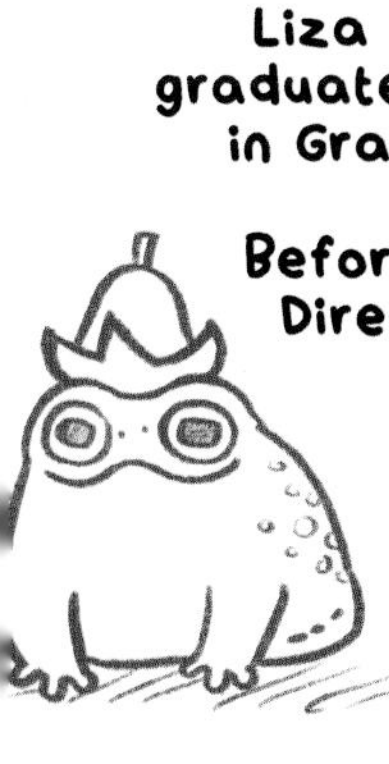

www.SiberianLizard.com

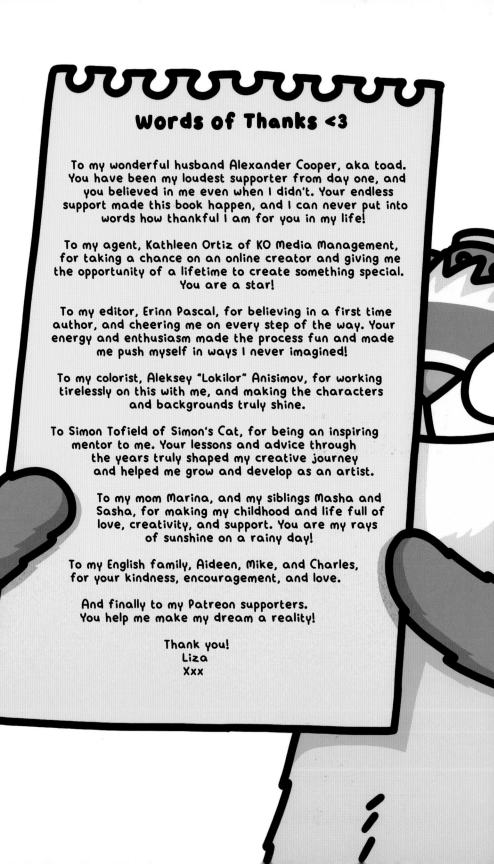

Words of Thanks <3

To my wonderful husband Alexander Cooper, aka toad. You have been my loudest supporter from day one, and you believed in me even when I didn't. Your endless support made this book happen, and I can never put into words how thankful I am for you in my life!

To my agent, Kathleen Ortiz of KO Media Management, for taking a chance on an online creator and giving me the opportunity of a lifetime to create something special. You are a star!

To my editor, Erinn Pascal, for believing in a first time author, and cheering me on every step of the way. Your energy and enthusiasm made the process fun and made me push myself in ways I never imagined!

To my colorist, Aleksey "Lokilor" Anisimov, for working tirelessly on this with me, and making the characters and backgrounds truly shine.

To Simon Tofield of Simon's Cat, for being an inspiring mentor to me. Your lessons and advice through the years truly shaped my creative journey and helped me grow and develop as an artist.

To my mom Marina, and my siblings Masha and Sasha, for making my childhood and life full of love, creativity, and support. You are my rays of sunshine on a rainy day!

To my English family, Aideen, Mike, and Charles, for your kindness, encouragement, and love.

And finally to my Patreon supporters. You help me make my dream a reality!

Thank you!
Liza
Xxx